GOBLINOPOLIS
THE TOL CHRONICLES

ROBERT G. FERRELL

ZETABELLA
☆ PUBLISHING ☆

ISBN 978-1-927384-18-3

Published by Zetabella Publishing
Toronto Canada, 2013
Printed in the US.
zetabella.com

For Ady.

Chapter One:
The Bloated Balrog

The races of N'plork all evolved from a distant common ancestor and developed their particular morphologies in response to the demands of the environments in which they lived. As a result, each can theoretically hybridize with the others, although the only relatively common such interracial assignations seem to involve ogres, trolls, and goblins. Half-trolls and half-ogres are still rare in the general population, but in certain densely urban areas of Goblinopolis (Tragacanth), Aspolia (Solemadrina), and Uzpleng (Nerr), they are not an uncommon sight.

—Excerpt from The Mythologies of N'plork,
CoME Cultural Sociography Series #27

Tol-u-ol dropped heavily into a chair crafted without evidence of skill from the posterior exoskeleton of an adult pseudomale Humphing Beast. Humphers had a single central gluteal muscle, since they had only one rear leg; the chitinous butt cheek made a fairly decent lounger if properly cleaned and exfoliated. This one wasn't, but Tol didn't give a smek. He was dead tired, and anything between vertical and supine was fine by him so long as it was an imbibing-friendly posture.

A barmaid slithered over. She was one of those eye-twisting orcish chimeras that caused such a stir when they first rose from the genetic cesspool called The Effluent. Despite their lumpish appearance, they were fairly normal as hybrid nightmares go. Folks had gotten pretty much used to them, but they

1

still made Tol flinch. He was too spent tonight for flinching, though.

"Hi, honey. An ubergourd of razzle to start with, please, and I don't want to see any straws or umbrellas."

Her ten inch razor-tipped tongue flicked around and neatly bisected a pencil wasp laying eggs in one of her ear flaps. "Razzhle comin' uph. Anythin' elsh?"

He waved her away. She disappeared into the murky darkness of the tavern, leaving a faint but discernible trail of slime behind on the worn glonkwood floorboards. Tol sat back and stared at it hopefully, waiting for some kobold or gnarlignome to come sauntering by and slip. None did. That figured. His day had been full of that very same lack of entertainment.

Tol was a cop. His beat was Sebacea, one of the roughest neighborhoods in Goblinopolis, the largest city and capitol of Tragacanth. It had been an incorporated area in its own right at one time, but was absorbed into the larger city when the Lord Mayor and Town Council were imprisoned *en masse* for drug dealing, smuggling, money laundering, tax evasion, fraud, counterfeiting, jaywalking, transgender sexual deviation, and felonious littering. Sebacea was not known for its gentility or subtlety.

Tol had been in on that bust. It had made his week. Under Tragacanthan law he was entitled to a share of the spoils, so he picked out a transmog unit. It was a little ratty-looking cosmetically, but it seemed perfectly functional. He used it mostly for domestic problem-solving, like zapping the next door kid's lapspider that was constantly raiding his meat garden into a can of old dried paint and setting it out on the curb with the garbage. He also turned the insulation voles living in the walls of his townhouse into cozy foot warmers.

Some of his colleagues in edict enforcement still used swords or magic; he'd long ago decided that a .44 neural disruptor was more his style. Let the long-haired old forensic mages cast their spells or pour their potions all over the floor after the situation was under control. He needed to get in, get the job done, and get out as cleanly and with as few complications as possible. If a three-meter greater ogress came at him with a sonic cleaver, he wanted to be able to drop her at a safe distance, not stand there waving his fool arms and chanting. That kind of nonsense got body parts separated from their owners toot sweet. A former partner of his had one of his arms torn off by a drug-crazed ogre while trying to activate a magic battle-axe in the back room of a bookie joint. Smek that nonsense.

The barmaid oozed back with his drink. He tossed her a five billme coin and told her to keep the change. Derision looks pretty much the same as any other emotion on a normal orc, much less a chimera, but this one managed to show it surprisingly well— no doubt due to all the practice she got dealing with the regular tavern clientele. Tol beamed a smek-eating grin at her and took a hefty swig from the gourd. Swishing the inferior grade razzle around in his mouth, he thought he detected a slightly bitter taste. Probably didn't bother to delaminate the gourd before putting alcohol in it. Smekking amateurs. Hopefully this wouldn't be one of those genetically modified gourds with the hallucinogenic properties. He hated getting stoned by himself in public places.

As the evening wore on, the *Bloated Balrog* began to fill up. It was located at a major crossroads, where the trade routes for various magic item components grown on ultra-high security plantations in the far south and the primary east-west techno-industrial interchange met. Sutha Magic Supply, headquartered in Qoplebarq, shipped most of its output to three sprawling complexes in the mountains of the far Northwest. Their exact locations were shrouded in secrecy and industrial-grade cloaking, as they were a source of almost unimaginable wealth for the mages who built and ran them. The Bungash Mountains in the East had most of the mines where raw materials for the technology trade were produced and shipped west to the great factory towns of Fenurian and Cladimil.

Those well-traveled highways met here in Goblinopolis, which was one of the reasons it was the most populated city in the realm, and specifically they met right next to the *Balrog*. That made this tavern situated on one of the most economically desirable real estate tracts in the country, a fact that was to prove alternately boon and bane to Terpitude Halftroll, the proprietor. Terp was a big smekker, with long greenish dreadlocks and breath that could drop an orc at ten paces. He was ornery, but honest for all that; Tol liked him. Terp had turned down obscene amounts of money for the *Balrog*, probably because he sensed even more obscene profits if he held onto it longer. He was constantly being hammered by agents for this or that development company, though, and this made him even crankier.

One night after a few gourds, Tol asked Terp where he got the name for his tavern. "What the smek is a 'balrog,' anyway?"

"I don't know," replied Terp, wiping down the bar counter, "It just came to me in a dream. And I figure anythin' called a balrog is bound t' be ugly and bloated, so there ya go."

"What had you been drinkin'?"

"Weren't drink. I had a couple puffs from one of those smekkin' gnome pipes—you know, just to be polite and all. The next day I stopped being polite and took to mindin' my own business."

Tol belched and held up his gourd. "Here's to keepin' your nose where it belongs."

Tragacanth wasn't exactly a kingdom, in the traditional sense—it was more of a Royal Technocracy. Whoever could wrest formal control of the Royal Network was declared King, although all of the new King's edicts were initially subject to review by the elected Council of Mages and Engineers (CoME). There were several academies of different sizes and levels of reputability scattered about which purported to train royal aspirants, but so far none of their graduates had gotten very close. Tol's little brother Aspet, or just "Pet," as Tol mockingly referred to him in the manner of big brothers universe-wide, had recently completed the curriculum at one of them, but Tol figured Aspet's chances of becoming king at somewhere between "no way" and "zilch." Not that he'd spoken to Pet much since he moved out on his own. Their worlds had diverged early, as his sibling was a techno-geek almost from birth and Tol had difficulty working the toaster.

One of the patrons in tonight's packed house was a hobgoblin Tol recognized. Pyfox was a professional criminal, you might say, which except for the "professional" part was mostly redundant where hobgoblins were concerned. The vast majority of the petty crimes that plagued Tragacanthan society were perpetrated by hobs; they seemed to have something of a predisposition for that sort of behavior. Although he had been under the impression that the hob was still in prison after his latest bust, Tol wasn't particularly surprised to see Pyfox here in public. He was probably at large on some experimental amnesty program pushed by the Tragacanth Prison Reform Committee, populated predominantly by social-crusading elves. Tol didn't have a lot of respect for elves, but he was prepared to accept that some of that was due simply to the age-old mutual distrust between his race and theirs. Even with his "edict enforcement officer's objectivity" turned up all the way, though, he still found dealing with the pointy-eared pansies rather distasteful.

Tol had no reason to suspect Pyfox was up to no good tonight—other than the fact that he was habitually up to no good—but decided to keep an eye on him, nonetheless, just to hone his skills. He was fairly certain his adversary had spotted him, too, so the playing field was level in that respect. Sure, Pyfox was sequestered in a horde of hobgoblins, but there was a saying on the force: *One Hobmob, One Goblin*. Handling hobs was like scattering scrubhounds—take a couple down and the rest head for the hills with all three of their tails between their legs (except that hobs only had the one tail, and it was really more of an elongated scab). Hobs like to dish it out, but they couldn't take it. When you're an EEO you have to know these things.

Pyfox was attached through a tortuous web of associations to an organized crime syndicate of hobgoblins, trolls, and ogres (not to mention the odd gnome or gnarlignome, and even a sprinkling of disaffected goblins) that called themselves the Belladonnas. Rape, extortion, murder, double parking—these guys were a million laughs. The Capo Belladonna was a grizzled old troll named Gramidius Contentius, but everyone in the family just called him Capo, or if they were in favor today and feelin' lucky, Grami. The Belladonnas were in and out of lockup so often several of them had their own reserved seats in the Ferroc Loca prison dining hall.

There was no scheduled floor show in the *Balrog*, apart from blundering inebriates and kobolds-on-the-make, but most evenings saw at least one spontaneous outbreak of entertainment, usually precipitated by a drunken dare or a goblinspouse who'd been left at home one too many times while hubby went out carousing.

About midway through the evening a spectacularly drunken ogress, or maybe it was a half-ogress—Tol couldn't quite tell through the dense haze of smoke—got up to sing a couple of bawdy songs to mixed approval. The smoke was from dongelweed, the favorite inhaled intoxicant of the many gnomes with their elaborately carved labyrinth-pipes who had filled up one end of the room an hour or so ago. Looked like a convention was in town, or maybe these were part of some work convoy heading for Cladimil. Gnomes did most of the assembly work in the tech factories; they had small, very nimble fingers and were swiftest of all the races to grasp the nuances of mechanical and electronic equipment.

At the conclusion of her performance, the ogress (it was apparent now that she was a fullblood) climbed up on the bar to dance—Terp had long ago reinforced that bar with timbers salvaged from the shipwreck of a commercial sea-going freighter in Myndrythyl Bay for just this eventuality—but before the bouncer could sweep her off with a huge metal claw designed expressly for that purpose an extremely loud and discombobulating explosion went off right outside the tavern. One wall blew in immediately, several large support beams fractured, and parts of the ceiling began to sway ominously. There was a moment of stunned silence, during which the ogress fell limply off the bar of her own accord, followed by a mad stampede for the door. Tol was too far away to have any hope of getting through the hysterical crowd. He shrugged and slipped unimpeded around the corner to the back door. Panic is a curious thing, he mused as he casually skirted the building to see what all the brouhaha was about. It makes people forget that they are sentient (where applicable).

The front side of the *Balrog,* or what was left of it, was a bubbling stew of confusion, liberally sprinkled with a wide range of body parts and erstwhile architecture for condiments. Gnomes were shaking their little fists, goblins were wailing, ogres were cursing; the few elves who had been in attendance (and a couple more who were passing through at the time) were weeping quietly off to the side. Tol pushed his way through the fractured throng to examine the blast area.

"Anyone see who did this?" he asked of the nearest circle of bystanders. An ogre wearing the livery of the Goblinopolis Transport Service, who ran the city's cabs, stepped forward. He was old and leathern, with gobbets of what had probably until recently been tavern patrons embedded here and there in the folds of his waxy skin.

"I seen 'em," he croaked, "I seen three elves come a runnin' out from behind that there buildin' and they drops this box undern th' winder there. Then they goes skeddalin' off that way and not more'n fifteen pops later there was the biggest boom you ever heard. Lucky I's next door by then or I'd jest be leetle lumps on th' pavement now."

Tol cocked his head, "Are you trying to tell me that *elves* blew up this pub?" The cabbie nodded vehemently in the affirmative.

He whipped out a notebook. "OK, oldster. Can you describe these 'elves' for me?" He tried not to sound too doubtful, but it was a struggle. The ogre didn't seem to notice, but then ogres aren't famed for their mastery of linguistic nuance.

"They's skinny as rails, wearing light gray shimmery-lookin' duds. One of 'em had on a hood with one o' them long tails on it. The other two was sportin' what looked like some kinda red sashes er wide belts. They mighta had a metal buckle or somethin' on th' front—I didn't see 'em from thet angle long enough ta tell fer sure."

Tol scribbled some of this down in his leather bound department-issued notepad. His writing instrument was a clever little biomechanical hybrid thing that some misguided genius had thought it would be nifty to endow with a limited form of 'domestic intelligence.'

"Skinny has two *n*s," it reported quietly, "and while we are on the subject of skinny, you are 14.5 kilocalories above your optimum intake for this week, and it is only Midweeksday."

Tol rolled his eyes. "Spare me the dietary editorials, will ya? I'm trying to take notes here."

There was a strategically-calculated pause, and then a very slightly affronted electronic voice replied, "I apologize. I am just a poor mechanical device attempting to carry out my programming as well as I am able. If I have offended or annoyed you in the process, I am sorry. I shall shut up now and go back to being an inert piece of elegantly crafted metal and apparently utterly wasted circuitry. Do not mind me. I shall be in 'silent' mode, hoping against hope that someday you will find even the smallest reason to validate my presence in the universe. The gods know I do not ask for much. I only live—wait, I am not alive, am I?—I only *exist* to serve."

Tol stuffed the pen back in the acoustically dampened lining of his overjack pocket (he'd had that lining installed specially and at considerable personal expense) and pulled his lower fangs across his upper lip in deep annoyance. He hated those stupid pens, but they were regulation for all field officers because the Edict Enforcement Commissioner's brother owned the company that manufactured the confounded atrocities.

He interviewed several more eyewitnesses to the bombing, but no one had seen the perps as closely as the old ogre. The others just spoke of vague figures that ran out from the shadows, dropped something near the pub window, and scurried away. They agreed that there were three of them (well, one witness said six, but he was obviously deep into his gourds since he addressed Tol as "you guys"), and that they took off in the direction of Elixir Street. No one else from EE had shown up yet—mostly because they avoided Sebacea whenever possible—and the trail was already getting cold. Tol realized that this was going to be his case for the simple reason that it already was. Every time he fought fate, he didn't even score a point.

He sighed and started sniffing around. Goblins had a pretty well-developed sense of smell; he could definitely catch a faint whiff of elf that led off in the indicated direction. It must be true, then: elves were responsible. He'd never heard of an elf willingly involved in a wanton destructive act like this. What was the world coming to? This could never have happened in the old days. He sighed again.

This time he heard himself sigh, and the sound made him realize what nostalgic nonsense he was thinking. People were people, be they elf, goblin, troll, or even chimera, and people were capable of just about anything at any given moment. They weren't any better or worse than they'd ever been. He was just getting more cynical. Being a street cop in Sebacea will do that to you if you keep at it long enough.

As he tried to track the rapidly-fading scent trail, Tol was a bit put off to discover that the cobblestone walkway he was treading seemed to be dissolving under his feet. The buildings also were behaving rather oddly, in that their exterior walls were bowing out and sucking in, as though they were engaging in respiration, an architectural function he'd somehow never noticed before. The stars peering from between patches of cloud were beginning to leave contrails when he moved his head. This wasn't normal, even for a goblin. Tol stopped for a moment and shook himself. The realization sloshed over him like a large wave of liquefied toffee that he *was* stoned from the smekking gourd. That would boost his detective aptitude, all righty. All righty, all reety, all reety-righty-roty. All de all de lall de lull de looloo.

He sat down abruptly on the sidewalk and began to hum a song from his childhood. The humming turned into singing, and that turned into not very skilled goblinwarbling, which woke most of the neighborhood, or at least that contingent who had managed to get back to sleep after the explosion. Somewhere deep in Tol's brain there was still a tiny capsule of sobriety and that capsule had just enough room for a single thought: *thank the gods that being stoned on the job isn't against regs anymore.* The Commissioner's sister owned a pharmaceutical company that specialized—under the table—in 'recreational hallucinogenics;' EE management as a result now tended to look the other way when officers 'indulged,' so long as no one got hurt or duties weren't *too* grievously impacted.

Tol finished a couple of songs and was about to launch into a third when a large and decidedly odiferous article of footwear came sailing out of a second-story window and plopped unceremoniously into his lap. He grinned at it and took a bite out of the upper. He chewed on it for a few seconds, rolling it around in his mouth like a dollop of vintage razzle. He swallowed with some difficulty and decided that further ingestion was not warranted at this time. It needed to age a bit more. He tossed it aside and got unsteadily to his feet (there being no one else's feet to get to).

He knew there was something he was supposed

to be doing—something important—but his attention kept getting diverted by fascinating little details like the patina on a corroding doorknocker or the way in which a rain gutter jutted out from the wall to which it was no longer firmly attached. As Tol stood there with his head cocked and one eye shut, staring at the empty space between gutter and stone, a liripiped figure crept up on him, silent as a worm, deposited a small package wrapped in paper near his feet, and disappeared just as quietly into the night.

He noticed it right away, as the accumulated precipitation from the cold mist that was now falling rather heavily caught the light from a street lamp and drew his attention. He knelt and picked up the package, fascinated by its sudden appearance. He turned it over in his hands; then his faced screwed up in exaggerated concern when his fingers encountered a greasy film that seemed to be emanating from within. Tol marched over to a nearby public trash receptacle and dropped the offending parcel inside. He turned away and had taken about seven or eight wobbly steps when the trash receptacle blew itself apart. The compound curves of the ornamental slats forming the outer structure of the container hurtled out in all directions, one narrowly missing Tol's head and embedding itself in a brick facade a half meter to his right. The pressure wave from the blast knocked him to his knees.

It took a few seconds to recover from the shock, and by that time he'd noticed a pair of luminous eyes peering out at him from a broken grate. He crawled over to the grate to investigate, serendipitously moving out of the way just in time to avoid being crushed by a gargoyle dislodged from its rooftop perch by the explosion. The stone monster shattered on the sidewalk about two meters behind Tol, spraying berzal nut-sized chunks every which way. The eyes vanished into the pitch-dark recesses from which they'd materialized.

Tol got to his feet and brushed off the gargoyle debris. He picked up one of the chunks and regarded it briefly, wearing a frown that looked like concentration but really was more akin to hangover, and dropped the fragment absently into his overjack pocket. The gourd buzz was beginning to wind down, and he felt a growing sense that something wasn't right. He examined the shattered remains of the gargoyle and peered up at the shadowed skyline trying to ascertain where it had fallen from. The mist had turned into light rain which streamed down his EE helmet and into his eyes. He snapped the collapsible brim into place and pulled his collar up as far as it would go against the chilly dampness. Then he remembered what he was doing out in the wet night.

He backtracked to the last place he'd been sure of the elves' scent and tested the air. The rain had done a thorough job of erasing any definitive trail; all he could register was a faint hint that might or might not be elf spoor. Sighing, Tol picked his way along, relying as much on professional intuition as physical evidence.

Back at the site of the ruined gargoyle, a thickish

mist, faintly blue in color, formed near the center of the debris and slowly began to rotate. It intensified and grew more substantial as the swirling increased in velocity. After half a minute the rotating column was a goblin-foot wide and the center of it radiated a strong white light that suddenly erupted in a blinding flash. When it faded the gargoyle pieces had mysteriously reassembled. This time around, however, the monster was no mere piece of grotesque sculpture. It was quite definitely alive. It shook itself, sniffed the night air, and let out a low, mournful keening. Suddenly it leapt forward and ran along at a trot on powerful, compact legs, nose jutted forward like a hound at the scent. It left a trail of warm, blue liquid oozing from a hole about the size of a berzal nut in its left shoulder.

Chapter Two:
Arnoc, Ferrocs & Dubers (Oh My!)

The Council of Mages and Engineers was billeted in a rather stylish manor house at the east end of the smartly designed and landscaped Royal Tragacanthan Government Complex in Goblinopolis. The building had two distinct components: an elaborate conference suite and office block occupied by the Council and their staffs, and the heavily fortified open floor plan Royal Network Operations Center, known widely as Arnoc. This was the central nervous system of the kingdom, where four discrete network layers provided all the data and control operations for the Royal government. These layers were named for the prevailing color schemes of each: aqua, cyan, teal, and chartreuse (the chief design engineer, it later turned out, was quite color blind and thought he had picked contrasting hues).

Each of these networks had its own dedicated core of analysts, engineers, systems administrators, operators, and programmers. They were in constant rivalry with one another; getting into any of them, however, was the pinnacle of a career in the Royal Data Corps. They were 'the best of the best.' The rivalries were actively supported by senior management because they tended to keep the geeks occupied and too busy to think much about hacking the systems for their own advancement/amusement.

All of the functions of government in Tragacanth were controlled by one or more of these networks, whose terminal linkages with the rest of the country were under the oversight of either engineers or mages. Some of the interfaces were digital, some magical. A few swung both ways. There were five dual interfaces, to be exact; together they constituted what was known as "The Pentagorn." They were located one in each of the five administrative districts of Tragacanth, called *Ferrocs*. Ferroc Norda was in the North, Ferroc Sutha in the south, Ferroc Osta in the West, Ferroc Oria in the East, and Ferroc Loca in the central capitol district. Each of these had a dual interface, or *Duber*, and each interface was under the control of a Magineer, a cross-trained mage and engineer, of which no more than ten existed at any given time, by order of the Council: one primary and one backup for each Duber.

The significance of the Dubers was that they were the only points in the kingdom where the spheres of magic and technology truly overlapped. Magineers were equally well-versed in either realm, which made them the most valuable people around. It took a minimum of fifty years of study and an exhaustive series of progressively more demanding examinations to achieve the status of Magineers' Apprentice, the ranks from which a new Magineer was chosen to ascend by the Council when an existing member died or retired from government service (and most chose to serve for life).

The Magineers are imposing old farts. They've

spent the better part of a life getting to where they are, and they don't care who knows it. The last thing one wants to do with a fine sunny day is waste it arguing anything at all with a Magineer. You're hopelessly outgunned, because if they can't win you over with rational discourse they'll just turn you into an amphibian and let you hop about until you've seen things their way. That can be frightfully inconvenient if you've planned to tee off right after lunch.

Another useful thing to know about Magineer candidates is that they are required to live their entire lives in the district which they hope one day to represent. Each area has its own particular magnetic fields and arcanomorphology that have to be imprinted on the prospective's psychic template in order for him (no female had ever ascended; something to do with genetics, or so the official story goes) to be able to manipulate the Duber fully. The only way to accomplish this is for him to spend many years wandering the district, absorbing its auras and tuning his bioresonance to that of his Ferroc. By the time they've been aligning their neurons with the local universe for that long, they just don't give a wet slap about what lesser mortals think anymore.

Each of them is fanatically convinced that their district is far superior to the others, and they can work up quite a lather when someone dares to intimate otherwise. For this reason they are never allowed to associate with any of the Magineers or Magineers' Apprentices from outside their district, even in the unlikely event they retire from the office and are then theoretically free to travel. It would be like mixing matter and antimatter without the magnetic bottle: quite untidy for the local space-time continuum. A disagreement in person between Magineers would almost certainly result in rearrangement of the nearby landscape and possibly even one or two constellations.

The Dubers were located in highly ornate structures in the capitol of each district. The districts tried to outdo one another in providing facilities for the Duber and its Magineer, and so over the years the architecture had gotten more and more elaborate. In all four of the provincial districts now the Dubers formed the centerpiece of veritable palaces. It takes two years to fully train those who aspire to be guides for assisting visiting engineers and mages in weaving their way through the baroque maze of a Duber complex.

The purpose of the Dubers is to provide a place for registered mages and engineers to access both the awesomely powerful Arnoc and the reservoir of magic known as 'The Slice' through far greater conduits than are available elsewhere. The Arnoc is a repository of all written or spoken knowledge, as well as an almost infinitely powerful computing engine.

The reason that the Royal Network is so powerful rests with the Magineers, or more precisely, their art. When the system was first designed and constructed, the highest level mages and most brilliant engineers in the kingdom collaborated. Every data transport buss in the network's massively parallel CPU array was suspended in a permanent temporal stasis spell that enabled the system to do its calculations, for all practical purposes, instantaneously: essentially infinity-1 flops. No matter how long it actually took to complete a calculation, the amount of time that passed in the native temporal frame was measured in nanoseconds.

It wasn't merely a matter of casting a spell on a piece of machinery, though. The interactions between subatomic particles operating at a quantum level and the flow of magic are extraordinarily complex; some pundits say, in fact, that magic itself is simply a manifestation of quantum energy states. It took many, many failed attempts before engineers and mages working together finally stumbled on the correct procedure, a procedure that became the most jealously guarded secret in Tragacanth. Any significant modifications to the system had to be performed by the only people with total understanding of both the technical and arcane aspects of the architecture—the Magineers.

Custodianship of this awesome resource was the principal job of the Magineer of Ferroc Loca. The Ferroc Loca Duber was located on the grounds of the Royal Palace Complex, only a stone's throw away from the Arnoc. While Duber Loca was the most heavily used interface in the kingdom, the Loca Magineer nevertheless spent most of his time hovering around the Royal Network. His status in the kingdom was roughly equivalent to that of the King, who was in reality the Chief Hacker, although the Loca Magineer had no formal duties as a policy maker. His influence on the king—and therefore on the king's edicts—was usually considerable, nonetheless.

In many ways, the Magineers were a form of clergy: they acted as priests who could commune with a higher power—the supernatural conjunction of magic and technology. Heaven in this mythos was that narrow band of overlap between physics and metaphysics, called *The Slice* by Tragacanthan philosophers. The Arnoc represented the temporal manifestation of The Slice: a place where cutting-edge technology and rarefied magic coexisted in one of the stranger and more sublime of all known juxtapositions.

The current Loca Magineer was, at 62, one of the youngest ever appointed, and he was a certifiable genius even among his esteemed peers. His birth name was Gepefrindos, but he'd bowed to ancient tradition and at his ascendance taken the name Cromalin, which from Old Goblish translates approximately to "Imposer of Order." In strict point of fact he was Cromalin II, since there had been a previous Magineer with that name, but the first Cromalin had served less than two years owing to an unfortunate fatal accident involving a spilled lightning potion and an unexpectedly well-grounded heating duct grating, so very few were even aware of him.

Chapter Three:
Magic Marker

The scent trail effectively vanished at the edge of a large urban park about a kilometer from the ill-fated *Balrog*. Tol made several sweeping arcs centered on the last position where he'd been certain of elf scent, but to no avail. He stood at the park boundary, wondering what to do now, when an ethereal voice washed over him like an invisible wave.

"Looking for something?"

Tol stood up perfectly straight and spun around very slowly. After a complete 360 he wrinkled what little forehead he had and grunted into the cold air. His breath made fog sculptures in the stillness.

"Maybe I am, and maybe I'm not. Who wants to know?"

"I'm positively devastated. Don't you recognize me?"

The sensation bugging Tol the last few seconds was not, as he had first surmised, jock itch. It was a dawning recognition that made his stomach knot up.

"Plåk? For the love of...I *distinctly* remember you being banished to the negative energy plane."

"Change is a fundamental force, Tol-u-ol. I found

a momentarily unguarded teleportal and slipped through. Okay, actually I made the whole banishment story up. You don't sound happy to see me."

"I'd be happier if I *could* see you."

A faint shimmering manifested itself in the air a short distance from Tol. He watched with a kind of grim resignation as it ever so gradually coalesced into a wispy generic biped. When it became apparent that the process had gone as far as it intended to go, Tol arched his eyebrows and chuckled.

"That the best you can manage? You must not be eating right."

"It's been nearly nine centuries in my personal reckoning since I possessed a physical body, goblin. I'm a bit out of practice."

Tol shrugged. "As I recall, you weren't much to look at before, anyway."

Plåk ignored the insult. "I repeat: are *you* looking for something?"

Tol rolled his eyes, "Nah, I just thought I'd go for a little midnight stroll out here in the frozen freakin' wasteland. Of *course* I'm looking for something! Looking for things is part of what I do for a living— if you wanna call this living."

"Would that something be three rather scruffy elves?"

A sharp involuntary intake of breath gave Tol a lung full of crisp, damp air. He coughed as the less sooty park atmosphere mixed with the polluted Sebacea glop resident in his lungs.

"Could be. What do *you* (cough) know about

all this?"

Tol's could feel his mental gears beginning to grind. True, they could stand a good lubing, but he was on the job and his favorite pub was scattered all over the sidewalk.

"About half an hour ago three elves made a quantum portal jump, right about where you're standing. Caused a lot of ripples. I followed 'em for a while, but they disappeared down a wormhole that I wasn't prepared to enter without damn good reason and a reliable map."

"Are you sure it was a quantum gate and not a magical door of some sort?" Tol asked, frowning.

"Quantum portal, for sure. No magical aura, no invocation. Just an old-fashioned temporal distortion with medium-frequency rippling. Seen a lot of 'em, back in my neck of the woods."

Elven teleportation: red flag.

"Someday you're going to have to tell me more about 'your neck of the woods.' It sounds like a weird place."

"Heh. That's exactly what my people would think of Tragacanth. In fact, I doubt if any of them would believe me if I told them about it."

"Tragacanth is the *real* world," Tol sniffed.

"Sure it is," replied Plåk, "as long as that's where you happen to be standin.' To me, this place is like a dream that can't make up its mind if it wants to be a full-fledged nightmare or just the aftermath of an over-spiced meal."

"Yeah? Well, the feeling is mutual. N'plork don't

need you around, anyhow. So, what brings you to our nightmare this time? Surely you didn't tromp across the multiverse just to report sighting three fugitive elves..."

"No, that was pure serendipity. To tell the truth, I came here to find you. I didn't expect it to be this easy, though."

"To find *me*? I must have gone up several notches on your list of favorite people since our last encounter. As I recall, you were none too fond of me then."

"Nothing to do with my fondness for you, or lack thereof. This is not a social call—it's all business."

Tol snorted. "*Business*? What possible business could you have with a goblin? You just said my world doesn't really exist."

"That's not what I said, at all. However, my business with you is predicated on an issue that is of vital concern to goblins, and in fact every creature on this entire planet. It concerns The Slice."

"What about it?"

"I have strong reason to suspect that someone is plotting to disrupt it."

"Disrupt it? How? Why?"

"How, I don't really know, not yet. Why, I can only guess at. I believe that someone wants to do away with magic on N'plork altogether by making it inaccessible, or at least reducing that access drastically."

Tol scratched his head, in that spot right between the temporal ridges that always got sore when he tried to think about things like The Slice.

"Magic is a meta-quantum phenomenon," Plåk

continued, "it exists in a continuum that bears the same conceptual relationship to quantum space as quantum does to the classical universe. That meta-state is accessible to creatures such as us, or rather, you, only via a narrow conduit that you know as The Slice. If something disrupts that conduit, which is actually a region of multidimensional overlap, you will no longer be able to invoke magic in Tragacanth. For example, on my native planet the only gateway was destroyed millennia ago. There is no stable access to magic."

Finally Plåk had said something that Tol could grasp and react to. Doing away with magic would severely disrupt every aspect of Tragacanthan society. That would be a bad thing.

"Why should I believe you?"

"Why would I lie?"

"Plenty of reasons. You're a criminal, for one thing."

"I prefer to think of it as a victim of circumstance. Either way, my 'crime' was not one of deception. However," Plåk paused, picking his words carefully, "I'm merely trying to make amends for my past actions by bringing you this warning. If you choose to ignore it, that be on your head."

"You're not telling me the whole truth."

"Perhaps not, but I'm not telling you any falsehoods, either."

Tol sighed. "Fine. So let's assume that you are telling the truth, at least as you see it. What do you expect me to do about it? I'm not a mage."

"No, but you are an edict enforcement officer.

Can't you report it to your superiors?"

"Report *what*? That a semi-corporeal fugitive from another dimension thinks that someone might be trying to sabotage the space-time continuum? Give me a break. I still have five years before I qualify for a pension."

"Surely someone in your organization understands issues associated with magic. Crimes must be committed using magic all the time."

"Yeah, but most of them get handled by regular jloks like me. We know how to secure a magical crime scene and canvass for magically-related evidence, same as for a physical crime. We leave the analysis to the Forensic Mages."

"Well, perhaps one of them will be interested in my report."

"I can relay it to the Forensic Mage in Charge at my Precinct, but I doubt ol' Derig will be all that interested. He's pretty much a by-the-book kind of gob. FMs are a crabby lot, too."

"It sounds as though you're telling me that no one cares about this threat."

"Oh, I'm sure they'd care about it if they believed it. Trouble is, it's gonna be a hard sell without any proof."

"I think I can supply that proof. Wait here for a few minutes and I will procure it."

"While you're out and about, can you look around for those smekkin' elves?"

What little there was of Plåk vanished abruptly, although Tol thought he heard the echo of a

28

chuckle. He sniffed and looked around. Snow was beginning to fall softly, covering the park in a finely stippled smattering of white. The flakes were tiny and powdery, making sharp outlines of the subtle contours in the surrounding landscape as they settled. Tol noticed that some of those outlines were in the form of regular impressions that appeared to be small footprints he hadn't seen before. They led up to the spot where the elves' trail stopped. He got down on his knees to examine them closely. They were too small for elves, but the wrong shape for kobolds or gnomes or any other races that would leave similarly-sized prints.

Tol reached rather reluctantly into his overjack pocket and extracted his pen. He winced involuntarily as he twisted the cap to activate it. "Pen," he began, clearing his throat, "provide data on any sentient species with the following pedal profile." He traced around the outline of the footprint with the pen.

"Your carpal extremities are cold. Would it kill you to wear gloves when it is snowing?"

Tol tried to be patient. "Please provide the requested data."

"Not in my onboard database. What do I look like, a central library server? I am searching for a compatible datalink. Hold on to your jack. And speaking of jacks, you have got a whopper of a condiment stain two point three centimeters below and to the right of your EE badge."

Tol glanced down at his chest. "Ha ha, made you look," chortled the pen. Its laugh was metallic and grated unpleasantly on the ear, like some ancient wheeled mechanism being operated without benefit of lubrication. He tightened his grip on the pen until something went *sproink*.

"Watch what you are doing, you big simian. Now I am going to need recalibration."

I'd love to recalibrate you with a sledge hammer. "What a shame. Any luck with that datalink?"

"Datalink (hic) established," the pen replied. Whatever Tol had damaged was causing the pen to shudder audibly every few seconds. It sounded a lot like miniature hiccups, and Tol couldn't help but snicker.

"Glad I could be so (hic) entertaining. Maybe next I will (hic) just detonate into tiny high-velocity slivers in (hic) your pocket. That should (hic) be good for a few (hic) hearty (hic) guffaws."

"No need to get testy. I'll get you adjusted next time I'm near the Precinct."

"A great com(hic)fort, I am sure. Your data returns (hic) are in. Footprint profile matches (hic) two species, within morphological (hic) and datametric margin for (hic) error: juvenile gnarlignome and (hic) alfar."

"These definitely aren't the tracks of a gnarlignome—even a young one. They're too shallow and the interior contours are wrong. What the smek is an 'alfar?'"

"An alfar," replied a voice that seemed to come from nowhere and everywhere, "Is a creature of fäerie. Distant kin to the elves, but from an entirely different, entirely magical, stock."

The voice startled Tol, and he dropped the pen

into the snow.

"Mmmfglrkk," it complained.

Tol picked it up and brushed it off.

"Sorry about that." He suddenly remembered why he dropped the pen. "His name is Plåk, and he's from another planet in another dimension."

"Right," replied the pen, its mechanical voice dripping with digital sarcasm, "And I am an unusually large and erudite microorganism with a slight limp."

"You seem to be a microorganism without the hiccups now, at least."

"Yes, the phase mismatch has apparently been corrected. I suppose you will claim that you dropped me intentionally with this goal in mind."

"Hadn't thought about it, but now that you mention it, yeah, I probably will. So, Plåk, welcome back from the outer limits. Did you bring me something?"

"Let us hope it is your medication," grumbled the pen.

"Shut up." Tol stuffed it back into his jack.

A wavy outline that vaguely resembled Plåk shimmered into view.

"Yes, I brought you a little gift," Plåk replied after a few moments. Something dark and shaped like an oversized partially-melted nine-pins ball swathed in a faint orange glow fell to the ground at Tol's feet. He picked it up. It was much denser than he expected.

"What is this blasted thing?" he grunted, letting it fall back to the snow with a heavy, wet plop.

"It's a magic marker: a benchmark created by

the first master mages millennia ago to establish the boundary between magical and physical space. It holds, or rather held, open one of the conduits between The Slice and the physical plane. It had a permanent inviolability spell cast on it before it was put in place."

"Not so permanent, it appears," remarked Tol, doubtfully.

"Aye, quite permanent. Try to damage it."

Tol shrugged and took out his .44. He aimed it squarely at the object and set the modulator to 'Fracture.' The marker absorbed the full charge without so much as a shudder. Tol frowned and turned the indicator to full power. Not even a scratch.

"That charge would cut a serving platter-sized hole hole in a ten centimeter marble gravestone," he said.

"Precisely. The inviolability spell is still quite effective."

"OK, fine. Does that mean the marker was created in this form, then?"

"No, it was once a perfect sphere. There were 24 of them, all told. Don't be frustrated—a conventional weapon one thousand times as powerful as your disruptor would have had exactly the same effect."

Tol raised an eyebrow. "How does one go about turning a magically inviolate perfect sphere into this pathetic melted glob?"

"One destabilizes The Slice, causing it to shrink. This was one of the outermost markers; it was caught in the metaquantum contraction. Essentially, it was melted from within, through a metaquantum anomaly rather like what engineers would call a wormhole, except that this wormhole connected two universes in entropic disequilibrium. The deformation of the marker demonstrates the considerable forces involved in such an event."

"But you don't know how this destabilization is being conducted?"

"No. I didn't witness the contractile event, only its aftermath."

"How do you know it wasn't some sort of natural phenomenon, then?"

"There are no 'natural phenomena' that could cause an event like this across the physical, quantum, and magical universes simultaneously. It just doesn't work that way. There has to be some sort of intentional outside influence that is driving the destabilization, and I'd hazard a guess those three elves were somehow involved."

"Yeah. How about this 'alfar' creature?"

"Ah, yes. The alfar are a race of small bipeds who inhabit a sort of 'off by one' alternate existence where magic is the prevailing natural force. They occasionally travel to both the purely physical and physicomagical universes via The Slice. Some of them spend most of their time in The Slice itself. Not much is known about them, because they tend to be quite secretive and are only rarely encountered, even by those of us who know where to look."

"Why would one be involved with this episode?"

"What makes you think one was?"

"Footprints. Here." Tol indicated the prints that ended abruptly a meter or so from the edge of the park. They were nearly obliterated by the snow now.

Plåk bent down to take a close look. "Well, they certainly do look like alfar prints. This is the spot where I witnessed the elves making the jump. I didn't see another creature with them, though. Strange."

"Maybe he didn't jump with them, or at least not to the same place,"

"Hmm. You may be right. But what was his purpose, then?"

"Ya got me there, sport. I'm just trying to work with what I have right now."

"I shall do some investigation into the matter."

"You do that. I need to get to the Precinct and file a report on all this."

"Then you desperately need to take a bath," said a small, distant voice.

Tol spun around. "Who said that?"

There was no one there. Tol stood for a minute trying to figure out what was going on when he heard a faint metallic giggle coming from his overjack.

"Why the smek didn't they make a 'mute' switch for these pens?"

Chapter Four:
Stone Deef

The operating system for most of the network infrastructure in Tragacanth was the Data Objects Operations and Retrieval System, also known as DOORS. It had been written over a period of several years by a team of Royal software engineers consisting mostly of dwarves and goblins, both of which races were adept at the type of logical, structured reasoning necessary to construct complex computer programs. The chief of this team was a dwarf named Amyr-it, who came from a family of programmers and engineers, including a distinguished uncle who was the sole dwarven member of CoME.

Not only was DOORS the principal operating system for the Kingdom's networks, it was the operating system for the Arnoc. Essentially that meant that anyone who could compromise and control DOORs had the skills to become the Sovereign Head of State for Tragacanth. No one knew more about that network than Amyr-it, and that made him the single most important person in the kingdom, politically speaking. He was only sixty when the network was completed and dwarves have a 200-year life span, so Amyr-it was looking at being the center of attention for a long time to come.

Because he was so knowledgeable of the mechanics of DOORS, Amyr-it had to be guarded at all times to prevent anyone from coercing him into helping them become King. The current monarch naturally had a strong interest in preventing this, so Amyr-it's personal guard always had a high priority in the annual Royal budget. Officially he was free to travel anywhere he liked on a lifetime Royal stipend, but in reality the necessity for heavy guard curtailed his activities drastically. He was in effect a prisoner; his every move had to be carefully orchestrated and involved numerous vehicles. The logistics of his life resembled an ancient dwarven epic poem about the complex workings of the universe.

Amyr-it tried to lead a normal existence. Dwarven culture dictated a large family, but he'd been too busy at first learning his trade and later executing the assignment of a lifetime to cultivate any serious relationships in his early adulthood. Now it was all but impossible to meet anyone, much less carry on anything vaguely resembling a romance. One of the reasons he'd been chosen as leader of the DOORS project was that he was a dwarf, and by Tragacanthan law only a goblin could assume the throne. Otherwise, he'd be pretty much of a shoe-in. Dark and insidious rumors had surfaced from time to time in the years since the first king had been crowned of a back door into the network secretly planted by

Amyr-it or one of his team, but no proof had ever come to light. Certainly Amyr-it had never made even the slightest move that could tarnish his reputation. Considering that such an act would be high treason and punishable by death, one can understand his reluctance to be seen displaying anything but the most salutary behavior in this respect.

Zyxyl, in contrast, was a half-ogre. Half-ogres were rare overall, but not so rare in Goblinopolis itself. Two things made Zyxyl stand out from his hybrid brethren, however: he was of above-average intelligence for the general population (which made him a veritable prodigy amongst half-ogres) and he was one of the *very* small number of his race in Royal Service. Not only was he in Royal Service, he was captain of Amyr-it's guard, which was in practice the third highest military office in the land, surpassed only by Chief of the High Command and, of course, the King himself. This was the loftiest post ever held by a half-ogre, and it made Zyxyl's most routine activities the stuff of legend for the kingdom's half-ogre population.

He was exceptional in other ways, as well, not least of which in that he was a confirmed pacifist. This may seem like an odd trait for a military leader, particularly one whose job involves, if necessary, hand-to-hand combat to the death using the traditional close-quarters weapon of the Tragacanthan Army, the ice tong-like *sklezaxe*. Zyxyl was quite prepared to do his duty, if it came to that, but he vastly preferred negotiation or even evasion to confrontation. Physical intimidation and bloodshed were the tools of absolute last resort in his repertoire, although he was quite adept at both.

This morning, though, Zyxyl had a problem that was more biological than military. This morning there was a lesser basking rok on the pathway that wound its way up out of the secluded glen where Amyr-it's stately home was situated. Now, ordinarily the soldiers in Amyr-it's guard would not have disturbed Captain Zyxyl for this sort of issue. Presumably members of one of the most elite military units in existence would be able to handle the relocation of a single head of wildlife. The problem here was threefold: first, a lesser basking rok had *two* heads, so they were already behind the curve; second, lesser basking roks weighed upwards of three and a half tonnes; and third, they were magical creatures that possessed a natural shield of missile reflectivity. This meant that any projectiles or magical directed attacks used against one were deflected back in the attacker's face.

The soldiers stood around the huge bulk of the creature, which seemed totally oblivious to their presence, discussing their options.

"Well, we cants shoot it, and we cants poke it. Cans we scare it?"

"Scare it? Wi' what?"

"Maybe we could shoot the big gun near one o' its ears. No shell—jest a blank charge."

"I heerd tell those things was deef as a post."

"Who shoveled you thet load of basilisk poop?"

"It were my brother, the one what went ta live

38

up i' the mountains."

"Yer brother wouldn't know a rok from a rooster."

"Here now. What's you gots to go speakin' calumny 'bout my brother fer?"

"I ain't speaking calumny, I'm just sayin' he don' know nothin' bout roks and they habits, on accounta they ain't many of 'em around no mores."

"I oughta belt you one, and good."

"Cheez it you horks, here comes the Cap'n."

Zyxl strode purposefully towards them, annoyance evident in his gait. Something was holding up the motorcade here and whatever it was, he wasn't happy that it hadn't been taken care of by the foremost troops. He hadn't gotten into position to spy the rok yet. He rounded a corner with his mouth open, prepared to bark out an order, when the full nature of the impediment to navigation hove into view. He stopped with his mouth still hanging ajar like a statue of a frog in mid-bug capture and gaped at the thing. It *was* pretty impressive—if you consider 3,500 kilograms of lard in a wart-encrusted slime-green leather bag impressive, that is.

There is evidence, the rokologists say, to suggest that roks were in the distant past capable of physical flight. Little nublets about where the shoulder blades sit were once wings, they theorize. As the creatures evolved the ability to fly using magic, however, the wings slowly diminished in size and utility. Now they were little more than ridges of flesh and cartilage, the underlying bone having given up the ghost after many generations of neglect.

Using magic for locomotion proved such a good idea from the roks' point of view that they decided to take it even further. They gradually started relying on magic for gathering food (they were strict herbivores) and eventually even for eating it. In the process they lost all need for useable limbs, and so evolved into the bloated, inert sacks of fat they had now become. When they got hungry, they just conjured some food into their mouths, or, in the case of the laziest specimens, directly into one or more of their half-dozen stomachs. Roks didn't possess a great many magical abilities, but the ones they did have were finely-honed.

The lesser basking rok was called 'lesser' because it wasn't quite as bloated as the greater basking rok. It was called a 'basking' rok because that's what it liked to do best: bask. And eat. Perhaps 'somewhat less bloated basking and constantly eating rok' might have been a more precise moniker, but that didn't fit on the little plaque at the zoological gardens.

True to form, basking and eating seemed to be the sole items on this particular rok's itinerary, much to the chagrin of Zyxl and the other members of the procession. They were due at a state function at the Royal Complex in little over an hour, and getting there with this adipose deposit in their path was going to be problematic at best. Zyxl tried to coax it out of the way. He tried to intimidate it. He tried to reason with it. He tried the friendly approach. He made up stories about his tragic childhood to try to win its sympathy. He went into a stand-up comedy routine he usually reserved for regimental parties after a bit too much fuzzfruit razzle. Nothing engaged the rok in the least; it kept contentedly chewing on Yamlop leaves it had teleported up from the southern archipelagoes.

Finally Amyr-it himself came forward to see why they weren't moving. He appeared pitifully small next to the hulking half-ogre.

"What's the holdup here?" he asked Zyxl, who was standing there looking peeved.

"This rok here doesn't want to move out of the way." He gestured at the huge beast chewing placidly and staring out into space.

"What have you tried?"

Zyxl recited the list. Amyr-it smiled, reached down to pick up a small stone, rubbed it on the rok's skin, and flung it suddenly and with considerable force at one of the creature's heads. Instead of being deflected, it struck squarely on the nose of the right-hand head. The rok looked very surprised, stopped chewing, seemed to notice all the people around it for the first time, and levitated heavily into the air, disappearing after a few seconds as it teleported to a less crowded basking and eating spot.

Amyr-it wiped his hands together, smiled at Zyxl, and walked off, leaving the Captain blinking and speechless. "Deflection doesn't work if the rok's aura is on the projectile," he called over his shoulder.

"Told ye they was stone deaf," whispered the soldier.

Chapter Five:
Prootwaddler

The Effluent was a dismal place. Through a diabolically efficient combination of magic and engineering, it had become the dumping ground for Tragacanth. Any refuse—solid, liquid, gel, colloidal suspension, liquefied aerosol, you name it—that wasn't close enough to be piped in was teleported there by sanitation mages (the lowest rung on the professional ladder, just above street illusionists, who were considered mere tradescreatures). Located far out on a miserable spit of land in the least inhabited area of the kingdom, the Effluent literally wallowed in its own, and everyone else's, filth.

Since all the garbage of the kingdom ended up here, the place had probably the oddest magical aura in existence. Broken but still magically active remains of every conceivable spell book, potion, amulet, ward, phylactery, charm, symbol, rune, and talisman were scattered randomly about, interspersed with many thousands of tonnes of shattered technical equipment. A fair amount of radioactivity was present, as well. All in all, it was the ideal breeding ground for strangeness, and the sentient creatures which found themselves evolving there against their wills were anything but happy about it. 'Somebody will pay!' was their rallying cry.

In the third year of the reign of Haxxos IV, citizens of Dreadmost, the nearest settlement to the Effluent, began to report odd happenings. Given their proximity to the Effluent, these folks were not unaccustomed to weird goings-on. They were hard to impress this way, in fact. However, the events that were occurring were definitely twisted enough to cause some stir, even amongst the more hardened senior denizens. Some of these old-timers could even remember what it was like before the Effluent forever changed the landscape, not to mention the air and water quality.

It started innocently enough, as these things often do, with some missing pets. No real shock there; the native conventional wildlife in the area was perfectly capable of absconding with the occasional small fur-bearing quadruped or unwary juvenile ornithosuchian. No, what really made the locals sit up and take notice was the way their missing pets kept turning up later with different body parts than the ones their owners remembered them having previously.

No matter how enchanted you are with your loveable little miniature duck-billed dragonette, when it disappears for a couple of days and then shows up scratching at your door equipped with jellyfish stingers and a musk gland, the honeymoon is probably over. Tragacanthan pet owners are fickle that way.

The phenomenon got so widespread that a new temporary industry sprung up overnight in Dreadmost:

itinerant veterinary surgery. Wandering surgeons, most of whom had no surgical training apart from carving at the dinner table, would go door to door looking for distraught pet owners and convince them to shell out a few billmes to have the odd wing, fin, or bioluminescent sexual organ removed. Sometimes, by an extraordinary stroke of good fortune, the pets even survived these procedures.

Despite a boatload of hypotheses, the majority firmly in the 'crackpot' category, no one had yet figured out what force was behind the mysterious somatic enhancements. Some thought they were merely accelerated mutations, brought about by the decidedly unhealthy environment of the Effluent. Others opined that the extraneous body parts were attached by some feral magic or a crazed mage running rampant in the area. None of the armchair theorists seemed inclined to do any field research in support of their various propositions, however.

One resident not intimidated by the situation, or indeed much of anything else, was an ancient gnarlignome named Qrud. Gnarlignomes are known for being stubborn, irascible, and just downright ugly, even to other gnarlignomes. One additional trait of the species is an obsession with privacy; little factual information was available concerning how—or even why—they breed. Most people were entirely satisfied with this situation.

Qrud's favorite pet, a near-blind burrowing hound he'd imaginably named "Digdog," came home one winter's day with rabbit's ears grafted onto its rear end, and this pissed Qrud off something fierce. He pulled himself up to his full regal one meter height and marched out into the frozen wasteland brandishing an old bent walking stick his grandfather had told him was a magic staff. He stomped around for half an hour or so, challenging anything within earshot and waving the stick menacingly.

No foe rose to meet his challenge, and eventually he got tired and headed for home. Not more than thirty meters from his yard he heard a strange melodic whirring and traced the sound to a small rock outcrop. Approaching it cautiously, with staff poised and ready to strike, Qrud leapt onto a boulder with surprising grace and stared disapprovingly down at a wide fissure in the table rock below him.

There was a metallic blob in there; a rambling piecework of a robot studded with blinking lights and seemingly constructed from spare parts intended for a wide variety of instruments and machines, none of which were robots. Indeed, the only electromechanical apparatus Qrud could visualize not represented by one or more of the thing's components would be a functional automaton. It didn't seem to have all the right parts for what it was trying to be, no matter what that was.

The chimeric robot chirred away, seemingly unaware of Qrud or his misgivings. It had what appeared to be spotlights aimed out the openings in the fissure on either side, except that they were putting out very little light. It was a soft, fuzzy, blue luminescence, barely detectable by Qrud's eyes. He realized it must be mostly ultraviolet.

As Qrud wondered what, if anything, to do about the metallic monster, he saw movement off to his right. Crouching instinctively, he watched a rather nice specimen of prootwaddler approach the crevice as though compelled. Proots were eight-legged segmented porcines—roughly a cross between a centipede and a pig—created as a practical joke by some ancient mage. They had proven quite adept at reproducing, and so were now firmly established as a species. Qrud realized that his mouth was watering: proots made for fine eating, at least if you're a gnarlignome and you roasted them long enough to burn off the fused chitinous shell. Stinky business, that.

The animal scuttled up to the opening in the rock without fear. Its attention appeared to be riveted on the spotlight, which was obviously a powerful attractant and seemed to have a mesmerizing effect as well. It stuck its snout just inside the crevice, sniffed a couple of times, and ambled on in. There was a muffled squeal followed by a low frequency static noise; the robot's lights dimmed momentarily. The unmistakable odor of frying bacon filled the air, sparking naked hunger in Qrud.

After a few seconds Qrud heard a scratching noise coming from the vicinity of the other side of the crevice. He peered down into the darkness and suddenly a small figure emerged into the soft radiance of the spotlight. It was the proot, except that it now seemed to have something growing out of its back.

While Qrud puzzled over the extra appendages, it suddenly unfolded its new wings and flew unsteadily off into the night, flapping the bat-like membranes in heavy strokes.

"Uch," Qrud grunted, "Cherry t'warn't a praper porker, or I dinna care tae tink what mayn befall. Flyin' porkers canna be a gud ting." He opened his palm and swept his hand upward in brief supplication to the gnarlignome god Arfsweener, protector of the world, asking for his purification of this bizarre villainy. From somewhere high above him, Qrud heard a thin scream that grew louder and more resonant until at the last possible millisecond before impact Qrud leapt agilely to the left. The rock on which he was standing cracked and split open, scattering lithic debris in all directions. Qrud was thrown clear by the impact. Standing up and brushing himself down, he peered into the newly-opened crack. There was a glowing fragment of meteorite embedded deep in the fissure with steam rising from it, positioned precisely where he had been standing a moment before.

Qrud's malformed brow knotted and he stared up at the sky, hands on hips. "Missed me, ya uld sut," he barked, shaking his fist and making a rude gesture with his multiple ear lobes. A deep, booming sound that could have been laughter echoed off the tortured landscape and died away like the memory of a miserable and protracted illness.

The impact had triggered a mini-avalanche in the crevice where the robot was lodged. When the dust settled, Qrud peered into the opening but saw naught save rubble. The spotlights were broken, one of them separated from its stanchion and lying in pieces on the ground. He heard no noise nor saw any evidence that the robot had survived the experience. Qrud grunted in satisfaction and waved his staff over the rock pile as though he were commanding it to stay sealed. He looked into the sky again, gave Arfsweener a thumbs-up, and then hobbled home, alternately grumbling and chuckling under his breath.

"The committee will come to order. Now!"

This last word was spoken with sufficient emphasis that the five other participants seated around the giant toadstool stopped throwing fairy buttons at one another and directed their attention to the speaker, an imposing figure of vaguely elven features, yet stockier and less angular. They were a curious bunch, this Committee for the Restoration of All Magical Privileges, also known as CRAMP: three weather-beaten elves, a kobold, an elderly ogre mage, and a leader of indeterminate race who dressed entirely in black (except for a single elaborate gold earring).

They met in a stereotypical sylvan glade, complete with faerie ring, in which their meeting table was the largest object. They had temporarily scaled themselves down to fit, both for secrecy's sake and to save money on refreshments.

CRAMP was indeed a secret society. They

took great pains to maintain their anonymity and conceal the existence of their organization. The few woodland creatures that passed by during the meeting knew something was up, of course, since you didn't often see bipeds reduced to this size, but woodland creatures are, on the whole, not really interested in anyone's business but their own. Most merely gave the proceedings a curious glance and a wide berth.

"Gentlemales...and lady," the speaker began, nodding to the female elf among them, "Fellow Tragacanthans and members of our esteemed committee," he paused to adjust his breeches, which seemed to be migrating around to one side of his hips—it's hard to get clothes that fit well when you're not even ten centimeters tall. "We are met here today to discuss recent developments in the struggle to restore magic and magical talent to the social pinnacle they once enjoyed in our fair land. Three among us have struck a resounding blow for the cause in Goblinopolis, only narrowly escaping one of the dark agents of technology." At this the three elves looked uncomfortable and fidgeted. One of them rubbed his arm self-consciously.

A large iridescent green dragonfly drifted up and landed on the toadstool, directly in front of the speaker. It settled and began to clean its front legs. He rocked to the right and left, trying to see around it to continue his oration. Finally the kobold impulsively leapt upon the mushroom and kicked the dragonfly's thorax, just behind the wings. The insect swiveled its head around and regarded him with inscrutable prismatic compound eyes, then took to the air with an angry buzz. It circled the meeting a couple of times and darted off into the woods. The kobold huffed and returned to his seat. The other participants tittered.

When a modicum of decorum had been restored, the speaker continued. "As a result of the efforts of these three gallant heroes, we believe a dangerous and highly subversive obstacle to our cause has been removed." The ogre mage raised his arm. "If yer referrin' to Pyfox, I saw the divil only yesterday. He was veer much alive."

The speaker stared at him for fully ten seconds, lower jaw quivering a little.

"If true, this is indeed unfortunate."

"Ov curz it's true. Ozervise I wedn't hev sed it, pootis."

The speaker turned to the elves, "I thought you said your mission was a success."

The elves looked at one another. One of them finally spoke up, "Our *mission* was to plant the bomb. We did that, and we heard it detonate. We placed it as close as we could to where Pyfox and his gang were seated. After that we were rather too occupied with escaping to ascertain if we got him or not."

The speaker closed his eyes, took a deep breath, and then said, simply, "If you will excuse me for a moment." He turned and walked to the perimeter of the faerie ring, disappearing in a little flash of golden sparkling luminescence. A few seconds later an agonized warbling drifted across the toadstool from somewhere off in the woods. The speaker reappeared shortly thereafter and resumed his position behind the improvised acorn shell lectern. He seemed to be about a centimeter taller than before. The other members of CRAMP tried to look nonchalant, drumming their fingers and whistling.

The speaker lifted his head and attempted to regain a somewhat dignified air, despite the sea of raised eyebrows facing him. He paused for a few moments, pretending to shuffle his nonexistent lecture notes, and finally cleared his throat to speak.

"It appears our itinerary is not quite so far along as I had believed. However, we shall not allow this minor setback to deter us in our struggle. We shall overcome!" He paused again, looking through his notes.

"You said you planted 'the bomb.' What about the backup device?"

An elf who hadn't spoken to this point piped up, "I dropped that one near a goblin we saw leaving the pub after the first device detonated. He looked like he might be in cahoots with Pyfox."

"*Looked like*? Did you observe him actually talk to or associate with Pyfox in any way?"

"No. But he was in the pub at the same time. He could have been an accomplice."

"And of course," added one of his compatriots, "he *was* a goblin."

The speaker eyed him with a frown. "Please do not target any more unauthorized civilians. It makes for bad public relations."

A strange whooshing sound at this moment was followed immediately by a loud splat that shook the toadstool like an earthquake. An enormous deluge of thick white fluid splashed up and out, very nearly suffocating CRAMP *in toto*. As they gasped and thrashed about in the foul-smelling muck, they glimpsed high above them a large sea-avian soaring gracefully back toward the ocean. At a lower altitude they saw the green dragonfly circle twice and disappear. It seemed as though a thin reedy laugh floated gently on the wind from its direction.

"I ne'er did take to those wee green beasties," muttered the kobold.

Chapter Six:
A Magical Beast

Tol stared at the report on his desk. It was giving him a colossal headache—but with a head the size of a goblin's that is about the only kind of headache there is to get. He cradled his throbbing supraorbital ridges in his hands and tried to make sense of the words. "Forensic examination of the explosive residue indicates that the device was composed of an outer shell of finely ground carbonaceous material enclosing a phase-transduction hypermagical thermal core." This last term was giving him trouble. He read it out loud slowly, trying to pronounce all of the words, one syllable at a time. It was rough going.

He stood up and paced in small circles in his cramped office, puzzling over the report. Three elves had planted a magical bomb wrapped in a jacket of charcoal outside a tavern. It had killed six people and injured thirteen more, covering everyone else in the vicinity in a fine spray of something like pencil lead. No one claimed credit, and no obvious motive for the act existed. He had tracked the elves to a park, at which point they had apparently escaped via a quantum portal—not an easy thing to come by in Goblinopolis, or even all of Tragacanth, for that matter. The peculiar mix of magic and technology left him uneasy—most folks were in the habit of employing one or the other almost exclusively. Except for a Magineer, of course, but it was ludicrous even to speculate that one of those could be in any way involved in this sordid episode. They simply didn't have time or motivation. Besides, the only member of that illustrious order allowed in the capitol sector was Cromalin, the Loca Magineer. A Goblin of his lofty stature simply didn't get mixed up with petty plots of this sort. It wasn't even worth considering. Tol wondered why he wasn't convinced.

He suddenly felt a bit peckish and decided to go out for a bite. He grabbed his overjack off the rack and noticed for the first time that there was a long vertical slit in the fabric just below the shoulder blades. He scratched his head and wondered where *that* had come from. Examining the tear more closely, he found a flake of thick green paint adhering to the lip of the opening. A dim, fuzzy memory of the events following the pub bombing floated tantalizingly on the edge of perception. He seemed to remember things flying through the air, things possessed of the same lurid green as the paint chip. He recalled two shining spots that he at length identified as eyes. Gradually the gourd-induced obfuscation began to peel back.

With a start, Tol suddenly remembered the greasy package and the explosion that had torn apart the trash receptacle. It had clearly been meant for him. He hadn't even mentioned that incident in his report, mostly because he'd forgotten about it in the gourd aftermath. Someone had tried to blow him up. Was it connected to the bombing of the *Balrog*? What were the eyes he was remembering? It was hard to discern between actual memory and drug fantasy, but something about the clarity of those eyes led him to believe they were more than simply figments of a pharmacological hallucination.

He headed out the Precinct door and down the block towards his favorite deli. They had a triple-decker spumefish sandwich to die for. The night was cold and clear, with two bright moons overhead and a third just setting. Despite his recent struggle with recovered memories, Tol was in a decent mood. He started to whistle, but only got about three notes out before something slammed him very hard from behind, just above the superior ischial crest. He stumbled and went sprawling on his face, but rolled and came back up in a crouch, disruptor in hand.

There was nothing there. Tol frowned and rubbed his torn elbow. Well, *something* had sure hit him. That was no smekkin' hallucination, he thought, looking at the blue-green blood splatter on the sidewalk. *His* blood.

There was no evidence of any physical projectile. Was this some sort of magical missile attack? Nope, the aura was wrong for that. No trails, no residual harmonics. He sniffed the night air. There was a strong scent here, but it wasn't one he'd ever encountered before. It was feral, animal, yet strangely exotic. Arcane, in fact. A magical beast, then. If so, where was the thing now? Remembering the force of the blow with a wince, Tol shrank back into the wall of a building to guard against another rear assault.

The night was still and moist. Only the ambient sounds of Goblinopolis could be heard: a steady drone of nocturnal commerce punctuated by the occasional shout or hollow metallic clang. Every so often a less easily identifiable noise echoed across the urban landscape, but Tol had learned to ignore these in a city of several million creatures of a variety of races and cultural traditions. To do otherwise would be to invite raving paranoia, and Tol already had the regulation ration of that.

The strange scent suddenly grew stronger. Tol snapped into a defensive posture, every nerve tingling. He scanned the streets carefully, but the only movement was from a scavenging darkcrow, moving down the gutter looking for scraps. It scarcely noticed Tol, intent as it was on locating a meal. He watched it pecking along, feeling reassured by its apparent lack of concern. The avian suddenly stopped, tilting its head and casting an unblinking eye up at Tol, as though startled by something above and behind him. Without warning it bolted into the air, screaming an alarm call.

Something very heavy dropped on Tol's shoulders as if from a great height. It drove him to his knees and then forward before leaping off and disappearing into the shadows with blinding speed. Definitely animate, he thought through the curtain of pain from his spinal column, knees, and hands. This must be what it's like to be a stuntgoblin's landing pad.

Goblins are not delicate creatures. They have heavy bone structure, dense musculature, and very thick hide. They can take abuse that would pulverize most bipeds and come back for more with what passes in goblin facial morphology for a smile. After just two hits by his mysterious assailant, however, Tol wasn't smiling. He wasn't even smirking. He was hurting. This thing had all the subtlety of a speeding dray, but sported far better maneuverability and the apparent ability to climb buildings or fly. Besides a bruised and battered goblin, it left behind a very strange magical aura that Tol was beginning to find distantly familiar.

He still couldn't put his finger on it, but there was something about the *modus operandi* of his opponent that tugged at the shirttails of his mind. (This would be a lot more effective metaphor if goblins habitually wore shirts, of course.) The scent began to get stronger again and Tol decided he couldn't take another round of that punishment. He broke into a hobbled run for the alley. It didn't make much difference that he'd be cornered there—he knew he couldn't outrun the thing. At least he'd be covered on three sides. He found a small piece of ornamental stone cornicework that jutted out from beneath a window and ducked under it as a partial defilade.

Tol's entrenched position forced a frontal attack, which was a bit of a gamble. The previous two assaults had been little more than glancing blows. If the thing hit him full in the chest, who knows if he'd even survive. But at least this way he might have a chance to get off a point blank disruptor shot. He pulled out the weapon and set it to emergency overcharge. This would give him two or three pulses at above maximum power before the weapon fried itself. He figured the battle would be over by then anyway, one way or the other.

The scent of the beast was once again growing intense. Tol dropped into his best EE academy-approved defensive stance with both hands bracing the disruptor, and waited. The air was very still, and the night strangely silent. He could hear his own heart beating—it sounded like someone with a jackhammer trying to remove his eardrums from the inside.

Suddenly a massive quadruped appeared, as though out of thin air, less than a meter from his face. His reflexes were on overdrive, and without thinking he squeezed off a shot. The disruptor belched out a hideous blaze of brilliant blue that drove the gun into his solar plexus. The energy bolt hit the monster full in the neck, just below the chin. It had roughly the same effect as trying to stop a moving carriage with a torch beam. Tol knew then and there without any shred of doubt that he was finished. The beast advanced on him, slavering jaws agape, and he fired his last shot right down its throat. The beast hesitated for a second, although he didn't know if it had anything to do with his feeble attempt at defense. He threw the now useless disruptor into the hideous maw and waited for the end.

The little voice that had been nagging him now

told him to reach into his overjack pocket. He didn't have much else to do, in these last few seconds of life, so he decided to humor it. In that pocket was a hard, irregular lump that surprised him. He fingered it, and suddenly realized what it was. With a supernatural effort he launched himself sideways, squirming past the creature's reactive paw swipe, and bolted for a garbage collection bin about five meters away. As he ran, he tossed the object over his shoulder in the general direction of the beast. It inscribed a graceful arc, halting abruptly at the apex, where it began to glow with a golden radiance. The beast slammed the brakes on its pursuit of Tol and stood perfectly still. The now brilliantly glowing object moved slowly and purposefully through the air, heading for a dark, ugly chasm rimmed with bluish residue in the beast's left shoulder. It fit with fine precision into the gap, and as it made contact the golden glow spread until the entire beast was similarly illuminated. Tol could now see it for what it was. Not just an animate gargoyle. *A Guardian.*

The Guardian shook itself and stared straight into Tol's fascinated eyes for a moment. Then it rose majestically into the air like some great dirigible and dematerialized, leaving behind a faint golden mist that gradually dispersed into what Tol now came to realize was the rather fetid atmosphere of the alleyway. He slumped against the garbage bin and exhaled slowly. It was nights like this he wished he'd taken his mother's advice and gone into rock ranching.

Chapter Seven: Change of State

Aspet had been a studious, focused young goblin for the first several years of his education. He had discovered computers somewhere along the way and grew more and more obsessed with them. He wasn't very athletic, but nevertheless possessed the usual intense competitive spirit of his race. He found that engaging in ever more complex computer challenges allowed him to express his competitive instinct and achieve victory much more successfully than any physical activity would have permitted.

At first he'd been primarily interested in gaming. Online gaming was a huge enterprise in Tragacanth. Besides hundreds of local and regional hobbyist groups, there were two competitive professional leagues for games ranging from single-player-against-all-comers deathmatches to massively multiplayer pro-am games where amateurs competed for the right to join teams led by a professional gamer. It was very big business for the hosts, and very absorbing for the participants.

Aspet was a competent gamer, but gradually the thrill of simply fragging opponents, farming resources, and solving online puzzles began to pale for him. He hit upon modifying the factory configurations for the game console to optimize his experience. He spent his allowance on programming books and courses, and started hanging out in hacker areas on the net. He downloaded code and compiled it himself, then toyed with it to learn exactly how it worked. After a while he began to write his own utilities—simple at first, but becoming more and more complex as his knowledge base grew. He became adept at several of the most popular programming languages, but his very favorite was DOORS.

Before he was really aware of what was happening, Aspet had become a veritable expert at the ins and outs of programming in DOORS. He even created a small footprint subset of the operating system he named KNOBS (KineticNoodle's Object Brokering System, after his online handle), for use in portable devices. This was a wildly popular move, and made Aspet one of the better-known hackers. Of course, everyone knew him as kineticnoodle, not Aspet, but that was by design because his parents would have been highly disturbed if they knew their little goblin cupcake was a, gulp, *hacker*. Not everything he'd learned had gone into creating free tools for legitimate use.

After Aspet finished school, he was looking around for his first real job when he came across an advertisement for The Seminar. He'd heard about The Seminar all his life, of course, but never paid much attention to it because it seemed too far from the reality of his personal world. The full name was *The Preparatory Seminar for Aspirants to Royal Office*, which of course is why it was popularly known as simply 'The Seminar.' This was far more than simply another Continuing Professional Education course, though—it served as the initial screening mechanism for future monarchs of Tragacanth. The final day of the event was a laboratory session where students pitted themselves against a team of crack Arnoc NetSec techs. Those who managed to achieve a set number of strategic objectives in this contest were certified as potential Royal Candidates and allowed to petition the Crown for the Right of Challenge, subject to approval by CoME.

Tragacanth had not always been a monarchial technocracy, of course. Until the advent of the digital age a hundred years ago it had been a conventional monarchy, ruled by a member of one of the three principal noble families, who juggled the throne among them. It had been a fairly stable system, but suffered from the utter lack of accountability to which hereditary absolute monarchies are inevitably subject.

The Royal government took little notice when computers began to dominate the command and control landscape in Tragacanth. Computers were just electronic filing machines to the King and his staff—as such they lay in the realm of clerks and other menials, well below the Royal purview. That indifference ended abruptly one night in the midst of a crucial negotiation with neighboring Galanga over a border dispute. The Tragacanthan King at the time, Rexingrasha II, was in usual goblin style attempting to intimidate the Galangan monarch by rattling sabers all along the disputed territory. The Galangan Potentate, a cerebral gnome named Clorvos, wasn't having any. He ordered his highly-trained Silicommandos into action.

By noon the next day, Tragacanth was virtually without power, data mining, communications, financial transactions capability, or entertainment (other than the spontaneous massive public demonstrations protesting the Royal *faux pas*). Rexingrasha was furious, but he had little recourse but to back down, as his kingdom was in a crisis of chaos. Clorvos, to his credit, was fairly magnanimous about the whole thing. He wasn't the aggressive, posturing sort, unlike the goblin—once Tragacanth backed off he instructed the Silicommandos to undo whatever damage they were able. The damage to Rexingrasha's reputation, and to the noble status quo of Tragacanth, however, was irreversible.

For the first time, the citizens of Tragacanth realized that their leader, not to mention their information infrastructure, was vulnerable. Of course, they all knew deep down that kings were just people, with the same frailties and insecurities as everyone else, but up until now those shortcomings had been well-hidden by a combination of stellar public relations and the inherent goblin need to believe in the unassailable nature of their government. Suddenly their king, and by association their nation, had been violated by a foreign power—critically embarrassed on the world stage, as it were.

Goblin society does not tolerate weakness and failure very well. It wasn't long before Rexingrasha found himself the object of derision, rather than the adulation to which he and his forebears were accustomed as monarchs. The Royal Protective Corps began to pick up signs, in fact, that a popular rebellion might be gaining momentum. This enraged the king, who felt that absolute obedience and unquestioned loyalty were his due as the head of state. He ordered the RPC to round up anyone whom they saw leading, advocating, or even—at the end—*looking* as though they *might* support a demonstration against the regime. This sort of strong-arm tactic just led to more resentment; violence and even civil war seemed inevitable.

The tinderbox was on the verge of ignition when an extraordinary event took place. For the first time since the founding of the Magineers, the Loca Magineer, an ancient named Preotimast, made a public appearance and appealed to the angry mobs for peace. He made a simple proposal: if the people did not want to be outgunned in the computer arena, why not ensure that their ruler was not only cognizant of computer technology, but among the best hackers around? Let the king prove himself worthy of leading the people, or step aside in favor of someone more capable. Preotimast had never been particularly impressed with Rexingrasha as a leader, anyway.

Such a radical proposal would have been met with scorn at best, exile at worst, if made by anyone else in the kingdom. The Loca Magineer, however, was in many ways the spiritual leader of Tragacanth; he commanded as much if not more respect than the king himself (especially under the current circumstances). Rexingrasha was predictably shocked by what he saw as Preotimast's treachery. He ordered the Magineer's arrest on charges of high treason, but the RPC seemed strangely reluctant to follow his command. They'd never had to arrest a Magineer before; they weren't even sure such a thing was possible, given the defensive capabilities of the Loca Duber.

This reticence from his own household troops was the final straw for Rexingrasha's mental health. He left the palace with his personal guard hurrying to keep up, rode to Royal Proclamation Square in the heart of Goblinopolis, and in a shrill and almost hysterical oration declared Preotimast a traitor to the Crown. The crowd that had gathered turned instantly hostile, and the king's bodyguards were on the verge of being overwhelmed by the angry mob when the 'traitor' himself appeared again. The antagonists faced each other in silence in the center of the square for several minutes. Finally Preotimast spoke.

"It would seem, my Lord King, that you have reached an impasse. While I wish you no ill will, I cannot allow you to subvert the office of Magineer of Ferroc Loca. Nor, it appears, will the people of Tragacanth."

Rexingrasha was vain, petty, officious, and occasionally callous, but he was not altogether dim. He added up the odds using all thirteen of his primary digits, realized that they weren't even in the approximate neighborhood of good, and started looking around for a way to back out without losing what little face he had left. Not that a goblin face, even a king's, would be any great loss.

By this time the Tragacanthan Army had rolled up to join the party, but they were disinclined to act once they saw how the wind was blowing. Backing the right horse has always been the goblin prime directive. The situation had degenerated into a whole lot of goblins (and a smattering of other races) standing around watching the king look for a hole to crawl into. This is actually the sort of thing that passes for popular public entertainment in Goblinopolis. A few enterprising bookies were giving odds and taking bets along the periphery.

Preotimast stood motionless, watching the king through barely slitted eyes. Actually, as he admitted to an Apprentice later, he had nodded off, but even in vertical repose he was a commanding figure, as old geezers go. Rexingrasha was meanwhile making a mental note to execute whoever had suggested he get out of bed this morning.

There's not much to say about the rest of Rexingrasha's day—it sucked. By the time the last sun set, he had come face to face with the fact that he was going to have to fight to keep his crown. *Fight*. Rexingrasha Lungmuch, the sovereign of Tragacanth by right of birth. It just didn't seem possible that the duly-consecrated monarch of the most powerful goblin nation in the world should have to justify his position of authority—all because of a little worm of a gnome and his sniveling horde of nostril-excavating computer weenies.

A couple of days later a Royal Proclamation was issued inviting any adult male goblin of pure blood native to Tragacanth to apply as a candidate to challenge the king for the right of ascension to the throne. Rexingrasha instructed his aides to screen applicants carefully and reject those who seemed to possess any significant computer knowledge. Preotimast, however, sent over an Apprentice to interview the candidates as a representative of the Magineers. The King's aides found themselves between a rock and a hard place when the Apprentice insisted on the right to review and supersede the aides' evaluation of candidates' suitability. They decided in the end that they were more afraid of the Loca Magineer than a likely lame dabbling-avian monarch.

The contest was scheduled for one month from the day the applications were closed, to give the candidates time to prepare (and to allow the King to take a crash course in hacking). Only about a dozen goblins signed up, most of them barely old enough to participate (Rexingrasha had set the minimum age at fifty, on the grounds that anyone younger than that brought up outside the Royal Family couldn't possibly have the depth of experience necessary to rule. Preotimast agreed).

Among the contestants was a youngish hacker of impoverished family background by the name of Carnilox. He was employed by the Royal Data Corps as a systems administrator for the Agricultural Support Services Network, perhaps the least prestigious unit of the RDC, although no less vital to the nation's economy for it. Carnilox's family were subsistence farmers and rock ranchers; he was proud to be serving in a job that provided them significant assistance. The ASSN kept track of harvests, requests for seasonal labor, subsidized seed allocations, fertilizer shipments, and other logistics related to food production for the kingdom.

Carnilox was not a dedicated hacker in the deep sense of the word. He was a network problem-solver who had very few government-supplied sophisticated tools to work with, so he'd spent his career making due. This had by necessity honed both his programming skills and his ability to think outside the box—talents that now promised to serve him well in his quest for the throne.

There were other viable contenders in Tragacanth, of course, but most of the highly skilled hackers were either too contemptuous of the establishment to have any desire to meld with it or too far underground to emerge safely. Only one of the other declared candidates had any real chance against Carnilox: a shadowy figure who went by the handle "Lempo." No one seemed to know his real name or anything else about him. He managed somehow to convince the screeners that he was a native Tragacanthan, and he was obviously male, a goblin, and over fifty. Since these were the only conditions the king had set forth for qualification to candidacy, Lempo was allowed to participate.

Carnilox was aware of his opponent by reputation only: as far as he knew they had never before met face-to-face. Lempo was fond of writing exploits that targeted specific computers owned by commercial concerns, then in the spirit of public service offering to plug the holes he'd demonstrated—for a tidy sum. It was a form of extortion, thinly veiled by Lempo's affectation of Samaritanism, but as yet it was not technically against Tragacanthan edict.

Carnilox found nothing about Lempo in person to change his less-than-favorable opinion. He seemed to be a self-centered, arrogant, crude, sociopath. However, none of this was material at the moment—all that mattered were Lempo's hacking skills, which Carnilox knew to be considerable. One problem he had in formulating a strategy for countering Lempo's probably superior programming abilities is that no one except the Arnoc security team who were charged with setting up the contest parameters had any idea what sort of format the challenge would take. After all, this had never been done before. There was a much better than even chance that Rexingrasha would take whatever steps he could to rig the contest in his favor; this went more or less without saying. With Preotimast looking over his shoulder constantly, and his Apprentices supervising preparations at the Arnoc, the king would have to be extremely crafty to stack the deck, though. As it turned out, craft and guile were piranhas that swam freely in the

Lungmuch gene pool.

"And this, Your Majesty, is a *pointer*. It's called a pointer because it points to an area in memory where a value is stored. It's important to remember that operations performed on a pointer do not affect the value to which the pointer points. If you want to get at the actual data, you have to do so by *dereferencing* that pointer."

Rexingrasha was struggling with several sensations at once: incomprehension, acute boredom, and incipient panic. He was so totally out of his league here that it felt as though he were learning a completely new language, being taught by an alien to boot. He sighed and tried to grasp what Sildran, the Chief Arnoc programmer, had just told him.

"So if I want to change the value in memory, I have to change the pointer, too?"

"No, not at all. If a house changes occupants, the address of that house doesn't change, does it? That's the same principle we're talking about here."

The king rubbed his royal temples. "I need a break, Sildran. I'm going to take a walk out on the parapets to clear my head. Amuse yourself. Write some code or something. I'll be back in a little while."

"As His Majesty wishes."

Rexingrasha strolled along the wind-swept walkway perched high above the Royal Palace. From here he could just see the sunlight glimmering off the Sea of Fleriz far to the northeast; to the southwest he could make out the dark wavering line of the majestic Espwe Mountains, to the east the heavily-wooded Bungash range was visible. The vast forbidding desert basin of Asga Teslu lay off to the west. Virtually every nook and cranny of the sprawling city of Goblinopolis could be observed from here, as well, especially through the array of high-definition telescopic surveillance optics spaced regularly up and down the guardrails of the ten kilometer-long parapet that completely encircled the Royal Compound.

Rexingrasha hadn't made very much use of the monitors himself—he preferred his network of spies and operatives on the ground—but his father had been a regular visitor to the security observation stations. The old boy had always been a bit of voyeur, though. The king chuckled at the thought of his father sitting in a room full of screens, his gaze eagerly darting to and fro among them.

After two weeks of almost non-stop study, it was becoming apparent to Rexingrasha that he wasn't going to be able to compete successfully in the upcoming challenge if it were a fair fight. He just wasn't the hacker type. Various possible solutions to this dilemma suggested themselves: sneak in a "pinch-hacker" (hard to pass off as legitimate); find some way to compromise the network beforehand (hard to arrange); see to it that the other candidates were "indisposed" (hard to get away with); or buy off one or more of the judges...yes. This last alternative was much more in keeping with his background, training, and inclination.

Money wasn't an issue. After all, he was the

king, and had the vast Tragacanthan Royal Treasury at his beck and call. No, the critical decision here was exactly whom to bribe, and how to broach the subject diplomatically. Discretion was obviously a key element, as was proper sizing up of potential bribees. Fortunately, Rexingrasha had for just such a contingency retained the services of perhaps the best practitioner of these ancient arts in the world: an antelf named Nessendar. The antelves were so called because they eschewed most of the character traits generally ascribed to their elvish kindred: kindness, bravery, non-violence, optimism, and goodwill chief among them. That's not to say that they weren't capable of expressing these characteristics, but they were not part of the normal antelf behavioral repertoire.

Nessendar had been the mastermind behind most of the truly successful underhanded foreign and domestic policy initiatives of Rexingrasha's reign. He was a genius, and fiercely loyal to whomever held the purse strings. He excelled as a spin doctor, and at arranging clandestine affairs of the heart or of state. Best of all, he was an absolute master at funneling funds to the proper destination without drawing undue attention. All in all, Nessendar was the perfect person to ensure that Rexingrasha retained the throne.

Not that his assistance would come cheaply. Far from it, in fact—he was bound to realize the critical part he was playing in the survival of the Lungmuch royal dynasty and expect to be compensated accordingly. It would be worth it, though. If anyone could save

Rexingrasha's Royal Keester, it was Nessendar.

The day of the challenge dawned a little later than usual, as both suns were retrograde that morning (considered by the superstitious to be an ill omen), but eventually daylight flooded the amphitheater adapted for the event. As expected, thousands of Tragacanthans and a contingent of foreign press were on hand to witness the spectacle. It wasn't every day you saw a hereditary monarch battle a dozen computer nerds to keep his crown. His Majesty was seated at a terminal in the center of the stage, the competitors arranged around him in a semicircle, facing the audience. The three judges sat at terminals off on far stage left. Spaced evenly throughout was a team of proctors who would keep all the candidates under close scrutiny during the competition.

Rexingrasha went into the contest with supreme confidence. Nessendar had assured him that the judges were "favorably disposed" towards him. All he had to do was run a couple of canned scripts that had been hidden on his workstation by a loyal Arnoc technician and wait to be declared the winner. That would show all those insufferable geeks who the boss of this kingdom was, once and for all. As soon as he was securely in power again, he'd have no difficulty suppressing any investigation if someone cried foul. He'd also make unauthorized hacking of any sort a crime and toss all those little turds into a deep, damp hole somewhere: he already had the Edict drawn up. His royal palms had gone all sweaty with anticipation at the mere thought. Carnilox was seated second from the end on stage right. He cracked his knuckles and surveyed his opponents. Lempo was on the other side, right next to the king. Interesting. The faces of the other ten candidates blurred together for him—he wasn't sure if it was the breakfast stimulants, the nervousness, or just that he didn't think any of them were serious contenders. Probably some combination of all three. That, and the fact he'd taken his glasses off to see the screen better.

The head judge made a hand gesture to the chief bailiff, who cautioned the crowd to be silent until the competition was at an end. The judges then went over the rules. All the workstations were identical, with the same operating system version, installed software, network adapters, and so on. The candidates had one hour to find a way into the Royal Network, to which they were physically attached but for which they had no credentials for entry. Once in, they had to find a specific file hidden in the network and change the contents so that the resultant checksum contained a unique string associated with their own workstation. The first person to do so would be declared the winner.

Sounded simple enough, especially since each workstation had the requisite software for manipulating checksums pre-installed. *There must be a catch*, Carnilox thought. He couldn't know how right he was, of course. To begin with, the computers in the contest had been specifically firewalled off from RNET. The only direct way in would be to defeat the firewall, and one hour wasn't much time in which to accomplish that. Carnilox decided not even to try, but to look for a vulnerable system that was already whitelisted by the firewall and tunnel through that way.

Five minutes into the contest he got a system message that several of his applications were being terminated. Odd. He didn't command that; in fact, he was actively using one of them to scan and evaluate a Royal subnet whose address range he'd had sufficient foresight to memorize. Carnilox frowned and fired them up again. With only fifty-three minutes left he didn't have time to look in the logs to see what the problem had been.

About ten more minutes of scanning and he had found a suitable node. It was in the personnel subnet, used mostly for time and attendance of Arnoc employees, so naturally it wasn't blocked by the firewall. Even better, he quickly found the credentials for establishing a secure connection between his box and the RNET, using the personnel node as a gateway. A few keystrokes and he was in. *T minus 42.*

RNET was a multilevel maze of mythic proportions. Finding the one file he needed was going to be a formidable task sans a good search strategy, but he didn't have time to plot one out formally. It would be great if he had a 'find' command that worked across the entire heterogeneous enterprise, but alas, that didn't exist. Carnilox stared off into the distance, wheels grinding furiously. Correction: didn't exist *yet*.

Before he could get very far with coding, though,

his apps got axed once again. He didn't have time to deal with this sort of smek right now—it was rapidly crossing the line from merely annoying to pissing him off. He reset the connection, reattached, and started up his proggies once more, but this time, on a hunch, he turned on a sniffer first and had it dump to a file in the background while he was working. *T minus 38.*

His idea was to combine 'all-scan,' a generic enterprise node identifier/enumerator used for network management and provided as a DOORS module, with the standard search utility 'fileseek.' Basically, it involved piping the output from the former into the latter—not exactly a revolutionary idea—but there was a fair amount of munging that would have to get done either just before or just after the pipe in order to produce any readily useful output. The formats were different, for one thing, as were the file types. It would take a few minutes of dedicated effort to hack together a working search engine. Time, unfortunately, was not a commodity with which he was blessed in abundance.

Lempo winced. He'd just gotten access to RNET—via a backdoor he'd planted some months earlier while working under contract to the Arnoc doing software quality reviews—when his applications all faulted at once, forcing him to restart the whole process. He figured it was an operating system glitch; they weren't all that uncommon on DOORS, especially given that he was using a stealth program that tiptoed around the usual OS checks and balances. While he was waiting he slammed out a script to automate the startup process, in case it happened again. Good thinking.

His strategy was to rank all the available locations for the target file by their probability as hiding places using an algorithm he'd concocted based on his experience on RNET. He knew the guys who set this contest up, and was pretty sure he also knew how they would think. Once he was back up and running, he set the search program to 'auto' and settled in to watch the results pile up.

His program scanned all the active RNET nodes and mapped out a probability hierarchy based on the dates of last modification of each directory. The odds are that the file in question had been uploaded quite recently. Of course, so had thousands of other files across the enterprise, but at least this was a logical starting point for his search.

He'd covered about 35% of the visible nodes when his apps exited abruptly. Again. This was getting irritating. He checked the system log for any hint of what was causing the kickoffs, but there was nothing to indicate unusual activity. Just a line stating that the apps had closed due to each receiving an 'end process' signal from the kernel. Damn stupid DOORS. This smek was really crinking up his neatly-planned schedule. He threw his restart script into gear and scanned some of the saved results as it did its thing. He noticed a couple of patterns that gave him a pretty good idea where to look next—if he could keep his stuff from crashing, that is.

Lempo glanced over at the king. He was looking a little bewildered—not at all like his smug and confident expression a scant ten minutes or so ago. Maybe he was having the same difficulty with this confounded operating system. He couldn't help smiling about that. Soon that happenin' jeweled band would be around *his* head, and then this cursed kingdom would get the 'tude adjustment it so desperately needed and richly deserved.

He closed his eyes and was momentarily lost in reverie as he visualized the vengeance being king would enable him to enact for various affronts against his person, real and imagined. The revenge of a goblin is never a pretty sight. The sudden realization that he wasn't quite on the throne yet yanked Lempo back into the here and now, and set his fingers flying over the keyboard.

Rexingrasha waited confidently for the official start of the contest. His strategy was simple: he had a script already in place to accomplish the objective, and an assurance that his blatant disregard for the rules would be overlooked by the officials. Nothing whatever to worry about. He coolly surveyed his opponents. Not a regal bugger in the lot. Most of them looked like downright peasants to the king, but then, just about everyone did. Coming from a long line of monarchs tends to color your vision in that regard. He couldn't even begin to imagine any of them wearing the Royal accoutrements. They just didn't have the proper bearing. The gods only knew what trashy third-rate educations they had, if any at all.

The signal to begin had been given. His Majesty decided it would be unwise to win *too* quickly, so he typed some random characters. He did it very fast, so it would sound as though he knew what he was doing. After three and a half lines of gibberish, he stopped. He wondered what would happen if he hit 'enter.' He shrugged, and did it. The computer seemed to pause for a moment, in seeming shock and derision, and then simply shut down.

For a moment Rexingrasha didn't comprehend what had taken place. He just sat there staring at the screen, waiting for it to come back on as though nothing had happened. When it didn't, he jabbed frantically at some more keys. Approaching a state of panic, he forced himself to calm down and remember what Sildran had told him about freeze-ups. He found the power button and recycled the system. After a couple of minutes he was back to the login screen. Whew. On the plus side, he felt that enough time had passed that he could now safely deploy the 'kingmaker' script without looking too suspicious.

The script in question was cleverly designed to simulate an exhaustive search, so that the inevitable audit of the system logs would corroborate Rexingrasha's legitimacy. The script itself, of course, would utterly self-destruct once its mission was accomplished, as would any incriminating temp files associated with it. He navigated to the place where the script was hidden and tried to start it up. The first attempts went awry, since he'd forgotten the exact syntax, but finally he got it right. The search simulation would take about three minutes, Sildran had said, so he just relaxed and pretended to be engrossed in his "hacking."

When the search finished, there was a pause while the last part of the script loaded. Rexingrasha knew it would all be over in a few seconds; he tried not to smile too broadly. Premature gloating might raise suspicions, after all. He closed his eyes and took a deep breath in anticipation of glorious victory. When he opened them again and glanced at the screen, something odd had happened. Instead of the little revolving dots that indicated a program in progress, there was a single printed line:

+++Program kingmaker.mod exited on signal t from kernel

What the phlenk was that? If the program exited, shouldn't that mean he'd won? Why hadn't the judges halted the contest yet? He pushed a few keys. Nothing changed. He tried listing the directory contents, one of the few commands he actually knew. It worked just fine. The script was still there, though, which was not fine. It meant that something had gone wrong, because it should have erased itself after completion. Rexingrasha had no idea what to do now. He stared dumbly at the screen for a few seconds, and then realized he had to do *something*, and soon. The only thing he could think of was to restart the script, which he did, apparently successfully. He couldn't even begin to consider the merest possibility of speculating on why his first attempt had been such a miserable fail. He could only hope it didn't happen again. With luck he still had time to beat his opponents to the prize.

Carnilox grinned internally. It was one of those huge face-wrapping grins you get when things are going really, *really* well, only he was keeping most of it inside so it looked like he was just smirking. His enterprise search engine was working even better than he'd dared dream. He'd already found six copies of the file; now all he had to do was figure out which was the correct one, calculate the proper changes to generate his signature, and drop the file in the designated judges' account. Everything was going smoothly now, it seemed. Just a few more seconds and...

He couldn't believe it. Just as he was mapping to the judges' drive, everything went down again. What in the name of Arfsweener's Pustulant Bunions was going on here? What could possibly be shutting down applications across nodes? It wasn't merely a simple OS glitch, after all. It was something much more mysterious. *T minus 17.*

He was getting a little frantic now. Surely everyone else was at about the same point in the process. He now knew in his heart that he was the best hacker in the competition—it would be exceptionally painful to lose due to some stupid machine malfunction. He looked around the stage while the system was coming back up. Everyone, including Lempo and the king, looked apprehensive. That was probably a good sign.

Lempo was closing in. He'd found two dozen directories that had files modified during the appropriate time frame, and narrowed down the potential candidates to about six, based on file size and type. He was already hard at work generating the necessary embedded signature. He figured three, four minutes, tops. That should give him at least seven or eight to spare. He glanced briefly at the rest of the field. No one was looking too happy right now. Good. That's just the way he wanted it. He checked network connectivity to the judges' shared node, where the properly tagged file was to be deposited. Everything looked fine. It was just a matter of time now.

Yes! He'd succeeded in embedding his signature. As he started the file transfer that would win him the throne, his apps dropped again. Lempo went through his entire sizeable litany of curse words silently, in alphabetical order just to be thorough. He jabbed at the restart button so hard it popped off on the rebound and skittered across the floor of the stage. A couple of people nearby glanced at it with raised brows; Lempo was not concerned with them. He only had eyes for the screen. *T minus 12.*

Carnilox shook his head in disbelief. It seemed like every move he made had been anticipated and prepared for. Could he have underestimated the king or Lempo or one of the other contestants *that* badly?

Was this an RNET employee's doing? The rules had explicitly stated that no one else was to be on the network. The judges would be only passively watching network traffic from their consoles. He looked at all network connections across the contestants' subnet and counted nodes. Twelve contestants, three judges. That added up to fifteen. Why, then, were there sixteen active connections?

He quickly eliminated all the legitimate nodes, leaving only one that couldn't be accounted for. It was a different type of network interface from all the others, as shown by the first eight characters in the physical address. Something was very weird here—there shouldn't be any heterogeneity on this network segment. That was by design; the segment had been constructed specifically for this contest. Someone had somehow slipped in an unauthorized machine. Either they were doing so with the tacit approval of the judges...or...*the judges didn't know they were there*. He slipped back to the OS shell and punched up the native network monitoring utility. The extra node was not visible to it! Good thing he always brought his own tools—an artifact of being involved in too many clandestine hacks with untrustworthy system binaries. He might well be the only one who knew about the intruder.

"Such a smekking *day* I'm having."

Rexingrasha was beating his head against the wall, mentally. Every time his script got close to completion, it would get terminated and he'd have to start again. The weirdest part was that it didn't seem to be happening at the same place every time. Not that he had any real technical clue here, but after a lot of stumbling around he'd found the debug utility's stepwise error log, and the last line processed before the kickoff was never the same twice. Even if he were a programmer, he wasn't sure what he could do to fix the problem. He glanced out at the audience and caught Sildran's eyes. With a tiny wiggle of his eyebrows he pled for help. Sildran looked uncomfortable for a few seconds and then abruptly left the audience seating area.

Well, at least the other contestants all seemed to be sweating profusely also. Maybe this confounded problem was affecting everyone. There couldn't be more than ten minutes left, and no one had yet claimed victory over him, so something was probably holding back the whole lot of them at once. None of the judges even had keyboards—he'd been watching them. Either one of the other contestants was responsible, or something odd was going down here. When Rexingrasha found out who *was* behind this inexcusable delaying tactic, at least one head was going to roll. First, though, he needed to wrap up this ridiculous contest and get back to being king.

Messages suddenly started scrolling across his screen. The script had restarted itself and was progressing much faster than usual. It looked as though someone had manually bypassed most of it, and was just running the portion that had so far failed to complete. Sildran! He owed that sniveling little geek. This time the script did finish, and the transfer took place. His Majesty relaxed.

Lempo had finally made it back to the transfer step. He started several instances of the file transfer program, to make it more difficult for whom—or what—ever to interrupt. He pressed the enter key for the final time, and sat back. Any second now. *T minus 4*.

Carnilox was logging every packet transferred between the intruder's box and the contest network. He was so engrossed in the intruder's movements, in fact, that he almost forgot about the contest itself. Shaking himself loose from the hunt for a moment, he set up a quick filter to slow down any attempts by the interloper to interfere with his processes and then sent the winning file over to the judges. This time it worked perfectly. He was so interested in the mystery hacker, however, that he scarcely gave his long-sought success a second thought. A few seconds later the contest was halted by the head judge.

"We have a winner," the head judge announced.

There was an avian in Tragacanth that lived predominantly in the mountains. It was a largish, solid black species, highly intelligent and tough as nails, but hard to observe due to its solitary and secretive nature. Avianologists had spent years just trying to map out the natural history of this bird, the Northern Boogla, but even today not a great deal was known about it. Local folklore held it in high esteem, though, ascribing to it the qualities of courage, wisdom, stealth, and speed. In the indigenous mythology of Tragacanth the boogla was credited with bringing knowledge and understanding, such as it was, to the goblin race. In these enlightened times, of course, no one but a few eccentrics who adhered to the old ways knew or cared about such things.

All of the keyboards were frozen the moment the contest was declared to be over. The judges would not be announcing the outcome just yet; they had to confer with one another and validate the winner's efforts. Rexingrasha and Lempo were each convinced they'd triumphed, and grinned knowingly at the crowd, the other contestants, and each other. Both of them were a little disconcerted by the other's smug expression, but didn't let it show.

Carnilox was still preoccupied with tracking the intruder. He'd switched over to his own stripped-down keyboard controller in time to evade the net admin's 'disable all' command. There hadn't been any activity from the intruder's box for a while. Maybe he had given up, now that the contest was over. The connection was still active, though. On a hunch, Carnilox punched up the sniffer. It was idle at the moment, but as he watched packets began to flow furiously. They were coming from the intruder's address and targeted the judges' station. He grabbed a few and perused them in detail. They seemed to be comprised of text, apparently formatted in tables or some other row and column-oriented manner. He ran them through his autoformat utility and gasped involuntarily at the results.

The judges conferred amongst themselves for a few minutes, then reached a unanimous consensus. They were about to announce their decision when their monitors suddenly flickered to life simultaneously. They watched as a transcript of sorts scrolled slowly across the screen. The same transcript was in fact also appearing on all the contestants' screens, as well as on the huge public screen provided for conveying messages and contest status to the audience.

0992.13: Node RNET_NOC_1 joined partitioned network CONTEST_NET via administrative override. Username: SILDRAN. Flags: stealth, no_id

0992.36: RNET_NOC_1 issued NET_BLOCK_ALL

0992.98: RNET_NOC_1 issued RCONTROL CONTEST_ NODE_1

0993.45: RNET_NOC_1 issued rrun kingmaker.mod -s 145

0993.94: RNET_NOC_1 issued serase −x kingmaker.mod; 34rt67km.temp; yt5e43km.temp

0994.55: RNET_NOC_1 issued rrun scrublogs; serase −x scrublogs

0994.78: RNET_NOC_1 issued rtrans sig.file > CONTEST _NODE_JUDGES_ALL

0995.02:RNET_NOC_1issuedstopRCONTROLCONTEST _NODE_1

0995.34: RNET_NOC_1 issued NET_RELEASE_ALL

0996.13: RNET_NOC_1 left CONTEST_NET

```
# show rtrans queue -t
    2 files in queue:
        File Name    Timestamp    Sender
        sig.file_11  0993.01      CONTEST_NODE_11
        sig.file_2   0993.34      CONTEST_NODE_2

#  show   users  -n  CONTEST_NODE_2,CONTEST_
NODE_11
        Node                    User ID
        CONTEST_NODE_2          lempo1
        CONTEST_NODE_11         carnilox
```

This public service message brought to you by Boogla. Glory to Tragacanth!

There was absolute silence for about ten seconds, and then a low murmuring began in the crowd, rising rapidly to a regular din. The audience was composed primarily of others in the data handling industry, since not many folks outside this field would be interested in a hack-off, even if it were being conducted for the purpose of choosing a new sovereign. Consequently, enough of them understood the implications of the posted log that public disenchantment with the king hit an all-time high in a matter of two minutes. The public in question, in fact, turned into rather an ugly mob (goblins tend to do that at the drop of a hat; it's genetic), and stormed the stage, demanding Rexingrasha's immediate surrender of the crown and/or various body parts.

The situation was deteriorating with each passing moment. The king's personal guard swept up and surrounded him, weapons drawn, in case the crowd decided to take matters into their own hands. Things were looking grim all around when suddenly the head judge stood up and raised his hands for silence.

"Fellow citizens of Tragacanth: in light of the evidence presented to us by the person who calls himself 'Boogla,' the veracity of which the judging panel has independently verified, and in strict adherence to the rules set forth for this competition, we now hereby declare the winner to be contestant number 11: Carnilox of Goblinopolis. Long live the King!"

The crowd murmured their approval, crescendoing into a cheer when Carnilox rose from his seat at the urging of the judges. It was beginning to sink in that he'd won, but something about the whole Boogla episode still had a powerful grip on his mind. He stumbled to the dais at the front of the stage and stared out at the sea of beaming faces. Finally he gathered his wits enough to address them. Fortunately, he'd memorized the canned acceptance speech beforehand, just in case.

"I humbly accept the charge that has been thrust upon me today, and promise that I will rule to the best of my ability, exhibiting neither malice nor undue favor toward any but those who have earned them by their actions. Further, I will devote myself utterly to the defense of Tragacanth against its myriad enemies, and to the betterment of all its citizens, be they rich or poor. This I, Carnilox, do now solemnly affirm and attest."

It was a speech right out of the public oratory textbooks, and it found wide favor amongst the crowd. Even Rexingrasha grudgingly admitted to himself that it was well executed. That was scarce consolation for his having lost the Royal Diadem to this pathetic little geek, though.

Despite considerable effort on his part, Carnilox, who took the name Haxxos when he ascended the throne of Tragacanth, was never conclusively able to prove the identity of his benefactor 'Boogla.' There were numerous theories and conjectures, but no definitive evidence ever surfaced. Boogla was such a superlative hacker that even the Senior Security Analysts at RNOC, the best of the best, were unable to track him. And so Boogla and his exploits passed into legend in the data handling community, the label 'Boogla' being applied reverently thereafter to all of the most technically proficient and audacious actions.

Chapter Eight:
Operation Tumble

Aspet knew this history, of course: knew it well. Learning it was required of every child attending school in Tragacanth, and one component of the orientation of attendees of The Seminar was another intensive review. He'd always been fascinated by the stories about Boogla, although in truth he didn't completely believe them. He knew from experience that legends have a way of expanding to fill the volume available to them, and in a field as esoteric as data handling that was a hefty volume. Still, the legend of Boogla was an inspiring one for someone with his aspirations. Aspet even dreamt one night that Boogla intervened on his behalf during his own challenge to the throne.

The day he finished The Seminar was also the day the messages began. They were cryptic and obscure, at first; even taunting. Despite his considerable prowess at the keyboard, he couldn't trace where they were coming from past the first couple of hops. The sender was obviously an expert at clandestine communications. He could only assume he'd been singled out for this treatment as a successful alumnus of The Seminar, although that information was supposed to be secret until and unless the student chose to challenge for the crown. Still, someone with the computer acumen of his taunter probably wasn't seriously put off by the access controls placed on the Seminar attendees' database.

Aspet decided to ignore the messages initially. They weren't really threatening or disturbing, just enigmatic. After a few days, though, the tone of the communications began to soften and Aspet felt a trickle of compassion for the anonymous author. He was apparently frustrated by some societal constriction, although he never made it clear what it was, exactly. He was obviously a *very* talented hacker, and despite the fact that it was contrary to his own interests, Aspet couldn't help replying finally, asking the mystery person why he didn't compete for the crown himself: he was definitely well-qualified.

There was no direct answer to his question, but from that point on the messages were friendlier: gone was the derisive rhetoric and underlying current of hostility. The mystery correspondent now provided shrewd political insights, valuable snatches of code the like of which Aspet had never before seen, and even the occasional bit of humor, so Aspet replied in kind. After a few more weeks they had developed an online friendship of sorts. Aspet had noticed that his pen pal never signed his messages with any name, so one day he wrote:

"Hey, I'm a little tired of just saying 'hey.' What

do you want to be called?"

It took much longer than usual for the reply to come back. He hoped he hadn't inadvertently insulted his new friend. When the response finally did come, it was brief and to the point:

"I am called Boogla."

Aspet was taken aback for a second or two, but then he chuckled.

"Sure you are, dude. And they call me Mordik, Goblin God of Fertility."

Still, he had to admit that 'Boogla's' hacking skills were considerable. He'd like to meet the guy, no matter what he called himself. After all, having a rampant ego wasn't exactly a foreign trait in this arena.

He couldn't help but be a little sarcastic.

<B So, what have you been doing with your-
self since the days of Haxxos I? You must be
quite old by now seeing as how that was, oh,
five or six kings ago. ;-)

He hoped he wasn't being too offensive, but surely anyone naming himself after a demigod had to expect this sort of reaction.

There was an even longer pause this time.

B> It is wrong of you to assume that there can
be only one named Boogla for all time.

Aspet scratched his head. I guess he had a point there.

<B So, you're like, Boogla III or something?

He was still considering this exchange humorous,

but not quite so humorous as before.

B> Boogla IV, actually. My great grandmother was the original.

 Aspet did a double take.

<B Whoa. Your great grand*mother*? Are you telling me that Boogla was a *girl*?

B> Indubitably. As have been the other three Booglas since.

 Aspet wasn't handling this well. His hands shook a little as he typed.

<B You're saying that *you're* a girl, too?

B> That is indeed what I'm saying. You appear surprised...

 He sputtered out loud to himself for a few moments. "Well, I, uh, yeah...I am."

<B Sorry—didn't mean to offend you. I'm just not used to thinking of girls as hackers.

B> Understood. We're discouraged from pursuing that goal for our entire lives. Yet some of us, probably many more than you realize, nevertheless feel the pull. Males have no monopoly on technology, no matter what they tell themselves in order to feel superior. It is taught in our circles, in fact, that the very pinnacles of hacking are obtainable only by females; males lack some certain combination of genetics and behavioral conditioning that prevents them from entering into the mental state necessary for the most esoteric work.

Aspet rolled his eyes. This was getting rather ridiculously dogmatic, in his opinion.

<B Whatever. You've got skillz, I'll give you that. But I think making it a sex-linked trait is going a bit out on a limb.

B> Perhaps. I have no real opinion on the issue, one way or the other. It's just what we are taught. But I will say that I have never met any at our level who were not sisters.

<B What do you mean, 'sisters?' Are you all related?

B> Sorry, no, I meant 'Sisters of the Code.' A secret sorority of female hackers.

Aspet wondered if this was some sort of elaborate practical joke, or if he had indeed stumbled across an uber-underground unknown to the conventional underground. A sub-basement of the hacking community, as it were. He needed some time to realign his world-view.

Pyfox shrugged noncommittally. He wasn't going to get involved in a petty political dispute just now, not when he had issues of far greater magnitude to address.

"Pyfox wants hobs to take it somewhere else

now. Pyfox has thinking to do. Hobs make too much noise arguing all time like children."

He adopted the classic deep urban hobgoblin disdain for pronouns. It was an affectation for him; he spoke perfectly well when the need arose. Speech affectations of one sort or another were something of a fashion in Tragacanth. Most who spoke this way had a tendency to drop out of it when stressed. Pyfox seldom got stressed. Even the recent attempt on his life elicited little reaction. The other hobgoblins cleared out of the room immediately. They knew better than to ignore the boss.

Spread out on a table in front of him were a series of diagrams—flow charts, in point of fact. They depicted a complex sequence of events, each annotated extensively in the margins with lots of cross-references and explanatory doodles. It was difficult to make out exactly the overall objective of the mapped-out processes, but given that Pyfox seemed intently interested in it, it was no doubt quite illegal.

He spent almost an hour poring over the charts, his face a model of hobgoblin concentration. Finally he jabbed his stubby little finger near the bottom of one and traced a rather shaky path around and across two others until he wound up at last at an apparent finishing point. "Stalash!" he said, with great emphasis. "Then will Pyfox have victory over the magic-using swibs. No more magic except through Pyfox. Hobs will be in charge. Sweet days for Pyfox then, no?"

As he was relishing the sound of his own little oratory, there was a knock at the door. Pyfox slid open a narrow reinforced spy panel at his eye level and stared out, contorting his body in an attempt to look at something apparently at or near ceiling height in the foyer. He grunted after a moment and opened the door. The visitor had to stoop severely to enter the room. He was a troll, of ancient lineage, if appearances were any indication. Hobgoblins aren't particularly puny by Tragacanthan standards—a little smaller, on average, than goblins, but bigger than most of the other races. Next to the hulking troll, however, Pyfox looked pathetically insignificant.

"Hail, Pyfox, savior of the people," the troll boomed in greeting. Pyfox raised his eyebrow, but said nothing in reply except, "Pyfox welcomes Fen." The two returned to the table where Pyfox had been examining his flowcharts.

"The agents of Pyfox relay that the plan has reached stage three, with stage four expected by next week. What news does Fen bring?"

The troll puffed up his already smekking impressive chest.

"I bring news of high import, O great one. A total of six spheres have now been located and the attack venues established. We have probable coordinates for six more."

"Pyfox is pleased. Fen will return to Astflanar base and tell the Liberators to continue the mission. Fen will also deliver an artifact to the Liberators."

Pyfox handed Fen a bundle wrapped in a soft grayish fabric.

"Fen will handle the artifact with great care and guard it well, for it is one of the ancient keys to The Slice, obtained at immeasurable personal risk by Pyfox himself."

The hobgoblin had, in fact, bought it from a clueless gnarlignome at an auction for practically nothing some years ago, but he had a mystique to maintain, after all.

The troll's already enormous eyes grew even larger. He bowed reverently in the downward direction of Pyfox and took the bundle from him carefully, as though it were made of finely spun crystal lattice. One of the things Pyfox liked best about trolls was their trusting nature and the ease with which they could be manipulated. They were habitually polite, too, which was a real plus for creatures strong enough to crush an adult hobgoblin's head in one hand.

"I will lavish the artifact with tremendous care and keep it safe from any harm, 'ere I deliver it to the Liberators two days hence."

Pyfox rolled his eyes almost imperceptibly. This particular troll had learned hobgoblin from an itinerant thespian, and so his mode of speech was a bit disconcerting at times.

"Pyfox wishes Fen to begin the journey. *Now*."

The troll nodded subserviently and scrambled for the exit, nearly taking the door frame with him as he miscalculated the degree of ducking necessary for successful negotiation in his haste to do his master's bidding. Fen clutched the precious bundle to his chest and lumbered away, the growing knot on his huge misshapen head merely reminding him of his sacred mission.

Pyfox watched him go and shook his head. Having a troll devoted to you was like having a three meter-tall scrubhound. As long as you gave him specific instructions and never let him do anything on his own initiative, he was pretty reliable. Unlike scrubhounds, many trolls were even housebroken (so long as you didn't overly excite them).

The artifact Pyfox had entrusted to Fen was, at least as far as he and his 'consultants' could tell one of the original keys used to lock The Slice in place thousands of years ago, when the ancient Archmages introduced magic into the world. Neutralizing the inviolability spell *in toto* would of course require all of the keys, but possessing even one should make it easier to destroy the spheres which marked the transition from physical to magical space. Once the field was sufficiently weakened, a concentrated attack of adequate proportions should do the job even without the remaining keys.

Fen would take the key to Pyfox's elite commando unit the Liberators (so named because their mission was liberating money from everyone else into Pyfox's pockets), who operated from a secret base beneath the slopes of Mt. Astflanar in the Espwe range, the highest peak in Tragacanth. The Liberators had been laboring for some weeks now on their mission, which was to tear down the border separating magical space from physical space, effectively destroying access to The Slice and rendering magic inoperative, except through one conduit controlled by Pyfox. Their motive was basically that Pyfox told them to, although he'd also filled their heads with propaganda about the evils of magic and how much better the hobgoblin lot had been before it came along. Hobs made notoriously poor magi—something to do with their lack of patience and shallow intellect. Still, for the most part they were just following orders, something that hobs did fairly well. The stuff about hobs having been better off before was pure speculation—magic had been introduced to Tragacanth millennia ago, before there were many written records. No one alive today really *knew* anything about conditions in those distant days. Pyfox had an ulterior motive for the destruction, as he had for most anything he did: his own profit.

Fen was an orphan who'd been befriended by Pyfox years ago, and he had proven to be a most excellent messenger boy and courier. Trolls were not exactly stupid, but the rivers of their thought did not run deep. Some of them had surprisingly large vocabularies, for instance, but they employed them almost exclusively in the conduct of utterly pedestrian small talk. They had no real concept of morality and tended to become fixated on a single idea or goal, which of course made Fen the ideal errand boy for Pyfox's criminal organization. One drawback is that trolls are purely incapable of lying; Pyfox had to be certain that he did not ask Fen to do anything *too* illegal, else run the risk of him being picked up and unwittingly confessing, possibly revealing sensitive operational details in the process.

Pyfox returned to his charts. Everything was coming together nicely, despite the pathetic attempts to interfere with his plans by killing him with a magical bomb. He didn't know who was behind that nefarious plot, but he was certain his spies would soon ferret out that information, and then he'd deal with the perpetrators in a suitably vengeful manner.

Meanwhile, he needed to send a more critical and secure message. He pulled out a small telecomm module and switched the encryption selector from "magical" to "quantum." Wouldn't do for him to entrust his confidentiality to a system he was actively working to decimate, now would it?

"Pyfox to Treqliw: Operation Tumble proceeding according to plan. Prepare to initiate stage four on my command. Transmit status report on this frequency at prearranged time. Pyfox out." Pyfox smiled. He always felt so deliciously high-tech and sophisticated when he used the telecomm module. Who needed magic? Technology was superior in every way, and he had a recurrent dream of emerging from the downfall of magic as technology's benevolent champion, bestowing technological bliss upon a grateful citizenry from his many factories. He would practically give it away at first—but as they grew more and more dependent on the devices only he could supply (he held most of the patents by acquisition or theft, and employed a large contingent of 'competition discouragement personnel'), prices and profits would rise accordingly. Of course, there would still be one magical access point remaining, and he would control that, as well. It was a classic case of externally-lubricated supply and demand. Pyfox broke into a delicious chartreuse sweat just thinking about it.

Chapter Nine:
Golem on the GRUE

"**I** dream a dream unvanquished; I soar with the buoyancy of a spirit unfettered."

Tol put down the file he was perusing and frowned. "What the name of Plegma are you babbling about?"

The pen let out an affronted huff—rather a disturbing sound coming from a writing instrument—and spit out a curt reply.

"I am trying to compose poetry here. Poetry is a manifestation of *culture*: I am not at all surprised you cannot comprehend it."

Tol snorted. "Poetry? Sounded like gibberish from this end."

The pen sighed, "Yes, well, that is just the sort of response I would expect from you. You have not a single molecule of literary appreciation in your entire wretched organic physical makeup."

Tol didn't like the direction this was taking. "I'll make a deal with you: you shut your smekking inkhole while I'm trying to think and maybe I won't 'accidentally' flush you down the toilet later."

"Spoken like a true vulgarian. I shall make every attempt not to interrupt your laborious mental grunting again."

Tol rolled his eyes. He noticed the hypersonic shredder across the room and idly speculated on what it would do to the pen.

"Do not even contemplate it, you crass barbarian," came a voice from his pocket, "I am departmental property, you know. You can't afford to 'lose' me."

He frowned in annoyance and turned his attention back to the file. It was a compilation of reports from citizens who'd observed suspicious activity in and around the park where he'd lost track of the elves. They ranged from the innocuous to the raving paranoid (aliens with thin pink skin and no armored ridges—right), but a couple caught his attention. One described a small, delicate, elf-like being seen flitting through the flowerbeds—possibly this "alfar" thing Plåk had told him about—and the other was a rather detailed account of mysterious 'energy fields' or something that the reporting party had seen on several occasions in one specific area of the park. The same area, in fact, where the trail of the elves had disappeared.

He studied the reported observation times. No apparent pattern. His detective's seventh sense was buzzing, so he dragged out the computer and started looking for matches between the reports and significant events in the activity database. It didn't take long before he'd come up with some interesting hypothetical correlations.

Some of the possible connections were a bit

silly, like the kidnapping of eight juvenile fruit-eating grunzagas from the zoological gardens. Others were just plain unlikely, such as the murder by electrocution of a sanitation worker on the job in the posh Goblinopolis neighborhood of Eshvodsi.

Then Tol came across this little tidbit:

Shortly after sunset I was strolling along the southern edge of the park, near the Trokkle gate, when I saw three bright flashes of light about two meters off the ground above a hedge. There was a crackling or spitting noise, and a strong smell was in the air, like that odor during a nearby electrical storm.

The time stamp of the report coincided almost perfectly with a strange rift in the magical matrix, reported to the CoME by numerous lower and mid-level mages. CoME provided copies of these reports to the EE community as part of a cooperative information-sharing agreement.

Way back when he first signed on with the force it had been a different story. There was little contact between edict enforcement and the Council then, and even less mutual trust. However, with the adoption of more and more technology (and even a few magical items) in criminal investigation work, the two camps drew closer out of expediency. Eventually the department began to hire CoME personnel as consultants. The crossover brought the two organizations together in a new way, and with the increased cooperation came a concomitant increase in mutual understanding that led finally to the beneficial symbiosis they enjoyed today. The holiday picnic fireworks, in particular, had vastly improved.

Tol realized he was mentally replaying the text of a departmental briefing word for word and snapped himself back to the case in annoyance. He had these periodic bouts of photographic recall, but they almost always involved stuff that he really would rather not remember. He shuddered and poured himself a shot of uberrazzle from a small flask he kept in a desk drawer.

Assuming there was a solid connection between the rift and the sightings, the salient question would seem to be, which came first? The time stamps were in close enough proximity that either event could have preceded the other, given the inexact nature of timekeeping among the general public of Tragacanth. He tried a little deductive reasoning. If the rift had been the result of whatever caused the flashes, then the reported odor was probably of a magical nature. On the other hand, if the rift occurred first, the flashes and odor were not necessarily magical in origin.

Tol was not very experienced with magic, but in his limited exposure he'd never heard of a magical process that left an electrical storm odor, although he was aware that magically-induced weather phenomena were possible. He also knew that they were extremely difficult to carry out, given the huge drain on the magical energy sump. It would take a high-level mage to perform such a ritual. One thing he did know was where to get the skinny on high-level mages: the office of the Loca Magineer. He decided to pay it a visit.

Public transportation in Goblinopolis is a haphazard affair. Some areas are serviced only by nominally licensed cabs, some by the ponderous underground system known as the GRUC (Goblinopolis Regional Underground Conveyance), and some are best reached on foot or by magical teleportation. This last means of transport is discouraged, though, because of the remote but still very real chance of materializing inside a pedestrian. Goblinopolis is a busy city, with an enormous amount of foot traffic. It simply isn't possible to reduce the threat of unintended magical hybridization, which always has embarrassing, if not disastrous, consequences. Even the dedicated teleportation booths didn't work, because gangs of ruffians took to hanging around them and preventing anyone who appeared in one from leaving until someone else zapped in on top of them. They got a real kick out of this. It cost too much to assign an edict enforcement officer to each booth to prevent such episodes, so the government just threw up its hands and warned anyone traveling via teleportation that they did so solely at their own risk, promising dire consequences if any bystanders were injured in the process.

Tol had his own personal pram—it had seen its best days during his father's career on the force, though—but parking was at a premium in the crowded metropolitan area and prams had delicate engines which needed to be looked after. You couldn't just pull up and leave one there indefinitely without any attention. There were draycare centers (drays were the larger cargo-carrying vehicles) scattered around the city that serviced prams as well, but in Tol's experience they were never near enough his destination to make the effort worthwhile. Licensed public cabs tended to blow out his meager expense account; the unlicensed ones, besides being illegal, were prone to "accidental" wrong turns and stranding their fares in bad neighborhoods, where they were soon relieved of the burden of fiscal liquidity. He usually found it easiest to travel around Goblinopolis by GRUC (most people just called it 'the Gruc').

For one thing, there were GRUC terminals just about everywhere. You were never more than a hundred meters from where you wanted to be when you stepped back up into the open air. And it was cheap—free for him, in fact. The department bought all detectives and foot patrol officers annual passes for business use. So, GRUC it was, dingy cabins, unidentifiable odors, and all.

Entrances to the GRUC varied from broad, palatial affairs with gold-plated banisters and marbled floors to cramped abruptly-sloping cave-like concrete corridors barely wide enough for two abreast, depending on neighborhood and anticipated clientele. Tol usually ended up in the latter—something of an occupational hazard, it seemed. Today, however, he was going to take the No. 23 to the 'Royal Complex: East' stop, one of the gold and marble varieties. He wore his least damaged helmet and even polished his disruptor with an old sock. After all, one shouldn't look *too* shabby if one is going to pay an official visit to the seat of government (unless one is there asking for more money for equipment and clothing, but that wasn't Tol's mission, on this occasion).

When his carriage rolled up, he was pleased to see that it was one of the newer ones. That meant fewer and less intense odors and less likelihood of mechanical failure during the ride. He had a minor case of claustrophobia that he could usually control without problem, but being trapped in a ten meter-long, two meter-wide sausage full of weird smells and weirder people in a dimly-lit tunnel twenty meters below the surface had a way of intensifying the irrational closed-in feeling rapidly. He'd found the best way to cope was to close his eyes and sing, but that degraded the quality of the experience even more for everyone else. Still, sometimes you just gotta look out for number one...

This carriage was quite clean inside, in stark contrast to most of the ones he'd ridden. There were only a couple of gnomes and another goblin already seated when he got on. Well, not many people rode the GRUC into the RC east stop. Most of the day-to-day government business offices were accessed from the south or west termini. He wondered idly where the gnomes were going. He noticed that they had matching toolboxes with *Zzingler Technologies* decals on them. Probably some sort of repairmen, most likely heading to the CoME Data Center or one of the public data cubes scattered around the East Complex.

It was a *little* odd that they were on the GRUC, since most of these companies had their own corporate drays for the sake of customer convenience, if nothing else, but it wasn't sufficiently strange that he felt justified in registering alarm. Paranoia was part of his job, but like his claustrophobia, he had to keep it under control.

No one spoke. The gnomes looked around and fidgeted a bit, but the other goblin sat absolutely still, like a statue. It was a bit disconcerting for Tol. If the guy was asleep, he was managing it with his eyes open, not that such a thing was unheard of since goblin outer eyelids were more or less transparent, anyway. Whatever he was doing, it was creeping Tol out. He fixed his gaze out the windows at the murky kinetics of the tunnel wall as it smeared past and tried not to think about the zombie across from him.

After a minute or two he caught some nearer movement out of the corner of his eye. One of the gnomes got up with his toolbox and shuffled to the far end of the carriage. Maybe he had a (silent) spat with the other one. Gnomes were hard to figure sometimes. He continued to stare out the window. A minute later, the other gnome took his toolbox and headed off to the opposite end. Tol chuckled.

A faint but engaging noise was beginning to make itself audible. At first he couldn't figure what it was or where it was coming from. No one else showed any indication of detecting it, although he had to admit he couldn't read ol' stone face at all. Bet that guy was positively deadly at poker.

The sound remained a mystery until something in his pocket began to vibrate. He realized that it was his pen, and at the same moment suddenly recognized the noise as the pen's alert signal, conveyed to his brain and his brain only by skin surface induction. This had better not be another malfunction, he thought as he pulled out the pen and a notepad to go with it. Departmental regulations stated that he was not to make it obvious that the pen had uses beyond scribbling descriptions of alleged purse snatchers. The jury was still out on that veracity of that claim, as far as Tol was concerned.

This time the pen was not making any smart remarks, however. It was all business.

"I have detected a dangerous situation," it stated quietly. "The ambient magical flux aboard this carriage has suddenly risen to a potentially catastrophic level. A spell with significant energy components is being cast in the immediate vicinity."

Tol shrugged and looked around. The two gnomes, at opposite ends of the carriage, seemed supremely unconcerned with anything but staring off into space. The goblin was still semi-comatose. Tol was beginning to wonder seriously if he were even alive at all. Failure to act on that suspicion would haunt him later.

"What sort of spell?" he whispered.

"Unknown. It is drawing considerable energy from The Slice through two transient nodes that seem to be separated by a little less than ten meters."

Tol blinked. The scales at the back of his neck started chafing the way they always did when he was getting a bad feeling about something. The "ten meters" part of the pen's warning was gnawing furiously at him.

"Pinpoint location of nodes relative to my line of sight."

"Approximately three and nine o'clock."

Of course: the gnomes, or more likely, their toolboxes. Funny: gnomes weren't usually known as mages. They generally preferred technology over magic. It was possible that they didn't know their toolboxes were the epicenters of some powerful juju, but he didn't think it likely. Gnomes also made for notoriously poor patsies. They were too astute and naturally suspicious of strangers.

That left two gnomes who were purposefully harboring and most probably actively participating in magical activity strong enough to slam a terminally smart-aleck pen into "just the facts" mode. That alone was pretty disturbing. The ten thousand billme question was, *why*?

"Any data on probable intent?"

"Insufficient data for statistically significant analysis, but my trick ink cartridge tells me that something dramatic is about to take place."

"Yeah, I'd gotten that impression from you

already. Any idea who or what the target might be?"

"I would suggest you find a highly reflective surface and gaze soulfully into it."

Tol snorted. "Me? Why would two gnomes be after *me*?"

"Insufficient data to draw any meaningful conclusions about motivation. The fact that you are an edict enforcement officer with many enemies does seem somewhat germane, however."

He tried to think of any gnomes he might have pissed off...there was that one he'd caught trying to rewire the betting machines in a South Sebacea casino. He'd been one utterly stoned gnome, though. Probably didn't even remember the crime, much less the arresting officer. Tol doubted the gnome he was recalling had the intellectual capacity to plan his route to the chemist's, much less hatch and execute an elaborate revenge scheme. No, if they were after him, they had to be coming from a different angle.

His introspective criminological analysis was interrupted by another, more ominous warning from the pen.

"The bifurcated magical energy stream has ceased. Shortly before it did so, I detected a unification which seemed to be focused directly at your 12 o'clock position."

Tol looked up, surprised. All he saw at 12 o'clock was the motionless goblin, who was still looking mighty inert. Something *was* strangely amiss, however. For a few seconds he couldn't put his finger on what it was, but then it hit him—the gnomes had disappeared, leaving their toolboxes behind. Since they had positioned themselves near the doors, it was logical to assume they had slipped out that way—but silently, and while the carriage was moving? Somewhere back there must be a couple of vaguely gnome-shaped splotches on the tunnel walls.

"The gnomes have vanished," he told the pen.

"That explains the transient spikes before the streams rejoined. They must have teleported."

Teleported? Why bother to ride public transport in the first place if you have that capability? Something wasn't making a lot of sense here.

"Forgot their tool boxes, it seems."

"I believe they were left behind intentionally. They probably contain some sort of local magical amplifiers. I am seeing regular residual pulses in several wavelengths of the magical energy spectrum from their locations."

"So I've got two pulsing toolboxes and a comatose goblin threatening me. When is the part where I'm supposed to feel intimidated coming up?"

"Judging from the energy dispersal pattern, I would say right about...now."

On cue the suddenly animate goblin across from Tol stood up and lumbered toward him menacingly. Tol couldn't help but notice that his assailant's eyes were glowing red. He stood up and whipped out his badge.

"Edict enforcement officer. I'd advise you not to

come any closer."

The goblin completely ignored him. He was looking in Tol's direction, but his disturbingly red eyes did not seem to be focused on anything in particular. He drew back one fist and smashed it into the back of the carriage seat where Tol's head had been a second earlier. It put a hole completely through the seat and dented the metal wall behind it rather badly.

Tol pulled his disruptor—time to nip this nonsense in the bud. It was set to "disable," the standard default setting dictated by departmental regs. He fired point blank at his attacker on his next swing. Didn't even flinch. Puzzled, he jacked it up to "full stun" and fired again while rolling out of the way of a full body lunge. Got him right in the chest. The red-eyed goblin shook it off as though he'd been shot by a child's water pistol.

Tol was beginning to get worried. This guy wasn't right. He longed for the days when firing his disruptor actually accomplished something besides using up a charge.

Luckily, ol' scarlet eyes didn't move too fast. As he was pivoting around for another go, Tol barked into his pocket.

"What exactly is that thing? It sure doesn't act like any goblin I've ever seen before."

"Strictly speaking, it is not a goblin, per se. It is a magically-animated construct known as a *golem*," replied the pen. "The body is that of a goblin, but the force which drives it is not metabolism, but rather magic."

"Great," Tol huffed, setting his disruptor on 'liquefy,' "I suppose that means that this won't do any good, either."

He fired at very close range into the golem's face, narrowly avoiding being caught in a crush hold. The shot ripped away half of the flesh on the golem's head, spewing not blood and tissue but a weird spongy gelatinous glop like pale greenish-beige packing material all over the carriage. The golem shook its gory locks and, despite now having no functional ocular apparatus, came unerringly for its quarry, who was rapidly running out of self-defense options.

"Gah. Sometimes I hate being right." He shoved his obviously useless disruptor back into its shoulder holster. "Any advice on what I should do now?" he yelled into his pocket as he dove out of the way of another powerful roundhouse.

"Discretion, it is said, is the better part of valor."

"What the smek is that supposed to mean?"

"Employing the vernacular, it is time to split."

"Gotcha."

Splitting was going to be problematic, unfortunately. The carriage was traveling at quite a respectable clip through a tube specifically designed and constructed to house a speeding carriage of these dimensions and nothing else. The gap between outer carriage skin and tunnel wall was never more than about fifty centimeters. That just wasn't room for a full-grown goblin, even one in relatively good shape like Tol. He reached above his seat and pressed the "Emergency Stop" button. That would bring the carriage to a halt at the next exit, be it a station or just a service access tunnel, where GRUC authorities would be waiting. Theoretically, anyway.

He had no idea how far it was going to be to the next possible stop, though, and it was promising to be quite a challenge to stay out of the way of the rampaging golem until then. He found himself devoting a fair amount of energy to that goal. As he began to tire from the constant dodging, his strategy got necessarily more creative. Perhaps he could lead the golem to one of the doors and trick it into leaping out. After barely escaping a particularly vicious lunge, he decided now might be a good time to try it.

Tol jumped up and stuck out his tongue at the golem, making a derisive noise with his lips and lower nostrils. When the enraged monster came after him, he led it toward one end of the carriage. As he approached one of the toolboxes, he heard a muffled exclamation from his pocket.

"Use caution. Something has just triggered a transient planar magical power flux perpendicular to the long axis of the carriage."

At that moment Tol encountered something invisible but very, very solid about a meter from the exit. It left him rolling on the floor in pain, which at least made him a more difficult target for his less than agile pursuer.

"A smekkin' force field. Ow."

"I *did* warn you."

"If you'd learn to speak plain Goblish, your

warnings would be a lot more comprehensible."

"Look, is it *my* fault that you have the vocabulary of a caged mimic-bird?"

"Ya know, if your little pen body happens to get smashed beyond recognition during the course of this encounter, no one could blame me."

"My exoskeleton is composed of reinforced anthratanium. It would take a blow of approximately 1,250 kilograms of force per square centimeter to deform it significantly. Such an impact would pulverize your biological structure utterly. In other words, anything that manages to 'smash my body beyond recognition' would do far worse to you, although one might argue that any such action would present no serious detriment to society at large."

Tol looked up and saw the golem heading in his direction. He waited until the last possible moment before leaping aside. The golem smashed into the force field with considerable momentum, losing several large skull fragments in the collision. His head was now reduced to less than half its original mass, and had gone from horrific to faintly ridiculous. The golem lined up on him, and again Tol leapt aside. The force field was becoming increasingly spattered with magical golem guts.

"Hey, I could start to like this," Tol chuckled as he jumped again and watched his literally mindless assailant lose yet another round with the force field. Golem debris was beginning to pile up at his feet.

"How long can this thing keep attacking? I mean, how many parts does it have to lose before it gives up?"

"It will never 'give up.' So long as there are any contractile muscle fibers remaining, whatever body remnants contain them will continue to strive in your direction. Think of it this way: each cell in the golem's body is under magical geas to kill you—alone, if need be."

"Super. The quest for the holey gore," Tol muttered.

"I beg your pardon?"

"Nothing. So, what can bring an end to this geas, other than my untimely demise?"

"Not much. You could incinerate every last cell of the golem, or get a mage of sufficiently high level to cancel the spell."

"How high a level?"

"Depends on the level of the caster. From the nature of the energy being drawn from The Slice, I would venture to speculate a very high level indeed."

Suddenly the golem's fist came crashing down on Tol's shoulder from the side. He hadn't expected that move, since his assailant had been lumbering straight at him up until now. The force of the blow drove him to his knees.

The monster immediately followed through with a blow to Tol's head, which fortunately didn't fully connect because Tol was in the process of slumping to one side at the time. The fist missed his head and hit his other shoulder, driving him fully to the ground.

"I...can't feel either of my arms," he said through

gritted teeth.

"Trauma to the suprabrachical plexi," the pen diagnosed, "sensation will return in a few minutes if there is no further damage. Roll around randomly on the floor; it cannot anticipate your movements, and it has not the dexterity to hit you if you roll quickly enough."

"Oof," Tol replied as he rolled, "Ugh...mmf... argh...ow..."

He sat up and struggled to his feet, bleeding from several new wounds. "I beg," he began, narrowly avoiding a hit that tore a seat from its moorings, "to differ."

"Odd," replied the pen, "reference data indicates that golems are strictly reactive—they depend on movement and detection of the magical aura of living creatures to track their targets. It should not be able to hit you if you keep moving in unpredictable ways."

"I'm thinkin' your definition of 'unpredictable' and his aren't the same, 'cause he keeps putting his fist right where I'm ending up."

"Interesting. I will need more data to revise my initial analysis."

"Too much more data collection and I won't be around to read the final report. How about some data on how to *stop* this thing before it kills me?"

"Very well," the pen sighed, "I will scan the databases for more specific details."

"You mean you haven't done that already? What

the smek *have* you been doing?"

"Proper analysis of a real-time tactical situation is complex and requires correlation across a broad array of information matrices."

"Have I ever mentioned how smekkin' worthless you are?"

"I believe the sentiment has been expressed previously."

"Good. I'd hate to think you were operating under the mistaken assumption that you served any useful purpose."

The feeling returned to Tol's arms at last, and he wrenched a mangled iron bar from a destroyed seat. He used it to deflect a particularly ferocious onslaught by the golem, slicing off the lower third of the leftmost appendage: there really wasn't enough left to call it an 'arm.'

"Ole!" Tol shouted, twisting out of the way of the golem's counterpunch.

"What does 'ole' mean?" asked the pen.

"Err, nothing. It's just a word a friend from another dimension once taught me."

"It does not appear in any of my dictionaries."

"Because it's not of Tragacanthan origin, I told you. Forget about it and concentrate on saving my skin, will ya?"

"If I must," the pen sniffed.

"Well, it might possibly justify your existence. Certainly your prowess as a writing instrument hasn't filled the bill."

"If *you* were a little more adept at the actual process

of writing, *my* utility might be drastically improved."

"Will you for the love of Gammag stop being defensive and focus? This thing isn't slowing down, but I am."

"Very well. Stand by."

"Easy for you to say."

Tol had taken to staying up on the seats. The golem apparently couldn't negotiate climbing, and was reduced to swinging at his legs. Of course, any hit that incapacitated him would put him within easy reach of his adversary, so Tol was really dodging just as much as before. Not having constantly to duck away from blows to his head and neck was a relief, though. As he was bracing for another attack, Tol caught a glimpse of something whizzing past the carriage. It took a few seconds before his brain registered just what he'd seen. It was a maintenance portal. The carriage should have stopped at it, but obviously it didn't. That probably meant that the emergency stop system had been sabotaged. Made sense; he should have anticipated that move.

The situation seemed a great deal less hopeful than it had a short time ago. He was trapped in a small cylindrical prison with a virtually immortal magical opponent eager to rip him limb from limb and/or beat him into a gooey pulp. There was no realistic hope of stopping the carriage, and attempting to escape it while moving would be suicide. His only ally was a wise-cracking writing instrument with an attention deficit disorder. How much bleaker could things get?

There is an old goblin maxim to the effect that one should be careful what sorts of rhetorical questions one poses, even mentally, lest they lose their rhetorical nature. As if to illustrate that nugget of wisdom, the gods chose that moment to answer Tol's question in an unequivocal manner. The golem caught him just behind the knee in another surprise move and slammed his relatively intact fist into Tol's ribs as he buckled. He managed to roll away from the next blow, but his pain level had increased logarithmically.

"I have good news and bad news," said the pen suddenly, its electronic voice a bit muffled from the makeshift bandage Tol had wrapped around his cracked ribs.

"I *hate* it when people say that to me," replied Tol through gritted teeth, "what's the bad news?"

"According to my sensors you are losing blood too rapidly to sustain consciousness much longer."

"What did I say that sounded like 'raise my stress level even more, will you?' And the good news?"

"My power consumption curve has leveled off. That means my ambient energy conversion cells have finally stabilized to their mature values."

"Remind me to throw you a smekkin' party in celebration. Looks like I'll have to do it from the afterlife, though, since I won't actually be alive much longer."

He dropped to his knees as he spoke. The lack of blood was overcoming him. The golem wheeled around and moved in for the kill.

"Oh yes, I have one more bit of news, as well."

"I can't wait. What is it, did you discover some heretofore undetected mocking module in your onboard ROM?"

"Not exactly. I have detected the presence of a magical singularity."

"Would I regret it if I expended my last conscious breath to ask you what the smek you're talking about?"

"I am talking about him."

"Him? Him who?" Tol gasped weakly, and swiveled his head around. There in the middle of the carriage was a small fragile-looking creature about a meter tall, with bluish skin and casting a faint pearly radiance. He looked like a tiny glowing elf seen through the wrong end of a spyglass.

"Great. Now I'm hallucinating. What's next, flying purple seabeeves in sequined tutus?"

"You are not hallucinating, on this occasion. There is a creature now present in the carriage that is, as far I can tell from my telemetry, a manifestation of The Slice itself. A sort of living personification of magic, if you will."

Crazy though that sounded, it jiggled something in Tol's memory. "Is there any record of such a creature in your databases?"

"Yes. I have identified the species for you before. It is an alfar."

The alfar had been standing motionless, regarding the golem closely. The golem appeared confused, and stamped back and forth beating the air feebly with its fist and stump. It did not seem to be able to detect Tol's aura any longer, probably due to the overwhelming magical presence of the alfar. Tol laid there on a seat, barely conscious from blood loss but still fascinated by this near-mythical being a scant three meters from his face.

The alfar moved slowly, deliberately, with supernatural grace. It raised a delicate arm, spread the four fingers wide, and pushed against an invisible wall. The golem flew up into the air and crashed into the back of the carriage as though it had been hit dead-on by a fully-loaded dray. It slumped to the floor and gradually disappeared, leaving behind only a grotesquely distorted outline that gave off a soft greenish glow for some seconds before fading.

The being turned its gaze to Tol. It had youthful, almost infantile, features, yet the eyes were infinitely deep, pools of unimaginable power and wisdom. Tol shuddered, despite his weakened condition. Here was a creature who could be the ultimate foe or the best possible ally. Tol hoped fervently for the latter. Either way, though, there was nothing he could do about it now. His field of vision narrowed, and the world began to get fuzzy around the edges. He saw the alfar raise both hands in his direction, palms up. Then darkness took him.

Chapter Ten:
Spot the Brain Cell

Aspet sat slumped in his chair and fixed a blank gaze on the calendar hanging a little crookedly on the wall next to his computer. He had finally gotten up the gumption to file a challenge to the throne; it was set to take place in a little less than a fortnight. For years he'd dreamed of what it would be like to be king, but now that the prospect was finally staring him in the face, he wasn't sure he could handle it. He wasn't worried about the hacking part; he'd been doing that most of his life and as long as he thought of it as just one more online death match, he'd do fine. No, he was worried about what would happen if he somehow *won*.

In his younger days, being king had sounded like the ultimate glamor job: royal treatment, royal privileges, and royal luxury. After enduring The Seminar, though, he now realized that being head of state was nothing like he'd imagined it. It was stressful, demanding, and often exhausting. You give up any hope of privacy, as well as any expectation of a full night's sleep for weeks at a stretch. Your life is largely defined by your responsibility to the kingdom, and you must be unfailingly and fluently diplomatic to everyone. Any slip-up could start a war or uprising.

Now Aspet was doing some serious soul-searching, trying to get to grips with whether or not he was prepared to live under these terms for the rest of his life, or at least until he lost to the next challenger. That would be no sooner than two years from now, though, as that was the time a new king was allowed to serve before fresh challenges could be set forth. The Council of Mages and Engineers had some influence over whether or not a challenge, once issued, was accepted as valid. Neither Aspet nor most of the rest of the population of Tragacanth understood the precise nature of CoME's role, only that they were somehow involved. He assumed their decision had something to do with how well they thought the current monarch was governing the nation. Whatever the case, he was gratified they'd accepted his suit. At least, he *thought* so.

He'd had a brief flurry of exchanges with Boogla, then silence. Not that this was unusual behavior for a hacker, especially one as enigmatic as the legendary Boogla (or a direct descendant thereof), if that's who she really was. After a while he'd almost forgotten about her, but never completely. She'd established a beachhead on a remote lagoon in his mind—a presence both simple and elegant. He knew she would find him if the urgent need arose.

As he sat and fidgeted at his computer, weighing the wisdom of his lifestyle choice, Aspet absently surfed over to the "Tragacanthanem," a sort of underground alternative news and views site run clandestinely from an obscure branch of the Royal Network situated on an archipelago off the southeast coast. The authorities probably knew about it, but chose to look the other way because it was very popular and you didn't risk pissing off thousands of goblins unless you had a really good reason. They'd been thrown from that humpher before. (Humphers were extremely good at throwing riders because with three legs in the front and one in the back they could buck in several directions at once.)

Protest underway at Dreadmost Town Hall. Chimeras want larger voice in local government.

Amusing, yet disturbing. Amusing because the tone of the story was faintly derisive and mocking, along with the pictures that accompanied it. Disturbing because it was a political issue he'd have to take seriously were he to become king. As he was ruminating over this unsettling reality, he idly scrolled down the page, staring at but not really taking in the photos, until he came to the last one. It seemed innocuous, even nondescript, at first glance— just a picture of two rather scruffy chimeras holding blurry placards. It wasn't the chimeras or their fuzzy manifesto that caused Aspet's double take, though. It was the cloud formation in the background.

Another of Aspet's passions besides hacking

was meteorology. He loved studying the wide range of weather phenomena to which Tragacanth was subject. Wind-walls, spinners, ice curtains, washes, fogflows, heat bullies, ocean titans—he was fascinated by them all. He'd even spent one exciting season as a volunteer spotter with the Central Tragacanth Storm Tracking Squad. The rapid rotation of the planet N'plork, on which Tragacanth, Galanga, and three smaller nations constituted the largest of four continents, coupled with various unusual topological features such as a range of 20,000-meter mountains, several massive canyon complexes over 3,500 meters in depth, numerous volcanic hotspots scattered about the globe, and a series of truly gigantic, periodically reversing ocean currents of wildly different temperatures generated some dramatic and highly variable weather patterns.

This complex climatic milieu resulted in an extensive catalog of cloud types, ranging from the utterly commonplace to the vanishingly rare. It was one of the latter that Aspet was sure he'd spotted in the grainy photograph on the 'anthem page. It wasn't just that it was a rare type, though: it was the mechanism by which that particular type was created that captured his serious attention.

The annual journey of N'plork took it perilously close to a large and densely populated swarm of planetoids and smaller chunks orbiting rather haphazardly around N'plork's twin suns. The scientist types of Tragacanth had gotten pretty good at tracking these beasts, turning them over to the Planetary Defense Mages for magical deflection or destruction when they got too close to N'plork's orbital path for comfort.

The widespread use of magic on N'plork had, over time, established an aura around the planet somewhat akin to a magnetic field. Some of the smaller near-miss asteroids—those too small to be detected and destroyed before they entered N'plorkian space— grazed this arcane envelope and took on random magical properties. In exceedingly rare instances, the property a passing 'stroid picked up would be that of weather modification. This had only happened once in recorded history, as far as anyone knew. On that occasion the disintegration of the 'stroid, probably no bigger than a ripe plognik fruit, in the N'plorkian atmosphere had released a weather disruption spell of epic proportions that had modified weather patterns all across the planet for well over a month.

The only warning sign that had preceded the weather weirdness was a peculiar cloud formation generated by the ionization of the air around the plummeting space rock, enhanced by its magical properties. The result was a strange oval streak with periodic corkscrew shapes emanating from it at acute angles. Aspet had first seen the only surviving photograph of that phenomenon as a child, and it left a deep impression on him. Deep enough, in fact, that he instantly recognized the 'anthem photo as strikingly similar.

It was similar, but from what he could make out on the low-res picture, far grander in scale. The original cloud had been only a few tens of meters in length, with perhaps a dozen three meter-long emanations. Judging by the apparent scale of the 'anthem shot, this example was at least an order of magnitude larger—over a hundred projections extended twenty or thirty meters from the main cloud trail, which itself appeared to be over a thousand meters in length.

He wasn't sure what this meant, exactly, but he had a hunch they were, at the very least, in for some unusual weather. It was the wicked stepmother of all hunches.

"Curse yar blotchy hide, Jizrag, I tol yer t' hol' thet sign up so's th' cam'ra kin see 'im."

"Garn, eat yer maggots an' shat up, that's what I sez. I was holdin' th' bleeder up as far as I could. 'T'wadn't my fault th' little snorg was filmin' in the wrong d'rection."

"Nog y'are, an' nog yuv allays been, sez I. T'would be a blessin' for the res' of us if th' ground jus' opened up and swallowed yer."

"Speakin' o' blessins', why don't I jus' open up yer 'ead right now wit' this 'ere sign?"

While the two chimeras settled their differences in what was apparently the traditional manner, the camera crew took a break. They'd been filming all morning and were getting tired. A little lunch and something cold to drink sounded mighty good right about now. Besides, most of the demonstrators had wandered over to watch the combatants and cheer them on.

Selpla, the reporter covering the demonstration, sat in a citrum-green folding chair under a natty paisley umbrella and chewed thoughtfully on her hydroponically-grown ogrecress sandwich. Tragacanth harbored a number of different races who lived together in something approaching harmony most of the time. There seemed to be significant resistance to the chimeras' attempts to integrate themselves into mainstream society, though.

Of course, even by exceptionally tolerant Tragacanth standards chimeras evinced an utter lack of social graces; this tended not to endear them even to the other inhabitants of Dreadmost, where the chimeras' initial contacts with the rest of society were taking place. Offending the Dreadmost populace was something of an achievement in itself, since most of the inhabitants were already on the crude side of uncouth. The outpost was a popular spot for unsavory characters, sociopaths, drifters prone to violence, and those with shady pasts looking for a refuge from the public eye. They weren't, as a rule, known for their strict adherence to the protocols of polite society. Most of them believed spitting to be an acceptable form of greeting.

The mere fact that the chimeras were having trouble getting along with the Dreadmost citizenry was a strong indicator of just how few inherent social skills they possessed. In their defense, they *were* the product of random hybridizations triggered by errant magical processes. Those combinations which produced fertile offspring were now more or less self-sustaining, however, although their magical origin did give biology a little boost where fecundity was concerned.

One of the most enduring of the hybrids was that of orc and crusher eel, a nasty and wholly unnatural intersection if ever there was one. Orcs were a rarity in Tragacanth, having been virtually eradicated over a thousand years ago after a particularly vicious swarm very nearly succeeded in taking over the entire continent. There were only a couple of closely-watched colonies remaining, both in the south: one outside Dreadmost and the other on the coast east of Qoplebarq.

Goblins and orcs shared a relatively recent common ancestor, but goblins lacked the insane aggression and utter absence of morality that marked their slightly smaller cousins. No love was lost between the two species, shared family tree or not, but this was a tendency found throughout Tragacanth. No one got along with orcs; no matter how tolerant people were, sooner or later the orcs would completely and irrevocably alienate them by enslaving their children and roasting their pets; sometimes the reverse.

Crusher eels were, in many ways, the orcs of the marine world. They were bad-tempered, aggressive, and basically fearless. The random mutation that paired them genetically with orcs was a stroke of pure, unmitigated evil biological genius. There was widespread speculation amongst what passed for the intelligentsia of Tragacanth that this was the way politicians and personal injury barristers were originally conceived, as well, but critics of this theory pointed out that most true chimeras left *visible* slime trails.

The ragged mob of protestors Selpla and her crew had traveled to Dreadmost to film was composed mostly of goblin/domestic animal crosses, since those were the two most common gene pools in the area. This particular hybrid tended to be ungainly, ugly, and rock stupid, as evidenced by the sudden near-riot now taking place along the formerly united picket line. The crew straggled back to the demonstration scene and shot a few minutes of footage of the altercation just because they were already there, but violence amongst chimeras was hardly news: mild entertainment, maybe.

The news crew had resigned themselves to heading home substantially empty-handed, but they were suddenly greeted by more news than they bargained for. As they were packing up their equipment rather half-heartedly, one of the techs noticed a faint glow on the horizon. He tapped Selpla on the shoulder and pointed at the spot. As they watched, it lost much of its diffuse quality and sharpened into an increasingly intense blister of light.

Regarding this new development with interest, Selpla felt a faint prickling on the back of her neck. She reached quickly for the spot, to shoo away whatever noxious beastie was causing it, and discovered that no beastie, noxious or otherwise, was there. The sensation continued, and she recognized it as the kind you get from being too near a substantial source of static electricity. At this same moment the bright point of light began to elongate, sending fingers up toward the zenith like a hand grasping at the sky. The crew stared open-mouthed as the central digit of the hand passed right over them and stretched to about halfway towards the far horizon before halting abruptly. For a brief moment nothing happened, then a bolt of blindingly intense, brilliantly blue lightning leapt from the end of the finger. The point at which the bolt made contact with the ground melted in a blaze of pale blue flame and thick, oily, inky smoke.

Throughout the suddenly treacherous sky other fingers were discharging their bolts, and Selpla felt as though she were watching some eerie and nightmarish battle. She stood on a little hillock and looked out over the smoking marsh, which still reverberated with the occasional strikes and the hollow, cracking sound that accompanied them. Even the bickering chimeras had taken notice of the storm and were scattering like leaves in a gale.

The camera crew had recovered from their initial awe and were busily breaking out the gear again when Selpla felt the prickling sensation once more. This time it was much stronger, as if someone were vibrating the stiff scales on the back of her neck. She twisted around and saw a new finger soaring up towards them. She followed it as it raced across the sky, and felt a large, cold lump in the pit of her stomach when it stopped dead over their heads. She yelled a warning and dived awkwardly beneath the nearby pram. As her palms and knees skidded roughly on the chunky surface of the roadway, a mind-numbing flash of light and heat overwhelmed her and she found herself involuntarily curling up in a fetal position. Swamp gas and vegetation went up in flames all around her. Even the very soil, soggy though it was, seemed to be melting. Heavy black smoke belched up from the blasted ground and threatened to choke her.

Selpla coughed and gagged, and finally decided that she had to get out into the open to breathe, lightning be damned. She scrambled out and found a patch of ground relatively free of melted rocks and topsoil. The fingers seemed to have spent themselves, she noticed with some relief, but they were being replaced by huge, roiling clouds, apparently forming from nothing. In a matter of seconds the sky was overcast. The clouds were heavy, pendulous things, deep blue to deep green in color; they hung ominously low. The air suddenly became still and oppressive. Nothing moved, and she found herself poised for flight, though to where and from what, she wasn't entirely certain.

Without warning the air around Selpla positively exploded with rain. It didn't seem to fall from the sky so much as create itself spontaneously from the impossibly moisture-laden atmosphere. Certainly a lot of it seemed to be creating itself inside her undergarments. She shaded her eyes rather ineffectively from the torrential precipitation and sloshed about trying to find something resembling shelter. There really wasn't any.

Seeing as how they were already on the edge of a marsh, it didn't take long for the area to flood. Selpla's news instincts were quickly inundated as well, but they were fighting an increasingly pitched battle with her sense of self-preservation and concern for her crew. She finally hustled everyone into the pram with her cameraman perched on top getting as much footage of the deluge as possible as they evacuated. Various chimerae clung to their vehicle as they struggled to escape the rising muck.

Along with the rise in water levels came an accompanying drastic increase in the disagreeable odor of the swamp itself. Deep pockets of stagnant scum not disturbed for decades were being roiled and churned to the surface by the diluvian turmoil. The stench threatened to overwhelm them as Selpla fought to get herself and her companions out of the flood plain and up to the comparative safety of the elevated roadway. The soil, already treacherously unstable from the water table only a few centimeters below its surface, was rapidly evolving into an immensely viscous and adhesive glop that pulled powerfully at the wheels of the pram. Even at full throttle their progress was excruciatingly slow. Despite the hit she knew she would take from management if she came back to the station without the expensive pram, Selpla was considering abandoning ship and making a run for it if conditions did not improve soon.

When one of the uninvited chimera passengers slipped and fell into the muck only to disappear completely from sight a moment later, however, she wisely ruled out that course of action. Best to keep on sloggin'.

After a few more pram-lengths of progress various subsystems on board began to overheat and shut down, and Selpla realized that they were going to have to hike the rest of the way, good idea or not. Fortunately, it was no more than a dozen meters to the roadway, although it would be a dozen meters of leg-sucking deathpit.

"Everybody out," she said, "we'll have to hoof it to the road from here."

"What, and leave the pram? Kurg'll kill you. How will we get back to the studio?"

"Hang the pram, and hang Kurg. If we don't get out of here right now, we might not make it back to the studio at all. The mud is rising and we're stuck. If it rises much more we won't have any chance of escaping this buggy before it becomes a death trap. Now *move* it."

"Yo' da boss."

The pram had stalled on a slight downslope, which meant that the muck level was too high in the front for the passenger doors to open. They would have to evacuate via the cargo door in the rear.

Scrambling over the seats with her equipment, Selpla struggled to stay calm and lead her troops through the crisis. Her sound tech was having trouble with the rear door.

"What's the holdup, Drin?"

"Somethin's jammed against the door on the outside. Look like one o' them chimera thangs."

"Oh, for the love of Hork. Push it off."

"It don't wanna budge."

"Both of you work on it. Put your backs into it. We're running out of time."

The chimera was spread-eagled on the rear of the pram, balancing on the narrow bumper and holding on tightly to the gutters above the windows on both sides. He seemed frozen with fear, and was resisting fiercely the increasingly desperate attempts by the vehicle's occupants to dislodge him. The watery mud was already lapping at his feet. Another minute or two and even the cargo door would be virtually impossible to open against the weight of the encroaching muck.

While the boys struggled with the blocked door, Selpla acted on a sudden mad impulse and started beating on the windshield with a tripod. She managed to cover it with a spider web of cracks, but no actual holes were appearing. She turned the tripod in her hands and used it as a battering ram, finally shattering a fist-sized opening. The glass was, unfortunately, of the new self-sealing variety (the studio got an insurance break for that); the hole knitted itself closed before she could reposition the tripod for another go.

Frustrated and now scared, Selpla felt herself on the verge of tears, which is not a place any goblin ever wants to be, gender notwithstanding. There was very little tolerance in goblin society for open admissions of weakness. The only way to mask her feelings was to get her mind on something else. She slipped between the boys, braced her legs against the cargo net brackets, and pushed for all she was worth.

For a minute it looked like they were winning, but then the chimera suddenly took a deep breath and fought back even harder. The muscles on his long arms stood out like chiseled stone as he renewed his efforts to maintain his perch. Finally the trapped crew could push no longer and took a breather.

"We all goin' ta die, ain't we?" asked Drin.

"No. Someone will save us. I don't who, or how, or even precisely when, but it will happen."

She didn't believe a word of this, of course, but she felt obligated to play the stalwart optimist to the end.

"Whoever it is has about two minutes to get their ass here," replied Lom, her lighting tech, dryly.

As fear and panic were being replaced by numb acceptance of what seemed their inevitable fate, they heard a bumping noise coming from the roof of the pram. It started near the front, but progressed in a series of thumps towards the rear. Suddenly there was a dull thud just above the rear door and the chimera slipped bonelessly into the churning muck. The door popped open and a head peered in at them from above.

"You guys probably ought to think about cruising out of there pretty soon, before the gunk gets too high."

It was Prond, the cameraman, about whom they'd totally forgotten.

"I got some great footage. Um, sorry about bonking the passenger back there, but he was sort of blocking the door and I didn't think he would listen to reason."

"Prond, you magnificent bastard!" yelled Lom, "We owe you a pint of razzle. C'mon, let's blow this heap."

"Make that a case," Selpla said, smiling, as she crawled out through the door and stepped gingerly into the swirling mud.

"Smek," Prond replied, as he slung camera and tripod over one shoulder, "if I'd realized booze was involved, I'd have hung out on the roof more often."

The muck was deep and treacherous and insistently upwardly mobile, but all four of them managed to reach the roadway with nothing worse than pulled ligaments from fighting the ridiculously viscous undertow. Selpla stumbled once along the way when her foot caught on something solid but oddly elastic. She forced herself not to speculate too long on what it might have been.

They found themselves on a narrow asphalt island in a sea of stinking slop. Oddly-shaped protrusions jutted out from the black mess at irregular intervals, but whether they were tree limbs, fragments of former dwellings, or something more macabre was hard to pin down. Drin grabbed at one as it slogged by. It grabbed back and he shook free of it violently.

"Not gonna do *that* again."

"Wise decision. Anyone have a comm on 'em? I think mine is still in the pram somewhere." Selpla gestured toward their erstwhile conveyance, the only remaining evidence of which was a narrow band of silver with a luggage rack on it.

"I think there's one in my camera case," Prond answered, rummaging in the anodized metal container hanging around his neck by a thick strap. "Ah ha. Here it is." He handed the palm-sized communications unit to Selpla.

She puzzled over his cryptic address-filing system for a few moments, but finally deciphered the code sufficiently to find the station manager's entry.

"Bewl? Selpla. Is Kurg available? Yeah, I know the weather's gotten very weird. That's what I want to talk to Kurg about. He's where? Well, can you get hold of him and ask him to send someone down to Dreadmost to pick us up? We're having, uh, mechanical trouble with the news pram. Oh, and ask him to hurry. We're sort of running out of solid ground here. Yeah, I know it takes half a day to get here. We're holding on fine for now, but we can't do it forever."

By now the odiferous muck was lapping at the roadway, about ten centimeters of an asphalt/concrete mixture seven or eight meters across. It was dotted as far as the eye could see in either direction with clumps of refugees fleeing from the ongoing deluge. That was going to make their rescue an extremely protracted affair, so Selpla decided they could speed things up a bit by striking off in the direction of town while they waited.

Hefting their equipment, the ragged little news crew set off toward Dreadmost. The rain hadn't slacked off any; the wind was picking up now, as well, just to make things a little more interesting. They sloshed their way through the growing tempest, dodging knots of chimeras and occasional members of other races who had gathered on the asphalt to escape the rising waters. Every so often one of them would recognize Selpla and gush. She would do her best to be as diplomatic and cordial as possible under the circumstances.

"Sheesh. Who knew they even *got* news broadcasts out here?" she remarked after they'd left one such fan excitedly telling anyone who'd listen that he'd just met *the* Selpla.

Lom chuckled. "Honey, I don't think these people get a lot of celebrity visits. You're probably the only show business personality any of them've ever seen. You're a major star here. Enjoy it."

"It'd be a little easier to enjoy it if I weren't soaking wet and miserable."

"Ah, but look on the bright side. You're in such scintillating company," Lom replied with a smirk.

"The best and the brightest," agreed Prond.

"Whazzat?" added Drin.

"And the hits just keep on coming," Lom said

with a moist flourish.

"Shut up and trudge."

Bewl finally tracked down Kurg. He was already far south of the city with a cameraman, getting footage of various wacky weather phenomena. "I tell ya, Bewlie, we got snowflakes the size of smekkin' dinner plates, wind vortexes running every which way, and rain comin' down so hard it's put a concave indentation in the hood of the pram." Kurg sounded so excited he was falling all over himself.

"Get a grip, Kurg. Selpla and her crew are stranded down in Dreadmost and need someone to come pick them up."

"Selpla? What the smek happened to her pram?"

"She just said they were having 'mechanical trouble.' By the tone of her voice, I'd speculate that it was pretty thoroughly out of commission. She also mentioned something about 'running out of ground,' whatever that means."

Kurg looked south, towards Dreadmost. The clouds were black as midnight there, and stacked so high in the sky they seemed to touch the edge of space itself.

"I think I know what she's talking about. It looks pretty nasty down that way."

"Can you go get her, or should I try to find Weewit?"

"Smek. I'm already halfway there, so I guess I'll rescue the fair damsel. It'll be a tight squeeze getting her whole crew in here, but we'll manage somehow."

"Thanks, Kurg. I'll let her know you're coming."

He turned to the cameraman in the jump seat. "Looks like we're off to Dreadmost, Hnuppa. Hope you didn't have any early dinner plans."

"I'm just a piece of driftwood on the wayward tide, boss."

"Come again?"

"I'm free for the evening."

"Oh, good...smek!"

Kurg suddenly jerked the pram hard to the right to avoid a two meter-diameter ball of glowing gas that appeared in front of them and rolled straight down the centerline of the highway at a respectable velocity.

"There's something you don't see every day," Hnuppa remarked casually as he extricated his face from the cargo restraining net.

Kurg pounded the nav console. "Will someone please tell me what in the smek is going on with this weather?"

Hnuppa shrugged, "Maybe it's some sort of global warming."

As if in response, large sheets of ice began to fall on them from somewhere far above. They smashed noisily onto the pram and shattered like thin glass, propelling thousands of frozen shards in all directions.

"Or, maybe not."

As they neared Dreadmost several hours later, the ball lightning and ice sheets gave way to ever more torrential rain. The windshield wipers were useless, so Kurg switched on the hydro-repulsing ion field. It got overwhelmed, as well, so there really wasn't anything left to do but to drive very slowly and squint a lot. Fortunately, as a veteran news editor Kurg was a master squinter.

A few kilometers north of the city they started running into refugees. There were only the occasional clumps at first, but as they drew closer to Dreadmost the density increased dramatically. The standing water accumulation in the fields bordering the road was steadily growing from pools to small lakes as they approached the city limits.

Navigation was getting to be a real problem now. Not only was the weather atrocious, pedestrians were trudging along the roadway in ever greater numbers, their heads bowed against the driving rain. Needless to say, they were somewhat inattentive to oncoming traffic.

The Southern Reaches were remote and possessed some of the least hospitable lands in all of Tragacanth. They were populated predominately by hobgoblins, ogres, half-ogres, and dwarves, with one isolated orc colony. As was the way of minorities, they tended to clump together in small to medium-sized enclaves, each with its own set of traditions, cuisine, mores, and distinctive architecture.

While a great chunk of the Southern Reaches was sparsely-vegetated and uninviting, there were oases of a sort dotted across the landscape, where fresh water, abundant vegetation, and at least minimally arable land combined to support isolated knots of civilization. The only improved roadway linking the Reaches with the rest of Tragacanth snaked its way through the plains and mountainous areas of the region, passing through or near as many of these outposts as possible on its way to Dreadmost, the de facto capitol and economic hub of the southern peninsula.

Random acts of hardship and the tribulations of the natural world were nothing new to Reachers. The winds seemed to blow harder, rain fall with more gusto, and the seasons generate more pronounced extremes here than anywhere else in the kingdom. Whenever there was a shortage of some raw material or manufactured commodity, here was where it was felt most keenly. As a result, those who lived in the Reaches, by choice or necessity, were a resilient and determined lot with finely-honed survival skills. The current weather, while admittedly harsher than any of the inhabitants had previously experienced, did not faze them. They simply bundled up in their oiled skin cloaks and boots and rode it out.

Not everyone in the Reaches was a native or permanent transplant, however. Perhaps due to its very inhospitability, the area attracted a small number of enthusiastic tourists annually. Mostly these were deep urban types who yearned to escape from the cities for a while, to experience nature in a relatively unspoiled and pristine landscape while still having access to basic conveniences fairly nearby: weekend adventurers, as it were. They were almost always part of a carefully herded tour group. While not overly supportive of the influx of strangers, the Reachers found the considerable income they generated attractive and so made some small accommodation for them.

There were also, of course, a few hardy souls who truly wanted to get away from it all—those with atavistic leanings, paranoid survivalists, hermits, fugitives, and even a few out and out crazies. They were for the most part loners, fiercely independent and rabidly protective of their homesteads, such as they were. The natives knew to leave these folks alone; encounters were few and far between. Tourists occasionally ran afoul of the Wilders, as Reach inhabitants called them, but so far no serious trouble had erupted as a result.

Ballop'ril was a bugbear. That alone made him something of an outcast, as there were only a few scattered settlements of that species in Tragacanth. Bugbears, with their odd guttural language and even odder social customs, were difficult for the other races to understand; misunderstanding inevitably breeds mistrust. Consequently, in many places bugbears were automatic social pariahs, a distinction that did nothing to conventionalize their somewhat bizarre world views.

This particular bugbear had been some distance from the cave he called home foraging for his favorite snack, fleggen worms, when the rains struck. The water came down with such ferocious intensity that the path leading back to his grotto became a raging torrent in short order, so raging that he was unable to trudge his way home against the current. He cursed the weather roundly and stumbled down the hill as the stream that had been his garden path swept him along before tons of water, mud, and debris. The flood finally deposited him, bruised and waterlogged, at the bottom of the hill. He wasn't exactly in high humor. When a few seconds later it became apparent he was also now more or less trapped, by dint of multiple mudslides in all directions, in the middle of a major highway, Ballop'ril's disposition began to sour.

It was at this point that Kurg's pram came chugging around the bend. Kurg and Hnuppa were both busy ogling the huge mass of water and splintered timber that was cascading down the hill, threatening to overflow the roadway as it crashed headlong into an overburdened culvert. Kurg totally failed to see Ballop'ril until the bugbear was scarcely three meters from the pram—the heavy rain and mist rising from the road would have obscured him even if he weren't only a little over a meter tall and the same color as the mud. Swerving madly, Kurg careened up onto a guardrail, actually drove with one wheel skirting it for a few meters, then dumped the pram fairly gently over on its side. It slid to a halt, pirouetting on its door handle a few times as an encore to the soggy automotive ballet.

Ballop'ril, who dove out of the way at the last second, picked himself up and pointlessly wiped the pouring rain off his fuzzy forehead. He walked over to where Kurg and Hnuppa were extricating themselves from the crippled vehicle.

"Peers as though you boys had yerselves an accident," he said flatly, rain dripping from the matted hair tufts shading his ample ears.

Kurg glared at him in silence for a full ten seconds, soaking wet, thoroughly disheveled, and bleeding from a respectable laceration engendered by a chance meeting between his cheek and the shattered windshield.

Hnuppa expected a blistering barrage of invective from his boss, but Kurg merely continued to glare malevolently at the bugbear as he gathered up his scattered notepads and equipment. Maybe he was too angry and shaken to verbalize, although if so this represented the first time Hnuppa had witnessed such an occasion. He would have opened a bottle of vintage razzle in celebration if he had one. None was available, however, so he settled for watching the show in saturated bemusement.

"Why are you just standing around?" Kurg snapped at him abruptly, like a domestic scrubhound suddenly made aware of a rodentcatcher on his backyard fence. "Get the cameras and your other junk and let's get out of this smekking rain."

Hnuppa surveyed their surroundings, blinking against the hydrological onslaught. "How do you propose to do that, exactly?"

"Easy. I've got the Amulet of Dryness that mage in Dresmak gave me."

"You mean the one who told you never to darken his doorway again, even if he were dying and you were the only living creature who could help him?"

"Um, yeah, I think that was the one."

Hnuppa grimaced. "I'm just gonna step over

here for a moment."

"Wimp."

"Let's just say I have a robust survival instinct."

Kurg made a rude noise with his lips and pulled out the amulet. It was an intricately worked silver arc, beneath which were three copper spheres suspended by fine chains. He squinted at the activation phrase, etched on the rear of the medallion.

"Yestwe collnud meshwa resnam," he chanted unconvincingly.

Nothing happened, except the rainfall rate seemed to increase a bit. Ballop'ril, who was too far away to understand what was happening, chose this moment to shake himself like a dog, spraying bugbear-flavored rainfall all over the already saturated Kurg.

Kurg scowled even more deeply and shook the amulet, as though to wake it up. Hnuppa chuckled. "I don't think you're doing something right."

"Brilliant deduction, detective. Maybe I wasn't forceful enough. Yestwe collnud meshwa resnam!"

It suddenly began to hail. Pea-sized, at first, but the plummeting orbs of ice were gradually increasing in diameter as the three of them scrambled for shelter in the wrecked pram.

"Are you sure that thing is a *dryness* amulet?" Hnuppa yelled over the hailstone barrage.

"That's what what's-his-name told me. I suppose he could have been pulling my leg."

"That wouldn't surprise me. If I recall, he wanted

to pull your legs clean *off* at the time."

"Show it to me," commanded Ballop'ril. Kurg growled. "What does a *bugbear* know about magic amulets?"

"One may as easily ask, 'what does a goblin know of them?' Obviously nothing." Ballop'ril replied.

While Kurg worked this one out, the bugbear coaxed the amulet from his grasp. He stared at it for a moment, then, holding it tightly in his right hand, chanted.

"Resnam meshwa collnud yestwe."

A bluish radiance leapt from the amulet, slowly spreading until a hemisphere formed over them, repelling all rain and hail in a three-meter diameter.

Ballop'ril smiled a toothy smile and handed the talisman back to Kurg.

"Inscribed incantations are read right to left. That's Magic 101; glad I could be of service, oh great and powerful mage."

Kurg glared at him from under his bushy eyebrows for a few moments, and then began to make a repetitive gasping noise. At first it gave the impression that he was softly gagging, but then Hnuppa recognized that the sound was not of Kurg choking, but rather his peculiar way of chuckling. Kurg was *amused* by the cheeky bugbear.

The chuckle escalated to a full-fledged guffaw. Laughter is, as a rule, easily communicable amongst nearly all sentient species. This rule ordinarily fell flat on its pimply face when applied to Kurg, however, as his expressions of mirth were barely recognizable as such, not to mention as a general rule altogether unpleasant to experience. Ballop'ril was not put off by Kurg's odd laugh, though, and soon he lent his own throaty tenor to the opera. Appalled by the sudden cacophony, Hnuppa retreated to the far perimeter of the magical barrier and tried to find something to stuff in his ears. Fortunately, before he could seriously contemplate damaging his aural apparatus, the noise died down and the two jocularists gazed at one another with dawning affection.

Hnuppa noticed the upgrade in diplomatic relations and wasn't happy about it—Kurg was difficult enough on his own. As part of a duet he could be well-nigh impossible. He rolled his eyes.

"I hate to put a damper on the party, but we need to figure out how we're getting out of here. And someone still has to pick up Selpla and company."

"I know that. Don't you think I know that?" Kurg fumbled with his comm. "Bewlie?

Bewlie, can ya hear me? Confound it, what's wrong with this smekkin' thing?"

"I think the freaky weather and this magical shield together are interfering with the signal," Hnuppa said, "Try switching to 'arcane' mode."

"Whuzzat?"

Hnuppa sighed, "Main Menu>Options>Mode >Arcane. It uses magic to heterodyne the radio frequency transmission and boost it."

Kurg punched at his comm until it took on a faint orange glow. He looked pleased with himself.

"There. Got it."

"Yer a reg'lar jene-yus," Ballop'ril chimed in.

Hnuppa frowned. "Yikes. Don't encourage him."

The bugbear grinned at him.

"Bewlie? Bewlie, this is Kurg. We had a little setback on the road. The pram's gonna have to have some, uh, work. Yes, this one, too. I need you to send someone down with the remote broadcast dray to get us. No, I haven't made it to Selpla yet. Yes, it's still raining. No, we're sort of dry: I used an amulet. A dryness amulet. No, he's fine. Listen, tell whoever to get his rear in gear. We're just north of Dreadmost, on the main road. Hard to miss."

During Kurg's conversation, Ballop'ril had been fidgeting with something in his pocket. Hnuppa noticed a pronounced bulge in that location, but he wasn't sure that it hadn't been there before, so he said nothing. Bugbears weren't known as thieves, particularly—not that he knew much about them at all, of course.

"Looks like we've got an hour or two to kill," Kurg reported. "What shall we do, play a game?" He clapped his rather misshapen hands together in a childlike way.

Hnuppa cocked his head and peered inquisitively at Kurg. It was sometimes hard to tell if his boss was kidding. "*Capital* idea," he enthused sardonically, "Let's play 'spot the brain cell.' I'll go first." He shielded his eyes with one hand and made a half circle, as though scanning the horizon. "I got nothin,'" he said, shaking his head and making an exaggerated sad face.

Ballop'ril started laughing at this *bon mot*; at least that's what Hnuppa assumed he was doing. Kurg wasn't laughing with him this time, though. He was staring in stunned amazement at something over Hnuppa's right shoulder.

Hnuppa noticed Kurg's odd behavior after a few seconds and swiveled around, following his gaze. His initial impression was that a new mountain had somehow formed behind them—he was relatively certain there hadn't been one there previously. There could be no debate over its existence now, however. As Kurg continued to gape, Hnuppa couldn't help but think that he'd seldom, if ever, seen his boss at a loss for words.

It became apparent after a minute or so of gawking that this was not a sedentary topological feature but in fact an animate object. It moved toward them visibly, albeit gradually, the lower half of it undulating slightly as it progressed. The occasional bouncing boulder or small rock slide punctuated the behemoth's slow and deliberate movements.

Hnuppa glanced over at Kurg. He still seemed disinclined or unable to speak, so Hnuppa decided to take the reins.

"What *is* that?" It was not a profoundly-worded question, but it needed to be asked.

"Don't you worry none. It's for me." The reply came from the bugbear, about whose presence Hnuppa had momentarily forgotten.

Both Hnuppa and Kurg turned to stare at him.

"What the smek do you mean, it's 'for you'?" Kurg exploded, his dumbness apparently having finally worn off.

"I mean," Ballop'ril explained calmly, "That I summoned it. Well, not so much 'summoned' as arranged to have it meet me here. It's under geas to find me."

This was obviously too much for Kurg. His mouth slammed shut and he sat heavily in a puddle, splashing Hnuppa up to the knees. The dryness amulet clearly had no influence over water already inside its effect radius.

"Let me get this straight: you placed a *mountain* under geas?" asked Hnuppa incredulously, wiping his soaked pants without much efficacy.

"Yeah. I live in that mountain and I'm sort of a homebody, see? I figured if I'm ever more than a kilometer from home, I'm probably lost. So I put a geas on my home to come and find me when that happens."

"OK, ten out of ten for convenience, but an entire mountain? Why not just enchant some object to lead you back—a wooden avian or whatever?" His eyes suddenly narrowed, "Where did you get a magical artifact of sufficient power to do this, anyway? I've never seen an enchantment on this scale in person before."

"It weren't no artifact, at all. It were a spell I conjured up on me own."

"*You* cast a geas that affected an entire

mountain?" Hnuppa was torn by skepticism on the one hand and the incontrovertible evidence of his eyes on the other.

"Yep, I did." It was a matter-of-fact reply, and Ballop'ril apparently felt no need to explain further. The bugbear turned and headed off up the newly-arrived versant, leaving Hnuppa unsatisfied and sputtering. He suddenly felt a hand on his shoulder.

"I just recognized that guy," Kurg said, softly. "That was Ballop'ril of Qoplebarq."

It took a few seconds for the name to register, then a few more to overcome the incredulity. "*Ballop'ril?*" Hnuppa finally managed to squeak out, "Shouldn't he be *dead* by now? He was an old legend when I was in school."

"You'd think so. However, I suppose when you're the only bugbear ever to reach Magineer status, you have ways to keep yourself from growing old at the usual pace. How long do bugbears normally live, anyway?"

"He wasn't actually a Magineer, though."

"He never officially held the office, no. But the Council agreed that he was qualified, despite not being a goblin. He just decided not to commit himself to a life of being in the constant spotlight, I guess."

"Hmm. Teacher told us he was involved in something that the Council didn't feel was proper for a Magineer, and that's why he was asked not to accept the position."

"As far as I know, the only unsavory activity he was involved in was simply being a bugbear in the first place. That in itself was enough to give the Council heartburn. They're pretty conservative when it comes to any race but goblins occupying the magineer positions."

"Maybe we should have asked him give us his side of the story."

Kurg stared thoughtfully at the lumbering mountain receding in the distance. "Something tells me he wouldn't have been happy about that," he replied finally.

The rain was intensifying. Flooding on a massive scale seemed imminent, but Kurg and Hnuppa didn't see much they could do about it. They found the highest ground that still allowed them to watch the roadway and hunkered down, trying not to slip in the mud. The amulet kept rain from soaking them directly, but it didn't stop runoff water cascading down on them from higher elevations. Hnuppa was thinking about the lowlands that lay around Dreadmost.

"I hope we can actually *get* to Selpla when the dray does finally make it."

"Huh? What do you mean?"

"The water's pretty deep even here. It looks like it's all been coming up from the south, too. It's liable to be seriously flooded down Dreadmost way. The roads may not even be passable."

"I don't care if the roads are open or not. We've got to get Selpla and her crew back."

"I had no idea you were so gung-ho about the wellbeing of your employees. Maybe I've been misjudging you all this time."

"Don't be ridiculous," Kurg snapped, taken aback, "Selpla has footage that we need for the weekend broadcast, and I won't have time to string together enough stock if we don't get it from her."

Hnuppa grinned. "Ah, good. My world view is still intact."

"What the smek is that supposed to mean?" Kurg sounded more ticked off than Hnuppa would have expected. He must be stressed by their run of bad fortune.

"Nothing. Hey, look: here comes the dray!" What excellent timing. He owed whoever was driving a pint of razzle for helping him dodge a Kurg-shaped bullet.

The driver to whom the pint of razzle was owed turned out to be a lugubrious old gaffer named Slud. Most of the time he was a shadowy denizen of the labyrinthine catwalks above and below the studio sound stages, but occasionally he ran errands for Bewlie. Dreadmost was probably a little further than he was accustomed to driving on these clerical excursions, but this was something of an emergency, after all.

The dray clattered to a halt in the dead center of a large puddle, making it impossible to get to any of the doors without wading. It was a large and rather cumbersome-looking vehicle, originally designed to hold all the equipment for remote broadcasting but now refitted with bench seats and used primarily to cart investors and major advertisers to and from the overland carriage station and hotels during their periodic visitations. These visitations—which were really more akin to inspections—Kurg was fond of claiming were the principal reason for his ever-growing ulcer collection (goblins have complex stomachs with up to six chambers, so there's plenty of room). He motioned for Slud to pull forward out of the pond, but the old goblin ignored him. Throwing up his hands in disgust, Kurg slogged through the dirty water toward the dray, followed closely by Hnuppa, who was chuckling as quietly as he could. It wasn't quietly enough.

"What's so smekkin' funny?" Kurg growled, stepping in a pothole and splashing water in his face as he stumbled. Hnuppa tried to restrain himself, but the sight of Kurg soaking wet with the still-activated dryness amulet hanging around his neck was too much.

"Bwaaahahahah!" he bellowed, unable to frame any actually coherent reply.

Kurg glared evilly in his direction, but Hnuppa couldn't stop laughing. He was still chuckling as he climbed into the dray next to his soggy boss.

"There's about a gumjillion goblins who'd love to have your job, you know," Kurg said, arms folded across his chest.

"Maybe," replied Hnuppa, "but that's only because they don't fully comprehend the working conditions."

The dray chugged away through the ankle-deep water.

"What, you mean slogging through the torrential

rain?"

"No, I mean putting up with you as a boss."

"All right, that's it. You can just smekkin' walk. Pull over!" Kurg barked at the driver. Slud ignored him. "Pull over, I said!" No reaction.

"What, is this guy smekkin' *deaf*?"

"Pretty much. He's also my uncle, incidentally." Hnuppa started chuckling again.

Kurg sat there and steamed in his own pungent juices. Hnuppa knew there'd be a price to pay for this later, but right now he was going to enjoy Kurg's discomfiture as much as possible.

They still had a few kilometers before reaching Dreadmost itself, although they weren't sure exactly where Selpla was at the moment in relation to that fine metropolis. They figured their paths would intersect somewhere along the road.

Selpla had a certain odd knack for finding company vehicles under difficult conditions, as evidenced by the time several years prior when she'd managed to pick a pram driven by Kurg's ex-boss out of a crowd of some three hundred vehicles at a rally for charity. She'd broken a talon trying to pry open a package of dripple-beast chips in the stands and wanted to get a manicure as soon as was goblinly possible. Seeing his car approaching, she made one of those split-second judgments for which she was infamous and leapt down onto the road. She avoided getting run over by the other racers somehow, then flagged him down and managed to convince him to leave the rally to take her to the manicurist. When asked later how she'd accomplished this, Selpla replied, "I don't know. He was very cooperative. He seemed sort of quiet, though, like he was thinking about something real hard."

That person left the station's employ shortly thereafter, and Kurg was promoted to take his place. In a way, then, he owed his job to Selpla. It was common knowledge around the station that Selpla had something of a crush on Hnuppa, so Kurg put up with more than he ordinarily would from him for her sake. There was nevertheless a limit to his indulgence, but Hnuppa was quite adept at pulling back just a hair's breadth from crossing that line.

He was amused by Kurg's brusque manner, and pushing his buttons had become one of the twisted little pleasures that kept Hnuppa relatively happy in his job. Kurg seemed to take that in his stride, at least most of the time. Once he'd suspended Hnuppa for a day as a result of a practical joke gone somewhat awry, but Hnuppa looked at it as an unexpected day off (sans pay, admittedly) and held no grudge. Besides, he had gotten one smek of a good laugh out of the episode.

The rain seemed to be getting worse, if that was possible, as they drove south. Hnuppa couldn't even see the pavement from his vantage point in the back seat, but Slud seemed to be having no difficulty keeping the dray on the road. He steered rather stiffly, but he obviously was totally focused on his duties. Hnuppa knew that once Slud committed himself to a thing, only some great act of divine wrath could pull him away from it. He couldn't imagine a better pilot for this sort of weather.

Kurg didn't know Slud very well and wasn't nearly as confident in the gnarled old goblin's navigational prowess. He gripped the armrests of the front passenger's seat as though he were struggling against a gale force wind. Hnuppa thought about suggesting that he relax but thought better of it. Kurg seemed to thrive on high anxiety.

Chapter Eleven:
Needles and Pincers

Selpla sneezed violently. She had never been very ladylike when it came to expelling vapors. Her brother Grelm had been fond of comparing the sound to airbrakes being released on a heavy industrial transport dray, in fact. She wiped her nose on her sleeve and trudged along, sniffling. Water rolled down her in uninhibited abandon while she splashed in the rising river that had once been a highway. She wasn't in a particularly good mood.

"Where the smek is Kurg?"

"The weather's a bit inclement, in case you hadn't noticed," replied Lom, "He's probably fighting the rain just like we are."

"Cept he prolly drier," added Drin, ruefully.

Selpla shook her head. Water flew a full two meters in a semicircle around her face. "Thanks for the weather report. I'll be sure to grow an umbrella and gills in my next life."

Ahead of them a few meters, Prond was kneeling with his back to them. As they approached him he stood up, cradling something. He turned around to face them, and pulled his arms down a bit so they could see what he was holding. It was an utterly bedraggled battalo, or tree-bear. They gawked. None of them had seen one outside a zoo. They lived exclusively in tree tops of the dense southern forests that stretched from Tillimil to the Bungash Mountains.

"Where did you find that thing?" Selpla asked, her maternal instincts struggling with her desire to be anywhere dry and warm.

"Swimming in little circles," Prond replied.

"That's a battalo. They don't swim."

"Well, this one does," he said, showing them the pronounced webbing between the furry little creature's toes.

"Something of an odd adaptation for a canopy-dweller isn't it?" asked Lom. "I mean, not a lot of aquatics involved in their lifestyle, to my knowledge."

"Odd, all right," agreed Selpla, "And not, I suspect, a natural mutation."

"If not natural," asked Drin, "What, then?"

Selpla frowned and scrutinized the shivering furball closely. It was still weakly paddling with its back legs.

"Magic. A form of chimera."

Prond cocked his head in puzzlement. "How did the little guy even get here in the first place? It's a good seventy or eighty kilometers to the nearest deep forest."

"Yeah," Lom chimed in, "all the chimeras we saw earlier were concocted from locally occurring specimens. Maybe he escaped from a zoo?"

"Zoo? There's no zoo in Dreadmost," replied Selpla, "I don't think they even have a sewage plant."

Prond snorted. "Dreadmost *is* a sewage plant."

"Jest coz we only see chimeras in marsh, it not mean they not happen anywheres else," blurted Drin.

The other three turned to look at him in astonishment. Drin wasn't known for his intellectual prowess, or volubility, for that matter. Selpla sometimes wondered how he managed to find his way to the studio every day.

"That's quite true, Drin," Selpla said, finally, trying not to sound patronizing but failing rather badly, "We'd overlooked that possibility, it seems. Perhaps the mutations are spreading."

"What," Lom frowned, "Like some sort of pathogen?"

"Could be," replied Prond, "There is some evidence that wild magical outbreaks follow epidemiologically predictable vectors."

"Wah you say?" asked Drin, shaking his head.

"He said that magic and sickness can spread the same way," explained Selpla.

Drin nodded in agreement, but seemed disinclined to comment. He was behaving rather oddly, Selpla thought. It suddenly struck her that she knew next to nothing about him. He'd just appeared in the station one day. The muckety-mucks hired him and assigned him as a general gofer for the reporters. Senior management weren't in the habit of explaining their personnel decisions to the rank and file, so Drin became part of the team with nothing beyond a basic introduction. He never said much, and what communication he did engage in was a bit shy of sophisticated; Selpla and everyone else had naturally assumed he was uneducated and simple. He'd never done anything up to now to dispel that notion.

Selpla's ruminations on the true nature of Drin were interrupted by the sudden arrival of an obviously hysterical hobgoblin. She ran up to Selpla in the pouring rain and started gibbering about a mountain, switching back and forth between Goblish and Higglin, the most common dialect of the Hobgoblin language.

Selpla, Prond, and Lom huddled around the shrieking hob, trying to figure out what she was saying using a combination of translation and context. It was an uphill struggle. They got the "mountain" part, and something about "motion" or "movement." None of them were adept at Higglin, unfortunately, so the comprehension was tetchy, at best.

"A moving mountain," Prond said, at last, "Sounds like some sort of metaphor. But for what?"

The others shook their heads. "I can't imagine," replied Selpla, "But whatever it is, she's definitely put out about it."

"Escuse, please," interjected Drin, who had wandered over, "She not speaking metaphorically. She say she saw a mountain moving across the landscape like some great animal. To the north. It passed from west to east less than an hour ago."

Once again, Drin had impressed them. "Drin, do you speak Higglin?"

"Drin speak many tongues," he replied simply.

Selpla shook her head. It had been quite a memorable day already, and the end was nowhere in sight.

"Okay, she saw a moving mountain. Ask her if she's taking any sort of medication," said Lom. Prond looked at him sharply. He expected Selpla to chastise Lom for his bluntness, but she did not. Instead, she and Lom both peered at Drin expectantly.

Drin spoke to the hob in what sounded to Selpla like fluent Higglin. They conversed for nearly a full minute—she, rapidly; he, more deliberately.

"She say," relayed Drin, after taking a moment to sort out the translation, "that she hear deep rumble noise off to the west. After about five minutes of noise, a large mountain came out of the rain and fog and moved from west to east maybe hundred meters in front of her. It did not change shape as it moved. She say is a trail of broken trees to show if you want to see." He raised his one eyebrow comically. "Oh, and she also say she not take any medicine. She want to know if you recommending some."

Lom and Prond burst out laughing at this. "Hey," Prond said, between spasms, "You should let her try one of your wipeout pills."

"Yeah," agreed Lom, "She'd be seeing whole countries stroll by wearing top hats then."

"Or maybe fly over," added Prond, making a

dramatic sweep with his hand.

"You're both about as funny as you are sensitive," replied Selpla, "Those pills were prescribed to me for my headaches, and you know it. Anyway, I think this lady may have a story. It's not every day you get to report on a portable mountain."

Lom and Prond looked at one another in astonishment. "You're not gonna take her *seriously*, are you?"

"Sure. Why not? Why would she run up to a bunch of total strangers in this deluge unless she was genuinely upset about something?"

"Maybe because she's as loony as a fruit-flapper," Lom ventured, "Do you actually think she saw a walking *mountain*?"

"What I think isn't important at this point. It's obvious that she believes that's what she saw. Our job is to take a look and report what we find. Nothing more, nothing less."

Prond threw up his hands. "What the smek. I guess we can't get any wetter."

Kurg still hadn't decided whether or not he liked Slud. The old goblin was quite annoying and seemingly completely immune to intimidation by authority figures, but he was also one smekking good driver. Weather, wind, and crashing obstacles that would have unhinged any other mortal pilot had no apparent effect on Slud. He braked, smoothly dodged, and continued along his way as though he were on an afternoon pleasure cruise through the Eshvodsi Garden of Botanical Surprises. Kurg couldn't help but admire that kind of unflappable competence, crotchety old insubordinate leatherbeak notwithstanding.

They were close enough to Selpla's last reported position that it was time to start looking out for her and the crew. The rain had not let up, even for an instant, but they found themselves acclimating to the poor visibility. Amazing what a goblin can train his brain to filter out when the need arises.

Kurg scanned from the passenger's side, and Hnuppa from behind Slud. They were seeing ever more frequent knots of what looked like refugees from the floods; presumably Selpla's crew would be recognizable from their unmistakable equipment. "Unless, of course," Hnuppa pointed out, "They abandoned it because of the rain." Kurg refused to consider this; he found it impossible even to imagine that anyone would abandon video and audio equipment of that value, no matter how dire the circumstances. Hnuppa had a sudden mental image of Kurg doggedly clinging to a huge shoulder-mounted camera as he slipped beneath the waves after some catastrophic shipwreck. His last words would be, "Hey, these smekkin' things come out of my capital budget! Blub blub." Hnuppa chuckled in spite of himself.

"Why don't you share whatever it is you find amusing?" Kurg growled at him, "I'm sure we could all do with a laugh right about now." Hnuppa caught the warning tone in his voice. "Uh, just clearing my throat, sir. Nothing funny here."

"Jolly, then you can return your attention to

watching for Selpla."

"OK—I'm looking, I'm looking. Sheesh."

Just then Slud jerked the dray rather violently to starboard to avoid a large tree that had been swept onto the highway by a sudden onrush of water. It rolled across the road behind them and down an embankment like a giant bottle brush. This time, however, Slud was unable to regain full control of the dray; it slid off the roadway and into a water-swollen ditch. No one was hurt, nor did the dray seem damaged, but it was thoroughly stuck in the viscous blue Dreadmost mud.

"Smek, smek, smek!" Kurg cursed, "If it ain't one thing, it's another. Hey, giggles—get out there and push us out of this muck."

"Me and what army? What do I look like, a troll? It will take both of us, and even then we'll be extremely lucky to get out of here."

"I'm too smekkin' old for this smek," Kurg moaned as he yanked open the door and a raw blast of wind-driven rain smacked him square in the face.

They heard a curious sound, like an ancient steam engine being powered up for the first time in fifty years. After a moment they realized it was coming from Slud. He was, for lack of a better term, laughing at them.

"Doesn't *anyone* around here laugh like a normal goblin?" Kurg grumbled. Hnuppa didn't answer—he was too busy trying to keep from ingesting a fatal dose of the water being forcibly driven into every exposed square millimeter of his body.

The big dray was thoroughly stuck. Kurg and Hnuppa realized more or less simultaneously that they would have to dig it out. It would be a long, dirty task, and one that neither of them felt particularly suited to perform. It was that or sit there for who knows how long, though. Reluctantly, they grabbed the small emergency shovels (more like large spades, really) from the tool box and started mucking.

"Are we sure this is the right way?"

"This is the direction she said."

"Ask her again. Drin, ask her again if this is the right way."

"Preshka nis cassrell mo?"

"Diji cassol nis."

"Yah, she say this path is correct."

Lom snorted. "When are we gonna pick up this trail, then? You'd think a mountain on walkabout would cut quite a swath." He paused to shake off a refuge-seeking dirt wrat that had apparently mistaken his leg for a tree trunk. The wrat floundered in the mud for a confused moment, and then splished off into what little undergrowth had not already washed away. Lom watched it go disapprovingly. Only a few seconds later, Prond, who was currently taking point, suddenly blurted out, "Downed trees ahead!"

"Did you say 'downed' or 'drowned'?" Lom asked.

"Is there an important difference?" interjected

Selpla, a bit crossly.

Prond opened his mouth to reply but at that moment the hobgoblin became visibly excited, shrieking and pointing.

"She say this where she see mountain," explained Drin.

"Yeah, we managed to get that part," Lom replied, dryly.

The scene was one of, as they say on the news, utter devastation. A broad path of botanical destruction swept across their field of view—in many places the trees, some of them as much as thirty or forty meters tall in happier days, were literally ground into mulch. Rain had floated away many of the smaller intact branches, but a plethora of tree trunks and limbs were scattered willy-nilly. There were deep gouges where immense rocks had apparently been dragged across the forest floor by some unfathomable force. Here and there piles of broken stone lay strewn in mute testament to the shattering impact of boulder on boulder.

The little party stood and stared in silent awe at the impressive sight, except for the hobgoblin, who had been yammering non-stop since they arrived. Even Drin seemed to have ceased listening to her.

Finally Prond took a deep breath, "Hard to argue that *something* pretty impressive didn't happen here." The others nodded. "The question now, I think, is 'what do we do next?'" He had to raise his voice to be heard over the hob, who was still having at it. Selpla started to reply, but then glanced at Drin.

"What in the name of Grund is she gibbering about?"

"Hard for Drin to understand, but sound like she keep repeating some kind of magical ward. Something about 'keep us safe from giants in the mountains.'"

"It's a prayer," said Lom, with sudden recognition. "*The Prayer for Protection from the Rock Titans*. My mother used to have it hanging on the wall when I was a whelp. If I remember aright, it goes like this:

Mighty spirits, hear my prayer,
You who dwell in realms of air:
From the mountains to the sea;
From titans cruel deliver me.
With sinewed arms, with trunk and stone,
They rend the world, tear flesh from bone.
So hear my plea with each new day,
Pray, keep those titans far away.

"Yah," agreed Drin, "That sound like what she saying."

"Rock Titans?" asked Selpla, "I thought they were extinct or something."

"Maybe. I've never seen one, at least. My mother's folks were quite nervous about them, though. I grew up hearing stories of the terrible destruction they were capable of inflicting when they were on a rampage about something. We had to leave them offerings at the equinoxes every year to appease their wrath. Must have worked, 'cause, as I said, I never saw one."

"What kind of offerings?" Prond inquired.

"Meat pies, mostly. Big ones. And a couple jugs of leggen nut razzle, although I realized late in childhood that these were more for my uncle Ikorn than the titans," Lom chuckled. "One spring I caught him up on the hill where we left the offerings, wandering around in his skivvies. He had one of the jugs in his hand; the other one was lying empty on the ground. He made me promise never to tell mother or aunt Follia about it. I did get a new pro kickball out of the deal, though."

Selpla looked thoughtful, "Do you think rock titans could have been responsible for this mess?"

Lom surveyed the scene. "I doubt it. First of all, no footprints. Second, spark carefully at the air. There's still a faint magical aura here. Titans are decidedly non-magical creatures. They're just huge and brutal. Whoever did this used magic, and a lot of it, by the look of things."

"There can't be many mages in Tragacanth powerful enough to wreak this kind of havoc," Selpla replied, crossing her arms, "I seriously doubt the Sutha Magineer threw a temper tantrum here... but if not him, who?"

"Equally puzzling," added Prond, "Is why?"

They stood there for a further minute. Finally Selpla shrugged and shouldered her bag. "I guess the only way we get any answers is to follow the trail."

"Just a minute, intrepid newshound," said Prond, "We're supposed to be waiting to be rescued by Kurg, remember? If we get so far from the road that he can't find us, there'll be smek flying every which way."

"Oh, come on, Prond, it's a *story*. You know Kurg will always forgive anything anyone does, so long as a good story comes out of it." Selpa turned her lower lip down in a rather unconvincing pout. Prond rolled his eyes and stuck out his tongue in response. She giggled.

"Yeah," Lom added, "besides, it could be hours before Kurg finally hauls his hindquarters down here to pick us up. We could probably be back before he even shows."

Selpla knew that these were weak arguments, but her urge to sniff out a scoop lent them considerably more credence then they would have garnered otherwise. "Right you are," she agreed, throwing prudence to the wind, "So let's move out."

Prond still seemed a little reluctant. Selpla turned to him.

"If you're that worried about it, why don't you hang here and wait for Kurg? We can manage without you for this trip. We'll meet you back here in a couple of hours." She gestured to the others, "Come on troops, let's march."

Prond started to protest, but then thought better of it. "Fine," he said, plopping himself down on a stone mileage marker that looked like it would make a decent stool, "Don't get yourselves lost."

Selpla held up his comm. "I still have this," she said, waving it in the air.

Prond smirked, but made no reply. They were already too far down the trail to hear him if he had. The rain picked up again, so Prond pulled the hood of his overjack over his face as far as it would go and stared at the deluge. Better to be sitting here than stomping around out there in the mud with Selpla the soggy newscaster. He whistled softly, watching a variety of waterlogged wildlife slosh about their daily business.

After about half a kilometer Selpla called her little party to a halt. She pointed to the ground in front of them. "What are those holes all about?"

The path ahead was riddled with pits maybe half a meter in diameter, all, naturally, filled with water. They were superimposed over the debris trail left by the retreating mountain, so presumably had been formed since its passage.

"Looks like a print from the world's largest cleated shoe," Lom observed.

"Someone or something had to be expending a lot of energy to get all these dug since the mountain passed through. Wonder what for?"

As they stood there puzzling, Drin suddenly spoke.

"Holes getting bigger."

Selpla was momentarily startled. She had forgotten the little guy was there again.

The holes were, in fact, growing. Each had widened by about ten percent of its diameter in the minute or so since Selpla and her crew first spotted them. They seemed to be getting deeper, too; water busily swirled down into the cavities with an audible sucking sound.

Selpla suddenly yelped as her right foot slid

forward and down a few centimeters.

"They're not only getting bigger, they're increasing in number," said Lom.

"Yeah, I noticed that," replied Selpla, shaking the mud out of her shoe.

"I'd venture to guess that they're sinkholes," Lom added after a moment's reflection, "Flooding and the vibrations from the mountain's passage must have dissolved the interstitial carbonates in the bedrock."

Selpla looked at him and frowned. "Do you have *any* idea what you just said?"

He bit his lip. "No, not really. I think I must have read that somewhere."

"Good. I wouldn't want to think you'd suddenly gone all smartsy on me."

Drin abruptly backed up and started on a wide circling path to the right. Selpla and Lom watched him for a couple of seconds, until they realized the wisdom of what he was doing and followed suit. He was skirting the geologically unstable area altogether rather than trying to traverse it, as had been their original intention. They'd gone no more than ten or fifteen meters beyond it when they heard a sudden roar of water and the crunching of a large volume of collapsing rock. Water rushed past their feet on its way into the gaping maw where they'd been standing only moments before. The return path to Prond and the highway now ran smack through a lake.

Lom chuckled, "Looks like a new swimmin' hole coming in."

"This whole *place* is a swimming hole," Selpla

snorted, "C'mon, let's keep moving."

They sloshed in silence for a few moments.

"Given any thought to how we get back to Prond now?" asked Lom, making his way past what looked like a tree stump with gently waving tentacles.

"We'll cross that bridge when we come to it."

"If it hasn't been washed out."

Drin, who had been taking point about twenty meters in advance of the other two, came back and gave his report.

"There is bridge up ahead."

Selpla looked smug. "See, what did I tell you?"

Lom put his hands on his hips and frowned. "A bridge? Over what?"

"Water," replied Drin, simply.

"Well, duh. I mean what was there *before* the flood?"

"Water. Else, why build bridge?"

"Who knows why people build bridges? There could be a ravine, or an endangered orchid, or even a pork barrel contract between a local administrator and his bridge-building brother-in-law," expounded Lom, pausing to shake his head to dislodge an accumulation of precipitation. He managed to nail Selpla with the effluvia. She slapped him on the occipital ridge.

"Watch where you sling that stuff, smekking surfdiver."

"Oh, like it really matters in this smekking deluge."

"It matters to *me*." She shot him a warning

look.

"Sorry, Your Highness," Lom replied, genuflecting broadly. "I'll endeavor in the future to keep my personal runoff from impacting the Royal Person."

"See that you do, bloody peasant."

Their fabulously clever repartee was interrupted by the decidedly odd sight of Drin hopping about wildly, as though the ground beneath him had suddenly grown red hot. Of course, if it had, the half-meter of water *covering* it would be steaming, so that obviously wasn't the case. They watched him leap and gyrate for a few moments, torn between compassion and entertainment. Selpla looked down into the turbulent water near Drin's legs and noticed dark shapes darting here and there.

"What are those things?" she asked, pointing.

Drin's trajectory took him near them at this juncture. "Needlefish," he explained, hopping away again.

His companions' eyes got wide. "Needlefish!" they both exclaimed in unison, and joined Drin in hopping madly about. "I thought," Selpla gasped as she jumped frantically, "That needlefish only lived in the (ouch) Molkpot river."

"Drin," Lom asked, matter-of-factly, "You said there was a (ow) bridge up ahead. Did it have a sign on it?"

"Ya. Two."

"What (ow) did they (ouch) say?"

"One say, *Molkpot River, No Swimming.* Other one say, *Danger! River Over Banks! Keep*

Away!"

"Aaggh!" replied Selpla, "Why the smek didn't you *tell* us?"

Drin looked at her and shrugged. "Didn't ask."

Selpla, Lom, and Drin eventually managed to thrash and kick their way to a small sandbar in the middle of the flooded river, but not without quite a collection of lacerations from the fish and bruises from submerged stones. They sat on a fallen tree breathing hard and rubbing their mangled feet. Lom was scanning the middle distance looking for some way back up to the road (he'd privately decided it was time to abandon the moving mountain story before it killed them) when something strange floating in the water caught his eye. It was a large, thin, vaguely circular mat or raft of rust-red, heading slowly but deliberately in their direction.

He stared at it for some time, trying to figure out if it was vegetation, or some sort of oil slick, or just what it was. Eventually the floating mat touched the small island where they sat and began to disintegrate. More accurately, the tiny creatures of which it had been composed started swarming over the sand and up the bark of the tree towards them. Suddenly it hit him what he was witnessing: the landing of a raft of voracious pincer ants, driven from their colossal nest by the rains.

Lom yelped and splashed back into the water, where he was immediately set upon by the circling needlefish. The others were momentarily confused by his apparent loss of sanity, but soon realized the reason for it and followed suit as the powerful ants descended on them by the thousands.

Caught between needles and pincers, their only option was to flee to high ground, the nearest example of which was about fifty meters to the southwest. They leapt, kicked, and stumbled their way across the expanse of water, avoiding a couple more rafts of ants along the way. Finally they flopped weakly on the far shore, too exhausted from their ordeal to care that they were now mired up to their elbows in dark blue muck.

Chapter Twelve: Chosen

Tol concluded that he must be dreaming. It was the only explanation, unless he was deceased, but he didn't feel deceased. What did being deceased feel like, anyway? He'd always assumed it didn't feel like much of anything. He definitely felt *something*, so he must not be deceased. He wasn't in a place that seemed to be adhering to the natural laws he'd come to know and respect, however, so he had to be dreaming. Odd. He didn't remember ever having realized he was dreaming before while he was doing it. You're never too old for a new experience, he decided. Or did he dream that, too?

He was in a sort of stadium or arena, surrounded by sloping white walls and a large number of floating opalescent orbs of different diameters. Whoa. What had he been drinking or smoking? Whatever it was, he hoped there was some more of it. He hadn't had a dream like this since he was a rowdy teenager smoking or swallowing just about anything passed to him.

He rested there on some species of rather comfortable fluffy cushion pad and stared at the orbs. They were moving lazily about, occasionally sending bluish streamers to one or more companions. He felt no urge to stir, not even to go to the bathroom. That tore it: he *never* woke up without having to go to the bathroom. This was, unequivocally and without any doubt, a dream.

After a while, as Tol slipped in and out of what he could only assume was some kind of meta-doze, one of the orbs touched down next to him and morphed into a vertical haze. Tol gawked at it dazedly and watched it resolve into a short, thin, blue-skinned creature. Obviously another product of his drug-enhanced imagination...but it *did* look a little familiar. It reached out a four-fingered hand and touched Tol on the forehead. He jerked involuntarily—it felt like he'd been suddenly encased in warm gelatin. Actually, it was a pretty pleasant sensation, once he got used to it. If he weren't already asleep, it just might lull him into taking a little nap...

This time the walls were dirty gray. They went straight up to meet a decidedly undecorative ceiling whose little acoustic-dampening bumps were detaching here and there, giving it a scabrous appearance. The sheets smelled like disinfectant with just the merest soupçon of mildew. A real comedown after his hoity-toity dream, but at least he knew where he was. The Edict Enforcement Infirmary in Sebacea was a drab little building that all district EE cops grew to know intimately over the course of their careers.

An infirmary tech walked into the room just then. "Welcome back to land of the conscious, officer

Tol-u-ol. Hope you had a pleasant outing."

Tol grunted, "Any chance of getting something to eat in this dive?"

"Well. You seem to be recovering nicely from your ordeal. Let me see if I can rustle up some victuals for you."

"Wait," Tol called, shading his still-dilated pupils from the harsh infirmary lights, "How long have I been...out?"

"Let's see," replied the tech, looking at a clipboard, "says here you were brought in from a GRUC tunnel on the 13th. That would be three days ago. We thought you were a goner for a while—you'd lost a lot of blood. Last night, though, you took a sudden turn for the better and now here you are, rosy-cheeked and ready to party. Congratulations, officer. You're one tough so-and-so."

Tol grunted again, and the tech left the room. He could still see the image of the alfar in his mind's eye as clearly as he did in the dream...or, whatever it was. He was grateful to whoever facilitated his rapid recovery, regardless of whether or not they were real. Reality wasn't anything to drop your pants and celebrate most of the time, anyway.

He took a little survey of his parts. Everything seemed to be working. A bit of soreness here and there, but nothing he hadn't experienced after a moderately successful night at the pub. He took a deep breath and sat up. Felt pretty good. He rolled his legs over the side of the bed. Some slight dizziness, but he could handle it. Now for the big one. He slid his butt ever so gently off the bed and stood up.

Admittedly, if the bed hadn't been there to lean on, things might have gotten ugly, but as it was he managed to stand on his own until the surprised tech came back with his soup and crackers. It did feel really good to lie back down, though.

They kept Tol in the infirmary for another 48 hours, just to be safe. Everyone agreed his recovery from such a beating was nothing short of miraculous. "One might even be tempted to say magical," said the surgeon who released him.

"OK, ya found me out fair and square, sawbones: I'm an archmage in disguise. For my next trick, I'm going to walk down the street and turn into a pub."

The surgeon smiled. "Lay off the razzle for a while, Tol. No point in pressing your luck."

"What good is luck," Tol replied, walking away and waving, "If you can't press it now and then?"

Truth be told, he didn't feel nearly as fit 'n' chipper as he wanted the infirmary staff to believe. Things were sore; muscles and tendons throbbed here and there. He had a little difficulty walking straight, too, which he took enormous pains to hide from onlookers. The staff weren't fooled in the least, of course. They saw cops come and go every day, and this was more or less the way all of them acted. The tough guy image was very important to EE officers, because it gave them an edge on the streets and in interactions with the criminal element. Plus, they just liked to think they were made of sterner stuff than the average jlok.

Once out of sight of the infirmary, Tol leaned against the side of a building. He was sweating from the strain of trying to look healthy. He closed his eyes for a moment, took a deep breath, and hobbled onward. The delicate aroma of deep-fried wrat fritters assailed his nostrils and reminded him that he was hungry. He sniffed around for the source of the odor and was pleasantly surprised to discover that it came from a pub—one he'd never seen before, to boot. He could have sworn there was a vacant lot here just last week. No matter. He loved exploring new pubs. Things were definitely looking up.

The pub's decor was, um, different. The ceiling was hard to make out, but what little Tol could resolve seemed to suggest swirling multicolored gas with stars mixed in here and there for good measure. The barmaids were of some weird smooth-skinned race he didn't recognize. Must be foreigners. As long as they had wrats and razzle, he didn't really care if they came from another galaxy. Immigration wasn't his beat.

He chose an empty table near the bar and plopped down in an exceptionally hard wooden chair. Glancing around, he couldn't help but notice that *all* the other tables were empty. Well, it was obviously a new pub, after all. Perhaps the word just hadn't gotten out yet. One of the barmaids came over to take his order. She was chewing on something—maybe a cud?—and every so often a strange thin bladder protruded from her mouth, inflated, then disappeared again with a soft 'plop.' It was distracting, to say the least.

"What'll it be, Mac?"

Tol blinked in surprise, or would have if he'd possessed opaque eyelids.

"I don't know what 'mac' is, but I'd love a pint of razzle and a plate of wrats."

"Coming at ya, bud."

Tol shook his head, but instantly regretted it because it hurt like smek. He was becoming aware of the rather disorienting tendency of the pub's furniture and appointments to flow around the room when he wasn't looking. Was this a residual effect of his recent injuries, or something intrinsic to the building itself? He'd never before seen this sort of behavior while sober. It was a little like finding sand in your shorts before you even get to the beach.

The barmaid brought his wrats and razzle in a commendably short time. The wrats smelled wonderful, especially after days of infirmary "food." He started scarfing with considerable enthusiasm. Tol tended to get tunnel vision when he was scarfing. The world receded into the distance and went about its affairs entirely divorced from Tol's comprehension while food consumption was underway. It was hardly surprising, therefore, that when at last he and the world were reunited, Tol suddenly became aware of a stranger sitting quietly at the table with him. His head flew up out of reflex, which induced a cramp that started at his occipital ridge and went all the way down to his coccygeal ganglion. Of course, Tol just called it a pain in his neck.

"Who the smek are you?" he grunted, rubbing the back of said neck vigorously.

The stranger regarded him for a moment. He was fairly tall, of indistinguishable age (at least, to Tol), and had shimmering white hair on his head and face. The rest of his visible skin was oddly smooth, like the barmaids, and pinkish in color. In his hands he held a strange stringed instrument with a curiously bent neck and a rounded back made of ingeniously fitted wooden slats. Tol found his tablemate's appearance quite frankly repulsive. He was glad he'd already mostly finished eating.

"I am called Oloi," replied the stranger, finally, "I'm glad you dropped in."

"Yeah, well, I couldn't pass up the chance to check out a new pub. How long you been here?"

Oloi seemed to be counting on his fingers, "About twenty minutes, roughly, I'd say."

Tol sighed, almost but not quite imperceptibly, "I meant, how long has the *pub* been here?"

Oloi's bushy eyebrows went up. "About twenty minutes, as I said. We arrived at the same moment."

Tol sat back and folded his arms. "You're telling me that you and this pub just... materialized in this spot twenty minutes ago?"

"Yes. We didn't want to miss you, but for... logistical reasons we could not arrive much earlier."

Tol didn't quite know what to make of this. "It sounds like you're telling me that you came here specifically for my benefit. I'm flattered, but why?" If this guy was a nutjob, it would probably be in Tol's best interests, given his weakened condition, to play along.

"Because you are the key."

Tol rolled his eyes. He hated cryptic mumbo-jumbo. "I am the key to what? Boosting your razzle sales?"

"No, to halting disconnection from The Slice."

"Mother of Goblins, not that stuff again. I'm about as far removed from the theory and practice of magic as any jlok you're gonna find in the whole smekkin' realm. What makes you or anybody else think I can have the slightest effect on something happenin' in The Slice? Smek, I'm not even sure just what 'The Slice' is."

"Saving The Slice does not require magic, officer Tol-u-ol. It requires good, solid, detective work."

"Izzat so? Well, as it happens, I'm not particularly solid at the moment. Someone tried to kill me with magic."

"And you were healed by the same mechanism."

"What makes you think that?"

"The alfar who did it told me so."

Tol struggled with his memories for a few moments, trying to separate reality from trauma-induced fantasy. It wasn't easy. He needed to correlate everything he could about the alfar, but he couldn't draw a clean line between what he'd actually experienced and his dreams. Maybe he could get some information from this Oloi character, who was now strumming his instrument quietly. It was a catchy tune, and Tol found himself listening for a moment before he remembered he had unanswered questions.

"Yeah? What did he tell you, exactly?"

"Merely that you had been the victim of a concerted magical attack and that he had rescued you, then helped you to heal."

"Not to sound ungrateful, but did he happen to mention why?"

"Because he is a creature born of The Slice, and therefore vitally interested in its welfare, of course."

"And saving me is somehow going to contribute to that welfare? I still don't get it."

"As I said, you are the key to saving The Slice. There are forces at work intent on destroying it, or at least this world's access to it, and thereby rendering magic virtually inaccessible. A side effect of this action will be to alter the 'ecosystem' of The Slice rather drastically. Stopping those forces is your preordained task. They are aware of that, and so they have been trying to neutralize the threat that you represent."

"Okay, I'm gonna go for the big one now—why?"

"Why are they trying to do away with magic, or why should you stop them?"

"Either. Both."

"The answer is the same for both questions: magic is integral to Tragacanthan society. In the millennia since access to The Slice was established, a subtle balance has been struck between technology

191

and the arcane arts, as well as the magical equilibrium of The Slice itself. If this balance were disturbed by the destruction of N'plork's access portals to The Slice, chaos would undoubtedly ensue. There are those who would take advantage of this social disorder, the vacuum, to seize power. Look for someone hording technology and I believe you'll find your perpetrators."

"Why me? Sorry to sound so inquisitive, but it's an occupational hazard."

"I do not know why you, specifically, were chosen for this task, Tol-u-ol. It was not my doing. You *have* been chosen, however, and you must answer this call for the good of all Tragacanth."

"No offense, but this is getting a little messianic for my taste. I'm just your average cop, working my beat and trying not to get knocked off in the process. I'm not cut out for saving the world."

"The fate of Tragacanth rests on your shoulders, be they worthy or no. We cannot always choose our own path in life."

Tol sighed. It would still be several years before he could take even early retirement, so there was nothing for it. He tried to think of a way to ignore the whole thing, but failed miserably.

"Thanks for not puttin' any pressure on me," he said, at last.

"I do not lay this burden on you lightly," replied Oloi, in a kinder tone, "I wish you all the best, and I will help you by whatever means I am able."

Tol could sense that Oloi was being sincere. It

embarrassed him.

"Uh, yeah, thanks. I expect I'll need all the help I can get." He got up to leave and fumbled in his pockets.

"How much do I owe you for the meal?"

"On the house. Consider it a goodwill gesture. Best of fortune to you, Tol-u-ol."

Tol frowned. He wasn't supposed to accept free stuff or gratuities of any kind. Ethics violation. He started to protest but stopped short when he suddenly found himself alone in the middle of a vacant lot. An ethereal voice said, "Drop by again sometime. We're always open when you need us." He stood there for a moment, mouth hanging open, then turned and walked back to the street as though nothing out of the ordinary had transpired. He only hoped the entire thing hadn't been some sort of illusion. He hated to think passers-by might have seen him sitting in this field talking to himself. Bad for his street cred, you know? As he walked away he heard, faint but clear, the sound of Oloi singing to his own melodic accompaniment. It was a sprightly yet haunting tune about someone or something called *The Baron of Eastmarch*.

Chapter Thirteen:
What Dreams May Come

Aspet grimaced. The reports coming in on the vid were confirming his suspicions about the nature of that weird cloud formation. There was quite obviously a hurrarcane moving in from the Southern Reaches. Widespread flooding had been noted, as well as a host of other, less conventional, magical meteorological manifestations such as scorching orbs and plasma devils. Well, at least it would give the Emergency Magical Operations Center folks something to do besides conduct spell mishap drills.

He wondered what had precipitated this magical weather. It may just have been a natural event—a space rock with magical properties passing through N'plork's atmosphere with just the right velocity and trajectory, as the cloud formation had suggested—but something told Aspet there was more to this incident than random astronomical pummeling. It seemed somehow contrived; a little too convenient; a setup, in other words.

All he could really do about it was button up his own dwelling and get back to preparing for his challenge to the throne, however. He only had a few days left before the big event; the pressure was building hourly. The current king was an accomplished hacker, although such skills tended to get rusty after a year or two. Not much time to practice the art, after all, when you're busy running a huge government like Tragacanth's. Nevertheless, Aspet's gut feeling was that it would be a bloody battle. The king had already fended off two challenges from decent code slingers Aspet had known through the underground. Both had since vanished. One of the undocumented but nevertheless widely-known issues with challenging for the throne is that if you lost, you were pretty much washed up in Tragacanth. The Royal Protective Corps made certain you were no persistent threat. Many challengers committed "suicide" or disappeared under mysterious circumstances, although a few later turned up in other countries, predominately under assumed identities.

Consequently, Aspet understood that he *had* to win. There was no reasonable alternative. Even if he backed out now, the RPC would consider him a potential future challenger. Everyone who attended The Seminar went on a watch list, but those who never actually challenged the throne were generally left alone, albeit under lifelong scrutiny. These weren't facts you took lightly when starting on the path to possible regal status, but Aspet had considered them carefully and decided the risk was worth it. He honestly thought he could do a better job as king than the current monarch, who was widely unpopular due to his arrogance and repressive policies. He seemed to believe that he could make economic and social issues resolve themselves just by issuing a proclamation to that effect.

Aspet sat down at his terminal and punched up the immensely complex schematics of the RNet. He needed to be able to navigate this maze with his eyes closed if he were to have any chance of success in the upcoming challenge. That meant memorization of the network architecture from every conceivable angle, like a medical student cramming for a gross anatomy final. He was so engrossed in his task that he didn't notice at first that a message had popped up in his inbox.

To: Asp37!cholinergia!goblinopolis
From: boogla!boogla!boo
Subject: Ur tim3 has com3

I just wanted to be the first to congratulate the new king on his imminent accession to the throne of our great nation. For too long Tragacanth has been ruled by elitists with no connection to the common people. Stay true to your roots, Aspet, and you will achieve greatness.

We will be watching you.

Aspet stared at the screen for a few moments, startled by the unexpected message. Finally he sat back, musing. "She's nothing if not an optimist," he mused out loud, "Unless she knows something about this that I don't." He had to admit that was entirely possible. The whole process was still mostly a mystery to him, despite The Seminar and countless hours spent doing research online and in libraries. The Royal Protective Corps did a thorough job of scouring the available resources and purging them of information deemed to be of a classified nature. Much of this information concerned details on the challenge ceremony or even speculations thereon.

Of course, the underground was constantly mutating and evolving, so as quickly as the RPC could bring down a site, another popped up to take its place. Tracking them all was a bit of a headache, even for those who knew precisely where to look. Fortunately, Aspet had been at this for a while and had developed some automated tools to help speed things along. They didn't do all the work for him, but they narrowed the scope of his search. More importantly, they helped obfuscate both his own location and the location of the rogue servers by channeling everything through a constantly changing series of zombie machines, the owners of which weren't even aware they were part of an elaborate electronic cat-and-mouse game.

Aspet sat and savored the dawning irony of the fact that, were he actually to win the throne, he would be on the other side of this struggle—trying to prevent aspiring challengers from gaining intelligence that could help bring him down. That was just the way things were, though. There wasn't much he could do about it, even as king. Or was there? He didn't get too far with this line of thinking before the urgencies of the present moment recaptured his attention, but a little seed had been planted.

He was seated alone on the pinnacle of a narrow cylinder seemingly made of glowing stonework, grass-topped and ringed with unfamiliar vegetation. He was impossibly high; the cloud tops lay spread out far below him—mounds of gossamer curds as far as the eye could see. It struck him that he'd never seen the tops of clouds before. They were beautiful and somehow otherworldly; foreign, exotic, yet compellingly familiar.

As he stared out over the majestic panorama, Aspet noticed a stirring in the clouds directly below his vantage point. Something slender and steel blue emerged from the cloud deck, rising slowly and steadily, leaving behind ripples that spread slowly to the horizon. It was soon joined by a ring of lesser pointed shafts, all of which proved after a few more seconds to be attached to an enormous ovoid shape. The ovoid had eyes: it was in fact apparently a head, though if so it was the largest one Aspet had ever seen or even imagined in the grip of a high fever.

The behemoth continued to float upward toward him, revealing ever larger areas of itself. Aspet could now make out the titanic neck which attached the enormous head to the staggeringly stupendous body. The thing was easily the size of the entire Royal

Complex, if not bigger. Even after most of it had emerged into the clear air, it was very difficult for Aspet to grasp the true expanse of the manifestation. It seemed to stretch into the unimaginable distance. It was approximately at this juncture that he noticed that retreat was not an option. There was nowhere to flee but down, and flight in that direction would involve more plummeting than experience had taught him was healthy. He had little choice but to face the Brobdingnagian creature and hope it was in a relatively good mood today.

When he and the gargantuan entity were eye to eye, as it were, it ceased to rise and just floated there serenely, staring at him with unblinking slitted pupils. Aspet stared back at first, but after a bit began to get uncomfortable about the creature's placid countenance. What did it want? Surely it didn't come all the way here, wherever here was, just to challenge him to a staring contest. There was never any doubt about the outcome, anyway—neither of them had true eyelids, but at least Aspet could look away.

Aspet couldn't think of much else to do, so he sat cross-legged on a small patch of soft grass and regarded the levitating colossus. He had to admit it was truly a magnificent sight to behold: a floating mountain with a flesh-like covering and soaring ridges of bone and horn framing deep crevasses lined with steel blue scales, each the size of rooftops. It had thin membranous wings, too, although they didn't seem to be playing any real part in keeping the beast aloft.

Just when Aspet decided that nothing further was

going to happen, he noticed that the beast's mouth was beginning to open. It was barely detectable at first, but after a minute or so the gap widened to impressive proportions. The effect was decidedly unnerving; Aspet could feel the sweat running down his supraorbital ridges.

Instead of horrible decaying meat stench, however, the air flowing out of the creature's now wide-open oral cavity had a rather pleasant odor— for levitating behemoth breath, anyway. Aspet stared down into the cavernous opening. It really didn't look much like the alimentary tract of an animal, not that he'd spent a lot of time investigating that particular subject. Instead of a barbed and quivering tongue, the glottal region resembled a rather smart stairway leading down into the cool darkness of the creature's pharynx. There even seemed to be a little handrail of sorts running along inside one cheek. He blinked and stared hard at the incongruity, suspicious that it was some sort of illusion meant to encourage prey to walk right into the predator's mouth, as it were.

The monster didn't seem to be trying to force him into its gullet, however. It floated there serenely, jaws cranked open in a perpetual gape. Aspet realized with some incredulity that he could hear faint music coming from somewhere in the black depths. It sounded like blandly insipid instrumental versions of current and past popular songs. Well, that definitely blasted his "attracting prey" hypothesis into tiny, tiny particles.

After a few minutes it became apparent that nothing else was going to happen. The creature had reached some sort of equilibrium. It made no further effort to move, except for a slight but definite regular expansion and contraction that Aspet decided must be the result of the thing breathing, or at least appearing to breathe. It was a standoff, or rather, a sit off, since he'd decided that sitting was a more comfortable posture from which to contemplate this weirdness. Come to think of it, the monster wasn't exactly standing (or sitting) on anything at all. OK, it was a *faceoff*, then. Satisfied with at last coming up with an acceptable term, Aspet sat back on the small patch of grass and waited. He didn't know what he was waiting for—a sign, maybe.

☙ *Patience.*

In the end it was boredom and curiosity that forced his hand. The sheer monotony of being stuck on this tiny pinnacle with no other avenue of escape wore him down mentally until he was ready to entertain the proposition of actually entering the massive mouth. He had noticed that, despite the considerable time which had elapsed since the jaws first parted, no drool seemed to have built up anywhere. That had to be a good sign. Maybe this thing wasn't really here to eat him, after all. Some part of his mind knew he was rationalizing now, and told him so, but Aspet decided to ignore it. Logic and reasoning had gotten him in some pretty tight jams themselves in the past; he saw no particular reason to rely on them now.

He stood up and wiped the thin dusting of soil off his pants, took one last look around at the dizzying vista, and stepped tentatively into the monster's mouth. Nothing happened; this encouraged him a bit and he took another step. Still no reaction. He figured he would pause there a moment and see if the creature started to salivate in anticipation of the coming feast—not that Aspet would provide more than a bite-sized morsel.

When no secretions were apparently forthcoming, he took a deep breath and started descending the stairway of the tongue. The decor took a turn toward wholly inorganic in the larynx, starting with the elegant rose-radiant crystalline globes of the epiglottis chandelier. The deeper he went, the less like the inside of an animal his surroundings became. By the time he was halfway to the stomach, the esophagus had morphed into a richly carpeted passage, lined with high gothic windows and framed by magnificent vaulted archways. Pretty impressive interior design for an alimentary tract. Aspet was beginning to believe that he wasn't inside a living creature at all, but some sort of giant conveyance made up to look like one. He wondered what powered it, and how it achieved levitation.

♀ Courage.

The deep carpeting kept noise to a minimum. The only sounds were his still somewhat ragged breathing and the soft ploof of his footsteps as he headed ever deeper into the monster's belly. A sudden distant boom startled him, and he stopped to listen, senses suddenly on full alert. After a few seconds it rang out again—the far-off reverberating clang of very heavy machinery being operated. If he harbored any doubts about his host's mechanical rather than biological origin, they lost their footing at this and slid into oblivion.

Aspet resumed his inward trek, keeping an ear cocked for the source of the metallic cacophony. It was definitely coming from ahead of him somewhere, and below his current level. It didn't seem to be getting appreciably louder, though, so he decided not to worry too much about it for the time being. There were far more interesting diversions popping up all around him. Literally.

A large bulbous mass suddenly detached from the roof and hit the floor in front of him, squelching heavily as it bounced. Aspet grabbed a tasteful mahogany settee upholstered with combed bonggong fur to use as a shield and waited to see if anything emerged from the huge quivering sac.

After a minute of standing there waving a piece of furniture at a giant beach ball, Aspet began to feel slightly silly. He slowly lowered the settee and at last sat on it, legs crossed, waiting. More minutes passed in total silence. Even the gobs with the oversized wrenches seemed to have taken a beverage break. Finally he could resist no longer. He reached out and touched the squamous sphere, ever so gently. The reaction was not one he could have anticipated.

The surface of the sphere closed around his hand as soon as he made contact, and seemed to flow over his entire body before he could effectively react.

Within a few seconds he was completely enclosed. Aspet gasped and struggled at first, but the interior of his prison gradually took on such an intriguing appearance that the adrenalin rush played itself out and he was left to goggle in wonder.

He was in a grand library; a room as big as the floating creature itself had seemed. He decided not to let the fact that he was in a place too big to be contained by the thing it was contained in worry him. The universe had obviously adopted, at least temporarily, a new set of rules and regulations that he would sort out later. He wandered along the edges of the opulent chamber, staring up at the endless shelves of books that stretched all the way to the ceiling towering far above him. There were hundreds of thousands, if not millions, of volumes here. He didn't know that many books existed in the whole of Tragacanth, goblins not being voracious readers as a species. He was rather fond of books personally, though.

ϙ *Adaptability.*

Aspet felt he could easily spend, if not all of his remaining days, at least a goodly chunk of them here in this bottomless well of knowledge. It occurred to him that there was so very much about life and existence he didn't know. He had one of those annoying 'hall of mirrors' moments at this point, watching himself observing himself being depressed about his ignorance, to infinite recursion.

Shaking it off, he selected a tome at random and

extracted it carefully from the shelf. The movement dislodged a fine particulate which dispersed and settled lazily on the enormous woven area rug that defined the center of the library. The dust made him sneeze; despite the cavernous size of the room the sound was absorbed almost immediately by a vast sea of organic bindings.

The book Aspet chose to peruse had a beautiful gold-tooled title on the spine that made no sense whatever to him. He just liked the craftsmanship and the soft pliable feel of the leather. He took it over to a richly appointed table seemingly carved from a single slab of some exotic xylem and opened it. The odor thus released reminded him of a long-forgotten banquet from his childhood. He tried to read the words, but instead of flowing into his brain via his eyes, the images and ideas seemed to be following other paths. He could feel, smell, taste, and even hear the events portrayed in the narrative, but the words themselves were meaningless.

He was trying to wrap his brain around this new form of literary exposition when the pages of the book began to dissolve. The sentences ran out onto the table and spilled down to the floor. He soon found himself crawling around on all fours under the furniture trying to keep up with the story. This was the hardest plot to follow he'd ever encountered, yet it was so completely engrossing that he couldn't give it up without a fight.

Aspet never really stood a chance, though. Next

the words and finally the individual letters all went their separate scurrying ways, like scavenger-bugs scattering in a sudden light. He got off his hands and knees and sat there on the floor, wondering what in the world had happened to his book.

♀ Persistence.

He stared down at his lap for a while, deep in thought. A slight but uncharacteristically chilly breeze eased him gradually back to the here and now. He looked around for the source and was quite surprised to discover that he was no longer in the library.

He was in a field of wildly dissimilar tallish plants, waving gently in the wind. The cool air was swirling with a complex mixture of scents: some vaguely familiar, some he never remembered smelling before. The table, the books, the library—even the creature itself—had vanished as though they had never existed at all. In their place was left a crazy botanical wilderness like none Aspet had ever conceived.

He stood there a long while, examining the curious plants, breathing in the heady atmosphere, and just generally not knowing what to do next. It was a situation to which he'd lately grown accustomed. Eventually he began to wander, pushing bizarrely-shaped, outrageously pigmented foliage aside as he moved. Occasionally a small creature would skitter or flap away when he disturbed it. Once he heard the throaty growl of a distinctly larger predatory-sounding thing, but it wasn't close enough that he felt it to be directed at him. He had no idea where to run, even if he were attacked. He swallowed hard and hoped it wouldn't come to that.

The plant community was thick and flamboyant, but penetrable. He found navigation relatively effortless, albeit he had no clue which way to go or what he would find when he got there. He just wandered aimlessly, pushing aside the huge leaves and ducking under the myriad multicolored flowers, seed pods, and fruits as he went.

He began to get peckish looking at all the fruits and vegetables hanging about everywhere, like the world's largest and freshest produce market. Trouble was, he had never before seen *any* of these, so he had no idea which of them might be safe to eat. He remembered reading stories of the first goblin settlers of Tragacanth, thousands of years ago. They must have faced a similar conundrum. Not that goblin physiology was exactly delicate: goblins could, and frequently did, eat things other races aggressively avoided.

He shrugged and reached out to break a small section off a particularly succulent-looking fleshy fruit. Before he could pop it into his mouth, however, there was a shrill sound and a large leafy stalk crashed rather hard across his neck.

"Arrrooo, now. Don't be pullin' and pickin' at that. It ain't ripe yet. When it's ripe it'll fall off, and ye can nibble on it then."

Aspet dropped the fruit fragment and rubbed his neck where the stalk had caught it. He looked around stiffly for the source of the voice. It had come, apparently, from the plant itself.

There was a sort of bulge near the top of the center stalk of the enormous plant, with a horizontal slit in it that might pass for a mouth. Aspet immediately began puzzling over why and how a plant would evolve vocal chords and some means of operating them when the plant spoke again. The noise did, in fact, seem to come from the little slit.

"Y' think...tooo much. Not goood t' think sooo much." The voice was thin and raspy, but still pretty intelligible for a plant, he thought.

"Don't plants think? It seems to me there's not a lot else for you to do."

"Nooo brain," replied the plant, a little sadly, it seemed to Aspet, "Nooo thinkin' wi'out a brain. Jest drinkin' and rootin,' bloomin' and fruitin'."

Aspet frowned. "Now, wait a minute," he replied, hands on hips, "If you can't think, how are you able to talk?"

"There's nay connection atween think and talk, nubbly. If y' were thinkin,' fer example, would y' be talkin' to a plant right now?"

"Hey, I didn't start this little discussion: *you* did. I'm just responding to you."

"Ah, but are y' thinkin' about it? I mean, if y' think about it, could y' *really* be conversin' wi' a plant wi' nae vocal apparatus?"

Aspet considered this. "No, I suppose not. But since you *are* talking, either you *do* possess such an apparatus or you're not really a plant, per se."

"Or, y' anly *think* I'm talkin' t' y'. I tol' y',

thinkin' is bad for y'."

"Ha, ha. I hope I'm not so far gone mentally that I'm imagining debating a giant globe-root."

Silence.

"Okay, okay, I apologize for calling you a globe-root. It was just a joke. What, you got something against globe-roots?"

♀ Benevolence.

He looked carefully at the erstwhile interlocutor. It was for all appearances just a common garden-variety giant plant now. Even the little mouth slit had seemingly disappeared. He shrugged. Giant reptiles that contain impressive libraries full of dissolving books and now talking plants that may or may not be actual talking plants...if this was a dream—and he very much hoped it was (the alternative being that he had gone firmly off the deep end)—it was a doozie. Not at all like his usual oneiric forays into mucky landscapes that clung to his feet, falling from a great height, or not being able to remember where his house/clothing was.

Pressing on, after a little while he came into a clearing. At first appearances it was perfectly pristine, but as he approached the center a ring of stones broke through the soil and grew with rather alarming rapidity. After a few seconds they were at least twice as tall as Aspet himself. He followed the line around a full 360 degrees. There was no break, no gap, no opening. He was trapped. Again.

It was a long while before anything else

happened. Aspet was alone, enclosed in a lithic arena about twenty meters across, give or take a couple. Nothing stirred, not even the air. There were no animal or insect noises; no clouds scuttled across the visible sky. It was as though the rest of the universe had dropped away, leaving only his little circular island. He wandered along the impenetrable stone barrier, checking for even the slightest crack. Finding none, eventually he grew despondent and sat down sadly on the bare ground, wondering what he would do for food and water in such a place.

He leaned against a stone and closed his inner false eyelids that were usually only employed to keep out light when sleeping. Rather than the customary swirling darkness, however, the scene before his eyes remained unchanged. He opened his lids and tried it again. The overall light intensity was slightly diminished with his eyes shut, but otherwise nothing was altered. Had his inner eyelids also suddenly gone transparent? He waved his hand in front of his face. He couldn't see it unless the lids were retracted, but the backdrop of stones and empty arena implacably remained, taunting him with staunch immutability.

Not being able to seek refuge from the world behind closed eyes was far more disturbing than he would have guessed. It was maddening, in fact, and he realized that madness was a very real possibility if he couldn't lean to cope, and quickly. But how exactly does one cope with a landscape that leaks directly into the brain?

As he was puzzling over this, Aspet noticed one

of the stones glowing softly. Excited, he nevertheless approached it somewhat cautiously. A diffuse bluish radiance shimmered over the surface of the monolith. As he drew nearer, a finger of blue projected itself from the aura in his direction. The closer he came, the longer the protrusion extended. Hesitantly, he edged nearer until the finger came in contact with his chest. At that moment the stone circle vanished and he was in free fall from an inestimable height.

♇ Logic.

After he got over the initial shock, he realized that he wasn't really falling: it was more like being suspended in midair. There were no visual clues as to *where*, precisely, he was suspended, however. The atmosphere around him was a uniform dull silvery-gray. He discovered that he could walk normally, even though there was no apparent surface supporting him. Occasional wisps of white floated past, but otherwise nothing moved. He was no longer trapped in a ring of stones, but Aspet soon came to realize that he was as much a prisoner in this new location as in the old. He could move about freely, but there was nowhere to go. The only reasonable thing he could think of to do was to pick a direction and set out.

Locomotion here wasn't elegant. One can't simply walk where there is no solid surface to push off from. One must, shall we say, *flounder*. Floundering, or at least competence thereat, was not a skill Aspet had so far managed to acquire in his journey through life. By dint of thrashing and flapping his limbs, he eventually began to move along a more or less constant vector, albeit seemingly a vector to nowhere.

After a while he got pretty good at it, and even began to enjoy himself a bit. It was, if nothing else, a decent workout. He became so involved in the physical exertion part, in fact, that he totally failed to notice when the world around him changed, yet again. He didn't become aware of it until his foot slammed into something that definitely wasn't in the least ethereal. The substantial something gave him a bruise and a right nasty toe splinter.

Aspet grabbed at his injured metatarsal and removed the splinter with his teeth (goblins are much more flexible than they appear). He looked around for the source of the offending sliver and noticed for the first time that he was now inexplicably in very dense woods. The canopy of intertwined branches was so solid that it blocked most sunlight. Only the occasional fugitive sparkle filtered down through the overhead thicket to interrupt the heavy gray stillness of the forest floor. It smelled unexpectedly and incongruously foul.

He stood up and took in this latest panorama. There wasn't much of one: the trees were too numerous to see more than a few meters in any direction. They were obviously very old trees, and hoar. They had enormous trunks and moss-encrusted bark of a kind he had never seen before. It was strangely reflective. He could catch glimpses of himself as he shifted position or walked past. More disturbing, though, were the fleeting glimpses of other people and things that were not actually there. At least, as far as he could *tell* they weren't there. He was startled more than once by the apparition of a creature with tentacles or wispy wings approaching over his shoulder in the bark's mirror image, only to spin in panic and discover that there was nothing visible in evidence.

Eventually Aspet grew accustomed to the irrational specters that appeared to be dogging his every step. The shiny bark held less and less of his attention as he concentrated on threading his way through the massive trunks toward some unknown destination. The air was gradually losing the stifling stagnant rotting vegetation odor that had been its major distinguishing feature since his sudden arrival in this fetid and festering forest. It was difficult to ascertain whether the air quality was actually improving, however, or simply that he was growing insensitive to the stench via acclimation. Whichever was the case, he was grateful.

৪ *Focus*.

He emerged from the forest abruptly. There was a narrow clearing, on the far side of which a massive barrier shimmered into existence as he approached. It seemed transparent, except that nothing was visible behind it, and stretched higher and further in either direction than he could see even while squinting. Every few seconds a vibrant jolt of random color shot through the structure. For the split second that the tincture was visible, he could make out vague scenes of crowded plazas, public ceremonies with cheering throngs, and other less easily interpretable panoplies. Aspet scratched his head and sighed. He seemed to have been assigned his own personal Enigma Fairy, and one with a penchant for putting in overtime.

He stood and watched the spectacle for some minutes. It was impressive, enigma or otherwise. At times he almost thought he caught glimpses of people or places he recognized, but the visions were so fleeting that he couldn't be sure it wasn't merely his imagination at work. He realized he was looking at the world's—possibly the universe's—largest cinema screen. He couldn't honestly say much for the plot, but the camera work and effects were compelling, especially given that cinema was still in its infancy in Tragacanth.

Aspet didn't see any way to go forward or much point in retracing his steps, so he sat down with his back against a tree and stared at the barrier itself, rather than at the images moving periodically across it. It was smooth and featureless on first inspection, but as he swept his glance back and forth across one particular area something geometric caught his eye. It disappeared utterly during the color flashes, but in the interval between them it seemed as though he could make out a vague rectangular outline, about a meter above ground level and slightly to the left of his position.

He stood up and walked toward it. As he approached to within five meters or so of the wall, however, the intensity of the images suddenly increased and the color flashes came much more quickly, to the point that they were almost continuous. He lost track of the anomaly in the heady visual overload. He backed up until the strobing returned to its former tempo and recalibrated. He scanned the barrier until he located the rectangle once more, memorizing its position relative to his own by triangulating it against distinctly-featured trees. Once more he approached the wall.

This time Aspet forced himself to ignore the light show and focus on the spot where he'd seen the outline, glancing back at the forest every so often to verify his targeting. He reached out and touched the barrier for the first time. The color and light seemed to flow through him like electricity; the images burned themselves directly into his brain. He jerked away involuntarily and stood for a moment, disoriented, temporarily blinded, and gasping for breath.

When his vision and composure had returned, he retreated a few steps and stared at the spot where he'd made contact. The rectangle was now plainly visible, outlined in black as though a door leading into a darkened room had been pushed open a few millimeters.

It was the closest thing to an exit from this place he'd seen, so pursuing it further seemed the logical course. Trouble was, he didn't think very much of the idea of coming in contact with that barrier again. It was just too much for even his sack-of-bricks goblin physiology to handle. He looked around and remembered that there was a forest only a few meters away. Aspet disappeared into it and reemerged a minute or so later carrying a limb-sized limb.

He broke off the smaller branches and twigs until he had a manageable tool not completely unlike a meter-long section of staircase bannister. Approaching the barrier somewhat cautiously, he moved the limb into position and jabbed it at the center of the embryonic opening. At once he was hit full force by the same sensory overload blast as before. Obviously the native timber was not a good psychic insulator. He stepped back and tried throwing the limb at the door. It simply bounced off, scattering bark in all directions. The bark pieces shattered on impact, like fine glass. They made a loud crunching noise when Aspet walked over to pick up the log and have another go.

℘ Resourcefulness.

Several minutes and quite a few heaves later he'd made some small progress, but he could tell it wasn't going to get him an open door any time soon. The only thing he could think of to do was to go back into the forest and look for a larger battering ram. He turned toward the trees and took three steps before a voice suddenly rang out. It was thin and ethereal, but quite clear nevertheless.

"Allow me to assist you, goblin."

Aspet spun around to see a bipedal figure floating in the air near the door. It was less powerfully built than a goblin, and disturbingly smooth-skinned. The wraith pushed open the door with one hand and extended the other palm down, gesturing toward the resultant gap in the barrier. Aspet paused, and then approached the newly-created portal. He stopped short and stared up at it. "Thanks for the help, whoever you are, but how am I meant to get up there? Do I climb up and crawl through?"

"I suppose you could," answered his benefactor, doubtfully, "But I'd recommend taking the stairs."

"Stairs? There aren't any stairs."

"Yes, there are. You just can't see them. Over here." He pointed to a spot about two meters to the right of the door.

Aspet walked over, a little skeptical, but the skepticism evaporated painfully when his shin banged into something hard.

"I *told* you there were stairs here." The spectral voice sounded annoyed.

Aspet stood on one leg for a moment, rubbing his sore shin. "So you did. Silly me for doubting that there were invisible stairs leading up to a mysterious door in a giant cinema screen that blasts passersby with psychic jolts. It's so obvious to me now."

"Well, at least your sense of sarcasm is intact," replied the visitor wryly. "That's good. I suspect you'll need it in the future."

"What's that supposed to mean?"

"Nothing and everything."

Aspet rolled his eyes. "I *hate* it when people answer my questions with smekking riddles."

"Sorry. It's the nature of the beast, I'm afraid."

"What sort of beast would that be? And while

we're at it, who *are* you?"

"I'm your doorman. Your escort, as it were, to the other side."

"The other side? What, am I dying now? "

"No, no, I merely meant the other side of the barrier. Through the doorway."

Aspet let out a tiny sigh of relief. "Well, noble escort, have you a name?"

"I have several names. Were you looking for any one in particular?"

This was beginning to get annoying. "How about I just make one up? I'm thinking 'Captain Evasive' fills the bill pretty well."

"Ooh, a promotion. Now I'll have to upgrade my doorman's uniform." He shimmered a little brighter for a moment, but not long enough for Aspet to make out any real details. "If it will make you more comfortable, you may call me Plåk."

Aspet considered for a moment. "No, I don't think that would make me feel any more comfortable. I'll stick with Captain Evasive."

Plåk chuckled. It was a very strange sound, like hearing the wind laugh. Aspet found it even more unsettling than his ghostly appearance. "Knock that off, will you? You're giving my goosebumps the creeps."

"Very well, goblin. Now, ascend the stairs and pass through the door. Try to avoid coming in contact with the barrier itself, though."

"Yeah, I think I can groove on that," answered Aspet, "My last couple of encounters were something less than pleasant. By the way, *my* name is Aspet."

The strangely spooky sound of spectral giggling filled the air once more. Aspet shook his head and tromped (carefully) up the stairs. He collapsed himself into as narrow a profile as a well-fed goblin can present and inched carefully through the doorway, trying his very best not to touch any piece of the barrier as he inched. Rather than a simple portal through a narrow wall, however, Aspet found himself facing a corridor that stretched off into distant grayness.

He stepped into the passageway a little hesitantly. Nothing happened. He walked a few more steps and jumped when the door closed behind him. He resisted the urge to grapple with the knob for a couple of reasons: first, he didn't want to take a chance of experiencing those visions again; second, there wasn't any knob.

The hall was dark, but not pitch-black. It seemed wide enough for several goblins to walk abreast, not that there were any other goblins around to test that hypothesis. He was alone, as usual, which made him a little irked when he remembered what Plåk had said. "*I am your escort to the other side,*" muttered Aspet bitterly, "Some escort."

"I beg your pardon?" came a voice from the direction of the ceiling, "I believe I'm doing a perfectly marvelous job. You haven't gotten lost yet, have you?"

"Lost? In order to be lost, presumably one must first be found. That's not a condition with which I've been afflicted in quite some time, so no; I suppose you couldn't really call me *lost*."

"Ah, see? I'm a stalwart escort. I'll have you there in no time."

"Where, if I may ask without regretting it, is 'there?'"

"Tragacanth. Your home."

♀ Determination.

Aspet was silent for a moment, taken aback by the linear reply. "Just when I'm all set for some circular logic or oblique riddle, you have to go and give me a straight answer."

"I'm simply jam-packed with surprises. Like this one, for example."

Without warning, the floor of hall dissolved into liquid and Aspet found himself vigorously treading water.

He sputtered and jerked his head around this way and that, looking for Plåk. "Hey, Captain Evasive! You don't happen to have a boat handy, do you?"

Ethereal laughter floated across the water, but this time it was more of a slightly evil chuckle. "I'm afraid I'm not that sort of captain," Plåk answered, "Fortunately for you, it isn't far to the shore." Aspet found the concept of a hallway having a shoreline a little difficult, but he was grateful when after a moment of scanning that very topological feature hove into view. He made for it, splashing madly with the peculiar, rather violent, swimming stroke favored by goblins, the gob-smack. A few seconds later he pulled himself panting onto the slippery, slimy, vaguely malodorous beach mud.

As the viscous muck drained slowly from his ventral scales, Aspet huddled on the water's edge and spoke to the circumambient air. "So, you've stalwartly guided me into a river and now a meadow full of mire. I can hardly wait to see what new and execrable destination awaits me next. Forgive me if my recent trauma has created some false memories, but I seem to recall some mention being made of Tragacanth."

"As it fortuitously turns out, Tragacanth is where you are now." Aspet looked around suspiciously at the featureless gray landscape stretching out to the horizon in all directions. He shuffled through his mental index cards for a moment. "Sorry, I don't believe you. I've never heard of any part of Tragacanth that looks like this."

"Perhaps this will refresh your memory," replied the spectral voice. An oval object suddenly appeared in front of him. He plucked it out of the air and examined it. It was metallic, with a fine filigree pattern covering one side. He turned it over and realized with a shock that it was...a mirror.

Aspet awoke with a start. His neck was stiff and his head stuffed with cotton, as though he'd been drinking heavily the night before. He thought back, but couldn't remember any recent celebrations that would have necessitated significant razzle intake. His mind was a blank for a few seconds, and then suddenly the dream hit him all at once, a neural tsunami crashing ashore without warning. He struggled to a sitting position, but the dream was passing in front of his eyes so rapidly and in such vivid detail that he lost situational awareness and was unable to make it any further. All he could do was sit there, arms stiffly braced on the mattress.

Finally he rolled out of bed and staggered to the kitchen for a very large gourd full of stankabru. He needed it after last night. He couldn't remember at the moment what he'd had for dinner the previous evening, but as soon as his memory returned whatever it was went on his 'do not eat before bedtime' list. That dream was totally weird and completely different from his usual nighttime cinematics. It was as vivid as the memory of a recent trauma, and showed no signs of slipping into the oubliette of vague, misty recollection where the vast majority of his dreams ended up by the time breakfast was finished.

Aspet had never really been a devotee of the 'dreams mean something' school, but then he'd never experienced a dream of this clarity before, either. It had taken control of his mind in a way he found highly disturbing but completely irresistible. He sat in his breakfast nook and stared vacantly out the bay window into a small vegetable and herb garden he maintained as much for relaxation as thrift. It was beginning to rain; the droplets ran down tall reddish plant stalks and hung glistening from their leaves as tiny liquid globes. They looked like planets to him: entire worlds where countless creatures passed their lives and died, unaware of and unconcerned about all the other droplets around them, or the larger world beyond.

He shook his head and frowned. He never used to see things that way—what was wrong with him? Was the dream somehow involved? He got up to pour himself another gourd of stankabru. He was seeing everything a little differently this morning. Even his trusty ol' bru gourd seemed to have taken on a new dimension since yesterday. He saw textural details and tiny irregularities in the handle he'd never noticed before. As the steaming stankabru took hold and nudged him fully awake, Aspet realized that everything within his field of vision was clearer, more ambiguous, and less easily explainable than he remembered. He'd heard that certain pharmacologically-active substances could have this effect, but two facts kept hammering at him, militating against the theory that he was under the influence:

1) He didn't recall ingesting any such substances; and

2) He didn't have the munchies.

As the day wore on, he found himself wandering aimlessly around his house and grounds, puttering with this and that but unable to concentrate on anything but the dream. The unwavering monomania was really getting to him. He unwittingly reviewed every minute detail of the night's events over and over, until he was ready to scream. Aspet finally decided to go online and try to get his mind on something else before he plunged precipitously over the frigid falls into incapacitating insanity.

It was waiting for him in his inbox. The message. He'd gotten some pretty odd messages since he announced his intention to try for the throne of Tragacanth, but this one was just...out there.

To: Asp37!cholinergia!goblinopolis
From: RCLiaison!FerrocLoca!CoME
Subject: Oneiric Profile Exam

Congratulations. You have passed the final qualifying examination for ascendancy to the Throne of Tragacanth. Your tournament will be held at 0900 hours three days hence at the Royal Network Operating Center Tournament Hall (South entrance). Please be there by 0800 hours for judging briefing and security checks.
Your disentanglement trigger is Fimbolu lagra premnalb
It must be activated orally, and repeated thrice.

Sincerely,

Faxol Brokk
Royal Candidate Liaison
Tragacanth Council of Mages and Engineers

Oneiric profile exam? What the smek did that mean? He hadn't taken any sort of exam. In fact, it had been awhile since he'd even heard from CoME or anyone else associated with this Royal stuff. It was weird that he'd spent so much time and effort honing his mad skills and preparing mentally for this, the challenge of his life, yet suddenly it all seemed so distant. That damned dream was sucking his psyche dry. He glanced down at the message again. What was that globber about a 'disentanglement trigger?' Aspet felt himself getting irritated at the sheer paucity of explanatory information in this communication.

After a brief but frantic search he located a disc containing the extensive collection of docs he'd been given when he attended the Seminar. Scanning the table of contents scored no hits, but after a global search using the right string, this popped up:

At the conclusion of the Oneiric Profile Examination, a trigger phrase will be supplied which should be repeated slowly and clearly out loud three times to disentangle the examination implant from the candidate's subconscious mind. This procedure *must* be carried out within one diurnal period of the exam termination or the subject will risk severely diminished mental capacity.

Rereading this part several times oddly did not help to form any cogent mental image for him. He saw the words but found it increasingly difficult to comprehend them, as though they were changing into a foreign language right before his eyes. After a few minutes it seemed prudent to stop trying to understand the nuances and just concentrate on absorbing the gist. Even this seemed more and more hopeless. Finally some small nugget of intellect holding on to a tiny shred of awareness fixated on the words "fimbolu lagra premnalb" and began repeating them in his head, over and over. A mental struggle between this bizarre phrase and the swirling juggernaut that was the dream ensued, driving him even closer to the edge of *non compos mentis*.

Aspet closed his eyes as tightly as he could, scrunching down until his face sported one long wrinkle across the ocular axis. He made a monumental effort to suppress the dream just enough to bring the phrase his brain was chanting at him into focus so he could grab it. Succeeding for a fleeting moment, he began to mouth the words, quietly at first, but louder as he gained confidence.

Fimble lagga premal....fimbala laggar premnob... fimbola lagra premnal...fimbolu lagra premnalb... fimbolu lagra premnalb...fimbolu lagra premnalb!

A loud snap reverberated through his skull and suddenly the dream was gone. Totally. No trace. As though it had never happened.

Aspet sat in stunned confusion. He was relieved at suddenly having control of his mind handed back to him, but the sucking hole left by the dream as it was ripped out of his consciousness gave him a wicked case of mental nausea. Except he couldn't make it better by throwing up. He put his head in his hands and took deep breaths, instead.

Gradually the gaping chasm vacated by the dream got filled in by granules of real memory and fragments of fancy, leaving him a little disoriented but no longer acutely traumatized. He rubbed his eyes to improve focus and looked around. The world seemed to have dropped back into routine mode: comfortable, familiar, boring. Not that boring was bad in this case.

He noticed the post on his screen and read it again. It still didn't make his top ten most lucid communications, but it was no longer the jumble of nonsense it had seemed minutes earlier. Well, except for the *Fimbolu*... business. He had no idea what that was supposed to mean. The gist seemed to be that he had been the subject of some sort of test, which he had apparently passed. The whole episode jogged something; he figured it was a crumb he'd picked up in The Seminar but forgotten about due to extreme lack of engagement. The Seminar's presenters were not exactly scintillating, and nor was the subject matter terribly gripping. It was mostly officious government-speak interspersed with hefty dollops of rules and edicts. Throughout most of it Aspet had struggled simply to keep his eyes open.

He scrolled through the electronic documents he'd brought home with him and read the entire section on the 'Oneiric Profile Examination.' Apparently it was a deep psychological examination conducted on candidates shortly before they were scheduled to make an attempt at the crown. A dream scenario was magically injected into the candidate's neural stream just prior to the initiation of the dreaming part of the sleep cycle. The reactions of the candidate to various situations and problems posed during the dream were carefully scrutinized by a team at CoME to determine if the candidate was suited for ruling and that he had no vengeful itinerary or other ulterior motives for wanting to be king. Aspet wasn't sure *why* he wanted to be king, other than feeling he could do a better job than the current monarch, but he felt reasonably confident that he wasn't harboring any repressed sinister aspirations.

The fact that he now had less than three days to make final preparations for his attempt at the throne suddenly squirmed its way through the crowd of thoughts and ruminations currently milling about in his consciousness and shocked him into action. He had a lot to do, and a short time to do it in.

Chapter Fourteen:
Null Magic

Tol sighed. As expected, he wasn't having any luck convincing his superiors that there was an imminent threat to The Slice. He had stopped short of telling them about Oloi and the phantom pub, though. He just got out of the infirmary and the last thing he wanted was to be sent back forcibly, under restraint.

The walls of his cramped office were closing in on him, as they often did after he'd met with the duty sergeant. The only cure was to hit the streets. Besides, he wasn't going to make any headway on this problem sitting at a desk.

It was raining, as usual. Goblinopolis really wasn't all that wet a place, except when he needed to walk and think. Then you could guarantee precipitation of exactly this sort: deliberate and drenching. Something about the way they were falling enabled the individual drops to wriggle into areas they weren't supposed to be able to reach, at least according to the marketing claims of the rainwear garment manufacturers. He snuggled down into the flipped-up collar of his departmental trench overjack and stared grimly at the rain-slickened sidewalk as he trudged along en route to his favorite destination: nowhere in particular. Tol had a standing reservation for a window seat.

He decided on a whim to wander down by the docks. Not his Precinct by a long shot, but what the smek. Goblinopolis was inland, but built on a river that had been widened and dredged repeatedly over the years to accommodate larger and larger vessels. As a result, the vast majority of traffic on the waterway below the city now consisted of huge barges plying their way back and forth between ocean-going freighters docked in deepwater Myndrythyl Bay and the extensive municipal warehouse district. If there was a logical place in the city to conceal horded technology, or anything else for that matter, the block after block of massive freight storage buildings in the warehouse district was it. Most of them also had connections to a labyrinthine underground routing facility that occupied nearly a square kilometer of the area below the district's streets. A goblin could thread his way through that maze for days, even weeks, without ever seeing sunlight.

The rain slacked off as he approached the eastern wharfs. These were the only ones designed to handle passenger traffic, the others being dedicated solely to freight. It was getting late; the last disembarkation of the day had just taken place and people returning from holiday or shopping on the semi-autonomous Halo'jn Isles just east of Lumbos streamed past with luggage, boxes, and bags. Tol dodged and chuckled as a wizened old gnome crone with a particularly wide load went scooting by, hurling gnomish obscenities in his direction for having the audacity to be in her way.

Tol decided just to wander up and down the commerce-choked streets until something interesting happened. Having grown up not far from here, he knew it wouldn't be long. Sure enough, after less than a minute a curious parade came around a corner and wound its ponderous way up the street in front of him. At its head was what would appear to the uninitiated to be a horribly disfigured monster, tentacles waving wildly. Behind this apparition trailed, in orderly single-file, a procession of diminutive robed monks. As the tentacled thing came abreast of Tol, he took off his helmet respectfully and spoke to it. "Glorious day to you, Exalted One. On visitations?"

The convoy halted as the Exalted One ran a leathery sucker-encrusted tentacle over Tol's face. It withdrew and a thin, trilling voice emanated from somewhere deep inside the giant barnacle of a body. "Tol-u-ol. It has been many risings since last we met. You have matured;" a pause, then, "and you have been...injured."

"Yes, Exalted One. Several times. Occupational hazard, I'm afraid."

"Life is too brief to spend battering away at one another, Tol-u-ol. Have you not learned this?"

"I generally try to avoid it whenever possible, Exalted One. There's just something about being an edict enforcement officer that makes people want to batter me."

"Some of your injuries run much deeper than mere broken flesh, Tol-u-ol. Flesh heals with time;

spiritual wounds often do not."

"I appreciate your concern, Exalted One, but I don't put much stock in that spiritual mumbo-jumbo. I'm just a simple cop."

The Exalted One made a strange thrumming noise that Tol only just recognized as laughter. "Yes, Tol-u-ol, you are a simple creature. But one destined to leave his mark amongst the very stars themselves, nonetheless."

This prediction took Tol by surprise. He grappled with his thoughts for a moment as the Exalted One and his retinue moved off down the street. Tol frowned and called after him.

"Wait, Exalted One. I have an important question to ask you!"

"Your answers sleep shrouded in darkness, Tol-u-ol. Seek them where childhood dreams are hidden. Fare you well!"

"Wait. What?" Tol scratched his head. "Smek. I hate puzzles. Why can't these guru types ever talk in plain Goblish? I'd better write that down before I forget it." He felt in the pockets of his overjack for a pad. Unfortunately, the only pen he could find was one he thought he'd 'accidentally' left locked in the desk drawer in his office. He groaned as he realized it was going to nag him.

"My internal navigation system indicates that you are 2,354 meters from your assigned district. Is this extrajurisdictional activity authorized? I see no such orders on file."

"Hey, I'm tryin' to save the world or somethin' here. That goes beyond departmental policy just a little, doncha think?"

"As usual, I have no idea what you're prattling on about. I suspect you don't, either."

"Eh, put a cap on it, pencil brain."

Tol wandered aimlessly through the narrow streets of the warehouse district, trying to comprehend the underlying meaning of the cryptic message the Exalted One had given him while simultaneously ignoring the strident running commentary emanating from his overjack pocket. It was a bit like trying to make out with a date on the front porch while your mother nagged at you through the closed door. As he passed within a few meters of a wharf, he had a sudden overwhelming urge to hurl the pen far out into the dark lapping water—but the thought of having to account for it come equipment audit time stayed his hand once again.

"Where childhood dreams are realized...shrouded in darkness..." He repeated the words under his breath. "Sounds like the closet in my bedroom as a kid."

"There was no mention of layers of discarded food and crumpled, soiled clothing; the resemblance to your bedroom closet escapes me," opined a muffled electronic voice.

"For the love of Gammag Palindromia, will you please shut up? I can't think with your constant inane jabbering."

"I expect your inability to think considerably predates my 'inane jabbering,'" the pen replied in a hurt tone.

"Hey, ya know, I think that would be a good

name for you. Inane Jabberer, or 'Eyejay,' for short."

"My designation is 'PDWA/AI Model 36, serial number 409427,' not 'Eyejay.' How barbaric and typically insensitive."

"Eyejay it is, then," replied Tol, beaming, "It's a good name for you. The *right* name."

The pen clicked in irritation, a sound Tol hadn't realized it was capable of making. He chuckled. It wasn't often he scored a point on the little digital smekker. He hoped the victory didn't prove too Pyrrhic.

He stopped for a while to watch a cargo vessel being unloaded. The spectacle of those gargantuan cranes extricating huge containers from deep in the bowels of a freighter and plopping them deftly on flatbed transport drays never failed to enthrall him. As a lad he'd spent countless hours down here watching the great dhowmats divest themselves of their treasure, trying to imagine from what exotic ports of call it had been brought back through impossibly turbulent seas and vicious pirate blockades.

Out of curiosity he pulled out his departmental-issue optical enhancement goggles and slapped them over his eyes. They brought the lettering on the side of one of the containers up close and into sharp focus. *Extruded Polychitin Dental Polish Applicators, 1000 Gross*. Serious buzz kill. Smek those truth-in-shipping-label edicts.

Ignoring the bitter disenchantment of a childhood dream shattered, Tol hurriedly shifted his gaze to the ship in the next berth further along. Unlike the first ones, these containers had a brightly-colored logo splashed on them. He recognized it as belonging to a well-known toy manufacturer. The sight warmed the cockles of his heart (the cockles reside just below and to the left of the auricles in goblin anatomy) and brought back even stronger memories of his juvenile phase. His rose-colored reminiscences were once again dragged into the stark glaring light of reality when one of the crates slipped out of its sling and crashed awkwardly to the dock. It burst open at a seam and what came tumbling out was definitely *not* intended for children.

Instead of brightly-colored animals and wooden vehicles, the broken crate disgorged bundles of boxes with stenciled labels like *Programmable Field Generator, 1 ea* and *Opto-Mechanical Transducer Array*. Tol's eyes narrowed and the 'something wrong with this picture' alarm in his head started ringing. Only seconds after the accident two furtive-looking hobs came scuttling over and rounded up the spilled merchandise, hastily nailing the crate back together and securing it with metal banding. Tol decided he would follow the suspicious container to its destination. He blended with the shadows and settled into the pursuit.

He'd only been watching for three or four minutes when a lifter driven by a surly gnarlignome rolled over to the crate and hoisted it up on two extensible prongs protruding from the front like flattened tusks. With insolent skill he whipped the whole assembly around and drove off with surprising speed down an aisle crowded with crates and barrels of varying sizes. Tol leapt to his feet and scrambled to keep sight of his quarry as it disappeared into the dockside maze. He clambered over barrels and around shipping containers, stubbing his foot on an exposed plank. Cursing silently he hobbled along, trying not to lose the crate. He thought he'd blown it for a moment, but rounded a corner and spied his target being loaded onto one of the lesser flatbed drays, beside a smaller crate.

He skittered around a couple of shelving units and positioned himself near the exit, leaping onto the bed of the dray as it lumbered by in the darkness and wedging into a narrow space between the two crates. They took a corner rather faster than was prudent and it threw him roughly into a cargo tie-down ring. He lay there rubbing his bruised pelvic ridge and foot, muttering. "Ow. I'm getting too smekking old for this smek. Where'd you learn to drive, you smekking lunatic...by correspondence course?"

The dray bumped and bounced along for another minute or so, then swung abruptly into a dark garage. Tol struggled to a crouch and waited for the vehicle to slow enough for him to dismount. As it clattered to a stop he jumped down rather awkwardly and rolled behind a large metal water tank with peeling red paint. The dray backed in and an overhead block and tackle was maneuvered into position to relieve it of its cargo. Tol watched as the crate was lifted off the dray and lowered onto a wheeled pallet. Four hobs pushed the pallet away into the gloom of the warehouse, forcing Tol to dodge and weave his way through the boxes, crates, barrels, and assorted junk piled throughout the building in order to keep up. After thirty meters the haphazard caravan passed through an archway and the floor beneath them suddenly sloped forward, becoming a ramp leading down into the inky subterranean blackness.

The good news was that the blackness made it a lot easier for Tol to trail them without being seen. The bad news was that, even though the amount of junk piled up along the walls had lessened considerably since they entered the tunnel, the absence of illumination virtually ensured that whatever debris remained would find its way into Tol's path undetected. Every time he stubbed toes, ankles, or knees on one of these hidden hazards and cursed softly to himself, he heard an odd twittering noise. After a few repeat performances he realized it was coming from his pocket. The smekking pen was *laughing* at him. The next time he stumbled, he steered himself intentionally into a wall and smashed the pocket holding the pen into it as hard as he could. A gratifying silence ensued. He smiled grimly and turned his full attention back to the pursuit.

The downward slope of the tunnel seemed to be increasing. They must be pretty far underground by now, Tol reckoned. The passage was throttling down also; as it narrowed the amount of goblin-obscuring junk tailed off as well, forcing him to drop further back into the darkness to avoid detection.

The floor suddenly leveled out and the

narrow hallway widened into a vast musty cavern honeycombed with storage nooks and piled to the darkly invisible ceiling with crates, chests, barrels, and containers of every size and color imaginable. He panicked briefly as he crossed the threshold without a fix on his quarry, but breathed a sigh of relief a moment later when he heard them shuffling off to his left. He darted behind a pillar of crates and peered around the corner just in time to see the hobs shovel their cargo into a large steel container and lock it securely.

Surveying the scene, Tol noticed a number of other crates nearby with the same paint scheme and cryptic markings. He cooled his heels until the hobs had retreated topside, then inspected the containers. They were all identical, all locked. He didn't recognize the logo stenciled on them, so he reached into his pocket and hauled out the pen. It was still sulking and refused even to acknowledge him. Tol grinned at this unexpected turn of good luck and whistled softly under his breath, which annoyed the pen even more.

"What now? I suppose you are going to use me to pry open that box?" The voice was as icy cold as a metallic speech synthesizer could generate. "In a manner of speaking, yes, I am," replied Tol, cheerily. "I want you to search through the commercial tokens database and identify this logo." The pen said nothing. "*Now*, Eyejay. Don't make me use the override sleeve." It seemed to shudder at the suggestion.

"Processing," it snapped vitriolically, "Positive

match discovered. Smekker."

"What was that last part, again?"

"Nothing. The emblem is registered to Pyfox Consolidated Industries."

"Pyfox. Hmm. What an interesting... coincidence. All right, access any registered shipments made to this port by Pyfox Consolidated Industries in the past thirty days. And keep the solid state pejoratives to yourself."

"Port Authority records show an anomalous increase in PCI deliveries beginning eleven days ago. Manifests range from children's toys to housewares."

"That don't tell us much. Manifests are fictional documents even under ordinary circumstances for Pyfox and his ilk. The increase in deliveries itself, though, is another matter altogether. Eleven days ago would fit neatly into the timeline, too. I guess I'm just gonna have to open one of these crates."

"I should think your breath alone would do it."

"Oh look, Ma—I found a talking bottle opener. Too bad it's so smekkin' ugly." The response was an extended electronic raspberry. Tol grunted and slipped the offending instrument back into his overjack.

He snapped on his pocket torch and started rooting around in the dim clutter for something to use as a pry bar. After a couple of minutes of kicking boxes and cartons out of the way, he found a length of reinforcing rod.

"Payola!" he exclaimed, extricating the improvised tool from the framework of a broken packing crate.

He scraped its coating of rust onto a nearby tarp and inserted the rod into the hasp of the lock securing one of the PCI containers. It took a couple of sharp jerks, but he finally succeeded in breaking apart the lock, sending metal bits and a cloud of oxidized iron particles in all directions. He heard the unmistakable sound of coughing from his overjack pocket.

"Oh, stop it. You don't even *have* lungs."

"Good job, too. You'd have ruined them long before now if I had."

"You make that sound like a bad thing."

If the pen made any further remark, Tol didn't hear it. He was busy cracking open the newly liberated lid of the shipping container. The manifest attached to the crate read *Culinary Utensil Assortments*. He reached in, pulled out a sealed box, and slit it open. A shiny metallic unit with several dials and switches tumbled out. He picked it up and examined it.

"Wonder what sort of 'culinary utensil' they expect me to believe this is?" he mused, turning it over to discover a small label on the underside. He read it out loud: "*Multimodal Dweomer Repeater/ Concentrator. Caution: High Voltage. No user serviceable parts inside*. What the heck is that?" He waited a few seconds, and then cleared his throat. "Ah hem. I said, 'what the heck is that?'"

From his pocket came a voice dripping with sarcasm. "Ah, yes. It would be a serious error on my part to assume you were intellectually capable of posing a rhetorical question." Tol screwed up his face in a scowl and started to reply, but postponed it when the pen switched to its data readout voice.

"Simplistically, a multimodal dweomer repeater/concentrator, colloquially known in the industry as an 'emdrec,' is an electronic device for intensifying and focusing magical activity. It operates on the Quantum Equivalence principle, essentially providing a duplex inductive gateway between magical and conventional electrogravitational energy fields."

"More magineer stuff. What's Pyfox up to? Bidding for a major CoME supply contract?"

"That would be highly out of character for him."

Tol grunted in agreement and proceeded to break into all the crates he could find with the PCI logo on them. Not a single one contained anything like what was listed on their manifests. "You'd think at least one of these would have gotten inspected at the docks. I think maybe it's time to pay a little visit to the Port Inspector General's office. Make an inventory of each crate, the merchandise it contains, and the corresponding manifests, and we'll throw that to the PIGs."

"Already done." If the pen had eyes, it would be rolling them.

Tol chuckled. "Eyejay, Eyejay: just when I think it's time to trade up to a crayon, you turn out to be somewhat useful, after all."

"A crayon? I wouldn't think you were qualified to operate anything so sophisticated."

Tol held the pen up and looked at it. "Yeah, you've got a point. I'd better just stick with the simple stuff."

Eyejay seemed to be working this out while Tol

went about cracking open one last PCI container he'd stumbled across, this one a barrel rather a crate. Inside was a single cylindrical unit apparently made of a solid metallic core with a large collection of pipes, conduits, wires, and less identifiable gadgets encrusting it. Tol was a pretty meaty goblin, but even he had difficulty lifting the thing out of its protective packing cocoon. "What in almighty Plegma *is* this contraption?" He turned it around, looking for a label. There was nothing but a small plaque with a serial number and the words *zZingler zZ-1*. He read it out loud for the pen's benefit. "You got any buzz on this?"

"I've been upgraded to insect now, have I? I suppose that's better than crayon."

"Hey, I said crayon was a *goal*. Any results yet?"

Eyejay harrumphed—yet another sound Tol hadn't been aware a pen could make—and after a few seconds began again.

"There's nothing in the product registration database, but I did find one reference to a prototype bearing that designation on a military Requisition Ticket For Materiel issued a couple of years ago. It doesn't seem to have been accepted by the government, though."

"Hmm. Any descriptive language attached to that RTFM?"

"Just a general *Statement of Proposed Functionality*. It reads as follows:

A flux generator for dampening quantum fields within a given radius to modulate or eliminate

242

magical activity."

Basically, a null-magic device."

Tol furrowed his unibrow and paced. "Since when does Pyfox give a wet sloppy smek about magic or technology? He's always been more the contraband/money laundering type, with a side order of protection racketeering."

"First-order pattern analysis suggests some sort of infrastructure involving a magical interface along the approximate lines of a Duber, albeit presumably minus the Arnoc node."

"Surely even Pyfox wouldn't be presumptuous enough to try to build his own private interface. What's in it for him? He can't charge Magineers to use it—they can already access the government ones for free. *Gotta* be an angle here somewhere..."

Tol kept adding up the numbers in his head but he couldn't make the balance sheet work. He frowned and started to move crates around.

"If I asked you what you were looking for, would I regret it?"

"I don't know. I just have a gut feeling there's another important piece of this puzzle lying around in here somewhere."

"A gut feeling? Ah, I can see your point. The central nervous system hasn't been performing at all well as a decision-making organ, so why not try the gastrointestinal? Especially when there's so much of it."

"You know, if you were any funnier I'd rent you out to emcee at funerals."

"That would a violation of departmental pol-"

"Clam up, diode butt. I'm workin' here."

Tol was tossing crates around willy-nilly now, blindly following his cop's instincts. There was something almost palpable just on the verge of coalescing into a concrete thought dancing around in his subconscious, and he wanted to give it as much opportunity to solidify as possible. Besides, as long as he was making this much noise he couldn't hear Eyejay's color commentary. He redistributed a new layer of wooden boxes and suddenly something caught his eye. It was a row of barrels identical to the one he'd just examined. He shoved a stack of crates aside and found even more barrels. As he continued clearing away boxes and crates, he ran across more and more of the barrels, each with the same *zZingler zZ-1* label. All in all, after over an hour's hard work, Tol found at least a hundred of the zZ-1 units, most in a tightly-packed raft camouflaged by dozens of boxes and smaller crates.

A hundred magic-dampening units, emdrecs, field generators, transducers. Even a technically-challenged EE grunt like Tol could begin to see a pattern here. "Eyejay," he said, biting his lower lip, "Correlate all the devices we've so far discovered and tell me what industrial or scientific enterprises they would be appropriate to. Discount, at least for the moment, the possibility that they might simply be warehouse inventory."

"Stand by," the pen replied, "My comm link is cutting out. I need to do a spectrum scan and lock onto an alternate primary biphasic carrier."

"Knock yourself out. Just try not to take all day doing it."

"I shall endeavor not to take up too much of your precious time. I would not want to be accused of impeding the march of idiocy."

"Did I say, 'knock yourself out?' How thoughtless of me. Please, allow me to do it *for* you."

"That sounds considerably more in line with your personality and acumen, although I do worry that it might tax your intellect." Eyejay noted the rise in Tol's blood pressure and respiration rate, and continued hurriedly, "I suggest you postpone it, however, so that I may parse and deliver the new datastream."

Tol smashed a huge fist into his palm, took a deep breath, and answered with a curt, "Go."

"While there are multiple feasible scenarios in which this particular collection of instrumentation might be appropriate, the most likely explanation is that Pyfox is planning some sort of large-scale disruption of access to magical space."

All at once a large chunk of the puzzle assembled itself in one corner of Tol's mind and plopped down in front of him. Thoughts of pen-directed hostility were tossed aside as he considered this new information.

"Disruption of magical spa....wait a smekkin' minute! That guy with the face fur and smooth skin in the pub. He said somethin' about a plan to whack The Slice. Maybe Pyfox is mixed up in that somehow. But what's in it for him? Doin' away with magic would screw up everything. We'd either have to figure out how to get along without it, which would be a disaster, or find some way to get it...back..." He tailed off as the full significance of this scenario hit him. Tol trudged the rest of the way up the ramps in silence, chewing on this.

"I wonder," Tol mused several minutes later as he stepped once more into the light of day, "If that horker could actually pull it off?" As though in answer to this question (which it was), Eyejay chirped from his pocket. "By my best estimation he could, given judicious deployment of personnel and equipment. The key would be effectively neutralizing the existing Dubers while maintaining the security of the null magic generators. I have calculated only a 0.023% chance of that being a successful tactic over the long term, however."

"Not very good odds," Tol reflected, "but...what if The Slice were somehow rendered inaccessible except through one heavily fortified portal controlled by Pyfox?"

"Feasible. Collapsing the quantum gateway in all but a narrowly-specified position would take both enormous energy and an intimate understanding of the transdimensional architecture involved, however. There are few, if indeed any, living creatures with that sort of knowledge at their command."

"Yeah, Pyfox couldn't cast a spell even if it was printed in large block letters on the back of a racing form. So, who gave him the guts of this scheme and why?"

"Logic would suggest it was someone who stood to profit from the outcome. Or perhaps, given the nature of the individual in question, some degree of coercion was involved."

"I'd say that's a pretty sure bet. Pyfox rarely employs the art of gentle persuasion when brute force will do. But who would know enough about this stuff to help him, coerced or not?"

"There are a few possible candidates in my database, but they are all very remote. The one who seems most likely under the current circumstances is Clostridius Perspice."

Tol rolled his eyes. "Right. I don't think Pyfox has that kind of clout."

"Perhaps not, but Gramidius Contentius quite possibly does, and Pyfox is known to have strong ties to the Belladonna organization."

"What could even Grami do to convince someone with Perspice's power and influence to participate in a caper like this? I know Archmages are traditionally amoral, but jacking around with access to magic is not something he'd be likely to do."

"Certainly such an action would not seem to be consistent with his self-interests or prior behavior patterns. However, organic creatures have a marked tendency to grow increasingly irrational with age and Archmage Perspice is well over two hundred years old now. There is ample evidence that, at least in the past, Gramidius considered the archmage to be a close personal friend; it is not illogical to presume that this friendship persists and may even have strengthened. Gramidius himself is, according to public records, 247 years of age."

Tol made no reply because just then a shadow passed over them and he found himself staring up at a huge, heavily-muscled, oddly familiar beast. It did not seem particularly pleased to see him.

"I've had it up to the dorsal hump with that thing. What the smek does it want from me now?" Tol yelled as he dove behind a traffic signal box. "It is a Guardian," Eyejay explained calmly, "it was created to protect something or someone. I would speculate that it considers you a threat to...whatever it has been put under geas to guard."

"What, by just walking down the street minding my own smekkin' business? What the smek is it guarding?"

"Good taste, perhaps?"

"Har de har har. The electric tweezers made a joke. Laugh this off, fun-o-matic: that thing weighs as much as a good-sized pram, and if it stomps me *you're* going to end up looking like the blade of a palette knife, no matter what kind of fancy-schmancy alloy you're made of."

"That possibility has occurred to me, in abeyance of which I therefore suggest you move approximately one meter to your right as soon as is practicable."

Tol leapt aside, looking over his shoulder as he did to watch a huge paw come crashing down and leave a gaping, crumbled hole in the sidewalk where he'd been standing a moment before.

"I wish to smek you'd learn that complete sentences are not always optimum for communication in tight spots like that. I...*we*...could have been flattened."

"Next time I will be more succinct. Duck!"

Tol mouthed Eyejay's last word with a puzzled look on his face until peripheral vision afforded him a glimpse of the stone-gray oblivion swinging towards his head. The meaning of the reply became crystal clear in the split second while he dropped to his stomach and rolled, getting clipped in the noggin in the process. "I guess I asked for that," he muttered, rubbing the throbbing grutch egg blossoming in the fertile ground just below his inferior occipital ridge.

"I suggest you either run away with considerable alacrity or go on the offensive, because the energy aura surrounding this Guardian is intensifying rapidly."

Tol whipped out his weapon and snapped off the safety. "I've never been very good at retreating. Something to do with being clumsy running backwards." He dove to avoid a vicious claw slash, tripping in the process and ending up in a crumpled heap.

"Yes, I can see that would be an issue, given your level of grace in forward movement." "Who the smek programmed you to be sarcastic? What kind of desirable trait is that in a personal digital assistant?" He fired point blank into the gaping maw of the beast as it narrowly missed taking off his head with a single awe-inspiring chomp.

"I was not *programmed* for sarcasm, as such. I was programmed to be adaptive to the social milieu in which I operate. Sarcasm is simply a logical adaptation to being constantly in your vicinity."

"Yeah? Well you'd better be prepared to adapt to being in the vicinity of carrion because this thing is eating my lunch. The disruptor doesn't do smek against it."

"Naturally. It has no neural system to disrupt. You may as well be discharging it at a concrete pillar."

"Great. Smekkin' great. So how am I supposed to go on the offensive? Body odor?" He waved his arms back and forth in the general direction of his assailant.

"That would be an extremely viable tactic in your case, were the Guardian biological. Enhanced olfactory sensitivity is a component only of specialized golems created for tracking purposes, however, and that does not appear to be one of the primary functions of this creature."

"How did it find me, then?"

"I would posit rather that *you* found *it*."

"Twice? In totally different parts of the city?"

"The triggers can be placed anywhere. Tripping them will summon the Guardian instantly; location is immaterial to the process, as they teleport through transient directional wormholes."

"So, basically, you're saying," Tol yelled as he narrowly avoided being eviscerated by a well-aimed paw swipe, "that I just blindly blundered into some random tripwire? Why aren't the sidewalks littered with the bones of the other hapless jloks who've done the same, then?"

"It appears to be trippable only by you. Tol-u-ol-specific, in other words."

"Why *me*? Who would go to all this trouble just to knock off a tired old beat cop?"

"Pattern analysis indicates that these attacks are meant primarily to dissuade you. Your termination is likely no better than a secondary intent, if the primary goal fails."

"Dissuade me from what? Walking down the street?"

"The strategic goal is not clear."

"There's sure nothing unclear about the tactical go..." His last word was cut short as a section of stone facade on a nearby building crumbled under a glancing blow from the Guardian and landed on him. He lay there out of breath, trying desperately to come up with something, anything, to combat this seemingly unbeatable leviathan. The beast assessed the situation and moved in for the kill.

"I would suggest that now might be the appropriate time to activate one of the null magic devices in the adjacent warehouse. The field effect should be sufficiently strong at this range."

"How am I meant to do that, then? By telepathy?"

"Telekinesis is one option, of course, but generally it requires a considerably more advanced cranial morphology than you possess. My advice is to make use of the remote control device in your pocket."

"What the smek are you talking about?"

"The small round object in your right overjack pocket. You picked it up in the warehouse and slipped it into your pocket, probably without thinking, as is

251

your wont. In this case paucity of neural activity may prove to be life-saving. It is a remote control device locked to one of the null magic units you examined. Press the rectangular button near the outside edge."

Tol reached into his pocket skeptically and was astonished to find that there *was* a small, hard, round thing in there. He fumbled with it for a moment, trying to find the rectangular button by feel, but finally gave up in disgust and drew the object out to examine it in the light of day. It proved to be his watch.

"Wrong pocket," Eyejay explained.

Unfortunately, the diversion gave the Guardian just enough time to lay in a new and more devastating attack.

The sun was suddenly only a fond, distant memory. A blackness the depth and intensity of which Tol had never even suspected possible now covered his visual field from horizon to horizon. The air smelt strongly of sulfur and concentrated perspiration.

"What the smek is happening?" He shrank down, arms over his face, in a reflexive attempt to ward off the smothering darkness. Eyejay's voice sounded muffled, "It would appear that we are being...sat upon," came the doleful reply.

"Aaagh! What do I do?"

"Push the smekking button."

Tol scrambled around in the other pocket and found the device. He pulled it out and frantically stabbed at it as the immense derriere closed in. At the last possible moment he found and pressed the correct switch. The rapidly narrowing gap between him and the huge butt abruptly stopped narrowing. He held his breath and continued to cringe for a few seconds for good measure. When it became apparent that gluteal demise was not so imminent after all he crawled out from underneath the now inanimate beast and peered at it with a mixture of trepidation and relief.

"Wow," he remarked, turning the remote over in his hand, "this thing really comes in handy. Maybe I should carry one all the time."

"I hasten to remind you that the device is merely a remote controller. The actual functionality is provided by the null magic unit down in the warehouse, the construction details of which render it rather unsuitable for portable use."

"Too smekkin' heavy to carry around, you mean."

"I believe that is what I said. You are, in fact, extraordinarily fortunate that the power supply was present and armed. I suspect it was meant as a demonstration unit."

"So anyway, what happens to Rover, here, now?"

"Eventually the null magic burst will dissipate and the Guardian will return to its native state. It would be best if you were no longer in the vicinity when that occurs."

"Not a problem. As it happens, I have a date with a balrog."

Chapter Fifteen:
Seize() the Day

Aspet winced. The review program he'd established was just short of impossible to carry out in the short time he had left to study, but he felt as though he owed it to himself and to his potential subjects to give it his best shot. It wasn't a review of computer hacking techniques or esoteric network architectures, however: it was the social and political history of Tragacanth, along with a ponderous volume titled *The Precepts of Governing* by a well-known political scientist of a past generation. Hacking he knew a lot about—it was the process of ruling a nation where he felt woefully inadequate. The fact that no previous contender for the throne had worried about that aspect until after he'd won would have been irrelevant to Aspet even if he'd known about it. That wasn't acceptable behavior in his world view. He knew he couldn't hope to become any sort of expert in policy-making in less than three days, but he nevertheless had to give it his best effort.

The hardest part, he soon came to realize, was staying awake. Most of the material was a little...

dry. He found it useful to bang his head against the table every so often to renew his focus, although he also discovered that too much enthusiasm in this activity led to headaches, fuzziness, and a sticky tabletop.

Cranial abuse notwithstanding, Aspet stuck to it like the trooper he aspired someday to be until he decided he'd better wrap things up and realign his brain with the technical challenge ahead. Besides, all this political theory was generating weird cobwebs in his mind. He was beginning to feel a strange compulsion welling up to draft an election committee or organize a fundraiser dinner. It creeped him out.

There would be a total of four candidates for the throne, including of course the present monarch, Trellior I, who had assumed the kingship six years previous. He had been a first-rate hacker prior to his ascension, but it was widely believed he had grown rusty in the three years since his last challenge. It isn't easy to keep your mad skills pumped while playing lord over all you survey, after all.

Still, Aspet wasn't harboring any delusions about the challenge he faced. The king had the 'home field' advantage and was defending his regime, not to mention the lifestyle to which he had grown accustomed, so there was little doubt he would put up a fierce fight. Also, two previous challengers, both of whom Aspet had known, had mysteriously vanished after failing in their royal bids. This was especially worrisome to him, but he didn't know what, if anything, he could do to prevent it happening to him—apart from winning. A complete transcript of that challenge and the one which gained Trellior the throne would prove useful, if one could be had. Fortunately, he *had* one right here, supplied by the mysterious but ever-useful Boogla. It was weird having a powerful fan you've never met and really haven't done anything to deserve. Weird: but oh, so useful.

It was clear from the outset that Trellior was a search-and-destroy hacker. He wasn't concerned with finesse or elegance, just brute force and aggression. The transcripts showed a predictable pattern of reconnoiter/decoy/attack/dodge that Aspet found rather simplistic, although obviously successful. It was a tactic he'd seen and defused before; he could only hope His Majesty's strategy hadn't evolved any since the most recent transcript. That seemed pretty unlikely, given that all candidates for the throne came under extremely intense scrutiny by the king's personal staff. They probably knew just about everything there was to know about him, Aspet mused, and that meant they'd studied his tactics at least as closely as he'd studied Trellior's. That was all right, though, because his personal strategy was nothing if not fluid.

The morning of the challenge dawned overcast and drizzling. Aspet was up before the light, readying himself mentally and going over fine details of the Royal Network one last time. He was so absorbed with his preparations, in fact, that he almost missed the message that popped up on his screen.

To: Asp37!cholinergia!goblinopolis
From: boogla!boogla!boo
Subject: Good fortune

Be wary of the unexpected.
Seize() the day.
All things come to those who wait().

Aspet rolled his eyes and chuckled. "Another cryptic communiqué brought to you by the great and mysterious Boogla." He stared at the words a moment longer, but could wrest no more meaning from them and went back to his review. A few minutes later he looked up and realized it was time to leave for the Arnoc. He closed his notebooks, shut down his computer, and said a little goblin prayer for luck.

He had an escort to the challenge site from two Royal Protective Corps agents, as was normal procedure for all aspirants to the throne who made it this far (to ensure they arrived safely at the Arnoc and, he suspected, in order to discourage last-minute cheating). They weren't a very talkative pair, so the trip was made in silence. That didn't bother him; he needed to concentrate, anyway.

Challenges to the throne were a rare occurrence overall, and this combined with the monumental nature of the contest made them quite important to the Goblinopolis social calendar. The South entrance to the tournament hall was secured and reserved for official personnel only, but the area surrounding the North, public, entrance took on a carnival atmosphere in the days leading up to a challenge. There were barkers, biters, jugglers, jongleurs, illusionists, delusionists, contortionists, extortionists, daredevils, dust-devils, acrobats, fruitbatters, and a whole host of other entertainers and profiteers. Just about every semi-sentient race on N'plork was represented in the teeming throng.

Aspet had witnessed this spectacle once before during the last Royal Challenge, but not being willing to mingle very long in such a vast assemblage he hadn't really comprehended the full scope of the event. This time he only saw the crowds from afar, as the RPC kept everyone back a considerable distance from the disembarkation area for official vehicles. He felt a little strange being hustled up the carpeted runway surrounded by goons in RPC tactical gear, but it wasn't an altogether unpleasant experience.

Inside the Arnoc tournament hall, Aspet was taken directly to a security station where he was searched, given a lecture on security measures in the presence of the Royal Personage, and required to sign the formal Intent to Occupy the Throne documents. Then it was off to the Master of the Tournament for a briefing on the rules and expectations for candidates. Finally, there was an all-too-short interval where he was allowed to familiarize himself with the equipment he'd be using and the secure network partition established for the purposes of the challenge. Very soon it was show time and the ornate curtains were drawn aside.

His opponents, including the current king, were lined up every five meters along a semicircular console with a huge four-way split screen placed out in front so the audience could see what all the candidates were typing but the participants themselves could not. Between each pair of candidates was a read-only network traffic monitor/recorder with a judge at it. Each kept a separate copy of all packets passing across the net and allowed that judge to replay any exchanges for analysis, looking for suspicious activity. The system had been fine-tuned by every challenge that went before, as something new and unanticipated occurred with every contest. Cameras, other than those belonging to officially-sanctioned and thoroughly vetted commercial media, were strictly forbidden in the audience to discourage elaborate cheating scenarios that had taken place in the past. Several highly-trained RPC agents with optical reflection detectors were stationed on a platform overlooking the crowd, watching for traces of the illegal devices.

The spectators were a seething pie wedge splayed out within line of sight of the giant display boards. With a growing population of computer geeks in the kingdom, hacking had become rather a popular pastime, even to the point of being considered a bona fide sport. The Tragacanthan Royal Challenge was the de facto World Championship of hacking on N'plork. There were many other competitions, but none with stakes this high. This one was for all the marbles: absolute (more or less) ruler of the largest and most prosperous nation on the planet. For a split second Aspet sat stunned in awe and terror at being part of something far beyond his station, but he quickly reverted to his long hours of training and focused his thoughts solely on the task at hand, shutting out all distractions. He could never forgive himself if he did anything less than his absolute best here today, no matter the outcome.

There was a bit of ceremonial hoo-hah involving the Loca Magineer and various court officials, mostly for the benefit of the crowd, that allowed the contestants a bit more opportunity to become intimate with the physical and logical layout of their workstations. At length Cromalin II waved his Scepter of Office in a blessing-like gesture and the challenge was on.

The objective of this particular challenge was a form of capture-the-flag scenario. Each contestant had an encrypted token in a randomly-chosen location on their local system known only to him. They were charged with protecting this token from the other challengers, while capturing and holding as many of the other tokens as possible. Points were awarded every time you captured an opponent's token and deducted every time your own token or one you had captured was taken by someone else. The contestant who possessed all of his opponent's tokens or, if no one had achieved that, with the highest number of total points at the end of one hour was declared the winner.

Aspet started by building some stout walls around his token. He changed the name of it, hid the properties by embedding it in a deceptively constructed shell that looked like an incidental system file, and set up reactive sensors throughout the system that would warn him if anyone got close while at the same time relocating the token automatically, giving him valuable time to take active countermeasures.

Next he ventured out into the network, looking for easy targets. He found one almost immediately. It was so blatant, in fact, that he knew it must be a trap. He could simply skirt around it, but first he crafted a little time bomb of his own and tossed it into the mix.

A little further on he found a remote process being advertised that he knew had a couple of old vulnerabilities. He pushed against the first one and nothing happened. The second, however, proved to be incompletely patched and he slipped smoothly in through the resultant hole. Knowing a conventional system search for the token was probably both pointless and dangerous, he dumped the raw directory tree with full file attributes directly from the kernel and sorted it three times: by date created, date modified, date last accessed. Most hackers were skilled enough and had the presence of mind to change all three accordingly when fabricating file metadata, but under the intense time pressure of the challenge mistakes will be made.

Aspet did some quick further refining of his sort algorithm and narrowed the pool of likely candidates down to about a dozen files. He created a new directory and tried to copy all of them there. One of the files refused to be copied. "Target acquired," he chuckled softly. Unlike all other files on the system, tokens could not be copied—only moved. He snagged it, erased his tracks, and beat a hasty retreat.

Just then an alert message popped up to advise him that an intruder was closing in on his own token. He sighed. There just wasn't time to plug all the holes, several of which he suspected had been left on the system intentionally. He slammed out a script that created a dozen encrypted decoys and shotgunned them throughout the file space. *That ought to slow him down a bit.* He kept one eye on the intruder's progress—better to let him waste time poking around fruitlessly than simply kick him out—and slid back out into the network, on the prowl for another token.

Almost immediately one, then another of his decoy tokens disappeared. Aspet chuckled. Those two would probably leave him alone now unless they discovered his deception in time to do something about it. He followed one of the data trails back to its origin, and found his counterfeit token in the same directory as the owner's genuine one. Shaking his head at the lack of defensive structure, he snagged the real token and beat a hasty retreat. Two in the bank, one to go.

The remaining token belonged to Trellior. The king had spent his time well so far, first erecting prickly defenses of his own, then building a sort of armored vehicle for invading and hijacking other candidates' tokens by brute force. Once His Majesty entered the field of combat in earnest, it didn't take him long to realize that he only had one real opponent here: Aspet. The other two had already lost their tokens to him, and the fools had even fallen for the old counterfeit token ploy. Clearly they weren't worth expending any additional effort on.

Trellior moved without any attempt at stealth onto the network and began to hammer away at Aspet's defenses as hard as he could. Aspet had expected this, given the king's predilection for direct action, and waited until his opponent was fully committed to the attack before playing his hand. He intentionally weakened his barricade at one specific point and hung back until Trellior found and exploited the hole. As soon as the king was through the opening Aspet snapped it shut and trapped the intruder in a 'jail' that appeared to be a root-level account but was actually an isolated user with no real access to system resources.

He knew Trellior wouldn't be held up long in there, but his brute force approach would actually work against him in these circumstances and prolong that time sufficiently for Aspet to do a quick search for the king's token. Knowing Trellior's style, Aspet simply looked for the most heavily defended area. It didn't take long to find it.

He circled the bastion warily, admiring the multiple layers of alternating passive and active defenses. It was beginning to dawn on him that no one, least of all a rusty coder like Trellior, could have thrown up such sophisticated barriers coding from scratch in the amount of time that had elapsed since the start of the challenge. There had to be prefab code blocks in use here, something that was strictly against the rules. At least, against the rules for everyone but the sitting monarch. The only person who could overrule him in this case was Cromalin, and the Loca Magineer would have to see concrete proof of the infraction in order legally to intervene. No, better to use the Sovereign's own duplicity against him in a more...*direct* way.

His Royal Majesty Tragacanth was peeved. The canned attack code he was deploying did not operate as expected, and as a result it was taking too long to break out of that snot-nosed little brat Asp... whatever's pathetic attempt at a trap. He pounded impatiently on his keyboard as he waited for a new process to fork and spoke quietly. "If you can hear me, Snarlox—and you'd better be able to—this tactical software you wrote is a load of rancid rok excrement. It's not properly pipelined, the processor overhead is bollocks, and the system footprint is far larger than you promised. When I get through here we're going to have a little chat about what it means to serve one's king." He smiled as he imagined his gnome accomplice sweating in the secret room above and behind him.

Snarlox was worse off than that, in fact, because he'd just come to the realization that the problems His

Majesty the Boss was experiencing were not actually his fault. Somehow, the software he'd surreptitiously stashed on Trellior's computer had been modified by parties unknown. The security had been airtight—unless—there had been someone else on the inside... no time to worry about that right now, regardless. He had to figure out some way to get his neck off the chopping block.

His audio communication with Trellior was one-way, to minimize chances of discovery by either the judges or some smartass in the audience with an RF-triggered scanner. He did have an illicit encrypted data tunnel into the king's box via a network control channel, however, although use of even that ran a certain risk of being picked up by the Arnoc traffic anomaly sensors. Part of Snarlox's job here was to serve as scapegoat if the cheating scheme was discovered; toward that end an elaborate series of fabricated clues had been planted, all of which pointed squarely at him and exonerated the king of any complicity. Snarlox himself had been conditioned to resist the standard interrogation methods employed by the Special Investigations Branch of CoME, who would be responsible for investigating any such allegations. Trellior had gone to great lengths to ensure that he did not lose this challenge.

Meanwhile, back on the playing field, Aspet was chinking away at Trellior's defenses. The king was employing a rather clever 'sandtrap' technique that filled in any gap as soon as it was opened. As he tried different approaches, Aspet began to realize that not only was the Royal strategy clever, it was darned effective, especially as a delaying tactic. Of course, Aspet could probably win the challenge now just by holding onto the tokens he already possessed, but he had a burning desire to bring Trellior to his knees for being such an utter turd. He strongly suspected that the king hadn't even written the code he was using to cheat. That was *much* less forgivable, in Aspet's eyes, than the mere act of cheating itself.

By the time Trellior managed to break free of Aspet's entanglements, he was dangerously angry. The frustration at being mired in his opponent's defenses, coupled with a perceived failure of Snarlox's (not so) Ultimate Tactical Software, was taking a heavy toll on the Royal composure. He decided an all-out assault on Aspet was in order. Instead of concentrating on searching for and capturing the other contestants' tokens, he turned to attacking the underlying operating systems themselves. Since the contestants' systems were essentially out-of-the-box non-hardened installs, taking advantage of known programming flaws was an easy way to escalate user privileges and eventually root each box. Even for a hacker with Aspet's obvious mad skills, it simply wasn't possible to sew shut every exploitable hole in the time allocated for the contest. All Trellior had to do was deploy his illegal vulnerability scanner to find a chink in the usurper's armor and punch through. Hard.

It didn't take that long. He found an exploitable remote service on Aspet's computer being advertised to the network and quickly used it to gain a shell account. Then, after a few false starts, he finally ratcheted himself up through the user hierarchy to root-level access. A few more keystrokes and the cursed usurper's system was history. As a bonus, once Aspet's computer went offline any captured tokens residing there would be automatically regenerated in their respective owners' systems, ripe for Trellior's own harvesting.

Aspet, meanwhile, had just about sorted through all the tricks His Majesty had used to protect his token when one of his own alarms went off. He switched back to his home screen and felt a strong jolt of adrenalin as he realized what Trellior was doing. He raced to find the exact location of the intruder in his system and cut him off, but he was too late. A warning popped up that said:

System shutdown imminent. Please save any files you have open immediately. Shutdown in 10 seconds.

No time to dump the process table to kill off whatever was controlling the shutdown; Trellior was probably smart enough to have several backups running to prevent this, anyway. He watched the counter click down to 7. There *must* be some way to stop him. Aspet's mind raced furiously, grasping at something just beyond reach, when a sudden calm came over him and the mental fog lifted. Seemingly in slow motion, he watched himself type

    $ wait(0) -PMA -9

The counter stopped decrementing at 2. He had overridden the shutdown with an undocumented failsafe kernel command that suspended all running processes except those associated with the current window. When he restarted the system he'd have two seconds to act. Plenty of time. He checked the process list and found the hostile PIDs.

```
$ wait(0) -R | seize -T [2347..2350] > null
```

Aspet hit the 'data submit' key and before it had returned to the fully upright position switched back to his attack window and slurped the Royal token over to his own system. Then, for the *coup de grace*, he forced Trellior's network adapter into an infinitely recursive local loop condition that escalated after a dozen or so iterations into a packet storm which brought the king's interface to a grinding halt.

From Trellior's point of view, he had initiated the shutdown of Aspet's computer and watched the countdown suddenly pause at two. It restarted after a few seconds and everything seemed to be working fine when suddenly his attack screen went blank. Switching back to the system screen, he discovered that all communications with any remote node were simply nonexistent. He was off the grid. As he stabbed frantically at the keyboard trying to understand what was going on, the bells started ringing. The Challenge for the Throne of Tragacanth was over.

Chapter Sixteen:
Dead Reckoning

Selpla and her compatriots finally reached the high ground overlooking the grotesquely swollen Molkpot River. The three of them sat in the muck breathing heavily after their narrow escape from the flood and its attendant wildlife perils. The mud wasn't just blue and sticky—it seemed almost sentient. Well, maybe not *sentient*, but at least more animated than mud was supposed to be in their experience. It was actively engaged in crawling up into their most intimate places, no matter how tightly sealed against the elements. Regardless of the discomfort, it was still better than being nibbled on by needlefish or shredded by pincer ants. There were still ants about, to be sure, but not in the concentrated mass of the floating rafts.

Selpla was the first to speak. "Well, that was fun. Guess we'd better figure out the best way to get back to the road. Without running that gauntlet again, I mean."

"Wonder how Prond is making out?" asked Lom.

"He's probably as wet as we are, but I'll bet he hasn't got quite as many, um, perforations." She was noticing the remarkable collection of holes various ravenous creatures had left in her hide. Good thing goblin skin was tough stuff. The goblin immune system was downright formidable, as well.

Drin had been scouting their position in a tight circle and suddenly made an announcement. "Road that way. We walk along ravine." He pointed down a water-swollen gulley leading off to the southwest.

Lom and Selpla looked at one another and shrugged. They sloshed off behind Drin, who led them as though he were fronting a grand parade. The path he chose down to the road wasn't exactly smooth, but it was marginally more navigable than the route up had been. When at last they stumbled onto the paved surface, it was barely recognizable under the layers of debris and displaced topsoil the flood waters had scattered across it. Now they just had to figure out which way Prond was from here.

The main highway was well maintained from Goblinopolis to Tillimil, but south of the river Tud it got a bit tetchy. It narrowed and widened sans any obvious pattern or logic, and even the quality of the paving deteriorated markedly beyond the Tudmash Marsh. There wasn't a lot of traffic between Tillimil and Dreadmost to be inconvenienced, however, which is probably why the Transport Council hadn't made road improvements along that route any sort of priority. That, and the fact that none of them lived anywhere near the place.

After some head-scratching and dead reckoning, they agreed that north along the road was the most likely route to where they'd left Prond, since the natural movement of the water that had swept them along was southeast toward the Gulf of Honkmin. Selpla was trying to take notes on their position so she could pursue the 'moving mountain' story further once they were again mobile, but the steadily streaming precipitation was making pulp of the leaves in her reporter's pad.

The ever-increasing deluge had finally convinced Prond to look for some real shelter. He scrambled a few meters up a muddy embankment and found a hole that after a little excavation provided a snug but relatively dry refuge from the flooding. As the daylight slipped slowly away with no sign of either Kurg or Selpla, he began to feel rather drowsy. The rain had slacked off to a gentle patter now, which made it all the more difficult to stay awake. Finally Prond could fight it no longer and fell into a deep, contented sleep.

Less than ten minutes later Kurg's dray chugged slowly around the bend, still sporting large outcroppings of thick blue mud on the rear wheel wells and bumper. Its noisy passing below him disturbed Prond's slumber a bit, but not enough to bring him to full consciousness as his snoring easily drowned out the rain sounds as well as those of Kurg's transit. In truth, he could have acoustically overpowered a medium-sized volcanic eruption. When he awoke half an hour later and saw tire tracks in the mud below him, Prond intuitively realized they had been left by Kurg. He scrambled down the incline and jogged off along the road in pursuit.

"Is that them?" Kurg shouted, gesturing at several figures off to one side of the road. Hnuppa shaded his eyes and strained in concentration.

"No, that's a couple of rocks."

"Those aren't smekking rocks! Are they? Oh, smek."

He trailed off as they drew nearer and the lithic nature of the figures became more apparent. Slud was making the odd honking sound they'd come to understand was his version of laughter. Kurg shot him a withering glance but otherwise ignored him. His attention was on something in the distance. He stared at whatever it was so intently that Hnuppa was worried he'd gone catatonic or something. He waved a gnarled extremity in front of his boss' face. "Kurg? You still with us, you ol' planker?"

"Quiet, smekhead. I'm tryin' to figure out what that thing is over there." He pointed to what appeared at first glance to be a distant hill. Hnuppa glanced over in the direction Kurg was pointing, but all he saw was a distinctly non-remarkable topographic feature. He shook his head and frowned at Kurg. "You take all your meds today, boss?" Kurg scowled menacingly, but did not take his eyes off the distant object. "You're gonna need more than meds if you don't shut your yap. Get your camera stuff and follow me."

"What, on foot?" Hnuppa complained. "Yes, on smekkin' foot," Kurg replied, "I'm not taking this dray off the road into that muck and risk getting it stuck again. A little rain won't melt you, or if it does, I'll see to it your smekkin' remains get flushed down a nice, tasteful loo."

"Thanks, boss. You're one smek of a great goblin."

"Don't I know it. Now get yer carcass movin.' We've got a mountain to catch!"

"Excuse me, boss. For a moment there I thought you said we've got a *mountain* to catch," Hnuppa said, shaking his head.

"That is exactly what I said, smekhead. We're following that mountain over there. I've been watching it, and it's moved a good half a mile in the last fifteen minutes."

Hnuppa stared in the indicated direction and confirmed that there was, indeed, a large topographic feature that was apparently ambulatory.

"OK, it's a moving mountain. Curious geologically, perhaps, but is it really front page stuff? I mean, after all is said and done, it's still just a pile of dirt and rocks."

"I don't give a damp smek about the mountain itself, smekhead. The thing is traveling far too fast to be a natural phenomenon. It takes a very powerful mage to cast a translocate spell to move something that big, and *he's* the story I'm after. Why is a mage of that caliber out here in the boonies? What purpose does the moving mountain serve? It has all the makings of a great goblin-interest story."

"Did it occur to you that a mage who goes around moving mountains might be a tad nutso and therefore sort of dangerous to approach?"

"Danger is part of this job, smekker. You knew that when you signed on."

"This isn't another one of your 'imaginary

infantry platoon leader' flashbacks, is it?"

"There's nothing imaginary about them! I *was* a platoon leader in the infantry, you smekhead."

"Yeah, at a supply depot outside Lumbos. The only danger you ever faced was in the chow line."

"That's more than you've ever had to worry about in your pampered life, smekhead, but you keep yakkin' and that's gonna change."

A ridiculously loud clap of thunder drowned out whatever response Hnuppa made to this challenge and changed the focus of the conversation dramatically. Actually, it wasn't the thunder that mattered so much as the associated lightning strike. It split a nearby gonsap tree neatly in twain, the larger fragment of which fell directly in the path of their dray, rendering any further vehicular progress in that direction problematic at best. Slud let out a sound like the air brakes on a large cargo transport and twisted around to stare accusingly at Kurg, who pointedly ignored him and clapped his hands.

"Isn't this great, kiddies? Now we *all* get to go on a hike. Don't forget your knapsacks and juice boxes."

"To say that 'you suck' would demean vacuums everywhere," Hnuppa mumbled.

Prond saw a lightning strike in the distance ahead of him and dove instinctively under a scraggly bush jutting at an odd angle from a nearby overhang.

The rain, which had slacked off considerably over the past hour or so, began again in earnest, pouring over him in great, drenching sheets. He resumed his slogging trek along the highway, now nearly obliterated by water, mud, and debris. If this was a typical weather pattern for the area, he reasoned, it wasn't difficult to see why the southlands were so sparsely populated. You'd need to be part amphibian to enjoy living here.

There wasn't much for it but to keep to his course. The rain apparently felt right at home here and intended to kick back and make itself comfortable. Prond figured he might as well get used to it. The first adaptation he made to his new semi-aquatic habitat, other than working out how to slosh more efficiently, was learning not to glance up in alarm every time thunder boomed out across the sodden landscape. Water was falling with such intensity that his custom of gaping at loud noises actually threatened to get him drowned.

He trudged about a kilometer in silence, slanting his head forward to allow supraorbital ridges to divert the flow of water away from his eyes. As a navigational technique, however, this left a little too much to the imagination and he continually careened into rocks, ledges, trees, and the occasional foraging hearth bear, which while potentially quite vicious were easily outmaneuvered as they were neither agile nor particularly aggressive. Especially when soaking wet and wading.

Prond stopped to rest in the mouth of a rather

dark cave under a rock overhang mostly obstructed by a dense tangle of vegetation. He found this refuge by literally blundering into it; otherwise it would most likely have escaped his attention entirely. He was grateful for the accidental discovery, as the constant drumming of raindrops on the external secondary tympanic membranes above his auditory canals was beginning to give him a headache.

As he sat there on a boulder waiting for his head to stop throbbing in rhythm with the rainfall, Prond noticed something rather odd about his chosen resting place. Bruised and broken plant parts were sticking out from under the rock flooring as though the entire cave had recently been plopped down on them from somewhere else. He contemplated the botanical devastation for some time, but couldn't make any sense of what he was seeing.

A sudden movement off to his right caused Prond to turn his head just in time to get beaned right above the eyes by a flat rock dislodged from somewhere in the darkness above the cave entrance. His vision blurred and he stood there cradling his pounding, bleeding cranium when more rocks came careening down around him. His free hand groped the rock wall for some anchorage as the floor began to shift and heave beneath him. He turned to run out of the suddenly treacherous cave but ran smack into a granite slab that seconds ago had been the floor of the entryway but now tilted up at a crazy angle, blocking the cave entrance and trapping him inside.

The barrage continued. Prond's only escape route

seemed to lead deeper into the cavern, although his common sense was screaming at him that this just *couldn't* be a good idea. Still, a rapid examination of the tactical situation convinced him to explain to his common sense that, while it was welcome to hang about and take its chances here, the rest of him was evacuating the landslide zone posthaste in whatever direction was available for that purpose. He scrambled over the increasingly obstacle-strewn floor, looking for a place not actively engaged in trying to flatten him.

Prond finally found a refuge of sorts deep in the bowels of the cavern. The occasional rumble still resounded off the stone walls, but actual rocks being heaved in his direction had diminished dramatically. As his eyes adjusted to the subterranean gloom, he began to realize that this was more than just a featureless hollow in the heart of the mountain. It was a complex arrangement of balconies, grottoes, blind corners, overhangs, and fantastic rock formations that stretched far up into the overarching darkness. A few places were faintly backlit, suggesting that someone or something might possibly live here. Prond scratched his head and contemplated what an extraordinary way of life that must be, residing deep underground with bits of the ceiling constantly falling around you. Headache medicine and a stout helmet would seem to be basic necessities.

He wandered aimlessly among the stalagmites and shimmering translucent curtains of crystal, marveling at their intricate beauty and wondering how they escaped being destroyed by the constant motion of their surroundings. Funny thing, though, is that in here the movement didn't seem nearly so pronounced as it had on the periphery. In fact, he didn't really notice it at all anymore. No stones had tried to meld with his head lately, either. He was puzzling over the curious kinetics of the mountain when he rounded a corner and came face to face with...the stairway to Paradise.

It was, in a word, magnificent: wide as a city street, helical, bannisters and steps carved from the very living rock with geometric precision by obsessive deep gnomes and slavishly polished to a high luster. It sparkled and glinted as though inhabited by its own animate light source. Prond stood there awestruck for a longish while, unwilling to break the spell cast by the unexpected architectural spectacle. Finally he approached the lowest tread almost in reverence and padded gingerly onto it. There was a marvelous, undecipherable quality to the experience—like stepping on an exquisitely resonant chime made of frozen clouds.

Prond followed the winding wonderway up and up into the stalactite-studded highlands, until he came at last to a grandiose balcony that circumscribed the entirety of the cavern. From this lofty vantage he could see many additional and even more astounding structures than were visible at the lower level. He wondered how such a fantastic subterranean palace as this could have remained totally unknown to the citizens of Tragacanth. "It's the best-kept secret in the country," he said out loud, shaking his head in amazement.

"And I'd deeply appreciate it if things remained that way," said a crackly voice behind him. Prond spun around to see a fuzzy little creature standing there he recognized after a few seconds as a bugbear. Hadn't seen many of those before. They regarded each other for a long moment. Prond finally broke the silence. "Did you build all this?"

"I was...responsible for the construction," the bugbear replied, "Although I didn't perform all of it personally."

"Wow," said Prond, simply. "Wow. This place is utterly amazing. Do all bugbears live like this?" He didn't mean it in any racist way; just trying to expand his cultural horizons.

The bugbear didn't seem offended. "Many of my kind do choose to live underground, but none, to my knowledge, have taken quite the same interest in...interior design as myself."

A light snapped on in his head and Prond suddenly realized his awkward social position.

"So sorry. My name is Prond. I apologize for trespassing. I ducked into what I thought was a shallow cave to avoid drowning in the deluge out there and sort of got herded further into the mountain than I intended to go."

His host noticed the falling rock contusions on Prond's head and shoulders and shrugged. "Yes, well, no permanent harm done, I suppose. The mountain does tend to be rather selective about whom it allows in this far. You must have impressed it in some way."

Prond raised his eyebrows. "The *mountain* is selective? Are you implying that this huge pile of rocks is somehow alive and aware?"

"Of course. The entire mountain has an active twelfth level sentience spell and geas on it. It took me over two years to cast."

Prond's jaw dropped. "*You* cast a permanent archmagical dweomer on this place? Who *are* you?"

"My name," the bugbear replied somewhat hesitantly, "is Ballop'ril."

Chapter Seventeen:
Answering the Call

Selpla and her companions sloshed north along the road. They were heading slightly uphill most of the time, which meant opposing the seemingly infinite volume of precipitation making its way down to the lowlands behind them. Progress was slow and taxing. The rain rose and fell in irregular rhythm, but never stopped entirely. None of them had ever seen this much water before that wasn't actually in the sea.

"Think it'll ever stop raining?" asked Lom, glumly.

"Not until spell is done."

They both looked at Drin. Selpla shouted over the noise of a fresh surge of precipitation. "What 'spell' are you talking about?"

"The spell that brought the rains. Is not natural rainfall. Magic aura very strong."

Lom rolled his eyes. "That's ridiculous. There can't have been more than a handful of mages in Tragacanthan history who could cast a spell of this magnitude. The power requirements alone are staggering, not to mention the amount of personal energy and concentration necessary. There's not a goblin alive today with that much dweomer."

"Not goblin spell."

"Whatta ya mean, 'not goblin?' Who else could possibly cast something like this? The arcanelementals have been extinct for millennia."

"Goblins are not the only users of magic on N'plork."

"I don't suppose you intend to elaborate further?"

They plodded along in silence for a few seconds.

"Cryptic, as always," Lom remarked, shaking his head.

Just then Selpla spotted something in the distance ahead of them. It looked like a large tree fallen across the road. They approached it. The crown of the tree was smoking slightly. She walked over to the smoldering lumber and inspected it, the ever-present rain trickling down her face.

"Lightning."

Lom had drifted to the opposite side of the road. "Hey, come take a look at this," he suddenly yelled to the others. They trudged obediently to his side and followed his pointing finger. He seemed to be indicating a nondescript pile of rocks. They regarded the manifestation for a long while until Drin expressed what he and Selpla were thinking.

"Rocks."

Lom raised his eyebrows with an audible squeak. "Yes, they're rocks. But notice something odd about them. They're the only rocks anywhere around here. The nearest mountain is too far away for them to have fallen down its slopes. Also, they are broken and scattered, as though they were dropped from a meter or two onto this spot."

Selpla surveyed the scene. "Yes," she agreed, "That is how it appears. The question would be, 'where did they drop *from?*'"

There didn't seem to be any reasonable solution to the conundrum until Drin pointed out a series of wide, deep gouges all leading away in the same direction. Selpla immediately seized on the discovery, dropping the current puzzle in favor of a far more intriguing one. "My moving mountain!" she exclaimed, "On the trail, trackbeasts!" and scrambled off along the gouge lines that disappeared over a nearby ridge.

Drin and Lom looked at one another, and then at Selpla, who was rapidly diminishing over the horizon.

"Something not right about Selpla," Drin said, as they started off after her.

Lom nodded in violent agreement. "I keep sayin' that, but no one listens. Trackbeasts. Sheesh."

Selpla's news instincts were seldom wrong, and her stick-to-itiveness once she was hot on an investigative trail was much less than half a tad below frightening. Lom and Drin had to break into a full run to catch up with her as she jogged along in pursuit of the montane migrant. The spoor it left did not require a skilled tracker to follow.

"Selpla," Lom asked as he and Drin jogged along beside her, "have you ever stopped to consider what, exactly, could motivate a mountain to take up a nomadic existence?"

"No, I haven't given it a lot of thought. I figure when we catch the thing we'll just ask it."

"That's a Selpla plan if ever I've heard one," Lom mumbled as he dropped back a bit. Drin looked at him quizzically but made no remark. The terrain was getting pretty rough by this time, and their focus was increasingly on minimizing the skeletal trauma that too often accompanied Selpla's pursuits of journalistic excellence.

You'd think a moving mountain would be fairly easy to catch, but all three of the intrepid newshounds were puffing hard with the effort after half an hour, with no bagged quarry to show for it. The trail had been crystal clear, but there was no sign of the mountain itself. They stopped to rest on a ridge that stuck up rather incongruously from an otherwise gentle upslope. Lom immediately found a semi-comfortable bank of ferns to lean against and proceeded to take one of his famous instant naps. Selpa stood on the highest point of the ridge and scanned the horizon for her fugitive topography. After a few minutes she seemed to experience an epiphany. "This way!" she shouted as she ran towards the nearest foothill.

Drin shook Lom awake. He struggled to his feet and together they scrambled after her. The route she had chosen became more and more strewn with increasingly larger boulders as it wound its way up the shoulder of a hill that was much steeper in the climbing than it had appeared on the approach. The boys stumbled and cursed whilst negotiating the tricky footpath, never really seeming to gain any ground on Selpla, when suddenly they rounded a corner and narrowly avoided colliding with her. She was standing motionless and staring open-mouthed at nothing at all.

Drin and Lom took up positions on either side of their feckless leader and gazed out at whatever was holding her in its rapt embrace. Lom was about to make a snide remark about her newfound fascination with hallucinations when all at once the bottom fell out of his brain: where a moment before there had been a rugged, rock-strewn hillside there now swirled a phantasmagoric fractal maelstrom, replete with darting crystalline insectoids and chromatic milk globule explosions. Lom and Selpla were utterly transfixed by the show. Drin started salivating. It began without warning to hail. The only shelter they could see was a rock overhang up a steep path that most certainly hadn't been there before the hail began. Selpla shrugged and started up, wincing from the bruises that were forming where the hard ice pellets traumatized even her tough goblin skin. Any port at all was welcome in this storm.

"It would appear," remarked Ballop'ril to his guest while staring intently at a glimmering bubble of magical televescence hovering between them, "That we have more visitors on the lower terrace." Prond had a look. "Ah, I was wondering where they'd got to."

Prond would have been considerably more

skeptical when Ballop'ril introduced himself had he not personally witnessed the moving mountain at very close terms. It was hard to argue with a calling card of that magnitude. Prond had heard of Ballop'ril, of course, but a cursory mental calculation put his age well beyond the normal goblin lifespan. He didn't know very much about bugbears, though. He decided it was both prudent and sensible simply to take Ballop'ril's word for his identity. He was evidently a powerful mage, whoever he was, and that in itself was a strong argument for maintaining an amiable relationship.

His host seemed pleased at Prond's unquestioning acceptance and offered to conduct a personal tour of his fantastic lodgings. (He had dropped the provincial dialect he habitually employed on the 'outside' to keep strangers from guessing his identity.) Prond nodded in silent assent and they set off. The entire mountain was riddled with chambers and catacombs, each more spectacularly appointed than the last. They wandered for hours among the grottoes of towering crystal, precious metals, and multihued magical luminescence. They passed through an endless array of breathtakingly splendid magnificence, punctuated occasionally by glimpses of more utilitarian spaces where the actual work of running the vast complex got done.

They stopped at last in a lavishly appointed library. Prond had no idea that many books existed on the whole of N'plork, much less in one room, enormous though it admittedly was. At the center of the expanse was a crystal globe, larger than a goblin, which glowed with an intense blue radiance. Ballop'ril invited his guest to peruse to his heart's content while he excused himself to attend to some pressing duty. Prond wandered in an overwhelmed daze amongst the hundreds of shelves that stretched up into the darkness of the arched cavern ceiling. Massive ladders that moved effortlessly on their tracks with a light touch were positioned every few meters for access even to the topmost tomes.

After an incalculable period of aimless browsing, Prond caught sight of an oversized volume far above on an upper shelf that seemed to pulse as would a beacon, beckoning him. He was a bit afraid of heights, but swallowed his fear and scaled the multitudinous rungs in pursuit of the object of his temptation.

The grail of his quest was a book with *Theoretical Magic: The Way of Mastery* embossed in cracked gold along an age-stiffened spine. It was musty and dusty and in all ways lived up to the stereotype of the forgotten tome of arcane lore. Prond carried it carefully back to one of the elaborately carved reading tables and opened it gently, half afraid it might disintegrate in his hand so ancient did it appear. It fell open to a passage about a third of the way through the fourth bound signature. He settled back in the padded leather chair and began to read.

Goblins developed what we commonly refer to as senses as a result of slow adaptation to their environment. Over the long history of life on N'plork, the demands of the physical environment allowed those creatures that could detect and respond appropriately to the constantly-changing conditions surrounding them to breed more successfully; with each successive generation these senses were honed until no reproductive advantage was to be gained from further increase.

As we have discovered throughout our intellectual history, there are many forces and phenomena present in the holoverse that we are unable to perceive without some form of interface to translate extrasensory information into stimuli that fall within our range of sensation.

Sight, sound, taste, smell, touch, spark, and the less common senses all evolved in response to survival pressures. We see the colors we see because of the nature of sunlight. We hear what we hear because of the range of frequencies generated by events that affected our survival and reproduction. We smell, taste, and spark in response to other natural stimuli, the processing of which enhanced our survival. Our sense of touch and the related 'subsenses' such as proprioception, balance, and visual echolocation are necessary to move through the environment, avoid danger, and gather resources.

'Magic' is a widely-used and for the most part poorly-defined term. Many different meanings have been assigned to the word, some of them with little regard for what I will call 'etymological fidelity.' While there are many manifestations of both the subjective mind and objective nature that have been referred to as 'magical,' I do not refute these *events, nor do I begrudge any for applying the term 'magical' to them. For my purposes, however, 'magic' will refer to the comprehension and controlled use of forces not ordinarily perceived by the unindoctrinated sentient. Perception is fundamental to the mage; one cannot control forces one cannot envision. Comprehension is next. Again, the mage must understand the forces the mage purports to control. The last and perhaps most difficult stage in the development of a mage is Direction. Not all mages are able or desire to advance to the level where they are capable of directing the flow of magic. Contrary to popular belief, in fact, relatively few mages choose this path. It is arduous and can lead to great danger for the mage, for Directing is a task that requires absolute concentration and total dedication. Anything less can be catastrophic, as some of the forces of magic are highly volatile and possess tremendous kinetic energy. Many of the greatest mages have chosen not to embrace the discipline of Directive magic, but this has not diminished their greatness.*

I have read of sentients who claim to call forth magical powers by using symbols, objects, and spoken incantations as substitutive Directors. I have no firsthand knowledge of such things, but I can say that this would be a very dangerous and rather ineffective method for exploiting the forces of which I speak. To call forth magical energy by any other means than straightforward Direction is a haphazard process and the results are left largely to the whim of

Chaos, of which we will now speak at length.

Chaos is a wholly integral part of the holoverse, one of the pillars upon which the fabric of reality rests, but it is in many significant ways an enemy of the Directive mage. Entropic balance requires that any increase in orderliness, such as that resulting from an act of Directed magic, be accompanied by a concomitant increase in disorder at some other locus of the holoverse. In the vocabulary of the mage, this offsetting chaos is called the backflux. In symbolic terms, then,

$$(\lor) + (\land) \mathrel{|>} (o\text{-}o)$$

where $(\lor)$ represents an act of Directive magic, $(\land)$ represents the equivalent backflux, and $(o\text{-}o)$ represents the entropically balanced holoverse. The symbol $\mathrel{|>}$ represents 'leads to' or 'results in.' Positive entropic imbalance, such as exists in the short time between an act of Directive magic and the balancing of that act by a backflux, is denoted by $(o\text{-}o)+$. Negative entropic balance, symbolized by $(o\text{-}o)-$, can exist only in a local context, but never in the forward flow of space-time, called by mages the ventroverse. Entropy is always increasing in the ventroverse except during the periodic nodal events called flux singularities, where the total mass of the holoverse returns to the primordial energy state and entropy is reset. The last of these nodal events is referred to by modern cosmologists as the 'Big Bang;' the next will occur when the total entropic load of the ventroverse reaches the level necessary to penetrate the temperospatial envelope in which the holoverse is contained (as symbolized by o))). When this barrier is breached, the positive and negative entropic components will cancel each other and a new envelope will be created in the first nanoseconds of the next cycle.

On Perception

The Goblin sensory apparatus is capable of a surprisingly broad range of signal reception and processing. The demands of survival, mating, and offspring-rearing (which are the driving forces for evolution) place particular emphasis on the range of signals we have come to think of as normal, yet these represent in truth only a subset of the total information that can be processed by our species. Evolution has, in effect, developed filters to enable us to shut out signals not immediately concerned with tasks of genetic continuity. Many phenomena go largely or even completely unnoticed until we have reason to pay attention to them.

Magic is one these phenomena, or more accurately, the effects of magic. Like wind, magic itself is invisible. The energies that constitute magic cannot be seen by normal eyes. Unlike things affected by wind, however, the manifestations of chaotic magic are most often themselves imperceptible because they operate along a different temperospatial axis from the one with which we are natively familiar. The very nature of magical events dictates that they seem to the unknowing observer to manifest themselves from *nothing; this could not be further from the truth. Magic flows along a conduit wrought by the mage from normal space-time to a vast extradimensional energy reservoir known as the Dark Energetic Continuum, or, colloquially, The Slice.*

At this point his studies were interrupted by the return of Ballop'ril. The old bugbear was both surprised and pleased that Prond had chosen this particular treatise with which to entertain himself. "This is a very old book," he said, reading over Prond's shoulder, "and one that I haven't seen for many years. Wherever did you find it?"

Prond pointed over his left shoulder. "Way up near the top over that way."

"How did you know it was there?"

"Not sure; it sort of called to me."

The mage twiggled his eyebrows. "Did it? Interesting."

Ballop'ril and Prond spent the rest of the day strolling the caverns, deep in conversation. Prond didn't consider himself any sort of intellectual, nor had he ever expended any real mental effort thinking about magic, but everything that Ballop'ril said made so much sense to him. Their brief relationship had opened up a whole world Prond had only dimly been aware existed. At the end of the evening Ballop'ril showed him to opulent guest quarters and, at the doorway, asked him a simple question that would have sounded utterly alien to Prond a scant few days ago but now seemed perfectly natural and reasonable.

"Young master Prond, you have proven a most pleasant and, more importantly, intelligent companion. Your mind is like a sponge, with a potential capacity for learning magical arts I've rarely encountered. With time and training you could quite plausibly take your place among the great mages of Tragacanthan history. Will you stay with me and be my apprentice?"

Prond's eye slits dilated to their maximum extent (something like overstuffed sausage casings) and he suddenly had trouble breathing. He tried to speak, but his host held up a finger. "A momentous decision, I realize, and not one to be taken on the spur of the moment. Sleep on it, and we will resume this discussion by the cheery light of morning, over a hearty breakfast. Good night."

With that he turned and strode down the hallway.

Prond stood there in stunned silence for a longish while, unable to remember how to walk. He finally allowed instinct to propel him forward in an awkward, no-knees manner toward what he assumed must be the bed, although from this vantage it more closely resembled the raised foundation for a new luxury housing project. A foundation swathed in costly velvet and fine linens, with a surprising array of overstuffed pillows. He half sat, half fell on the nearest edge and curled up in the goblin fetal position (which resembles a fossil imprint of an animal trampled by a much larger animal fleeing from something hideously brutal and ravenously hungry).

He lay awake for a few minutes, but the luxuriousness of the bed combined with his mental and physical exhaustion soon lulled Prond into deep slumber. It was anything but restful, however. He dreamed a dream of flying, being chased by dragons and four-winged demons. He dove and swerved through trees and spires of rock, but always the hot reptilian breath seared his eyes and nose. At last he swooped into a narrow cave his pursuers could not enter. It started as a vertical fissure barely wide enough to admit him, but soon opened out into a broad boulevard lined with soldiers in full dress uniform who saluted as he sailed past. At the end of the avenue was an elaborate dais, decorated with golden ribbons and a multitude of precious stones. On it stood a magnificent throne of the finest hardwoods, intricately carved with scenes from the long history of Tragacanth. Seated in the throne was a young monarch in rich robes, looking slightly ill at ease.

The king waited until Prond had landed at his feet, and then gestured toward him. The sovereign presented him silently with a staff encrusted with jewels, the gold-cast figure of an animal Prond had never seen before attached as a finial. The creature was powerfully built with four large paws. The ears were triangular and tilted forward. From the nape of the neck sprouted a generous tuft of hair that spread out around the head and upper body like a halo. The entire body of the beast seemed to be covered in short, thick hair, in fact. It was odd, but irrefutably majestic.

The dream ended abruptly when Prond awoke

wrapped so tightly in the silk blankets he could scarcely breathe. He struggled out of his cocoon, confused and disoriented, until awareness slowly trickled back. Eventually the stark vividness of the dream began to fade, but its images remained strongly fixed in his mind. For the rest of the night he relived the mystical experience over and over, pondering its significance. He was not prone to vivid dreams; the vast majority of his oneiric adventures evaporated before he made it to the bathroom in the morning.

By the time a complex series of mirrors set in shafts leading to the surface directed the first rays of dawn dancing through the glass skylights set into the roof of his bedroom, Prond was in a peculiarly conflicted state of mind. The surrealistic dream had temporarily driven Ballop'ril's proposal just below the surface of his consciousness and now, with the onset of the new day, it bubbled back up to take over his thoughts once again. The simple truth was that he still had no idea whether or not to accept the bugbear's offer. He could not help but feel that the Archmage had somehow confused him for someone else.

They took breakfast on a stone platform high above a wondrous grotto with many waterfalls and colorful rock formations, including stalagmites, stalactites, curtains, and glittering crystalline flows. Flitting to and fro throughout were magical blue, green, and yellow butterflies that left trails of glowing rose-colored sparks as they flew. Ballop'ril seemed in no hurry to reopen the subject of apprenticeship, and Prond was grateful for that.

Chapter Eighteen:
Astflanar

Three weeks after his coronation Aspet was finally beginning to settle in as king of Tragacanth. The ceremony itself was nothing short of overwhelming; he was glad that pretty much all he had to do was memorize his lines and stand on his marks. The presentation of the royal symbols, the swearing of fealty by officers of the court and high national officials, the investiture of lands, property, titles, and legal authority—each of these activities blended into the next in his recollection a fortnight and a half later. It was overload: an adrenalin-inducing blur.

The vicissitudes of running a kingdom as complex as Tragacanth were now Aspet's chief concern. He had to decide whether to keep the previous monarch's advisors or appoint his own, for starters. Some of the decisions were made for him when the incumbent advisors took the opportunity of a change in leadership to retire. His economic advisor, for example, was perhaps the leading economist of the day; Aspet didn't want to lose her and in fact offered her a raise in salary to stay on, which she gracefully accepted.

His most problematic cabinet position was that

of Magineer Liaison. This was the chief magical official of the administration and the primary means by which kings communicated with the Magineers, who operated quasi-independently of the royal government. Aspet suspected the current Liaison to have been involved in what he had good reason to believe was an attempt to cheat him out of the crown during the Challenge. Boogla had, in fact, provided him with clear and compelling evidence of this transgression his first day in office.

The ML didn't have to be a great mage himself, but he did need to have a strong command of the terminology and theory of both magic and technology in order to be able to interact effectively with the Magineers and their staffs. The Royal Transition Team had provided him with a list of Civil Servant Corps officers with adequate magical training, but Aspet wasn't enchanted by any of them. He paced along the parapets of the Royal Residence overlooking Goblinopolis and pondered the situation.

As he took in the dramatic sweep of the villas and inns crowding each bank of the wide, rolling green Mernal River that skirted the northern edge of the city, a tiny seedling of an idea took root and began inexorably to push its way up into the light. Aspet stopped and stared off into the distance, transfixed by this mental gestation. After a few seconds he blinked and a slow grin spread across his face. He turned abruptly on his heel and strode back to his office with renewed purpose and a sense of mission.

Having a good idea is one thing, making it a

reality quite another. He knew without the merest sliver of a doubt who he wanted for the ML position, but he didn't have any solid idea exactly how to move ahead with the recruiting process. For one thing, he and the candidate had never met face-to-face. For another, he had no idea at all where she resided, how old she actually was, or anything else about her, if indeed she was even truly a *her*. All he knew was that his gut told him she was the right person for the job.

To: boogla!boogla!boo
From: aspet!Palace!Royal!Tragacanth
Subject: Employment Offer

I need someone implicitly trustworthy and devastatingly intelligent to act as liaison between the crown and the magineers. Someone who has a great aptitude for technology, magic, and the interaction between the two.

The pay is pretty good, as are the benefits.

Interested?

A.

He didn't expect an immediate reply, of course. He wasn't sure if he'd get a reply at all, to be honest. He'd barely leaned back in his Alpha Humphing Beast leather chair with the Royal Seal of Tragacanth gold-embossed on the back when the reply popped up, nearly knocking him out of it:

From: boogla!boogla!boo
To: aspet!Palace!Royal!Tragacanth
Subject: RE: employment Offer

I'm all over it, Your Majesty. Where we can meet? I'm not very keen on public appearances. Someplace private and out of the way, perhaps?

B

Aspet pushed his chair away from the desk and stared at the screen for a long moment. He was so surprised that Boogla had accepted his offer, and so quickly, that his chain of thought was momentarily disrupted. Finally he overcame the shock and responded. They arranged to meet in a secluded Royal retreat known as Hikklew situated in the Bungash Mountains southeast of Port Zog. His Majesty Tragacanth found himself nervous and a little giddy at the prospect of meeting the legendary Boogla, even though he'd come to regard her as something of a friend over the past few months.

Boogla turned out to be younger than Aspet had expected, and also quite attractive. She had an aura of wisdom that belied her tender years, however, and an unmistakable current of powerful energy running just beneath the placid surface of her charming smile. He knew instinctively and immediately that she would be one very powerful ally if treated with the respect she was due. He had every intention of making sure that was the case.

Their first meeting was a little awkward for him, but he remembered halfway through that he was king and that helped a bit. Boogla seemed extraordinarily politically astute in addition to her obvious elite technical skills. Aspet was already beginning to think she would make a better monarch than he. When he told her so, she laughed out loud for a full ten seconds, and then chuckled for a while longer while she wiped the tears from her eyes. Aspet was a little offended. She noticed this and regained her composure. "I am flattered, really, but being king, even if it was possible for one of my gender and lineage, is not the sort of life I would wish to lead."

Aspet thought for a moment. "You are a wise woman; this I already knew. You have the life you want, and you got it entirely through your own skills, on your own terms. Why, indeed, would someone like that want to change anything at all? I am gratified beyond words that you chose to take on this high office. I believe Tragacanth will benefit immeasurably from it."

Boogla's first assignment was to meet with the Magineers and form working relationships with them. This was a tall order, and Aspet was curious how well she would do at it. Being an expert hacker did not qualify you as a diplomat, as had been pointed out to him rather strongly by his other advisors, but Aspet had a feeling that there wasn't much Boogla couldn't handle. She simply oozed confidence and competence (and a few other things, as well, but that came with being a goblin).

The Magineers seldom left their Dubers for a number of reasons, not least of which being that they were forbidden to travel out of their districts, so Boogla would have to travel to them. As an officer of the Royal Cabinet she was required to be transported in a Royal carriage or dray with an RPC escort detail at all times. She found this annoying and at first refused, but Aspet explained to her that it was for her own safety and the responsible thing to do, so she finally acquiesced. He allowed her at least to hand pick her security detail.

Stop number one was originally scheduled to be Tillimil, but the weather was reportedly quite inclement down there at present, so she diverted to Ferroc Oria, in Lumbos. It was only a day's journey by barge and carriage, and that would give her an opportunity to get acclimated to her RPC entourage as well as time to study up on the Oria Magineer, Kryptoq.

Tol sat down in the mostly repaired Bloated Balrog, at the bar rather than his customary table, and ordered a razzle on draft. He had a hankerin' to chat with the barkeep. "Looks like you got most of the damage squared away," he said, after the third pull at his brew. Terp looked up from polishing a glass. "Most of it. You nab the smekheads what done it yet?"

"Nope. But I have a good idea who they are, at least."

"The little smeks will be on the obituary page if I catch 'em around here again."

"I don't think you will, unless Pyfox drops by."

"Pyfox? What's that sleazy smekker got to do with it?"

"That's who they were after."

"What? You mean they blew the smek out of my pub trying to off that waste of breathin' air? Why didn't they just plug the smekker as he was leavin'?"

"Hard to say. I get the feeling this was their first attempt at the assassination game. Not exactly a professional job, if ya get my drift. Speaking of Pyfox, what do you know about him?"

"He's a scumbag with fingers in every slime pie in Sebacea and beyond. If it's sleazy and illegal, Pyfox is involved somehow."

"Sounds like you don't care much for the guy."

"Smekkin' brilliant deduction. You oughta take the detective exam."

"How would you like to help bring Pyfox down?"

"So long as it don't get my pub blown up again, I'm in."

"All you gotta do for me is keep your ears open. I've got a hot tip that Pyfox uses the Balrog as a messenger drop. His minions meet each other here and exchange information. You probably won't see his ugly face in here anymore, because he won't be likely to appear in public again after the botched smackdown. But, his toadies will be in and out of here regularly; I'd bet solid billmes on that."

"So, you want I should spy on them. D'ya know which ones they are?"

"Here are EE sketches of two of them. There's also rumored to be a troll named Fen involved—he's

302

been sighted with Pyfox before—but you may not see him. As you know, trolls don't come into goblin-sized establishments too often because they're not very comfortable for them."

"I gotta room in the back just for trolls, actually. Built it for my dad's side of the family. Don't advertise it outside the troll community."

"I never knew that. Well then, keep an eye out for Fen, too."

It was only two days later as Tol was walking his beat near the western edge of Sebacea, where the shanties graded gradually into farmland—although like the residents, the soil here was too poor to produce much beyond weeds—that a young goblin who worked as an errand-boy for Terp and several other merchants in the neighborhood came running up to him. Tol waited while he caught his breath.

"Officer Tol-u-ol," he gasped, "I have a message for you from Master Terpitude." He handed Tol a scrap of parchment with some scratching on it:

Pyfox sending messages back and forth to Astflanar

Tol raised his eyebrows and patted the gob on the head. "Thanks, kid." The messenger made no move to leave, and Tol suddenly realized he'd forgotten something. "Here ya go, sport," he said, handing the boy a billme note. The gob left his hand extended. Tol rolled his eyes and gave him another one. "Terp's definitely rubbed off on you, kid. Don't spend it all in one place." The little goblin grinned and jogged away.

Tol made a pollenbug-line back to the Precinct. He marched straight into the duty sergeant's office.

"Gotta an extrajurisdictional assignment request, Sarge."

"We ain't got much left in the pay pot for that sort of thing. Whatta ya need it for, and where?"

"I got a hot lead on the Balrog bombing case. There's somethin' going down on Mt. Astflanar."

The grizzled old cop looked at him over his rusty optics. "That's halfway across the smekkin' country. Just write up a report; we'll let the Southron Rangers handle it."

"Come on, Sarge, this is Pyfox we're talkin' about. That smekker is mine. I ain't handin' this over to those smekkin' backcountry yahoos."

"Sorry, did I make that sound like an option? You ain't goin' mountain climbin' on the city's billme. Period. End of discussion."

"Fine. I got a smekload of use-or-lose leave to take. Put me down for a week's worth, startin' tomorrow."

"You know leave requests have to be put in at least two weeks in advance, for schedulin' purposes."

"I ain't got two weeks, Sarge. Pyfox is on the move now. Give me leave, or not. I'm out of here either way."

"You're a smekkin' hardnose, Tol."

"Have you been behind this desk so long you don't remember what it's like to be hot on the trail of a slimy smekker like Pyfox?"

He paused, and then shook his head. "No, I ain't. All right, leave approved. Don't get yourself killed, Tol. Ain't nobody else on the force willin' to take your beat."

"Don't I know it. See ya."

The next morning before the sun crept over the horizon, Tol was waiting at the carriage station, backpack stuffed to the gills. He had seriously intended to leave Eyejay behind, but at the last minute changed his mind and stuffed it in a waterproof pocket of the pack. The carriage would only take him as far as the village of Cartlug in the Espwe foothills, with a three-hour layover in Tillimil. The weather was atrocious all the way down. The leading edge of the hurrarcane had reached the south side of Goblinopolis by then, so the trip was non-stop nasty. *At least*, Tol mused as he stared nervously out the windows of the savagely swaying carriage, *I won't have to walk my beat in this muck*. He purposely avoided thinking about the fact that soon he would be walking up a mountain in it.

As it turned out, the weather actually improved once they headed west from Tillimil. By the time the first bumps of foothill hove into view, the rain had slacked off to a steady drizzle and the wind had dipped below gale force to more of a stiff breeze. Tol felt for the reassuring bulge of his disruptor and the ten clips he'd brought with it. He had no real idea what to expect from this mission, but he was reasonably certain a little firepower would come in handy at some point.

The carriage passed through a short, but very dark, tunnel about twenty minutes out from Cartlug. When the lights came back up, Tol noticed a note pinned to the seatback in front of him. Odd. He was sure he would have noticed it if it had been there before, but he was equally certain no one could have squeezed by him during the blackout. It had two words written on it in neat block letters: DINING CAR.

The dining car wasn't open, though. The run from Tillimil to Cartlug was too short to have meal service. Tol shrugged and headed back, anyway. There was obviously something interesting waiting there for him, and a cop can't afford to pass up any opportunity to gather intelligence on a case. Fortunately, or maybe not, the car just in front of the dining car was totally empty. He drew his weapon and slid open the door.

At first glance the dining car appeared uninhabited. After scanning it for a few seconds, Tol spotted a single white-haired occupant seated at a table on the far end of the car. He holstered his weapon and sat down across from him.

"Hallo, Oloi. What brings you to a carriage heading for nowhere?"

"On the contrary, Tol-u-ol. You're headed for quite a fascinating destination. Pyfox has established an elaborate organization, the nexus of which is located in an ancient temple deep in the bowels of Mount Astflanar."

"Funny, I never pictured Pyfox as the big-time crime boss sort. He always struck me as a small change racketeer."

"He is. The brain behind this outfit, as you might say, is not Pyfox at all, but a much more dangerous entity known as Namni."

"Who or what the smek is Namni?"

"Namni is a transcendent mage: one that has crossed over from the physical plane and now exists primarily in The Slice itself."

"A lot like you, eh?"

"Astute of you, Tol-u-ol. Exactly like me, in fact. Namni and I were once brothers on the High Mage's Council in another dimension. Exactly like me, except that I have no wish to rule your world, or any other."

"This Namni character wants to rule the world, huh? Imagine that. What megalomaniac doesn't? What's his scheme?"

"He has convinced the fool Pyfox that he can make him immortal."

"Can he?"

"In a manner of speaking, yes. An 'image' of any creature can be taken by magic and stored in The Slice, to be used to construct an exact duplicate of that creature once it has passed from life. This process may be repeated as many times as desired, thus effectively rendering the subject immortal. There is a catch, however. The reconstructed creature will have no memories, knowledge, or skills garnered in the previous life. These must be relearned each time."

"Does Pyfox get that?"

"Namni has convinced him that he alone has developed a philter that will restore Pyfox to his full state each time."

"And I suppose that's malarkey?"

"Not entirely. Namni really is a very accomplished magic practitioner. I believe he has, in fact, developed such a talisman, but with one subtle difference. Pyfox will be largely identical during each reincarnation except that he will be entirely and utterly obedient to Namni. He will never realize he is being controlled; his thoughts will seem to be his own. But they will be the thoughts of Namni and Namni alone. Pyfox will be nothing more than Namni's automaton on the physical plane. The plan is that he will come eventually to rule not only Tragacanth, but all of N'plork with an iron glove— and the hand inside that glove will be Namni's. Oh, and one further incidental detail Pyfox is not aware of: reconstructs are sterile."

"Heh. That one won't be much of an issue, if you get my drift."

"Not given Pyfox's current lifestyle, no. But if he ascends to a position of power he may find it something of a drawback, as having children to whom to apportion resources can be of great advantage in ruling large, dispersed populations."

"That's not going to happen, not in Tragacanth, at least."

"That will be largely up to you Tol-u-ol."

"Why do you keep saying that? You make it sound like I'm some kind of savior or something. I'm just a simple city cop looking to bring down a lowlife."

"You misunderstand. This is not about you or your accomplishments or your intrinsic virtue.

You have been chosen by forces outside anyone's control, for reasons that no one can comprehend. You may only choose to participate or not. Even if you consciously choose not, you will still play some part."

"How about I ignore the 'chosen' thing altogether and just do my job?"

"That is probably why you were chosen. Best of fortune to you, Tol-u-ol."

"Hey wait, I gotta question for you, oh Archmage. What exactly is an alfar, and why would one be following me around?"

"Alfars are creatures of pure magic, native to The Slice and in service to the magical essence that constitutes it. One of them has been assigned, if you will, to be your protector where magical forces are concerned. This is another example of the significance of your role in this attack on The Slice."

"Assigned? Assigned by who?"

"To paraphrase a great sage from my own planet, there are more things in the universe, Tol-u-ol, than are dreamt of in your philosophy."

"What does that mean?"

"It means the alfar works for a boss beyond your, or even my, ability to comprehend fully."

"I'll have to take your word for that. What is this attack on The Slice I keep hearing about?"

"Namni, through Pyfox, is attempting to sever all connection between The Slice and the physical plane except through a portal controlled by him alone. This will effectively give him total dominion over the use of magic on N'plork. It will also grant him almost unlimited magical essence—manna—with which to carry out his evil schemes of domination."

"That would put a major bump in the road, all right. I'm still not convinced there's much I can do to stop a racket of that magnitude, but I'll give it my best shot."

"No one can ask more of you. Farewell, for now."

The carriage pulled into Cartlug station a few minutes later and a couple hours after that Tol parked his rented off-road pram next to an impressive darshu tree with a canopy that seemed to cover enough area for a sporting arena. He shouldered his pack, adjusted his weapon holster, and started off along the rock-strewn trail that wound its meandering way up and around the tallest peak in Tragacanth.

Mount Astflanar was a long-extinct volcano embedded in a tremendous limestone upwelling in the Espwe mountain range that ran from the Gulf of Wollu in the extreme southeast all the way to the arid region of Asga Teslu. It was the tallest peak on the continent of Esmia, upon which Tragacanth was the largest nation of five. The lower elevations were covered in lush vegetation and a popular destination for hikers, sportsmen, and nature-lovers. Above 3,000 meters or so, though, the going got decidedly tougher and the summertime crowds thinned out to only the occasional hardy soul: mostly antisocial outcasts or troubled loners trying to prove something to themselves.

Tol wanted no part of that scene. He paralleled the trail whenever possible, avoiding contact with other hikers. He was a city goblin, true, but a few years in the Backcountry Scouts as an adolescent had provided him with at least rudimentary wilderness survival skills. Well, he could duck behind a bush when he detected someone approaching, anyway.

This is precisely what he did when he heard a heavy thudding footstep coming down the darshu needle-strewn path toward him. It was a troll, albeit a fairly cheerful-looking one. As he passed near Tol's bush, he recognized the hiker as Fen, Pyfox's errand boy. He was definitely on the right path. Fen had a couple of hobs trailing him. They were about as noisy as creatures their size could get: stomping, snuffling, wheezing…Tol could track them during a nighttime thunderstorm with his eyes closed.

He waited until Fen and his noise boys had disappeared down the path and then moved cautiously along the trail, alert for any stragglers or even a second wave of Pyfox toadies. The air was getting thinner and more crisp as he negotiated the seemingly endless series of steep switchbacks. Finally, out of breath and lightheaded (which for goblins entails a faint actual illumination), Tol reached the trailhead and found himself facing an unnaturally smooth stone wall. There were numerous tracks of different sizes and shapes that led right up to and away from the wall; it was obviously a portal of some sort. Tol just had to find the triggering mechanism. He felt around for any imperfections or slots chiseled into the rock, but came up empty-handed. He started examining the nearby landscape for odd or out of place-looking structures that might serve as trips. No obvious candidates. He pulled on branches, moved rocks, stuck twigs in knotholes...nothing worked. He realized there was probably some magical mumbo-jumbo involved, and the only way he was going to get in was to camp out nearby and wait for someone else to open the door for him.

By the time that finally happened, Tol was snoring gently in a pile of darshu needles about ten meters away in a dense stand of trees and brush. The scraping noise as the ponderous stone door swung slowly open awakened him with a start. He leapt to his feet and hid behind a particularly massive trunk as he watched for his chance to slip in unnoticed.

There didn't seem to be anyone there. Tol watched in growing confusion as the door stood wide open with no one in evidence on either side of it. Finally he shrugged and made his way to the closest bit of cover, about three or four meters from the yawning doorframe. Since there still was no sign of movement, he darted into the darkened maw and dove for cover behind a large glistening boulder near the entrance.

No one ever appeared, so after ten minutes Tol decided to push on. He'd taken about seven or eight steps down the stone pathway when the huge door suddenly shut behind him with a powerful 'whoosh.' The rush of air and suspended particulates was so forceful it almost knocked him off his feet. "Shuts a smekkin' lot faster than it opens," he muttered, knocking the new layer of dust off his clothes. There was no direction to go now but further in.

The corridor was apparently well-traveled; the stone floor was worn smooth in the center by what must have been centuries of plodding feet. Tol wondered why he'd never heard of this place; a moment later he realized it was because he'd seldom left Sebacea, let alone Goblinopolis. There was no good reason for him to have more than a vague knowledge of the basic topography of the Southern Reaches, much less intimate details about secret passageways far up in the Espwe Mountains. He hated not being an insider, as it were: this made effective edict enforcement much more difficult. He had to keep reminding himself to relax because he was way, way out of his jurisdiction here, anyway—only a tourist.

There were myriad twists and turns, as well as a great many intersections, but Tol concentrated on the well-worn stone path and followed it scrupulously. It led at last and rather abruptly to a magnificent carved chamber that seemingly could host the entire population of the capitol city. Tol stood in the entrance and gaped in awe until his mouth got dry. He moved reverently among the shimmering stone columns and crystalline curtains, interspersed with carved monuments to unknown gods and heroes. The path led him past so many previously undreamt-of wonders that he ceased to be able to take it all in. Tol went numb.

The numbness disappeared when he heard talking in the distance. He shoved himself between a rock drapery and a large stump of stalagmite and waited. He saw a couple of hobs he didn't recognize and then a familiar voice drifted out over the tinkle of water dripping into unseen pools: Pyfox.

"When Fen returns, we will begin the final phase of the plan," Pyfox was telling the hobs, who seemed to be taking notes. He had dropped the hob speech affectation in favor of clarity.

"Where did he go?"

"He has one last message to exchange with our operatives in Qoplebarq."

"And then what?"

"Then Namni will appear and The Slice will be ours to control. Forever."

"What about the Magineers and mages?"

"They will have to pay me to gain access to their precious magic. I will be the richest person in Tragacanth, and eventually on N'plork. And I will live forever!"

"How you gonna swing that, boss?"

"Namni will make it possible for me to be reincarnated via The Slice each time my mortal body dies."

"Why would he do that?"

"Because I will make it possible for *him* to rule The Slice itself."

"What is there to rule?"

"Fool. The Slice is an entire realm that spans the firmament. It has its own cities and nations, all populated by beings created entirely from magic. Namni will be emperor over them all once we control the portals from the physical plane to The Slice."

"How will that make any difference?"

"Magical essence—what some call manna—is constantly bled off from The Slice onto the physical plane. This prevents any buildup of pools of magical force. With the portals shut down, the pools will form at each sealed node and spread into vast reservoirs. An entity skilled enough to do so may tap them to greatly amplify his own power."

At that point a strange resonant chiming filled the cavern. Pyfox looked up, excited. "Namni calls!" He hurried away, followed closely by the hobs. Tol tagged along as best he could in stealth mode. Something about Pyfox's story didn't sit right with him; he wondered if Namni had told him the entire truth. Evil mages are not traditionally very good at full disclosure.

Chapter Nineteen:
Lost and Found

"I don't think we're going to catch up," Hnuppa puffed, "it's moving away faster than we're walking."

"Then we'll need to walk faster, smekkers. Hoof it!"

Hnuppa shot Kurg the most withering glance he could manage under the circumstances, which actually more closely resembled a wince tending toward a grimace. He readjusted his pack and the tripod slung over his shoulder and redoubled the pace. Slud said nothing, but didn't seem to be laboring too hard, despite his age. Of course, he wasn't carrying any cargo.

After another few hundred meters, they caught a break. The mountain, which had been moving almost directly away from them, took a gradual turn to the right until it was traveling at right angles to its previous path. Kurg saw what was happening and urged them into a dead run. They reached the lower flank and leapt on the nearest moving boulders. All three lay there panting, unable to speak for a couple of minutes.

Finally a significant jolt convinced them to

struggle to a sitting position in order to prevent being catapulted off their hard-won perch. Hnuppa scrambled madly to corral all his camera gear, while Kurg sat and chuckled at him. Slud didn't seem to notice either of them.

"You could help me, you know," Hnuppa snapped at Kurg, "this is station-owned equipment."

"For which you are financially responsible, seeing as how you signed it out. Don't worry—I'm sure management would give you a discount, under the circumstances. Shouldn't take you more than four or five years of wage garnishment to pay it off."

"Wonder how long it will take to pay off a busted boss?"

"You and what goblin commando battalion, cupcake?"

"Looks like a cave," interrupted Slud.

Kurg and Hnuppa stopped glaring at each other and looked where he was pointing. There was indeed a cave there. Hnuppa was pretty sure it hadn't been there a minute earlier. Kurg stomped over to it and peered inside. There was a strange bubbling noise issuing from somewhere in its musty depths.

"Looks safe enough. Let's go."

"Since when are you any kind of expert on 'safe?' Oh, I forgot—your platoon leader experience. Squad! Wait for it...present shovels!"

If Kurg made a reply to this, the other two didn't hear it. He had already disappeared into the gurgling stone cavity. They shrugged and plunged in after him.

The first ten meters were pitch-dark. Hnuppa and Slud could hear Kurg's somewhat labored breathing ahead of them and followed it without speaking. Gradually the lights began to come up, although in a half-hearted way, as though they were too tired to give it much of a go. The narrow corridor they were following—really not much more than a gap between rocks—twisted and turned this way and that for at least a kilometer. Finally a light shone from up ahead. It got brighter as they approached, and suddenly they were back out on the mountainside. Kurg and Hnuppa stood blinking in the sunlight while Slud surveyed the area.

"Been here before," he said, pointing at the ground. They stared at the spot he was indicating; it contained footprints. Three sets of footprints. Familiar footprints. *Their* footprints.

"How in the smek could we possibly have ended up back where we started?" Kurg groused. "I have a smekkin' *great* sense of direction and we should have gone straight through that pile of dirt and come out on the other side."

"I don't think 'sense' and you have anything to do with one another."

"The first three words are the only ones in that sentence that matter, smekker."

Kurg stomped off back into the tunnel to give it another go. He was determined to come out somewhere else this time. Hnuppa made as though to follow him, but Slud put a hand on his shoulder. "Wait. He'll come out here." Hnuppa stopped and nodded.

"Yeah, you're probably right. Why tire ourselves out chasing after the old coob?"

Ten minutes or so after Kurg vanished into the darkness they heard a faint voice. At first they couldn't make it out, but a few moments later it resolved into the sound of Kurg roundly cursing at something or someone. Hnuppa considered going in after him, but thought better of it when a decidedly un-Kurg-like howling roiled up out of the cave mouth. Even Slud looked put off by it. They came to a nonverbal consensus that whatever Kurg had gotten himself into he could smekking well get himself out of.

The mountain, which had been relatively quiescent for the past half hour, lurched suddenly into motion again, throwing Slud and Hnuppa onto the boulders. They crawled out of the path of a minor rockslide and waited to see if Kurg would reappear. Another somewhat larger rockslide opened up a trail around the side of the mountain and they heard faint voices coming along it. Not knowing what to expect, they hid themselves behind a newly-raised stone barrier.

Hnuppa noticed in his peripheral vision that Slud was batting at something near his ear. He turned to look and saw little sparkling insects of some sort flitting to and fro. He smacked one between his hands and found nothing there. Soon the little glimmering bugs increased in number and as the voices approached to just around the corner a kaleidoscopic light show of colored pillars and swirls seemed to be accompanying them. Hnuppa realized after listening to the now very nearby voices that he knew at least one of them.

Lom seemed less bedazzled by the hypnotic light show than either Selpla or Drin (although with Drin it was hard to tell), so he assumed the temporary de facto leadership of the party. The hail storm had been short-lived, but when it had spent itself Lom discovered that the path leading back to the soggy plain from whence they had come was no longer in evidence. As they made their way in fits and starts along the winding trail in pursuit of the flashing lights, it was quite apparent to Lom they were being deliberately driven further and further up the hillside for reasons unknown.

Without warning the ground beneath them shifted, throwing all three off-balance and onto the rocky trail surface. At the same time stones slid all around them, changing the landscape dramatically and revealing for the first time that they were climbing no mere hill: it was a full-fledged mountain, one that apparently had decided abruptly to change street address yet again.

"Congratulations, Selpla," Lom said, rubbing his bruised backside, "I think we finally made it to your moving mountain."

Selpla seemed to come alive, as though waking from a dream. "Yippee! Let's get some pics and start cracking this mystery."

Lom took a few shots with his still camera while Selpla nosed around, peering under rocks and into crevices.

"What exactly are you expecting to find doing that?"

"I'm an investigative journalist. I'm investigating. Duh."

"Look more like prospecting to me," Drin observed.

"She forgot to pack her pickaxe," said Lom, dryly.

"Yeah, well, maybe I'll strike it rich, then. Either way I'm doing more than just sitting around on my duff waiting for Kurg to somehow find us."

"Which this little outing will render well-nigh impossible."

Selpla ignored the pessimism and moved steadily up the trail, poking and prodding whatever looked interesting. The light show was still underway, but she paid it little attention. There was a faint but growing rumbling under their feet which Hnuppa decided was the harbinger of another rockslide.

"Heads up! Stay away from loose rocks on the walls!"

They did a little dance figure to avoid not one, but two rockslides, the second more dramatic of which followed immediately on the heels of the first. Dusting themselves off, they resumed their trek. Drin had gone a little way off the trail and came back with an announcement.

"Another way open up."

There was, indeed, a broad new path revealed by the larger of the two slides. It looked well worn—as though it had been here for quite some time but got buried by rockslides. Selpla and Lom speculated on the nature of this anomaly as they walked along. They rounded a corner and came face to face with serendipitous destiny.

Hnuppa stood there for a moment trying to understand what was happening. As soon as he actually saw Selpla's countenance, though, he stopped wondering. He knew from past experience that when Selpla was involved the odds of this sort of coincidence increased drastically. She had a supernatural knack for making things work out this way; more accurately, when things worked out this way Selpla was usually somewhere in the vicinity.

"Hi, Selpla. Good to see you."

Selpla jumped, but recovered her composure in admirable time. She even managed to bat her eyes alluringly at him (or so she hoped). "Great to see you too, Hnuppa. What's going on here?"

Hnuppa shrugged. "Drin and I were just chilling, waiting for Kurg to come back."

"Kurg was here? Where did he go?"

Hnuppa pointed. "In there. We heard him cussing and moaning about something a few minutes ago. He should be back anytime now."

Selpla turned to Lom smugly, "Not so impossible after all, it appears."

Lom shook his head. "Your luck is smekking

supernatural."

A burning smell assailed their nostrils, followed closely by the appearance of Kurg himself. His clothes were singed in many places, outright burnt in others. Most of his incidental body hair (goblins don't have much) was gone. They crowded around him.

"Kurg, are you all right? Where have you been?" Selpla asked, sweeping soot off his back and shoulders.

"Of course I'm smekking all right. Where the smek have *you* been?"

"Oh, here and there."

"Where's your company pram?"

Selpla looked around. "Where's *yours*?"

"I asked you first."

"We had a run-in with some very sticky mud and some crazy mutants outside Dreadmost. The pram is still there, I suppose, although it's probably fossilizing as we speak. That's why we called Bewl in the first place."

"We'll have to go down there and get it, then."

"Be my guest."

"When I say 'we,' I mean *you*."

"Not gonna happen, Kurg. I'm an investigative reporter, not a roustabout."

"I don't care if you're a smekkin' root vegetable, you're going to retrieve that vehicle."

"Perhaps this discussion might best be tabled for the moment," said a voice that did not belong to any goblin. They all stopped and turned to face the source, which oddly seemed to be a large oblong boulder. As they had no prior waking experience in conversing with boulders, they waited to see if it would deign to speak further. It did.

"You are all my honored guests here today. I have an announcement that I think will be of interest, and which will affect all of you to some degree. Please step inside and be welcome to my abode."

They looked at one another, and then back at the rock, the surface of which was beginning to shimmer and ripple, fading into transparency. In its place there was now a very inviting portal into one of the most stunning architectural marvels any of them had ever witnessed. There really wasn't anything further to debate. They all marched in without hesitation.

Prond met them just inside, dressed strangely and beaming like a newlywed.

"Now, circle once more complete," declared Drin.

Chapter Twenty:
Velvet Gauntlet

The Royal carriage chugged out of Port Zog where it had stopped for refueling and began to skirt the ridiculously scenic expanse of Myndrythyl Bay, at the mouth of which sat Lumbos, Boogla's destination. The bay was lined with magnificent barktitan trees, some of which had been there for over a thousand years and had reached fully a hundred meters in height and twenty meters in girth. Each of these arboreal behemoths was its own self-contained ecosystem, with literally hundreds of species of animal, insect, and plant that thrived entirely within the confines of the tangled bark and extensive upperstory. There were rumors of other, more sentient creatures that made their homes in the trees, but no solid evidence of this had ever been provided to the Society of Sages and Mages ('SagMag'), who served as the official arbiter of natural history in Tragacanth, so the accounts remained purely in the anecdotal realm.

The water in Myndrythyl Bay was a glorious deep blue, kept crystal clear by the same minerals that provided the blue color: they dissolved in from the surrounding cliffs and precipitated out any suspended particulates in the coves isolated from larger ocean currents by the sheltered topography. In places you could see down twenty meters or more when the light was right. The marine life was no less diverse or spectacular than that of the woods. Blaze fish swam in huge schools, flashing their iridescent reds and yellows like littoral fireworks as they twisted and turned. Enormous seabeeves lazed along the pink sands, spaced almost perfectly every fifteen meters, the limits of their territorial range on land. A host of black and white saltchitters with bright blue beaks mixed with ponderous brown fish-storing pouchdivers wheeling overhead. At least ten other less well-represented species of avians lent their antics and voices to the saltmist cacophony.

All in all, it was an outdoorsgoblin's paradise, with numerous tourist accommodations ranging from simple bed and breakfasts to elaborate resort complexes dotting the landscape for a hundred kilometers along the paddle-shaped shoreline. Boogla was not here for the view, though. She had an important diplomatic mission of which this represented merely the initial step.

Lumbos was the oldest major settlement in Tragacanth, tracing its roots to the very first exploratory landings from the mother continent of Bazgush over four millennia ago. It was constructed essentially in concentric layers, oldest in the center, like a ripple expanding inland in three directions from the enormous harbor district. Ferroc Oria was an imposing tower of glass on the northern edge of the innermost circle. It was built using bricks made by melting the local beach sand in enormous furnaces and pouring the resultant slag into frames to cool. The unique mineral content of the sand lent these blocks not only great strength but also a pleasing appearance. They were opaquely crystalline and threw off rainbows when viewed from the correct angle relative to a strong light source. The edifice could be seen from quite a distance, and its visage was constantly changing according to the time of day and position of the viewer.

Kryptoq was the Oria Magineer. He had a reputation for being even more antisocial than usual for his ilk. True to form, he did not show up to greet the new Magineer Liaison, nor did he send anyone in his stead. Boogla waited there on the carriage platform until it became apparent she was not going to be escorted, counted to ten, then hired a pram to take her and her security detail to the Duber.

Her reception at the Duber itself was equally cool. Kryptoq was not impressed with some upstart little girl who had taken a semi-mythical hacker's name for herself and gotten a plum job out of the deal. She may have pulled the wool over the new king's eyes, but fooling a Magineer was something else again. He would simply have to make an object lesson of her, on behalf of the other Magineers. Once she'd learned her proper place in the pecking order, they could get along more amicably.

When Boogla arrived at the Duber, Kryptoq

did have the decency to send a minion down to the reception area to bring her up to his office. Boogla was diplomatic and courteous to her, and to everyone she met in the Duber, until she was seated across the elaborately-carved Teslu heartwood desk from the Magineer.

"I don't believe His Majesty will be pleased to hear that a Magineer was less than fully receptive to a visit from His Liaison, Doctor Kryptoq," she began, pleasantly. (Magineers were granted the rank of Doctor of Magical Arts and Letters upon taking office, if they did not already possess it. They also had to be Doctors of at least one Engineering specialty.)

"Ah, so? Well, I'm sure He'll get over it in due time. I have important work to do, and cannot always rearrange my schedule to accommodate messengers and their ilk."

"Verily. I have read your latest paper on computational transfiguration matrices and found it quite interesting. I believe if you'll examine your interspatial transformation algorithm you'll find a substantial error in the nonlinear fractal math, though. Correcting it alters the final magical flow pattern efficiency rather significantly and, I might add, for the better."

"I hardly think so, missy. That paper was thoroughly peer-reviewed and no one reported any such error."

"I certainly believe you. However, I'm *not* your peer."

"Well, it's good that you recognize that, at least."

"I don't think you understand. Check your math. I'll wait."

After a chat with the Oria Magineer—who turned out not to be Boogla's peer after all—that was in the end productive and congenial, the Magineer Liaison departed Lumbos for Tillimil. Kryptoq now knew precisely what the King expected of him and his office, and he accepted those assignments without reservation. Boogla had established herself as an intellectual and diplomatic force to be reckoned with, and the other Magineers knew it within minutes of her departure.

The road to Tillimil was somewhat arduous in the best of conditions; in the aftermath of the magical tempests its traversal became downright challenging. The carriage tracks were washed out on the southeastern end of the Ullglava valley, a wide, fertile plain between the Bungash and Espwe mountain ranges that served as the breadbasket for Tragacanth. It was almost entirely occupied by sprawling back-to-back grain farmsteads. The rivers and streams were lined with extensive vegetable plots. The land approaching the foothills of both ranges was occupied, in turn, by ranches raising the meat and dairy livestock upon which the Tragacanthan livelihood largely depended.

The Royal Transportation Officer assigned to Boogla arranged during the carriage trip down from Lumbos for a heavy off-road military dray to meet them at the last serviceable carriage roundabout, in the little town of Strix about forty kilometers beyond the Southern end of the Bungash range. The voyage from Strix to Tillimil was not exactly smooth sailing, but the large dray was quite accustomed to slogging through mud and debris and carried Boogla and her companions without complaining, albeit with numerous jolts and bumps.

Tillimil, and in fact virtually all of Ferroc Sutha, was in disarray as a result of the magical storms that had wreaked so much havoc during the past few days. Nevertheless there was a formal reception waiting for Boogla—she and her party were taken to the Duber in the Magineer's own conveyance, with two honor guards as escorts. This was much more in keeping with diplomatic protocol, and Boogla took mental note of the way things were supposed to work. The encounter with Kryptoq had apparently propagated to the other Dubers.

El-Asral was a cultured goblin of multitudinous accomplishment and impeccable breeding. He was courteous and engaging, and Boogla found herself both impressed by and strangely drawn to him. He was everything she had expected a Magineer to be. Despite the fact that he had a lot on his plate trying to analyze and counter the maelstroms and their aftermath, he met with her on her own schedule, patiently listened to her concerns and the instructions she conveyed from the Royal Seat, and responded appropriately and eloquently.

Boogla left the Sutha Duber in good spirits and ahead of schedule, so she took a little time out to sightsee. Tillimil had suffered some damage from the storms, true, but much of the charm of the old port city remained intact. The trees here were nowhere near as tall and magnificent as those in Lumbos, but they had a spreading stately majesty of their own. Encased in a silvery bark of wonderful carved intricacy, they threw their limbs out in all directions, creating an umbrella-like canopy that played host to myriad species of brightly-plumaged avian life. Long twisted tendrils of greenery cascaded from the higher limbs almost to the ground, like verdant streamers announcing some joyful forest celebration.

The trees swayed lazily in the wind, now that the gales had died down to the gentle salt-air breezes more characteristic of the area. The very essence of Tillimil was laid-back; even with damage from the recent storms in plain evidence it was still easy to imagine life as a mellow, rich experience, like a double dip of your favorite frozen confection on a summer's day. Boogla closed her eyes and drank it all in. She decided then and there to return to Tillimil someday and spend a lot more time getting to know the city and its people.

For now it was time to start the very long journey to Ferroc Osta and Cladimil on the far western coast. She had never been to that district, or seen the Noorprid Sea; Boogla was both looking forward to and dreading it just a little. She'd heard some disturbing rumors about the folk of the western shores, although they were merely hearsay, she kept reminding herself. The broad expanse of plains and shoreline beyond the imposing Masron Mountains remained something of a mystery to the rest of Tragacanth, as contact was traditionally rather sporadic before the introduction of modern communications and conveyances only a couple hundred years prior. The western peoples were mechanically, not magically, inclined, and kept to themselves. Gnomes were more numerous here than in the other districts. Boogla knew comparatively little about them or their culture; what snippets she had heard were disconcerting, but she was determined to give them a clean slate nonetheless and see the truth for herself.

There were no major cities at all on the rail line from Tillimil to Cladimil. It wound through hundreds of kilometers of farmland, skirting the northern edge of the Espwes, making a long straight run traversing the wastelands of Asga Teslu before crossing the headwaters of the mighty Zongat River, whose meandering channel formed the major portion of the border between Tragacanth and Galanga to the south, and then bent northwesterly. Beyond the Zongat, between the Masrons and the sea, lay the western plains, rich with volcanic soils that supported most of the herbs, root vegetables, and tuber crops grown in Tragacanth. A great majority of the producing fruit trees in the kingdom were also located within a band fifty kilometers inland from the coastline.

Asga Teslu was a vast desert area of rugged hills, gorges, and exotically colorful geological formations, but almost totally devoid of significant vegetation.

The Masrons trapped most all of the moisture that streamed in from the Noorprid Sea and precipitated it on the windward side, leaving nothing but hot, dry winds to sweep over the wastelands. While the desert had a certain stark beauty about it, Boogla had to admit she was relieved when the wind-carved sandstone chiaroscuros gave way to the verdant grasslands of the Western plains.

Cladimil boasted the highest per capita income in Tragacanth. Manufacturing firms wanted their corporate headquarters located here to be close to the vast gnomic talent pool and to take advantage of the abundant sunshine and temperate climate, as well as the expansive port facilities. The broad boulevards were lined with tropical trees and raised beds overflowing with brilliantly colored flowers. The buildings were all possessed of the same basic architectural facade by city ordinance, a tiled roof palacio-type construction that added to the overall exotic, well-to-do metropolitan ambience.

There was poverty and misery here as well, of course, but it was carefully hidden away from tourists and business executives in very strictly enforced ghettoes behind massive stone walls topped with gay foliage. The inhabitants were virtually prisoners in their own shabby neighborhoods; their comings and goings regulated by edict enforcement officers to minimize the negative impact they had on income-producing visitors, especially those from other continents who wanted to establish lucrative trade agreements with Tragacanthan firms headquartered on the 'Platinum Coast,' as it was self-billed.

The Ferroc Osta Duber was built in the same style as every other public building in Cladimil, only on a grander scale and with more attention to small architectural details. It was raised on a cliff overlooking a truly world-class panorama of the Noorprid, with the requisite complement of rolling waves, wheeling sea avians, and cavorting marine mammals seemingly on continuous duty. Dendrash, the Osta Magineer, had made it one of his agenda items to better accommodate visitors to the Duber. There were regular tours conducted from an elegant visitor center with a nice restaurant and easy access to the carriage station.

Boogla would have thoroughly enjoyed doing the tourist thing, but she had duties to discharge. Because of Cladimil's importance as a manufacturing center and major port for trade with the far western nation of Solemadrina, Ferroc Osta was of critical strategic importance to Tragacanth. His Majesty had a fairly extensive laundry list of topics he wanted Boogla to cover with Dendrash, and their meeting took most of the day. Dendrash was businesslike but not without a sense of humor. He and Boogla got along better than she had anticipated.

Just before dusk Boogla finally had the opportunity to stroll the kilometer-long boardwalk paralleling the beach behind the Duber complex. The salt air and warmth were very relaxing, and made it easy to see why so many people wanted to retire here. She had an excellent evening repast of seafood stew and tender bumpershoots wilted in karsi oil, accompanied by a vintage silverplum wine. It was only with great reluctance that Boogla boarded her private carriage for Ferroc Norda at midnight. She would definitely have to visit Cladimil again when she had more time to appreciate its delights.

The rail line to Dresmak threaded its way somewhat precariously through fifty kilometers of narrow opening between mountains known as Krubber Pass. The railway alternated between steep canyon walls and vertigo-inducing bridges with nothing but air on both sides down to the rock-strewn cirque far below. Boogla decided that since she was going to be keeping her eyes shut for the next couple of hours anyway, she might as well take a long nap. She did briefly bring herself to look down as they passed over the source of the mighty Mernal River. Here it was just a spring-fed trickle, augmented by melting snow and ice in the spring. Hard to believe this was the beginning of the kilometer-wide monster that eventually emptied into Myndrythyl Bay, carrying hundreds of thousands of tonnes of alluvium and fifty meter-wide cargo barges with it.

Dresmak was not an unattractive place, but compared with the sun-splashed splendor of Cladimil it was positively uninspiring from Boogla's perspective. The predominant building substrate here was granite—the nearby Masrons provided a wealth of easily-quarried raw material—and this lent the architecture an austere, classical feeling.

The city was laid out in very logical fashion,

predictable and precise. The Duber and city government buildings were set in a circular complex at the geographic center; the various municipal districts then expanded in exactly-placed concentric circles from this nexus like ripples on a pond, somewhat in the Lumbos model but with none of the freeform style. The Dresmak Mayoral pram that brought Boogla from the carriage station to the Duber took her past stately mansions, row after row of brick and stone townhouses, and a plethora of meticulously maintained parks and other public spaces.

Imber-ol, the Norda Magineer, was equally august, at least on the surface. Once he and Boogla were sequestered in the Magineer's Sanctum, however, he loosened up a bit, even joking now and then as they went over the King's agenda. Once they'd covered Aspet's topics, Imber-ol offered Boogla a drink of some excellent, difficult to acquire brandy that she couldn't refuse. He led her down into his quite impressive libations cellar and locked the door behind him. This put her on guard, but he quickly reassured her that his intentions were not evil. "There is a project underway here," he said to her as they wound their way down the stone stairs carved from the living rock itself, "known only to a select few. Indeed, I am not aware if, or to what extent, even His Majesty has been briefed, in truth."

"What manner of 'project' are you referring to?"

"To answer that, I'll have to give you some arcanophysical theory background. If you already know this I apologize in advance; please be patient and consider it a refresher in that event."

Boogla nodded.

"We've known since the time of the Archmage Ezcariel that a careful synergy of reflection spells could non-invasively extract a complete psychic clone of a person, which could then be stored in a properly prepared arcane crystal for a number of years before it began to degenerate due to entropic mutation. Within the last decade we've also been able to generate a complete genetic clone of that person. Both of these advances are generally known throughout the magineering community. What is not known, however, is that the process for magically overlaying the psychic template onto the cloned organism has been perfected."

Boogla gasped. "You mean you've figured out how to create an exact clone of a person, memories and all?"

"Yes and no. Yes, in that we could do this if we had a completely 'empty' adult shell into which to inject the psychic template. No, in that so far we haven't been able to raise an organism to the adult state without any learned behaviors or memories creeping in. If the template is overlain onto any existing information, the resulting discrepancies have unpredictable and often catastrophic results for the subject. In effect, since the template is an entire psychic blueprint, there is no 'room' for additional, contradictory, data. Either the incoming or the existing data is destroyed during the overlay procedure, according to the laws of localized nondeterministic entropic information theory—with which you are no doubt familiar. It is not possible to predict which will survive, or what the resulting effect will be on the subject's mental state. Another complication is that the template steadily loses integrity over time."

"Is there no way to simply wipe the subject clean, as it were, prior to the procedure?"

"Not as such, no. However, we have discovered another direction from which this problem may be approached. Unlike on the physical plane, artifacts transported to The Slice are not subject to degradation, since time as we understand it does not exist there. A psychic image stored in The Slice will not degrade—or if it does, the timeframe will be eons from our point of view—so a 'master copy' sequestered there should allow a person to be cloned again and again and restored to the same mental state each time. A form of immortality, if you will, and a way to correct progressive mental degeneration by resetting the person's brain to a known good state."

"Does anyone else know about this?"

"We suspect so. There is a class of archmages who have transcended the physical plane through their arts and now exist primarily in The Slice, although they can yet have limited interaction with our plane from time to time. They are probably aware of this technique, although it would likely hold little more than passing interest for them. As for N'plork itself, we don't think the magical community at large here has any knowledge of this, except perhaps as a completely theoretical thought experiment. Nothing in my long years of training hinted at it, at any rate."

"What happens to the memories and skills developed by the subject between the time the image is taken and the time it is restored to them?"

"Right now, as I said, that is the limiting factor for the process that renders it currently impractical. Eventually we will learn how to wipe them clean prior to the restoration. There is no way any of the research team can see to retain them without a high probability of driving the subject insane."

"If time does not pass in The Slice, are transcendent mages able to learn new skills or accumulate memories there?"

"We honestly don't know. There is a theory that the matrix of The Slice itself serves as a form of 'external storage' for the creatures that inhabit it, rendering additional neocortical function unnecessary, but that's very difficult to corroborate. There would seem to be a bandwidth issue, as it were, in accessing those memories, but our understanding of the arcanophysical limitations, if any, of The Slice is quite limited. Oh, and one more drawback to this process: as far as we have been able to ascertain, restored clones are sterile. We believe this has to do with the role hormones play in gametogenesis during early development. A cloned genetic template does not produce new gametes unless the image is taken prior to sexual maturity."

"Is there nothing to be done about this?"

"Actually, one of the most exciting sub-projects

underway here at present is one which extracts partial genetic and psychic images on a periodic basis throughout the life of the subject in order to restore them sequentially and thus preserve the entirety of the subject's biological meta-architecture."

"And that doesn't encounter the overlay discrepancy problem?"

"No, because each image is incremental to the previous: they don't overlap, at least in theory."

"What about the case where some injury has triggered the brain's plasticity to repurpose previously allocated structures?"

"Very astute point. You have an impressively broad range of knowledge, Your Excellency. The same plasticity that allows the brain to rewire itself to bypass an injury may work to our benefit—or against us. At this juncture we simply don't know."

"I see. Well, please keep us informed as to your progress. I will provide you with the private Royal Encryption keys before I leave; they make use of one-time pads that rotate every morning. A special messenger will deliver a new set once a month."

"Thank you, Your Excellency. May I presume that some Royal funding will be made available to us as well? So far we have made due with Duber research and development monies, but they are inadequate to fund the various projects over the long term."

"I will need to speak with His Majesty concerning this; I don't think He will have any reservations about backing this project fully, however."

The carriage trip back to Goblinopolis

traversed the vast northern woodlands. Hundreds of thousands of hectares of old growth forest resided here in pristine glory. Rumors abounded of many species of undiscovered wildlife and, as with other less well-explored areas of Tragacanth a few old legends persisted of unknown sentients. The vast area bounded by Dresmak, the Mernal River, and the Kopyrewt rain forest was relatively poorly charted, despite its proximity to two of Tragacanth's major urban centers. Kopyrewt was easily accessible by water, and harbored a great treasure trove of economically-important trees and herbs, so it was far better explored in comparison with the neighboring forest lands.

There was a movement afoot in Lumbos to have portions of Kopyrewt declared a national preserve before some unique species were lost forever due to habitat destruction, but so far it had failed to attract much attention in the capitol. Environmentalism was rather a new phenomenon in Goblin culture, although some of the other less thoroughly urbanized races had championed like causes for many years.

It was late in the evening when Boogla's carriage finally pulled into Loca Station. She left her escort at the entrance to the Royal Staff housing, thanked them, climbed the steps of her townhouse tiredly, greeted her servants and tumbled into bed. A good night's sleep was just what she needed after her grand tour of Tragacanth. As she drifted off into slumber she reflected on the differences and similarities between hacking and diplomacy. Hacking, she decided at length, was a lot easier.

Chapter Twenty-One: Aggravating Assault

Tol was grateful for the plethora of stone formations protruding at odd angles from the walls, ceiling, and floor of the caverns. They gave him plenty of easy cover. He followed Pyfox and his cronies by dodging from stalagmite to pillar to column; after a few minutes his clothes were wet and a little slimy from the thin coating of water on the living formations. Pyfox headed up a short, broad stairway and into a smallish chamber off to one side of the hallway at the top. Tol followed using his three decades of surveillance skill and sandwiched himself between two troll-sized boulders to watch. Pyfox stood in front of a carved wooden table on which sat a large crystalline sphere and thrice chanted some phrase Tol couldn't quite make out. At the very last word of the third repetition the sphere glowed with a rosy radiance. It seemed to enlarge as the light grew more intense, until the sphere itself took up half the room. Tol didn't know what to make of this, so he just made himself as small and inconspicuous as possible and waited.

The giant sphere shimmered impressively for a

few seconds, then a ghostly figure appeared within it and an ethereal, distinctly unpleasant rasp of a voice infested the small chamber like a dread disease.

"Pyfox, my loyal servant. Have you positioned your minions for the final assault?"

"Yes, Your Eminence. All of the Marker attack portals have been established and the mageslaves controlling them await my command."

"Excellent. You may proceed at will. Be certain to adhere to the attack pattern as planned."

Ballop'ril, wrapped in a rich scarlet robe emblazoned with mystic symbols, stood on a marvelously carved dais cut from some mystical bluish stone that seemed to glow from within. Prond knelt before him, with the others forming a semicircle about three meters out. The Archmage held in one hand a beautifully embroidered green sash and in the other an unadorned black orb of indeterminate composition that fit neatly in his gnarled palm. Prond was dressed in a simple white tunic with a thin silver chain around his waist.

Ballop'ril addressed the assemblage.

"Today we induct a new acolyte into the elite circle of mages. Prond has agreed to take on the sash of the Mage's Apprentice and to serve under my tutelage for so long as the relationship is mutually agreeable."

He stepped forward and bid Prond stand, then

tied the sash around his waist.

"This orb," he said, holding it up for all to see, "Is a magical energy sink mages formally refer to as a *speculum arcanis*. The orb may be invoked only by you, Prond, once we fuse it to your corolla integumenta—that's the magical aura that surrounds all of us—and you may then use it to draw magical essence, or manna, from The Slice and store it for future use."

He held the orb to Prond's forehead, raised his other hand palm up, and uttered an incantation. The orb began to glow, which progressed through yellow-orange-red, then all the color drained out of it and into Prond's forehead, briefly illuminating him from within down to the shoulders. Prond stepped back and staggered, but quickly regained his composure. He held the orb up and it glowed with a golden radiance that grew in intensity until a bright throbbing arc leapt out, the leading edge of which poured into an invisible tear in the fabric of the air itself. The orb began to accumulate manna as if it were literally being filled through a hole in the top.

At approximately the halfway mark the arc suddenly oscillated wildly then faded. Prond looked at Ballop'ril, puzzled. Ballop'ril put one hand on either side of his head and went into a mystic trance while everyone else looked on in concern. After a few moments he came out of it. The rocky floor beneath them began to rumble. They braced themselves; it was obvious the mountain was on the move again.

"We must hasten to Astflanar. The Slice is under attack."

It took about half an hour for the mountain to reach its destination moving at top speed. It was noisy and difficult to walk about during the journey, so the crew just found places to hang on without trying to converse over the din. Ballop'ril sat cross-legged in a trance, doing whatever it was archmages did at times like this. Prond in his new sash stood nearby, clutching the now inoperative orb and trying not to feel awkward and superfluous.

There was one final spasm of grinding and thumping, then all fell silent. Ballop'ril returned from his spiritual sojourn and stood up.

"Come."

He strode off into a small crevice in the wall. The rest followed somewhat hesitantly. They traversed a narrow but passable corridor for quite a while, until they came at last to what appeared to be the end of the line: a wall of very solid-looking unbroken rock. Ballop'ril stood there studying it for a moment, then raised one hand in a tight fist. He held the position for a few seconds, and then abruptly his fingers sprang open. The solid wall in front of them melted away like smoke dissipating in a sudden breeze. Ballop'ril strode through and motioned for the others to follow.

"Neat trick," Kurg muttered.

After only a few meters they came to a wide spot in the corridor. Ballop'ril halted and turned to address them.

"We have passed from my sanctuary mountain into the interior of Mount Astflanar. We are headed for a chamber deep in the bowels of the mountain where a puppet of the evil transcendent mage Namni is even now orchestrating a devastating attack on The Slice, or more accurately, on the portals that allow magic to flow from The Slice to the physical plane. As we approach the lair of the puppet Pyfox the path will be increasingly heavily fortified with magical traps. It is absolutely imperative for your safety that you follow my instructions to the letter. Any disregard may prove fatal. Are you all clear on that point?"

He looked at them expectantly. One by one, they nodded.

"Why are we doing this, again?" Lom whispered to Selpla.

"Because it's a story!" Selpla and Kurg answered, together.

"Sorry I asked."

Ballop'ril and Prond walked side-by-side. Prond held the speculum arcanis in front of him to serve as an early warning for magical activity. As they rounded a corner it suddenly began to pulse with a deep golden light. Ballop'ril put his hand up to halt the party. He scanned the area ahead of them systematically, from lower left and around. After about a minute he picked up a loose stone.

"Shield your eyes."

He tossed the rock in a lazy parabola down the path and at its apex a brilliant blinding flash of white light erupted from the walls of the corridor. The rock disintegrated into fiery dust and a strong burning smell permeated the air.

"Integrity disruptor. Only one charge, so we're safe to head through."

The rest of the party looked at one another in alarm. Ballop'ril raised his large eyebrows. "It's perfectly passable now. Behold." He walked down the path a few steps and turned to face them.

The others followed, a little hesitantly. Selpla stopped to pick up some of the rock dust. It was still warm and smelled like burnt charcoal. "Nasty trap."

A little further on Ballop'ril halted them once more. "Hug the right-hand wall. Do not touch any stone on the left." He stood between them and the left wall as they passed. Once they were safely beyond the danger, he pointed to something embedded in a stone slab on the left. It was the rear portion of a cave wrat. "Quicklith," he explained, "Instantly entraps and eventually absorbs any living creature that comes in contact with it." The wrat tail twitched spasmodically. "It can take a while to kill the victim. Not a pleasant death, either."

"Ugh," said Drin, "Bad magic."

"Bad magic, indeed," agreed Lom.

There were similar traps every five to ten meters along the passageway; avoiding being crushed, lacerated, sautéed, or impaled almost started to feel like a routine activity by the time they were approaching the crest of a rise beyond which

Ballop'ril had informed them lay the lair of Pyfox.

"There will most likely be one final trap near the entryway. I suspect it will be unlike the others. Stay back until I give the all clear."

Suddenly Slud let out a sharp exclamation. The others turned to see him being wrapped by a strange snake-like apparition, smothering him in a vaporous grasp. They rushed over to him just as Ballop'ril shouted, "Keep your place!" All but Lom stopped in their tracks, but he had too much momentum, stumbled, and grabbed at a protruding rock for support which unexpectedly folded back as if hinged. A deep gong rang from somewhere down the corridor. Ballop'ril waved his hand over the constrictor and a flash of blue energy from his palm popped it like a pricked balloon.

"We've triggered an alarm. Everyone be ready to fight or fly."

"I wish I *could* fly," said Lom.

"We glad to help you out with that," replied Drin, scowling.

"Shut up, both of you, and look for some kind of weapon," said Selpla, brandishing a bakkla melon-sized chunk of rock.

While he generally manifested on the physical plane as an old man in a long cloak with white hair and wild eyes, in his adopted native habitat—The Slice—Namni's appearance was nothing short of awe-inspiring. Depending on where you stood in relation to him, he appeared as a fiery jungle hunter, a magnificent predator avian with shimmering silver wings, or a towering iron-muscled rock titan with fierce glowing slitted pupils. The visual effect was a bit muted by the eye-twisting sight of The Slice itself, however. The fundamental geometry of The Slice was fractal in nature, with every discrete feature composed of infinitely recursive branchings of itself. Color was infinitely mutable here, with all chromatic information dependent entirely on the perception and visual acuity of the observer.

The fundamental underlying architecture was magic. Gravity, friction, thermodynamics, and all the other basic forces of the physical plane were superimposed on a magical manifold. Even the physical laws of the rest of universe were 'pseudo-fractal' here in that they seemed chaotically implemented on the macroscopic scale but were actually rigidly uniform at the microscopic level.

The landscape itself was breathtaking. Since geological features—if the term geological really applied to a realm not built on any solid substrate— were not constrained by gravity or structural integrity considerations, the sky was literally the limit. There were pillars and columns and spires in great number visible in all directions. Some were no more than ten or fifteen meters in height, but a few soared so far into the firmament that their upper reaches were invisible to even the sharpest eye. Between them were nestled great halls, temples, ziggurats, pyramids, towers, and other imposing structures whose very walls and buttresses seemed fluid and insubstantial until one approached quite closely.

The flora and fauna of The Slice were not readily apparent, but they were there in abundance for the careful observer. Most of them seemed to be corollaries of creatures and plants found on the physical plane, created perhaps by homesick transcendent mages, but a few were quite obviously native to the magical milieu. There was, for example, a whole family of species of photon-frogs who resembled small-to-medium irregular globes of light and fed on the regenerating fabric of The Slice itself. Their usual motion was a slow and deliberate creep, but when alarmed or excited they could leap up to ten meters away, leaving a glowing arc of charged, crackling atmosphere tracing their path.

The skies were populated by a variety of aerial creatures and several floating plant forms. The aerials were mostly delta-shaped squamous things with whiskers and feathery forked tails that seemed to employ some form of negative gravity for lift and propulsion. They whistled and screeched with abandon as they swooped among the spires.

The floating plants, in contrast, were the epitome of stately grace. They could change altitude, and did on occasion, but the transitions were extraordinarily gradual, on par with the elongation of a growing tree trunk. They were oval, sack-like, hued in warm colors, and shiny in a leathery sort of way. The bags would have been filled with hydrogen or helium on the physical plane, but here in The Slice their means of levitation was almost certainly more magic than simple positive buoyancy. Some of them had long, twisting tendrils that sparkled as though they were laden with precious jewels which proved on closer inspection to be spheres of some colorful liquid clinging to the string-like tendrils.

There was also weather of a sort in The Slice. At least, calling it weather was more descriptive than calling it much of anything else. At intervals fronts would move through, strewing fragments of old sloughed-off Slice fabric (The Slice shed its 'skin' on a regular basis) and leaving puddles of a substance that resembled runny legume-butter dotting the landscape. Rather than rain down from above, though, the precipitation seemed either to ooze up from the fabric or just congeal out of the atmosphere directly. On occasion all of the spires and columns in a given geographic area would suddenly begin to bend and sway in unison, as though a gale was raging, but no wind movement would be felt. It took some getting used to.

Namni was presiding over an operation that would give him unquestioned control over The Slice in its entirety. Scattered throughout the realm were twenty-four *specula arcanis majoris*: ten pins ball-sized orbs that were known colloquially as 'magic markers' because they delineated the boundary between The Slice and the physical plane. Each of them also guarded a portal to the physical plane, although those shunts did not correspond to any single location but rather were available on demand to any mage for drawing magical essence from The Slice.

In truth there were only twenty-three specula remaining, as one had been destroyed by a metaquantum contraction. These events were exceedingly rare; this was, in fact, the first instance since the specula had been put in place by the founding generation of mages over four thousand years earlier. Contractions were The Slice equivalents of major earthquakes, caused by unstable interactions between the magical fabric and the space-time continuum. The magical realm splintered off from the physical plane femtoseconds after the breakdown of stable supersymmetry at the dawn of the current cosmic cycle.

When the first mages discovered how to tap into The Slice (the name of which is actually a corruption of *Ta'slizh'I*, which meant 'energy source' in ancient protogoblish), they established permanent channels connecting it to the physical plane and kept them open with the specula, which had non-reversible inviolability spells cast on them to ensure that no future mages could alter them in any way.

Namni and Oloi were transcendent mages, magical practitioners of such great skill and knowledge that they had been able to leave their physical bodies behind and cross the magical boundary to live forever in The Slice, subsisting by extracting energy from its infinitely regenerative fabric in the same manner as the native inhabitants.

They were able to visit the physical plane for short durations by filling their persistent remnant shells with enough magical energy to render them semi-solid, but when their substantiality reached the minimum necessary for maintaining a physical presence as the magical fuel was depleted they reverted to The Slice.

They were more than just mages, however. The gods that rule The Slice, created in the same quantum event as the gods that rule over the physical plane, had selected a few of the most powerful transcendent mages to serve as their ambassadors and peacekeepers throughout the magical realm. Both Namni and Oloi had been chosen for this elite company, known formally as the Noil Emissaries. Namni had forfeited his place in the ranks of the Noils by abandoning its principles and violating his oaths in his own pursuit of power, but he retained most of the abilities they granted him as an Emissary by dint of some very dirty dark magic.

Oloi was aware of Namni's plots, but chose to let him hang himself with his own rope, as it were. In doing so, however, Oloi was taking a calculated risk. If Namni's military actions in Tragacanth actually succeeded by some mischance, his power in The Slice would be unmatched by any but the gods themselves. There was no way for Namni or Oloi to damage the specula by magic, but Namni had discovered a way to channel unimaginable kinetic energy by triggering geologic fault zones in Tragacanth through magical conduits directly into the specula, eventually igniting metaquantum contractions in them one by one until only Namni's personal speculum—the last of the original twenty-four—remained. While this would result in Namni controlling the flow of magic between The Slice, that was not the worst effect: it would trigger twenty-three major quakes in Tragacanth, causing a staggering loss of life and property. This, even more that the loss of magic, was why Oloi was determined to stop Namni. His ace in the hole back on N'plork was a simple cop.

Chapter Twenty-Two: Collateral Damage

"Good morning, Your Excellency. I trust your voyage of discovery went smoothly?"

"Yes, Your Majesty. I would say that it did. All four of the provincial Magineers have received your greetings and instructions. Three of them were genteel and professional."

"And the other?"

"The Oria Magineer has seen the error of his ways, I believe, and will treat Royal Functionaries more in keeping with their station in the future."

Aspet chuckled. "Kryptoq can be a handful, it's true. You didn't hurt him, did you?"

"Only his pride."

"That will heal in due time. Job well done, Magineer Liaison."

"Thank you, Your Majesty. Shall we retire to the 'war room' for my briefing?"

"Lead the way. I've arranged for a suitable selection of pastries and drinks."

"I believe it is the perks of this job I love the most."

The briefing lasted into the afternoon; most

of it spent talking about the secret project at the Norda Duber. Aspet had also received some disturbing intelligence concerning anomalous magical activities at seemingly random spots scattered about Tragacanth, none of them near any communities or dwellings where magic was known to be practiced. Not that mages didn't wander around and 'freelance,' of course, but the sudden upswing seemed suspicious and worrying to him. He plotted the locations of the activity on a large wall map of Tragacanth and he and Boogla puzzled over them.

"Not on trade routes, along rivers, a certain distance from population centers, or any other commonality that I can perceive. How about you?"

"Doesn't seem to form any magical sigil, glyph, or other symbol that I'm familiar with."

"Good. I hadn't thought of that one. What we do know is that each of these locations has some connection with a notorious inner-city hobgoblin hood known as Pyfox. What he's plotting here, if indeed he is behind this, is a mystery. Hobs are not generally known for their magic."

At that point there was a knock on the door. One of Aspet's personal guard detail leaned in. "Sorry to bother you, Your Majesty, but here is an urgent message." He handed a sealed envelope to Aspet.

"Thank you, Sergeant." The smartly-dressed soldier gave a crisp salute, turned on his heel, and resumed his post next to the door.

Aspet opened the envelope and read the missive. He looked gravely concerned, stared off into space for a moment, then handed the note to Boogla. While she was reading it, he walked over to the encrypted intercom system on the wall. He punched in his Royal passcode and spoke into the microphone. "This is Aspet. Scramble the Royal Disaster Corps. I repeat, Scramble the Royal Disaster Corps. I want encoded progress reports from each division chief to my Incident Tracking System account on the hour." A voice from the other end replied, "As you command, Your Majesty." A few seconds later sirens went off in the surrounding communities.

Four near-simultaneous major quakes had occurred, one in each of the outlying districts. A substantial part of the Northern port city of Fenurian had been destroyed. There were villages and hamlets throughout Ferrocs Sutha and Osta that had been totally leveled. The death toll was unknown at this point, but it would be considerable, especially in the Fenurian metropolitan area.

Aspet sat with his head in his hands. "What could possibly have caused four major quakes at once? They're not on the same fault lines. Smek, one of them wasn't even *over* a known fault zone."

Boogla had carried the message over with her to the map. She held it up and compared it with the geography of Tragacanth.

"I think I might know."

Aspet looked up. "You might? What's the common factor?"

"Pyfox."

The king's jaw dropped. "*Pyfox*? How can a

small-time thug like him be orchestrating geological disasters? And for what purpose? We haven't received any ransom notes or other evidence of extortion from him."

"His known base of operations is Sebacea. Why don't you ask your brother?"

"Tol? I haven't spoken to him since before I challenged for the throne. Do you think he even knows I'm the king?"

"He's an edict enforcement officer. I expect he's read the news feeds."

"He hasn't tried to contact me."

"Have you tried to contact him?"

Aspet looked a little sheepish. "No, but he's always been hard-headed and never understood why his little brother got involved with all that computer nonsense. You might term him 'provincial' in that respect. I sincerely doubt he's impressed."

"Impressing him is high on your list of life goals then, I take it."

"No! Well, yes, I suppose it is. Or was. I've got a kingdom and its people to worry about now. Tol doesn't cross my mind very often anymore."

"With all due respect, you're a liar, Your Majesty."

"Don't talk to me that way. I'm your king!"

"And I'm a trusted member of your cabinet whom you hired explicitly to tell you the truth, no matter how much it hurts."

Aspet looked away. "Touché," he said, finally.

"I'm sorry. I don't really mean to pry in family

business. Your brother could prove to be a very valuable asset in this investigation, however. He is bound to be familiar with Pyfox and may have some idea what he's up to."

"You're right, of course. If Tol can be of any help, I'll track him down. We have lives at stake here." He went over to the Royal computer terminal at the head of the table. A drop-down menu led him to the Goblinopolis EE headquarters, then another to Sebacea district. He messaged the Precinct Captain's office.

From: Royal Palace, Office of His Royal Majesty (**cryptographically verified sender**)
To: Goblinopolis Edict Enforcement Department, Sebacea District Captain

Captain,

I have an urgent need to contact my brother Tol-u-ol, one of your officers, immediately. Please arrange for him to conference with me via encrypted link at Goblinopolis EE headquarters, or preferably send him to the Royal Palace in person by the most expeditious possible means.

Aspet I, King of Tragacanth

"Sergeant, report to my office, pronto."
The duty sergeant hung up his comm unit and rolled his eyes. From his tone, there was no doubt the

captain was serious about this one. "Wonder which smekker screwed up this time?" He flipped over the *Back in a Few* placard, pushed himself away from the desk, and headed up the no-frills concrete stairs to the Precinct Captain's office. The captain was waiting for him with an odd look in his eye. "This can't be good," he muttered.

"Sergeant, where is officer Tol-u-ol assigned at present?" he began, without observing any social formalities.

"Uh, Captain, he works the roaming foot beat most nights."

"Where is he at this very moment?"

"On leave, Captain."

"Recall him immediately and have him report to my office. Highest priority."

"I...I don't think he's reachable, Captain."

"What do you mean, he's not reachable?"

"I mean he's off in...the wilderness, sir."

"*The wilderness*? Why would a hard-boiled city gob like Tol head off into the smekking wilderness?

"He...uh...just wanted to get away for a while, Cap."

The captain glared at him from under furrowed eye ridges. "Get. Away. For. A while?"

The sergeant looked down at his suddenly fascinating feet. The novelty finally wore off and he looked up again.

"Fine, he's chasing down a lead."

"Why would he need to take leave for that?"

"Because the lead is at Mt. Astflanar and we

don't have TDY money for that kind of travel. Smek, I can barely afford to give the lads overtime when they're on a hot case."

"Who or what has Tol taken it on himself to pursue to the middle of the Espwe mountains?"

"Our old pal Pyfox."

"Tol chased Pyfox to Mt. Astflanar for what...a speeding violation?"

"He just said he had a lead on something big Pyfox was involved in. As it was his personal leave he was taking, I didn't pry any further."

"Are you aware that officer Tol-u-ol is the brother of our new King?"

Sarge felt around on the floor to retrieve the jaw he'd just dropped.

"*Tol*? The *King's* brother? Smek me. I guess it don't run in the family."

"What doesn't?"

"Computers. Tol has no use for computers. Hates 'em. Files all his reports by hand or Dictaphone."

"Can't say I blame him for that. Whatever the case, I have a problem, which means that *you* have a problem. His Majesty contacted me personally a few minutes ago and said he wants Tol at the Palace toot sweet. Your job, therefore, is to go find him. Grab a couple of lads and get them on it. I'll authorize whatever it takes."

"Are...are you sure, Captain? This could get expensive."

"The smekking *King* wants Tol, sergeant. Do you understand what I'm saying? The *King*. Aspet the First. The goblin who controls our budget, not to mention our careers. This *will* happen, and it will happen in the minimum possible time. Get out of here now or you'll be spit-polishing patrol boots in the Precinct quartermaster depot until you retire."

"Squad deployed, Captain!"

"The first four seismic pulses have been triggered, Your Eminence. The engineers report a thirty-two percent energy transference efficiency. Your Hurrarcane worked perfectly, incidentally: the Seismic Coordination Center and Early Warning Network in Tillimil were completely disrupted."

The spectral holographic figure in the visiosphere nodded.

"Thirty-two percent is not as efficient as I would like, but it should suffice so long as the root disturbance is energetic enough. What method are your sappers employing?"

"We are using five kilotonne point charges combined with eleventh-level 'Dig' and 'Disrupt' spells, Your Eminence. There aren't enough mages with twelfth-level skill who were um, recruitable."

"I have just received word that all four of the initial specula were rendered inert. Congratulations, Pyfox. We are well on the road to victory."

"I have reports of over a thousand casualties as well, Your Eminence."

"Ah, well, collateral damage is unavoidable. What

happens on the physical plane is of little concern to me."

"Understand, Your Eminence, but it does matter to me."

"So long as mages and Magineers remain to pay you for access to The Slice, what matters the number of civilian casualties?"

"They are *people*, Your Eminence."

"People are expendable, Pyfox, and easily replaced. They breed prolifically. You must learn to focus on the mission and set petty sentimentality aside."

"Yes, Your Eminence."

"Now, the next set of seismic events is to occur when?"

"In ten minutes, Your Eminence."

"And the number will be eight?"

"Correct, Your Eminence. That will make twelve. Adding the speculum already destroyed in the proof of concept mission, we will have taken out over half of the access portals."

"Excellent. By your close of day we will have complete control. I'm already seeing manna beginning to pool near the ruined specula. It flows into me like a great river meeting the sea."

Behind the stalagmites, Tol's mind raced furiously. He wasn't sure what Pyfox meant by "seismic events," but the talk about casualties needed no translation. It sounded as though the action was taking place far from here, though. Maybe he could sabotage it somehow. But how? He could probably take Pyfox out, but would that do any good? Questions were easy to come by; answers were not.

The visiosphere swirled into life once more. Namni's ghostly form appeared. "Success! Eight more specula have imploded."

"Great news, Your Eminence. Five more are scheduled in ten minutes. That will leave us with six remaining portals: the five Dubers and our conduit here in Astflanar."

"We will bring the Dubers down at the same moment. It will be easier to overcome their defenses that way, as they will be unable to aid one another in the heat of the attack."

One of the other hobs approached Pyfox. "We got visitors, boss. Somebody woke the watcher."

Pyfox twisted around to face him. "Take care of them, fool," he hissed, "use the stasis runes."

"We're on it, boss."

Another hobgoblin ran up to them, slightly out of breath. "Just got a report in: the third wave has crested," he huffed.

Pyfox laughed and rubbed his hands together, then spoke into the sphere.

"Your Eminence, we've received word that the third set of quakes has been triggered."

"Yes," came the ethereal reply, "Yes, the specula have collapsed inwardly. They are disabled and their portals are shut. We are one step away from absolute victory. Is it not glorious?"

"Yes, Your Eminence. Glorious."

Although not visible to Pyfox through the nebulous veil of the visiosphere, the air around Namni began to swirl and suddenly tendrils of it solidified and wrapped around him tightly as he sat on his carved seat. He struggled, surprised, and a voice boomed out of a nearby spire.

"What mischief have you wrought, fallen one?"

Namni's eyes slitted. He shrugged and the tendrils flew off as though propelled by suddenly released springs.

"I am pursuing the path to glory you and your pathetic brethren had neither the foresight nor fortitude to follow, Oloi. Not only am I pursuing it, in but a few moments I will have achieved victory and that glory will forever be mine alone."

"The Noils are charged with maintaining balance and harmony between The Slice and the physical plane, fallen one. You know that I cannot allow your plan to succeed."

Namni pulled back a fold of his robe and extracted a statue of himself, half a meter long and seemingly carved from purest onyx. He held it up for Oloi to see.

"I have a replicast. It took me a hundred years to shape and enchant it. Even if you defeat me, I will retreat into it and escape you."

Before he'd quite finished his speech, Oloi spread out his hands and the replicast flew from Namni's grasp and was flung out into space. Namni leapt to his feet and a beam of light erupted from his hand, intercepting the statue and lowering it gently to the ground about ten meters away. He spun and with the other hand pushed a solid wave of bluish electrical fury directly at Oloi. The Emissary leapt over it and landed on a platform that formed itself out of the fractal fabric beneath him. He spread his arms wide and then brought his palms together in front. Two enormous spires, one on either side of Namni, crumbled and collapsed on top of him.

The pillar debris stopped just short of Namni and was propelled outward in a furious explosion. Rather than falling to the ground in a circle some distance away, however, it began to rotate en masse and draw closer together until it formed a tight eddy of fractal detritus that headed straight for Oloi, who flung his hands apart in response. Just before it swept him into its whirling maw the rotating debris split and spinning tails passed to either side. One of the vortices bent and flailed at near right angles as it passed, catching Oloi across the back and flinging him forward into a pile of rubble. Namni took advantage of this to leap for the replicast.

Oloi levitated up and away from the debris field. A ball of orange fire erupted from his hand and shot toward Namni, who dodged at the last second, losing his grip on the replicast as he did. It clattered to the ground and bounced into the scree. Namni executed a complete somersault and raised his arms to launch another barrage at Oloi when he suddenly lost sight of his target. He heard a noise behind him and spun around to confront a spectral likeness of Oloi that moved as though to strike him. Namni instinctively threw up his hands to block the blow. The ethereal golem's arms passed straight through him. As soon as Namni realized he'd been duped, he crouched and was scanning for the real Oloi when suddenly a cage made of glowing blue lines dropped out of nowhere and entrapped him. He tried to free himself, but contact with the bars affected him strangely and he drew back.

"That is a cage woven of manna-sponge," Oloi explained, hovering above him. "It cannot be broken by magical means, and if you touch it your manna will be absorbed."

"Why are you doing this?" Namni growled.

"You took the oath and accepted the mantle of a Noil, Archmage. When you concocted and carried out your plot against the specula arcanis majoris, thereby endangering the manna ecosystem of The Slice, you blatantly broke that oath. The Arcanum Magisterum has charged me with bringing you into their presence for justice. Without your assistance Pyfox and his rogue mages will be unable to complete the final ritual to seal off the Dubers."

He gently set down on the ground, then lifted his hand, palm up, and the cage floated free of the fractal landscape, following along as he walked away. Namni protested vocally, his language getting more crude and incoherent with time. Oloi paid him no attention. Their path happened to take them very near the replicast, lodged on top of a large heap of debris. Oloi realized that Namni had suddenly become very quiet. He turned to see that the prisoner's body had deformed into a long thin eel-like shape and was slipping between the bars. He rushed around to that side of the cage to stop Namni's escape only to see the last of his essence disappear into the replicast above them. He scrambled awkwardly up the debris pile, but just as he reached the statue it shimmered and vanished.

Oloi concentrated on the magical vapor trail left by the teleportation and saw that it led to Tragacanth on the physical plane. There was no time for him to construct a visitation ritual, so it was going to be up to whoever was present in Pyfox's lair to stop him. Oloi sat on a stone and eased himself into tenth-level meditation. He projected his astral self to scan the auras of Pyfox's companions and stopped with a jolt. He came out of the meditative state and smiled broadly. He had detected the presence of both Tol-u-ol and Ballop'ril. Namni was, in a word, doomed.

Pyfox was greatly concerned by Namni's sudden departure from the visiosphere. He knew that the final assault on the Dubers could not succeed without the augmented energy pulse Namni would provide to the remaining quake-triggering mages. The intruder threat had been neutralized by the deployment of stasis runes at the entrance to his chamber. They erected a powerful barrier that prevented both physical and magical trespassing. A motley crew had assembled on the other side, including the previously semi-mythical Ballop'ril, but Pyfox paid them no mind now that the barrier was up. Not even Ballop'ril could hope to weaken it before the final assault was completed. Presuming, of course, that Namni reappeared before the effect dissipated. He was beginning to get seriously worried when a brilliant flash lit the room and a small black statue appeared suddenly on the floor near the visiosphere. At the same moment the sphere flickered into life.

"When I am strong enough I will signal you and the operation can continue. Until then protect the replicast with your life." The voice was very thin and wavering, but unmistakably Namni's. Pyfox picked up the pitch black figurine. It was warm to the touch and softly thrumming. Little arcs of electricity leapt from it at irregular intervals, making a distinct crackling noise as they dissipated.

Just beyond the barrier, Ballop'ril was watching the proceedings closely. "It looks like a replicast," he narrated to the group, "Namni must have run afoul of someone extremely powerful to force him to retreat into that. Someone he anticipated, though, because it takes a very long time to enchant such a thing."

Pyfox heard his explanation and strolled over, replicast in hand. "Yes, it belongs to Namni, traitor. In a very short time he will be using it as the platform from which to launch the final assault on the Dubers. That will leave only my portal here in Astflanar for access to The Slice, access that will cost the mages and Magineers dearly. I will have a monopoly on magical sourcing for the entire planet."

"Careful you don't drop it, Pyfox," Ballop'ril said, "Or your boss will be so much latent magical energy spread across the cavern floor."

"Shows how much you really know, oh mighty archmage Perspice," Pyfox replied with a sneer, "this replicast has an inviolability spell cast on it. It cannot be damaged by any means."

"See those sparks coming out? That means the inviolability enchantment is not yet fully activated. Until they stop, you're just holding a porcelain figurine full of hate with an internal heating element."

Without warning a burly goblin wearing a trench overjack and helmet with the Goblinopolis Edict Enforcement departmental badge enameled on it popped up from behind a stalagmite and jerked the pulsing replicast out of Pyfox's surprised grasp. "Thanks for the scoop, your mageness. I hate to be an art critic, but this thing has got a date with a rock." He raised the statuette above his head. "No!" screamed Pyfox; he and two other hobs leapt toward Tol, but he body-slammed the first one into a stalagmite, dodged the others, and hurled the statue into space. The replicast inscribed a soaring arc over their heads and shattered against a large column of stone dripping with water seeping in from the ceiling. "Take cover!" shouted Ballop'ril. Tol ducked down behind the stalagmite again.

A pulse of pure white energy exploded from the fragmented replicast; the shock wave took layers of material off the surrounding stone facades and propelled Pyfox and his cronies against the walls of the cavern like rag dolls. The magical barrier bulged outward as the leading edge contacted it, and then punctured like a balloon shot with an arrow. An instant later the pulse had expended itself and all was quiet except for the moans and groans emanating from Pyfox. He had barely survived the explosion; one of his hobs was not so lucky.

Tol gave Pyfox first aid, and then pulled him to his feet. "You're under arrest for a whole buncha stuff that I'll sort out back in Sebacea." Pyfox grimaced at him. "I think we're out of your jurisdiction, smekhead."

"But not out of mine."

They looked up to see two more Goblinopolis EE officers accompanied by a third goblin in a brown and green uniform. His breast patch was the twin mountain peak & lightning bolt emblem of the Southron Rangers.

"Glad to see you gobs," said Tol, "how in the smek did you ever track us down in here?"

"Some weird smooth-skinned creature who called himself 'Plåk' not only told us exactly where to find you, he gave us a teleport right to the entrance."

"Good ol' Plåk. Makin' up for past indiscretions."

"What's that, now?"

"Long story. I'll tell you at the pub some night."

"Yeah, all of your stories are long when there's ale involved."

"I don't get it, Pyfox. How did your larcenous little brain ever come up with a scheme of this magnitude?"

"He ain't stupid," the surviving minion spoke up, "Namni said he would get rich and live forever

371

if he helped."

"Shut up, you idiot," Pyfox snapped, "He's raving. Must be the pain."

"I ain't in that much pain, boss. I just don't want 'em to sell you short."

The air off to their right abruptly took on a slight opacity and then Plåk himself shimmered into view.

"Yes, immortality would have been yours, Pyfox. But through what was no doubt an unintentional oversight the dearly departed Namni left out a rather crucial bit of information. Each time you were reincarnated into your cloned shell, your memories of anything that happened after the cloning would be eradicated. Further, and more to the point, Namni had modified the mental encoding of the clone such that you would be completely, unquestionably obedient to his every whim: incapable even of conceiving of questioning him, in fact. Forever a slave in word and deed."

Pyfox still appeared defiant, but a hint of doubt was creeping in.

"Oh, and one last tidbit. I was snooping about in Namni's lair while he was distracted by your little enterprise here and his rather entertaining battle with Oloi and discovered this."

He held up a glowing crystal cube with a red protrusion. "This, my immortal Pyfox, is a kill switch. It is magically linked to both your physical and cloned brains. Eventually Namni would tire of you and when that happened he would simply press this button. Poof! No more living Pyfox, no more clone."

"But...he swore to me that he would honor our agreement forever."

"Namni is for all intents and purposes a demigod. The gods, or at any rate those in the same neighborhood of the ethical spectrum as Namni, are not bound by pacts taken with mortal creatures."

Selpla stepped forward, her reporter's curiosity no longer containable. "So, Namni is dead, then?"

"Not truly dead, no. His energies have been dispersed over an ever-widening area. It is theoretically possible that he could nudge them back together eventually and reform, but that will take at least an Age or two. Nothing to worry about for a few millennia, at any rate."

"Who are you, exactly?"

"My name is Plåk. I am an...adventurer in The Slice."

"And a criminal," added Tol. "Reformed, it seems, but a criminal nonetheless."

"There you go, always hating—even after all I've done for you."

"I'm not hatin', I'm testifyin.' I am grateful for your help, by the way."

Plåk sighed. "Make a simple mistake and pay for it throughout eternity."

"You sank an entire island with three major cities on it!"

"It was a technical error, nothing more. I had no intention of harming anyone."

"Oh, I've *got* to get this story," said Selpla,

almost salivating.

"Morianella," said Kurg simply, from the rear.

Selpla looked confused for a moment, shook her head.

"*Morianella*? That disaster was caused by a quake almost a thousand years ago."

"Yeah," replied Tol. "Did it ever seem odd to you that scientists never figured that one out? That there are no faults or seismically active areas anywhere near where Morianella used to be? That's 'cause geology had nothin' to do with it. That quake was the result of not-so-Archmage Plåk here goofin' with something he didn't understand."

"That is so patently unfair of you, Tol-u-ol. I understood the Codex Lapidismotus intimately. I simply made a small error reciting one of the rituals. It was an honest mistake that anyone could have made."

"Except anyone else making it probably wouldn't have drowned a half million people."

"Well, it's obvious you're not in a pleasant conversational mood today, so I'm off."

Plåk disappeared, leaving behind a faintly sparkling outline that drifted slowly to the stone floor. The whole group began to move down toward the much more accessible entrance to the cavern used by Pyfox, who was positioned along with his injured henchman in the middle of the group as prisoners of the Southron Ranger, guarded by Tol and the other EE officers. Ballop'ril and Prond brought up the rear. Tol dropped back to talk to the bugbear.

"Beggin' your pardon, Archmage, but I heard Pyfox call you *Perspice* back there. What did he mean?"

Ballop'ril took a deep breath. "It is," he began, "one of those proverbial 'long stories.'"

"I think I may know some of it," Tol interjected, "if it involves the Belladonnas."

Ballop'ril nodded. "Indeed, it does. Gramidius Contentius, the Capo Belladonna, and I are…brothers."

Tol stopped short. "Not to seem disrespectful, Archmage, but is that even biologically possible?"

Ballop'ril laughed. "No, indeed it isn't, in the literal sense. What I mean is that we were brought up together. My mother and father were killed in a street riot in a Galangan border market when I was but a toddler. We had crossed over to do some shopping— my mother loved and collected Northern Galangan folk pottery—when a street protest formed right outside the shop where we were browsing. I don't think either of my parents realized how dangerously the situation had escalated. We had just stepped outside and were crossing to another shop when a mass of people came running down the street, fleeing government troops who were responding in large drays with horizontal rams affixed to them. My father flung me bodily onto the curb just as they were both slammed by a press of people trapped in front of the rams. I never saw them alive again.

Prond had never heard this story, either. He gasped in shock and horror. Tol just listened grimly.

He'd seen too many similar tragedies.

"Grami's family lived in that small town and saw what happened. When the casualties were laid out for identification and they realized I was the only survivor of my own family, they adopted me on the spot using the Galangan Declaration of Fostering. I grew up there with Grami as my 'brother.' Clostridius Perspice was the name they gave me as a child, but when I came of age they told me my original name had been Ballop'ril. His parents and I communicated up until his mother passed on; I don't know if old Terentio yet lives. Not surprisingly, they didn't approve of Grami's choice of occupation, or what comparatively little they knew of it. They didn't understand mine, either, but at least they were supportive insofar as it wasn't as morally questionable as his. Grami inducted me into his Belladonna 'family,' but I never felt comfortable there and did not associate with them often."

Tol was digesting all this when Selpla came bouncing up. Ballop'ril seemed relieved at the interruption and dropped back. Tol just let him go.

"Tol, can you give me details of the Morianella incident?" Selpla asked, sweetly.

"Sure, doll. All it takes is good ale and patience. It's ancient history, though. I did learn one thing from it: you can't prosecute someone who doesn't reside on the physical plane. The smekkers just skip out on you."

"I don't have any ale on me right now. Can we

make a date back home soon?"

"I hang out at the Bloated Balrog, on Pacinian in Sebacea. Drop by early evening, before my shift starts."

"I think your work schedule might be revised, Officer Tol-u-ol," interjected one of the Goblinopolis cops. "Sarge sent us to find you and bring you back as soon as possible. Captain wants you, and I mean now."

"Why in the smek would the captain want to see me? Did I forget to file some smekkin' paperwork or some smek?"

"Not sure. I think Sarge mentioned something about the king being involved. Seems a bit far-fetched, though, for the king to care about a Sebacea EE squad."

Tol rolled his eyes. "Smek, I forgot about him. It's not really as, um, far-fetched as all that."

The EE officer looked surprised. "It isn't? Why not? What possible reason could the *king* have for being interested in you or our squad?"

Tol looked annoyed and a bit embarrassed.

"He's my uh...he's my kid brother," he whispered. Their eyes got wide. "Keep it to yourself, all right?"

From somewhere in Tol's backpack they heard an odd twittering noise.

Chapter Twenty-Three:
A Knight to Remember

At the border between the Municipality of Greater Goblinopolis and the Southern Reaches, the Southron ranger formally handed over custody of Pyfox and his surviving accomplice to the EE officers. They thanked him for his assistance and headed for Sebacea. The news team split off at this point, with Selpla promising to contact Tol soon for the Morianella story. If she'd been aware of Tol's relationship to the King she probably wouldn't have been able to tear herself away, no matter how loudly Kurg commanded her otherwise. Access to anything related to the Royal inner circle was an irresistible draw for a Goblinopolis journalist.

As it was, Tol reported alone to the captain, who ordered him to the Royal Palace, a trip Tol made with considerable trepidation as he was immensely uncomfortable with the trappings of power, especially when the little brother he used to torment mercilessly now held that power. He popped into the Crown and Scepter pub just outside the curtain wall of the Royal compound for a little 'spiritual reinforcement.' Several large gourds of uberrazzle later, he made his somewhat unsteady way out the door and up the long, winding path to the Palace grounds.

The Royal Protective Corps eyed him suspiciously as he approached the Palace Antechamber. "Here! What's an EE grunt doing in the Royal Compound? Looking to cite someone for littering to fill your weekly quota?"

Tol cocked his head and eyed the splendidly-dressed guard tiredly. "Just tryin' to keep the peace. Got several complaints that the reflection from your fancy-schmancy brass buttons was blindin' people."

Another guard with stripes on his epaulets stepped forward. "Watch your tongue, citizen. You have no jurisdiction in the Royal Compound and we won't hesitate for a moment to slap you down if the need arises, badge or not."

Tol chuckled, "I don't think so. You'd have to get your nice white glovies dirty to do that."

"What is your business here, commoner?"

"You call me that as though it's some kind of insult. It isn't. My business here is that I got a Royal Summons. I don't know why."

The guard supervisor looked doubtful. "A Royal Summons? That's very unlikely. What is your name?"

"Tol-u-ol. Senior Edict Enforcement Officer, Sebacea Precinct One."

"Sebacea? How appropriate. I don't suppose you bathed before coming here, by any chance?"

"I was too busy saving the world for that, fancy-doodle."

The guard sniffed. "Saving it from hygiene and sophistication, no doubt."

"No doubt. Should I just tell the Captain you wouldn't let me in? Come to think of it, that works for me." He turned around and took a step.

The guard chuckled derisively. "I can't let anyone through whose name is not on the entry list, as yours, predictably, is not."

One of the lowered-ranked guards walked up and handed the officer another clipboard. The supervisor turned white and called after Tol.

"My sincere apologies, officer Tol-u-ol. Please, pass by all means."

Tol turned around, shrugged, and shuffled on through the gate grinning smugly. "See you boys in the hoity-toity parade."

As they watched him go, a third guard spoke up. "What list was he on, then?"

"Royal Gold."

"Holy smek. That's the one reserved for high officials of state and visiting Royalty. How did a scruffy inner city cop get mixed up in that crowd? Some kind of clerical error?"

"I don't think so. There's more than meets the eye to officer Tol-u-ol, I believe."

"The nose, as well, one would hope."

Tol sauntered up the increasingly elegant marbled corridor leading to the inner Palace. The walls were set with alcoves every couple of meters in which were nestled granite and gold busts of famous

Tragacanthans throughout history. The gilt filigrees and acanthus leaf tracings on every exposed surface were getting denser as he proceeded inward. Tol suppressed the very strong urge to turn and run. Why couldn't Pet have met him in a pub or something?

Finally he came to an enormous door—six meters tall if it was a centimeter—carved from some ridiculously exotic hardwood and decorated with dozens of bas relief figures sprinkled liberally with semiprecious stones set in gold and silver bezels. It seemed to relate the history of Tragacanth in mute narrative; a story Tol had always found singularly boring to recite in class. It wasn't much more engaging rendered in dead trees, beaten metal and polished rocks.

The door was locked, or at least it didn't seem to want to open, so Tol pulled the silk cord hanging in a narrow vestibule to the left of the doorframe. He heard a faint chiming somewhere beyond the portal and after a few seconds the ponderous panels creaked open. A large, elegantly dressed half-ogre stood there.

"Welcome to the Royal Palace, officer Tol-u-ol. His Majesty is awaiting you in the drawing room."

Tol sized him up and figured he could take him three falls out of five, despite his bulk. He relaxed a bit.

"Well, I hope he doesn't expect me to do any drawing. I ain't no kinda artist."

"Indeed, sir. I do not expect your draftsmanship will be called upon in the course of the meeting."

He led Tol along a lavish marbled corridor

and through an arched doorway into a splendidly appointed room where his little brother sat flanked by two stuffy-looking highbrows. Aspet had a shiny metal ring on his head and was looking far too pleased with himself.

"Welcome, Tol. It's great to see you again."

Tol sniffed at him. "Hey, Pet. How's it hangin'? Nice place you got here."

One of the attendants stepped forward and puffed up his chest. "You're speaking to His Royal Majesty Tragacanth. The proper form of address would be *Your Majesty*."

Tol raised a massive eyebrow. "Maybe for you. He's just my dorky kid brother to me." The attendants bristled.

Aspet raised his hand. "It's fine. I am still his dorky kid brother in some ways." He motioned for the attendants to withdraw, leaving the brothers alone. They regarded each other in silence for a long moment. Finally Tol spoke.

"I guess congrats are in order. I gotta say, I didn't really think you could do it."

"I wasn't sure I could, either."

"So, now what happens?"

"Now I try hard to learn this job and do my best for the people of Tragacanth."

"Good luck with that. I meant, why am I here?"

"Oh. Well, mostly because I wanted to see you... we haven't had any time together in a couple of years now. Also, though, I wanted to congratulate you on nabbing Pyfox. He's made himself quite a high-profile public enemy in the past few months. I understand you were instrumental in uncovering and terminating the conspiracy to destroy access to The Slice."

"Yeah. It's what I do for a living, oddly enough."

"Goblinopolis appreciates you for that. Speaking of Goblinopolis, come out on this balcony with me. There's a really nice view of the city you ought to see."

"I bet you got all sorts of nice views from this place. I never been inside a building this big before."

They stepped out on the balcony and Aspet quietly closed the door behind them. There was a curtain drawn around the edge of the balcony to above eye level. Tol chuckled. "Nice curtains. I especially like the little crowns. Did you order these yourself?"

Aspet smiled and pulled a silk cord, parting the draperies to reveal a significant proportion of the citizenry of greater Goblinopolis staring up at them. Tol was frozen in fear and awe. He instinctively reached for the door knob and escape, but his brother had locked it. His Royal Majesty Tragacanth held up a little key and grinned. Tol had nowhere to run, so he shrank back as far from the crowd as possible. Aspet walked to the edge of the parapet and began to address the assemblage.

"Good people of Tragacanth, loyal subjects of the Crown, I bid you welcome to this most joyful celebration. Today we honor a hero, a goblin who has played a pivotal role in preserving our way of life. For without his efforts, there would be no freely accessible magic. The Dubers would cease to function. All access to The Slice would be controlled by a tiny cartel whose only motive was obscene profit for themselves. This hero is one of your own. He is Goblinopolis Edict Enforcement Officer Tol-u-ol, and he hails from Sebacea."

At this, one area of the crowd broke out into wild cheering. Tol peeked over the edge and saw a lot of folks he'd met at one time or another in that cheering section. Seemed like everyone in Goblinopolis knew about this ceremony but him. He was a little annoyed at the gross failure of his street intelligence network, but he *had* been more or less incommunicado for a few days.

"One of my more pleasant duties as Monarch is recognizing those who have selflessly advanced the cause of peace; who have defended our civilization against those who would impose their will on the people without their consent. However, this particular hero is also my brother. I would not be accused of lavishing gifts or praise upon my own kinsman simply because of our familial relationship. I leave it, then, to you, the people of Tragacanth. Do you wish to see this hero honored by the Crown?"

There was a brief silence, and then a massive roar of *yes* erupted from the crowd in the central plaza, which Tol estimated contained at least ten thousand souls. Aspet smiled, turned to Tol and shrugged. "The people of your nation have spoken,

Tol-u-ol."

The King walked over to a small table draped with a velvet cloth and pulled back the covering to reveal an exquisitely worked golden medallion suspended from a blue and silver-striped satin ribbon. The medallion depicted the Royal seal of Tragacanth surrounded by a wreath of Sentallas leaves. Sentallas was the tree traditionally associated with the earliest settlers of Tragacanth, reputed to have provided them with shelter, food, and medicinal bark that enabled one of the first colonies to survive a brutal winter in the northern mountains near what later became the city of Fenurian. It was revered throughout the country for this reason.

Aspet lowered the medal around Tol's neck. "Tol-u-ol, in recognition of your inestimable service to the nation of Tragacanth, having put yourself in harm's way not only in recent days but over a career spanning decades, I, Aspet the First, in my capacity as Sovereign do hereby grant you the Tragacanthan Medal of Royal Merit. May it always serve as a reminder to the people of your service to our great nation."

Scattered applause began, but Aspet held up his hand. "Good people, this ceremony is not yet concluded." He unlocked and swung open the doors leading back into the palace. A military general officer in full dress attire walked stiffly onto the balcony, bearing an ornate sword and a pillow on which sat a gold and red garter. He stood beside Aspet opposite Tol, who by this time was almost too weak-kneed to stand.

"Tragacanth has long enjoyed an order of noble

Knighthood," Aspet boomed, "The Order of the Crimson. The red garter trimmed in spun gold has for hundreds of years signified our boldest warriors, our best and bravest defenders. It has traditionally been reserved for those serving in the military, but the actions of Tol-u-ol and others of the civilian sector have convinced me that now is the time to modify the charter of the Order, to expand eligibility to all citizens of Tragacanth who meet the lofty requirements of membership. I therefore today institute the accolade of *Crimson Knight-Protector*, open to civilian membership, to serve alongside the military accolades of *Crimson Knight-Bachelor* and *Crimson Knight-Commander*. In addition, I name Tol-u-ol of Goblinopolis as the premier recipient of that accolade. Kneel before me, candidate." He took the garter in his hand and the general placed the pillow on the tiled balcony floor.

It took Tol a second or two to realize that Aspet had given him a command. Then he shuffled forward, blushing a bright greenish-blue, and knelt awkwardly on the small pillow. Aspet cinched the garter just above Tol's right elbow, and then the general passed him the sword, hilt first, balanced on his forearm.

"Tragacanth recognizes its heroes, great and small, in many ways. For those who have given the ultimate effort, braved the fiercest foes, and triumphed against all odds is reserved the Crimson Accolade. Do you, Tol-u-ol of Goblinopolis, swear on the sanctity of your ancestors that you will hold fast to the edicts and traditions of Tragacanth, treat its people faithfully and with justice, and hold your unswerving fealty for now and all time to the Crown, as a true Knight should?"

Tol had no idea of the proper way to answer this, so he replied simply, "yes."

Aspet tapped Tol on each shoulder and once on the top of the head with the sword. "Then as Royal Monarch of the Noble Lineage of Tragacanth I do now hold you in fealty and elevate you to the rank and estate of Knight-Protector of the Crimson, to serve now and forever as Premiere of that Order. Arise, Sir Tol-u-ol, and greet your brethren of the accolades of Chivalry."

Tol got to his feet unsteadily and noticed that the balcony was now lined with Knights Bachelor and Commander, all impeccably attired in the dress uniform of red and gold reserved for the Crimson Order, each sporting their garter. The line stretched back into the drawing room. One of the Knights-Commander stepped forward and demonstrated the traditional grasp-punch greeting used by the Order and then ushered him along the line as he exchanged the gesture with each of his assembled brother knights. By the end he was getting pretty good at it. He was then led back out to Aspet, who pushed him forward to the edge of the balcony.

"People of Tragacanth, I give you Sir Tol-u-ol, Premier Knight-Protector of the Crimson Order!"

It was twenty minutes before the applause

and cheering finally died down completely; twenty minutes Tol would never forget. He stood there and swept his eyes across the crowd, noticing people he would never have expected to turn out for such a spectacle. He did a double-take and stared in gaping amazement at one point when he noticed The Exalted One and his retinue standing near the center of the crowd, with a respectful space encircling them.

Aspet gave a Royal Banquet in Tol's honor that evening. He had a new uniform designed for the Knights-Protector and Tol's first command as a knight in fealty was to debut it at the banquet. Aspet expected him to squirm uncomfortably all night, like a rambunctious child forced to wear a fancy suit to a family gathering, but to the king's surprise Tol took to it like a fish to water. He cut rather a dashing figure in the elegant silk and satin uniform of deep crimson, rich blue, and gold, Aspet had to admit. The garter rested in a custom-made harness of twisted woolen cords around his right arm, while the Medal of Royal Merit shone handsomely above the brilliantly-polished buttons on his chest. The splendid ensemble was a far cry from the tattered tactical fatigues he'd shown up in earlier in the day.

Tol spent the night in the Royal Guest Quarters, but early the next morning he insisted on returning to the Precinct. "I appreciate the glitz and glamor, really, but I'm still a working goblin and I got a job to do."

Aspet smiled and hugged him. "That's one of the reasons I elevated you, Tol. You don't let anything get in the way of your duties. You're Tragacanthan all the way to the bone." Tol gave him a rare look of affection. "You turned out to be one smek of a kid brother, didn't ya?" He picked up the custom suitcase containing his dress uniform (he was back in the fatigues, albeit freshly laundered) and headed for the door. As he reached it he turned around one last time. "Pet...Aspet...I'm proud of you." Aspet stopped cold and stared at him in shock. "I must take my leave now," Tol continued, "But I am ever your goblin." He paused for a moment to let the uncharacteristic language have its full effect, and then added, "Your Majesty," with a small, adroit bow. With that he turned and marched off down the hallway.

Aspet watched him go until he disappeared around a corner, then shut the door and sat down in his drawing room throne. He shook his head at the marvel of it all and began to laugh. He laughed joyfully, from the heart, and so loud that his Chamberlain came rushing in to investigate. Aspet wiped the tears from his eyes at last. The Chamberlain cleared his throat and said, "Your Majesty, you have a meeting with the Disaster Response Committee in the Blue Council Room in ten minutes. We should be on our way."

"Lead me then, good sir. I am well prepared for anything now."

Tol went home, dropped off the fancy duds, and changed into his EE duty uniform before he made his way to the Precinct. He wondered what sort of reception he'd get there. The situation was rife for extreme taunting, he figured, so he marshaled his retorts for the expected onslaught. Best just to pretend nothing has happened if he wanted to avoid stirring the pot any more than necessary.

He walked in and headed for the duty desk to report. Sarge regarded him in a strange, almost friendly, way. That unnerved Tol a little, but he took it in stride. "Mornin,' Sarge. Sorry I'm late, but I had to take care of some personal business. Smekkin' family stuff, you know."

"I heard. Cap told me not to dock you for it. We're good."

Tol fished some forms out of a column of wooden boxes attached to the wall. "I gotta get these reports done before I hit the streets." "Yeah, you do that, Tol," replied Sarge, going back to his own paperwork. Tol shrugged and headed for his desk. Sarge stared after him and his grizzled old countenance morphed into a surprisingly warm smile.

Tol had been working on the Pyfox arrest report for about ten minutes when he sensed someone was watching him. He looked up and saw the Captain standing there. He dropped his pen and stood hastily, almost knocking over his chair in the process. The Captain regarded him for a few moments then said, simply, "Follow me."

Tol was accustomed to instant obedience to his EE superiors; he followed without hesitation. They wound around past the Captain's office suite to the Command Situation Briefing Room, a room Tol had only been in once before, during a city-wide disaster preparedness exercise. There were a lot of cops in there, including some retired ones Tol hadn't seen in years. The Captain led Tol to the lectern, where a very important-looking official of some sort was waiting for them. Tol suddenly recognized him from a portrait in the EE headquarters entryway as the High Commissioner for Edict Enforcement for all of Tragacanth. *Why am I suddenly a smekkin' VIP magnet?*

The High Commissioner spoke. "Esteemed members of the Edict Enforcement community, today we are here to celebrate a very great honor bestowed upon our profession. One of our own, a career foot patrol officer, has been named the premier member of the newly-created rank of Knight-Protector of the Crimson Order. (Pause for energetic applause.) This reflects well not only upon the recipient himself, but upon the EE community at large. We have been recognized at the highest levels of Tragacanthan leadership as worthy of having a Knight in our ranks. The myriad benefits this will bring to our profession, and our budget, cannot be overestimated. We owe officer Tol-u-ol, *Sir* Tol-u-ol, a great debt of gratitude for both his service to the Precinct and his larger contribution to the advancement of Edict Enforcement in general."

Tol was getting really uncomfortable with all this flowery language. He wished the Commissioner would just make his point so he could get back to work.

"In order that we make most effective use of Sir Tol-u-ol's talents, I have decided to remove him from his post as patrol officer…"

Time froze for Tol at this point. He couldn't

believe what he was hearing. He'd been a patrol officer almost all his adult life. His entire existence was wrapped up in it. Without that anchor he had no idea what he would do. He was on the verge of panic before the Commissioner could even finish the sentence.

"...and appoint him to the office of Special Investigator. He will report directly to me and be responsible for high-profile cases that require complex investigative efforts. He will also act as a spokesgoblin for the EE community."

Tol shifted from one form of panic to another as this information percolated down through the layers of his awareness. *Special Investigator?* What the smek sort of job was that for a beat cop? He hadn't the first notion what a 'special investigator' did. He'd never even bothered to take the sergeant's exam all these years. And spokesgoblin? For the love of Gammag. He suddenly realized that the Commissioner was expecting him to respond.

"I...I thank you for this unexpected honor, Commissioner. I only hope I can, um, live up to it."

Whew. Tol found it really taxing to talk that way. The Commissioner seemed pleased at his response. Tol fervently hoped he wouldn't be called upon to say anything further.

"This appointment is effective immediately. Sir Tol-u-ol, your office will be located in Justice Hall adjacent to the Royal Compound, down the corridor from my own. Movers will be at your old office to relocate you shortly. Congratulations from the entire Edict Enforcement family on your knighthood and promotion."

Tol waited skittishly until the applause died down. Keeping himself from sprinting down the steps was, he would later reflect, possibly the hardest thing he'd ever done. He walked with as much dignity and restraint as he could muster down the aisle toward the exit. When freedom was a scant ten meters away, the applause started up again. This time panic got the better of him and he broke into an involuntary trot.

Outside he sprinted for about a block then leaned against a wall breathing heavily, trying to assimilate what had just transpired. His whole life had been turned on edge just because he decided to go after Pyfox. Smek, all he really did was hide behind a stalagmite, leap out, and smash a silly little statue. Compared with all the firefights he'd been in, criminals he'd nabbed at great personal risk, and street brawls he'd won in his long EE career, getting knighted and promoted for that seemed a little anticlimactic. Some small voice in the back of his head reminded him that glory was cumulative, but he wasn't particularly receptive to that logic in his current frame of mind.

By the time he got back to the Precinct, his old office was already stripped bare. All of his personal belongings had been relocated to the new office. He stood there for a long while, gazing dolefully at the well-worn walls. The cracks, gouges, and peeling paint strips seemed like comfortable old friends now, friends he would be leaving behind forever. Suddenly afraid he would get caught being sentimental over something so absurd, he turned and walked away.

His erstwhile coworkers peered out their doors at him as he passed. He felt their eyes regarding him with...what? Envy? Disdain? Sympathy? Goblins could be inscrutable at times. He had never felt so out of place before. Better just to leave now, before anyone made it worse.

Tol ducked out a side door and walked to the Sebacea GRUC terminal. He had expected some sort of goodbye, but maybe they all felt betrayed or something...or they figured having to attend that smekkin' ceremony was goodbye enough. Couldn't really blame them. He shrugged and got on the Uptown Express, wondering about this unexpected path his life had taken without his consent.

His new office was swanky. It was paneled in some exotic hardwood with swirly grain. The desk was big enough to sleep on. His chair was equally expansive, with a high executive back and covered in soft, wine-red leather. There was a huge arched window that overlooked the busy central square of the Royal complex.

Directly across the public concourse were the distant spires and intricate stonework of the Loca Duber. Four thousand years of continuous occupation had lent each of the spaces in Goblinopolis its own unique, complex architectural contours. The vast expanse of Royal Square was lined with innumerable columns, towers, arches, monuments, and pergolas that formed a living chronicle of the rise and fall of styles and cultures over the ages. Many of the pivotal events of Tragacanthan history had taken place here. Staring out over the sea of people, Tol could almost see the more familiar ones in his mind's eye: the coronation of Lodashim, who united the diverse Northern tribes under one shaky alliance; the fiery and defiant speech of the rebel leader Roj'nash before he was executed for crimes against the Crown; the splendid and magnificent wedding of King Qoplebarq (after whom the border city was named) and Princess Karelia of Galanga, ushering in an era of close relations between the two nations that lasted almost three centuries; and many more tableaus from the long and colorful journey of his native land through the twisting canyons of time.

Tol realized his reveries were waxing almost poetic and shook it off. He was determined not to let this new position turn him into yet another stuffy muckety-muck, which condition was somehow associated with waxing poetic via a connection he hadn't fully worked out yet. He remembered a poem his brother Aspet had written during his annoying 'literary' phase. It made no sense whatever, but Aspet had been very proud of it and had it pinned to the door of his room for years. Tol had seen it so many times he had it memorized totally against his will. He knew what almost none of the words meant, if they meant anything at all. It was utter nonsense as far as Tol was concerned: a pretentious vocabulary list, worse for the fact that he was pretty sure some of the words were just made up. To add insult to injury, it had won some local poetry contest, where the judges had called it 'daring' and 'cerebral.' Tol wondered how many of his own brain cells were permanently devoted to retaining this rubbish. He sighed. "It's not as though I got a lot to spare, either."

After he'd explored his ample new digs and gotten them arranged in some semblance of comfortable he decided to take a walk and familiarize himself with the surroundings. There could be no reasonable doubt that Justice Hall was built to be intimidating. Everything about it was oversized, over-decorated, and, he suspected, over-budget. From the marble floors and columns to the vast expanses of exotic hardwood paneling to the enormous, intricately-wrought chandeliers to the seemingly infinite niches filled with marble, bronze, and gilded busts of people he'd never heard of, this structure desperately wanted to impress; to overawe. In Tol's case it failed miserably.

A number of Very Important Entities were housed in this monument to institutional vanity, including the High Tribune, the High Courts of Civil and Criminal Appeals, the Adjutant General, and the Tragacanthan Council of Barristers. Tol strolled past each of their offices, which seemed to be vying among one another for the most conspicuously ostentatious elegance. Even the toilet paper had (biodegradable) gilt edges. He made his mind up there and then to have a little chat with his brother the king about responsible use of taxpayer money.

In contrast to inside of the Justice Hall, the surrounding grounds were literally and stylistically a breath of fresh air. There were tasteful granite fountains with benches encircled by shade trees, exquisitely well-maintained formal gardens with narrow cobblestone paths cutting through them, numerous topiaries, and some interesting statuary scattered here and there, mostly depicting scenes and personages from the various mythologies of the races which had inhabited Tragacanth for the past four millennia. Tol found it much more pleasant here than the interior of the premises. He fantasized about relocating his office to one of the little shady alcoves distributed seemingly at random along the many pathways.

He walked for a good couple of hours among the cool shrubbery and shaded cobblestone paths. At last Tol decided to head back to his office and see if they had any actual work for him to do. There was a single piece of paper on his desk. It said, simply:

Report to Egmesta Market. Large crowd gathering; possible riot in progress.

Next to the note was a set of keys and a small tag that read "57." They were giving him a departmental pram to use for the assignment, he figured. He hoped it ran better than some of the clunkers that belonged to the Precinct.

Egmesta was the principal market area in Sebacea. It had a public square surrounded by shops and farmers' stalls. Tol had considered it a sizeable area until now. It would fit into one small corner of Royal Square. He'd never seen anyone riot there, though.

Sebaceans tended to congregate in groups of no more than four or five in public spaces. It would take either some great perceived injustice or organized outside agitators to incite a riot there.

It took him a while to find the parking garage: it was entirely underground. That wasn't a common practice in Goblinopolis because the bedrock on which the city rested was solid and at least a hundred meters thick. Given the exorbitant cost of the Justice Hall, it really wasn't surprising they'd gone the extra kilometer and dug the parking garage under the building. Tol wondered what else was down there: he'd have to make that the subject of future exploration.

The pram in parking spot 57 wasn't exactly what he'd been expecting. It was sleek, so new parts of the interior were still wrapped in protective sheathing, and looked like something out of a spy thriller. He tried the key, not expecting it to fit, but it did. He just sat in the pram with the engine off for some time, wondering what all those buttons and knobs were for. There was an owner's guide, but it was even thicker than the Edict Enforcement Policies and Procedures Manual and Tol felt disinclined to tackle it at the present moment.

He managed to get the thing started without any trouble. The engine sounded like some great jungle carnivore growling throatily. It drove like nothing he'd ever previously experienced. After a few blocks, as he was beginning to get the hang of it, he suddenly noticed a brass plaque on the console just above the comm unit that almost made him veer off the road.

It had "Sir Tol-u-ol" engraved in fancy letters on it. This was intended as his personally assigned pram! Only bigshots got those. It dawned on Tol for the first time that he was a bigshot now. He wasn't sure how he felt about that yet.

He parked down the block from the market, in a position that would allow easy street egress if necessary. Cop training, and all that. He plopped the "Edict Enforcement Vehicle" placard on the dashboard as per policy; he really didn't fancy having his new car towed off. The emergency lights were hidden inside the grill and in a fold-down frame on the roof not obvious to passers-by.

Egmesta had a fair number of people swarming it, all right, but they didn't look as though they'd come for a riot. It looked more like some sort of celebration. Anything this size and location would require a permit, though, and Tol knew these shopkeepers well. They would not allow a gathering here that wasn't permitted properly because violations ran the risk of costly city-imposed fines and/or sanctions. EE HQ should already have the permit on file and be aware of the logistics. Something was a little odd with this. He walked over to one of the shopkeepers he knew played a leadership role in the local Merchants' Association.

"Afternoon, Zapu. What kinda shindig you got goin' here?"

The old Goblin regarded him kindly. "It would probably be easier to show you than tell you, Tol," he replied, and led him by the elbow to the head of one of the long series of tables set in the center of the square. His voice carried much better than one might guess.

"Denizens of Egmesta and wider Sebacea, our guest of honor has arrived. I give you Sir Tol-u-ol, Knight-Protector of the Crimson and the Hero of Sebacea!"

Tol blinked in surprise and scanned the crowd. The seats nearest him were occupied by, it appeared, every single person who worked in his old office. He wondered who was minding the Precinct. Beyond them he could spot dozens of the shopkeepers and ordinary citizens of the district he'd served all these years. He knew every one of them by name, and could recite their family histories on demand. The crowd milling around them were probably mostly shoppers from other districts who'd come for fresh produce or the finely-tooled leather goods for which Sebacea was widely known, but they joined in the celebration just the same.

They feted Tol for over two hours. There were at least a dozen testimonial speeches by people ranging from community leaders to ordinary citizens who'd been helped by Tol at some point. His embarrassment quota got overloaded during the first of these and he just sat there in stunned silence after that.

He never realized how much he'd meant to these people; how they depended on his day-to-day familiar, comforting presence on the streets to make them feel safe. His new position as Special Investigator began to pall for him. *This* is where he was needed and appreciated, not some gilded cage in the hoity-toity Royal district. He made up his mind there and then to do something about it.

They insisted on a speech, of course, but unlike with previous ceremonies, Tol actually wanted to speak at this one.

"Good people of Sebacea: I love each and every one of you. I have devoted my career to keeping your streets safe to walk and your businesses safe to patronize. I do not leave you by choice..." He stopped in mid-sentence to look them over for a moment. "In fact, I do not believe I will leave you at all." At this the crowd broke into wild cheering and began to chant his name.

He left Egmesta feeling really good about the world in general, and determined to figure out some way to spend most of his time in Sebacea. He ran over a number of possible strategies when suddenly he stumbled over the one that could not fail. He smiled broadly, flipped on the flashing lights, and put the pedal down.

Chapter Twenty-four:
Aftermath

His Royal Majesty Tragacanth stared at a map that covered most of one wall of his Palace Situation Room. It illustrated in lurid matter-of-fact detail the locations and extent of the structural damage done by the magically-induced quakes from Namni's monstrous scheme. It also listed casualty figures and reconstruction efforts underway. This was a large-scale project, by any measure. Since the damage encompassed all four of the provincial districts, Aspet had appointed a senior member of the Royal Engineering Corps in each Ferroc to oversee the project personally. He also had to deal with the offers of assistance coming from Galanga, Lardonica, Ovinis, Asmagon, and as far away as Solemadrina.

The parallel, and in many ways much more logistically complex, effort was going to be reconstituting the magical portals to The Slice. That would require a very high-level mage to lead the effort, the logical choice for which would be Cromalin. The Loca Magineer, unfortunately, was already swamped with handling greater than one fifth of the magical traffic for the entire planet, as the Dubers housed the only fully functional portals remaining and Loca Duber was the most heavily used of those.

That left Aspet with something of a conundrum: where to find (and recruit) a mage of sufficient power to assist with this vital effort. The question was preying on his mind heavily when Boogla entered the room and walked up and touched him on the arm.

"Your Majesty?"

Aspet jerked involuntarily at the contact. He also felt a tiny, unexpected thrill. He looked at her with wide eyes. She seemed nonplussed as well and stammered a bit. "I...I have...read your brother's report on the Pyfox case. I think there is someone in there who might prove helpful in our current crisis."

Aspet took the bound manuscript from her. "Oh? Who?"

"His name is Ballop'ril. He's a very high-level mage. My sources at CoME say he's probably the most advanced mage on the planet at present, in fact, and could become transcendent at any time he chooses."

"Meaning he could relocate himself to The Slice?"

"Essentially. Transcendent mages are able to manifest themselves bodily in The Slice. After a certain amount of time spent there, they lose the ability to return to the physical plane for any but relatively brief periods."

"Any sign that Ballop'ril is planning this in the

near future?"

"I don't think so. He's taken an apprentice by the name of Prond whose progression to full mage will require a number of years. I doubt Ballop'ril will want to transcend prior to that."

"Where is he located?"

"He owns an entire mountain in the Espwe range, adjacent to Mount Astflanar. His abode is apparently magically carved out of that."

"Wow. That's a lot of magic."

"It gets even more impressive. The mountain itself is mobile in at least a few dozen kilometer range. A Goblinopolis news team actually documented that."

Aspet gaped at her. "Okay, we definitely need this mage on the Recovery and Reconstruction team. Have a Royal Writ of Appointment drafted and I'll sign it."

"As you command, Majesty."

Something about the way she walked off stirred a primal instinct in Aspet. It was a thoroughly enjoyable experience and it precipitated a decision that had been latent for some time, waiting for the proper trigger.

"Boogla," he called after her, softly. She turned. "I would very much like to have dinner with you tonight. Not official business, just you and I and someplace quiet. We have...things to discuss."

"Is that a Royal Command, Your Majesty?"

"No, Boogla. It is a humble request."

She stared for a moment. "I accept. Eight?"

"Eight it is. I will send an escort for you."

"I'd prefer you came to get me in person."

"Splendid. I'll tell the RPC to take the night off. We'll have to stay on the castle grounds, but there are plenty of places to have some privacy. The Royal Chef will of course deliver wherever I tell him to."

She smiled slyly. "I have just the spot in mind."

Ballop'ril proved not only willing, but quite eager to help. "It will provide my apprentice a wonderful opportunity to experience some aspects of magic he might not otherwise be exposed to for a long while."

Re-establishing the destroyed magic markers was going to be a long and arduous road. The inviolability spell on each would take a minimum of a year to cast, and require a suite of extraordinarily rare ingredients as well. Ballop'ril, however, had an alternative solution. Rather than permanent, always-open portals, he proposed that the Dubers enchant wormhole talismans that created, in effect, on-demand access to The Slice. They took only a brief moment to connect, provided almost unlimited bandwidth, and could be disconnected with a single command. Since the Magineers had jealously guarded the marker-created portals anyway, the functional difference would be minimal.

In addition, portals that could be 'toggled' would be much less subject to the sort of attack that had brought the magical community to the current state of affairs. They would have to be activated regularly to bleed off excess manna from The Slice, but that shouldn't present a problem given how often they were used in the course of daily business.

After due floor debate in plenary session, the CoME accepted this plan and forwarded it to the king as a recommendation, with the endorsement of all five Magineers. The king signed the proclamation into effect, and the work of creating and enchanting the talismans began.

After the sea-avian incident, CRAMP had voted to have their meetings in a location a little bit less subject to wildlife intervention, so they chose an old deserted abbey overlooking the Mernal River, northeast of Goblinopolis proper. They also opted to retain their normal sizes this time around.

The Abbey of Serene Waters was abandoned two hundred and thirty years ago after the 'serene waters' raged across their lands during a millennium flood, destroying all crops and livestock upon which the monks depended for subsistence. The abbey itself was relatively undamaged, but without a nearby food supply the monks eventually relocated and the buildings fell into ruin. The chapter house was still nominally inhabitable, for the most part, so it was there CRAMP decided to convene.

The black-clad leader of CRAMP was in

reality a graying half-elf named Gipiont who had served at one time on the Goblinopolis Municipal Council as well as in the capacity of Warden for his home district of Eshvodsi. Not a mage himself, he nevertheless had made his fortune supplying the magical community with the vast inventory of paraphernalia and natural products used in the arcane arts.

Gipiont was in a far better state of mind at this meeting. "Fellow supporters of the magical arts in Tragacanth, I bid you warm welcome to our conclave. After much travail we have triumphed over our bitter nemesis Pyfox and magic is preserved. There was much ill done by the enemy; there are many scars that will heal only with considerable time and toil. But victory is nonetheless ours, and so the work of restoration shall be a labor of love."

Tamlokk, the ogre mage, leaned back in his somewhat less than structurally sound chair and smirked at Gipiont. "'Peers tae me thet we heven't triumphed over nothin'. 'Twere thet Tol-u-ol fella what did most of th' fightin.' We jest sat on our bumps and jawed abut how bad things wuz."

Gipiont glared at him for a long moment. "Yes, well, perhaps our role in the military action itself was more logistical than tactical, but the goals we set were met. Whether or not we were directly involved in their ultimate achievement is immaterial."

The kobold, who was called something like 'Vraklffth' (kobold names are often difficult to pronounce with only one tongue) raised his hairy arm. "Vhat do ve do now zat majic iz saved?"

"A motion has been brought to the floor that we discuss future goals for CRAMP. Do I hear a second?"

One of the elves stood up. "I second the motion."

"Seconded and duly placed on the agenda. Speaking of the agenda, the next item up is…future goals for CRAMP."

"Dint see thet comin,' nut ut all," chuckled the ogre mage.

"Irony does not flatter you, Tamlokk."

Tamlokk guffawed at this. His laughter brought to mind a forge bellows in strenuous operation. The kobold tittered. The elves stared.

"Future goals for CRAMP, as I was saying, are open for discussion. Does anyone have a suggestion?" He glared at Tamlokk. "A serious and physically possible suggestion, to be more precise?"

The only sounds to be heard were the breeze fluttering through the tangles of broad leafy vine dangling through holes in the roof. Gipiont rolled his eyes.

"Very well, if there are no compelling suggestions from the membership then I as chair will plot our next course. It has come to my attention recently that there are great factories hidden in the northern Masrons that spew out machines designed to circumvent magic by duplicating its effects, giving common people the ability to perform actions properly restricted to mages."

"Thet describes veer neer all machines, pootis."

"Tamlokk, you know I am offended by that nickname."

"'Tarnt a nickname: more lak a jub description."

"Well, whatever it is, I'd appreciate it if you'd just call me Gipiont."

"So, Jeepeeyawnt, whet do ye propose tae do abut these fact'ries?"

"I propose we travel there and picket them, in lawful protest, over their manufacturing policies."

"Nae bombs this time round, then?"

"I don't believe explosives or other ordnance will be required for this mission."

"Wahl, whet er we waitin' fer?"

"Indeed. CRAMP: assemble and march!"

They cut a strange, rather ragged figure tramping out of the ruined chapter house, their departure punctuated by the collapse of a portion of one wall opposite the door. A rodent-eater avian watched them recess from the rafters and waggled its feathered head to and fro mockingly. A large brush-wrat scurried suddenly from beneath the ruined lectern. The avian snatched it up and flapped out through a hole in the roof to have dinner.

Chapter Twenty-Five: Morianella

Tol's mind was working furiously as he drove the fancy new pram across town. His plan was a good one, but it hinged on his being able to locate someone he hadn't laid eyes on in many years. As a rookie cop he had come across one of those scenes where something just doesn't look right. On the northern edge of Sebacea there is a small luxury inn called Hillew House; it isn't widely known outside independent luxury hotel circles. Tol did a routine sweep around the building on an evening patrol and noticed footprints underneath one of the windows in the back, not visible from the street. The inn was swanky enough to have gardeners on staff; there was nothing necessarily odd about that. Tol decided to take a closer look, anyway.

He examined the window sill and noticed dried mud clumps on it. The window had pry marks along the bottom of the frame that someone had taken pains to conceal with fresh paint of a slightly different shade. Something was definitely going down here.

He called for backup and waited for them to arrive, keeping both the window and the rear entrance under close surveillance. He left two other officers positioned inconspicuously near the window and back door and headed around to the front. He found out the room number from the desk clerk and was told that a career diplomat by the name of Yarthros used the room for 'discreet meetings.' He stationed another officer in the hallway to keep innocent bystanders away, and then approached the door with his weapon drawn.

He knocked loudly. "Hotel maintenance, sir."

There were shuffling noises from inside and a voice with a foreign accent replied, "I do not need any maintenance, thank you."

"There is a potentially serious leak in your plumbing, sir. I need to repair it immediately before it floods the entire floor. Other rooms have already been affected."

There was a pause, then: "All right. Give me a minute to, um, put on some clothes."

The door was opened partway by a swarthy hobgoblin in a suit. Tol shoved his way inside, flashed his badge, and leveled his disruptor at the hob. "Edict enforcement officer. On the floor, face down, hands behind your head. Now!"

The hob reluctantly complied. Tol patted him down as he lay on the floor and found two disruptors and a wicked knife. He opened the door and summoned the other officer to watch him. "You're under arrest for possession of deadly weapons in violation of edict. You may request a barrister once we've reached the Precinct. Anything you say can and will be used against you before a Tribunal."

The hob spit at him. "Smek you. You cannot hold me. I have diplomatic immunity."

"We'll sort that out later. For now, don't even think about moving."

Suddenly another suited hob came running out of the bathroom. He pushed Tol aside and leapt through the window, shattering the glass and spraying hobgoblin blood all over one side of the room. Tol left him for the other officers.

Tol walked over to the bedroom door and found it locked. He kicked it open and discovered the diplomat, Yarthros, thoroughly trussed to a chair and gagged with socks. As he was being cut free, Yarthros gasped, "How did you know they had done this to me?" Tol thought about it for a moment. "I'm not sure. Something just didn't look quite right. Cop's intuition, I guess."

Yarthros was impressed. "You, my friend, obviously made an excellent career choice. I will put you in for a commendation with your Precinct Captain immediately. These people were going to take me under cover of darkness to a ship somewhere in international waters, from what I could gather. They wanted to persuade me not to back a treaty concerning more open trade with Solemadrina; failing that outcome, I suspect they would simply have tossed me overboard knowing that the ensuing disruption to the trade negotiations would set them back for a while at the very least. You have my eternal gratitude and admiration for your instincts.

If there's ever anything I can for you in return, I will take whatever steps are necessary to pay that debt. I do not forget my debts."

True to Yarthros' word, Tol did receive his very first commendation from that operation, one that hung on his wall to this day, yellowing a bit. Tol hoped that Yarthros was still around and that his memory for debts had not failed him.

Tol found his quarry after a bit of a search. He lived in a small but elegant home hidden far up a tree-lined cobblestone drive not more than three blocks from Hillew House. He was officially retired from the Royal Diplomatic Corps now, but still occasionally hosted foreign dignitaries at the request of the RDC because he was such a fixture in Tragacanthan diplomatic circles and knew the myriad details of entertaining dignitaries from a variety of cultures intimately. Yarthros himself genuinely enjoyed these formal social gatherings.

Yarthros had been following Tol's career rather closely and had even been in the crowd for his knighting ceremony, as it turned out. He remembered the debt quite well and was prepared to repay it however Tol desired.

"I knew when you busted through that door that you were destined for greatness, Tol-u-ol. I must confess I could not have predicted that you would be a Knight of the Crimson, but that status nevertheless suits you well, in my estimation. I am extremely proud to call you *Sir* Tol-u-ol."

"Thank you, Ambassador. I must confess the

title 'Sir' never entered my life's plans, even in a dream. However, we must play the cards we are dealt and my hand of late has been one that exceeds imagining." Tol was definitely getting much better at what he referred to as 'forsooth speak.'

"Indeed, and I can think of none more deserving. Now, what brings you here, beyond this most pleasant reunion?"

"I must humbly ask a favor from you, Ambassador. If you wish to consider it repayment of your debt to me that is your privilege, but for my part let me state again for the record that you owe me no such debt; I was merely doing the job for which the citizens of Goblinopolis pay me."

"I accept that as an expression of your personal philosophy, but from my perspective a great deed was done that day, and great deeds must be greatly rewarded in order for balance to be maintained. I am prepared to erase that imbalance which has persisted for these many years. What would you have of me?"

Tol explained to him the transfer to headquarters and how he missed his old beat. He also related the party thrown for him at Egmesta and the outpouring of affection from the people of Sebacea.

"I'll rot away like an old pot-gourd if I have to devote the rest of my career to being hoity-toity. I need an excuse to spend as much time as possible on the streets of Sebacea. Since I only get assigned to high-profile cases that can boost the EE community's PR efforts, I thought perhaps you could request that I head the security detail for your diplomatic receptions."

Yarthros considered this for a moment. "Yes, yes, I think I can finagle that. I'll need to approach it properly, but the EE Commissioner and I go back a very long way. And of course, you are brother to the king. That makes you a member of the Royal Family, which provides a great deal of lubrication for even the most recalcitrant wheel. Give me a week, no longer, and it should be arranged."

"You have my profound gratitude, Ambassador, and you may truly consider your debt paid in full for this kind act."

"It is little enough to trade for my life, Sir knight. I have a selfish motive, as well: it will allow me to see you much more frequently."

Tol blushed in spite of himself. "I look forward to that also. I must take my leave now, but know that I hold you in, if possible, even higher esteem than before."

"And I, you. Farewell, my friend. With luck we shall see one another again in under a fortnight."

As he drove back to his office, Tol could not stop thinking about something Yarthros had said. The term 'Royal Family' kept running back and forth through his mind. It had never occurred to him before that he now possessed that status. As with most things connected with his new rank, he wasn't yet certain how he felt about it.

Exactly a week later Tol received an official communiqué from the Commissioner's Office assigning him as Chief of the Ad Hoc Diplomatic

Security Detail for Extramural Ambassador Emeritus Yarthros. He immediately began to scout locations for his 'resident' office in Sebacea. Life was good again.

Tol's appointment was made public in the weekly EE Commission press release. That gave Selpla the perfect excuse to call him and ask for an interview.

"You already know the price," Tol replied wryly.

"Absolutely. The ale's on me. Seven at the *Balrog*?"

"I'll be there."

Terp was so happy and honored to have a Knight of the Crimson as a regular patron that he had a special table and chairs built for him, with "Reserved for Sir Tol-u-ol" carved along the top. He placed them in one corner with a view of the entire establishment and put up stanchions with velvet-covered ropes blocking off the area. Tol was shocked and embarrassed the first time he came in, but got accustomed to it pretty quickly. The service was fantastic, and he always got to try the new ales before anyone else. Terp's flyer now said,

The Bloated Balrog, Sebacea.
Good enough for the Royal Family:
Good enough for You.

To give credit where it is due, Selpla did ask a few due diligence questions about Tol's new assignment: what were his duties, what sorts of challenges did he expect to face, what was it like working closely with a legend of the diplomatic community? He answered them using EE-approved language, which he'd spent hours memorizing the night before (never having had occasion/reason to bother learning it in his prior role as a foot patrol grunt).

What Selpla was really after, of course, was the Morianella story. Tol grinned at her and summoned the waiter (it was so easy to do that here). "A pitcher of Uberrazzle. On her tab." When she returned with the coveted libation, Tol began his tale.

"Of course, I wasn't even born when this all took place. Not by a long shot."

"How did you get involved, then?"

"I'll explain that as I go. About fourteen or fifteen years ago I was serving on this task force looking at cold crimes: ones that had never been solved and were still on the books."

"Nine hundred and forty years isn't a cold case. It's frozen solid."

"Heh. Morianella wasn't even one of the cases we were looking at. We were actually reviewing the evidence for a murder that took place in an arcane bookseller over on Aslovava Boulevard."

"Oh yeah, I remember that shop. Toqualah's Tomes, right? Burned to the ground. Used to give me bad dreams just walking past the place as a kid. Creepy architecture."

"That's it. Toqualah was supposedly in the building when it burned. She was presumed dead, but no part of her body was ever recovered from the ashes. One of the few things we did manage to find intact in there was a book. It was a very old book, and apparently had some sort of defensive magic cast on it because it wasn't even sooty when we pulled it out of the rubble. It had *Codex Lapidismotus* on the spine in cracked gold tooling."

Tol paused to take a long pull on his ale. Selpla was busy scribbling in her reporter's pad. "Codex Lapidismotus, eh?" What kind of book was it? What language?"

"Dunno. We couldn't get it open. It was magically sealed. We took it to CoME and they told us it had been sealed by an archmage after it had been...misused. Apparently it was a very dangerous spell book that could cause, among other things, devastating quakes."

"Quakes? Did it have anything to do with all the recent quakes?"

"No, that was a totally different mechanism, as far as I know. Anyway, the Master Archivist asked if she could put the book in the CoME Library for safekeeping, and since I couldn't see it having much use as evidence I turned it over to her."

"I assume the book plays a further role later on?"

"Valid assumption. About a week, maybe ten days later, I get a call from the Archivist, who asks me to stop by because she has managed to get the book open and discovered something she thinks might interest me. What she's found is a sort of record embedded in the book's pages of the mages who have made use of it."

"Handy."

"Yeah. Apparently not unusual for spell books of that magnitude. Any mage powerful enough to use a book like that leaves a distinctive, unique 'fingerprint' behind that can be read by a mage specially trained in that sort of thing. The Archivist is one of those trained mages, and she told me the last person to actually cast spells from the book was an archmage named Plåk, who left quite an extensive calling card."

"How did you connect Plåk and the book to Morianella?"

"Part of the fingerprint mages leave is the last spell they cast. The Archivist—her name is Umsaxe, by the way—showed me his activity record; specifically the spell he was casting and botched, as well as when it happened. She told me the likely consequences of that screw-up and all the pieces just fell into place. Massive quake that submerged an entire island occurs in an area of no known fault zones or evidence of previous seismic activity at exactly the same time that a very powerful mage fatfingers a very powerful spell from a book devoted to shaping land masses… doesn't take much of a detective to put those clues together."

"Okay, so you have evidence that the tragic drowning of a half million people over nine centuries ago wasn't a natural disaster. Why would you think Plåk would even still be alive after all that time?"

"Because he was listed as a current library patron."

"What? No way."

"Yep. Not only that, Umsaxe said he came in pretty regularly. He had lived that many years by transcending, so he couldn't hang around very long, but he still made use of the reading room for an hour or so every week. Mostly read books about The Slice and chuckled a lot. All I had to do to meet him was come back and wait for him to show up."

Time for another pitcher. Selpla waited patiently while it was fetched and Tol had taken a generous swallow.

"What happened when you met him?"

"He told me the whole story, after a little wheedling. Then I arrested him."

"You did what? Arrested a thousand year-old archmage?"

"I didn't really have an option. He confessed to mass murder right in front of me. I'm a sworn edict enforcement officer. There is no statute of limitations for murder."

"How did he take it?"

"Actually, quite well. He surrendered peacefully; then, as we walked into the door at the Precinct he just…vanished."

"Wow. What did you do?"

"I cursed him out for a while and then had to explain to the duty sergeant why I was standing there with no prisoner. He laughed at me for a good ten minutes. In fact, he chuckled every time he saw me for the next year or so."

"That's one heck of a story. Is it true?"

"Every word."

"Most entertainment I'd had in a couple hundred years, as a matter of fact."

Selpla and Tol looked around to see Plåk standing there, grinning ear to ear.

Tol offered him a seat. "I know you can't hang around long. Can transcendent mages drink?"

"You bet your sweet glutes we can," Plåk replied. Tol motioned for another stein.

Selpla was trying her hardest to maintain journalistic detachment here, but sitting at a pub table with a Knight of the Crimson and a thousand year-old transcendent archmage made it quite challenging.

"What is it you were trying to accomplish when the 'accident' happened on Morianella?" she finally managed to squeak out.

"What? Oh, that. Well, ironically enough, the Elder Council of Morianella had hired me to unblock the principal channel leading into their largest port. It had been filled by a recent landslide and was majorly interfering with their shipping commerce. Not like they had dredge barges and soil transport bucket loaders back then, you know. I could probably have got it done with a long series of greater teleport spells, but that would have taken a couple of weeks altogether and they wanted the channel open toot sweet.

In my defense, I *did* warn them that magic at the level they were requesting could be potentially dangerous and unpredictable, but they insisted. Anyway, I stumbled over one of the tertiary incantations in the Codex Lapidismotus and instead of opening a crevice just wide enough to swallow the unwanted debris, I opened one that went under the entire land mass and destabilized the bedrock. There was a tremendous quake and then the whole island just...sank into the hole."

"How did you get away?"

"Same way I got there. Teleportal. I took all the nearby residents who would fit in the teleport field with me and tried to resettle them on the mainland. They were still in shock the last time I saw them. I lost track of them when I transcended; I suppose they lived out the rest of their lives there."

"Where did you take them?"

"Woklopen in Solemadrina. Nice city. Great public gardens."

"Never been. I'd like to see it, though."

Tol had been silent through this exchange. "I wonder if any of those people you rescued wrote anything about Morianella or the disaster?"

"I dunno. You could check the libraries and bookshops in Woklopen, I guess. That was over 900 years ago, though. Good luck. Oops. I gotta split. Thanks for the razzle."

He downed the remainder of his drink, and then held up a finger.

"Oh, by the way, Tol-u-ol, I've done my best to repay society—and you—for my little *faux pas*. I played an important role in your brother becoming king of Tragacanth, for example."

Tol frowned at him. "What role would that be,

then?"

"Ask His Majesty about it sometime."

With that, transcendent archmage Plåk dissolved once more into thin air.

They sat without talking after Plåk's departure: Tol drinking and Selpla scribbling. Tol was thinking back on everything that had transpired since the attempt on Pyfox's life. It wasn't that long ago on the calendar, but it seemed an Age to him. He wondered about Plåk's parting comment, but decided that he would leave sleeping scrubhounds lie, as it were. Selpla was daydreaming about winning a Lemishbin Prize for her investigative reporting. They wrapped up their respective reveries and stood up simultaneously.

"Thanks, Sir Tol-u-ol. I appreciate your time and willingness to relate the story for me."

"Welcome, doll. Any time you want to buy me ale, I'll fit you into the schedule."

"Nice that your pal Plåk dropped by, too."

"No extra charge."

Selpla laughed as she walked away, then turned and blew him a kiss.

"Good night, Sir Knight. Maybe we can get together again some time." She winked.

Tol practically skipped back to his fancy new pram. There was a priority message waiting for him on the onboard comm unit. He punched it up on screen.

His Majesty Tragacanth has announced that

he will be wed to Magineer Liaison Boogla on the twenty-eighth of next month in the Royal Cathedral. His Majesty further requests that Sir Tol-u-ol of Sebacea act in the capacity of Second to the Groom. Please respond as soon as is practical for rehearsal information.

Tol grinned one of those disconcerting tooth-filled grins that only a goblin can pull off properly. He was starting to get used to this knighthood stuff. It wasn't half bad.

Early one evening a few weeks after the wedding, which was one of the most spectacular events ever conducted in Tragacanth and literally involved a cast of thousands, Tol was driving around in the old neighborhood reminiscing. He drove a little teary-eyed past the Precinct, flinched as he cruised by the EE infirmary and did a double take at the vacant lot. There was a pub there now, a pub that looked familiar. A hand-lettered placard in the window read

Try our 'Guardian' Berzal-Nut Razzle.
Tonight Only!

Through the open door came wafting a haunting melody: something about a sorcerer's daughter. Tol smiled and pulled the pram up to the 'no parking' curb in front of the pub. He wouldn't be long.

As he walked up to the door a messenger gob slid to a halt in front of him. After he caught his breath, he held out an envelope for Tol. "Some lady asked me to deliver this to you right away, sir. I've been chasing you for the last six blocks!"

Tol took the envelope and handed him a five billme note. "An extraordinary effort deserves an extraordinary tip. You have my thanks, young sir." The gob's eyes got big. "You called me 'sir.' A Knight of the Crimson called me sir!" He bowed awkwardly and ran off at full speed, almost dropping the currency in his haste. Tol could hear him repeating as he ran, "Sir Tol-u-ol called *me* sir!"

Tol smiled after him and examined the envelope. It smelled wonderfully of some exotic, sexy perfume. In it was a perfumed page with brilliant gilt edges and beautifully calligraphed script in silver ink.

Sir Tol-u-ol,

I have uncovered some additional background on the Morianella incident. I would love to share it with you over some rather nice imported sparkling cherish-fruit wine. Can you meet me at my residence later tonight, say, 11 PM? I will try to make it well worth your while.

Affectionately,
Selpla

Below was a map to a house in the Tropsalla district of the upper west side. Very nice homes up there. Celebrities, sports figures, and politicians, mostly. Tol had no idea why a news reporter would reside in such a hoity-toity neighborhood. He felt it was his duty to accept her invitation and investigate this anomaly.

Tol smiled a special smile at the thought of seeing Selpla again. Still beaming, he positively bounced into the pub.

...like a nightingale piping in a green forest grove...

Acknowledgments

Goblinopolis began life in 2004 as a stream-of-consciousness serial fiction blog on LiveJournal. I used the Merck Index for many of the names, hence the seeming medicinal/chemical theme. I've always wanted to try my hand at a full-blown fantasy world. It requires a huge output of creative 'sweat and tears,' I will freely admit, but the rewards are great as well. Involving magic in the milieu is effectively adding another dimension, and the rules of magic add another complex standard against which all of the characters' actions must be compared for consistency's sake.

I would like to thank Corrie Bergeron, Marthe Moss Cole, Terry A. Harper, Lisa Sawyer, and Troyce Wilson for reading the manuscript at one draft stage or another. Marthe Cole, in particular, offered some invaluable comments that were sincerely appreciated.

The indomitable Elizabeth Moon, whom I am proud to count among my friends, served as a mentor and cheerleader during this journey. Her extraordinarily deep understanding of the publishing industry and processes thereto appertaining saved me years of trial-and-error, heartbreak, and general frustration. All of this coaching and patient explanation came at the expense of her own editing time; for this I apologize profusely. I am quite certain Elizabeth accomplishes more before breakfast than the rest of us do in a long day, which makes the considerable time she devoted to me doubly significant.

Aj Reznor is in some ways responsible more than anyone else for this book finally coming to fruition. Not because he read and edited chapters along the way; not because helped me find a publisher or led the marketing of my 'brand;' but because he gave me some place to go, mentally, to escape the claustrophobia and disorientation that accompany immersion in a different universe for long periods at a time. He was, in other words, my on-call reality check. Every author needs one of those, especially those authors who delve into deep places and obscure dark corners in search of plots or characters. Thanks, Aj. You're a true friend.

Robert G. Ferrell
La Vernia, Texas, USA
4 June 2013

About the Author

Robert G. Ferrell was born in Houston, Texas, USA, in 1957. He holds a B.S. in Biology, (almost) an M.S. in Avian Ecology, and has drifted in and out of graduate programs in Pre-Biotic Chemistry and Medicine. He has been writing for publication since the late 1970s, garnering recognition for technical writing, fiction, poetry, and humor. He was a finalist for the Robert Benchley Society Humor Writing Award in 2011 and a semifinalist in 2012. Robert has been published in three humor anthologies: "My Funny Valentine," "My Funny Major Medical," and "Open Doors: Fractured Fairy Tales." He was also a finalist for the 2012 Atlanta Review Poetry Competition, and his recent novella, "Theopraxis" was a finalist in the 2012 William Faulkner-William Wisdom Creative Writing Competition. He has been a popular columnist for ;login: magazine since 2006.

Robert lives with his wife Adrienne and roughly three cats in rural Wilson County, Texas. When not writing, Robert can be found engaged in ham radio, playing/recording music, reproducing medieval calligraphy and illumination, or doing the gob-smack in his pool.